Flight 3911

Billy Paul Smith

ALSO BY BILLY PAUL SMITH

Abuse of Process

Published 2001
Available on authors web site

www. Flight3911.com

Works in Progress:

Pro Se

Disbarred

Unnamed Sequel to *Flight 3911*

Willie C

Flight 3911

Authored by Billy Paul Smith

www.flight3911.com
www.BillyPaulSmith.com

Edited by Alice Eachus
Formatted by Billy Paul Smith
Cover Design by Berge Design

Dedication

Flight 3911 is dedicated to the real heroes, the passengers and crew of United Flight 93.

And to all the first responders, living and dead, who responded to the World Trade Centers and Pentagon attacks.

And to the United States military who deployed around the world to fight the war on terror.

And to the late Captain Hartwell Hubble who was a Navy aviator and captain with Delta Airlines who provided technical help with the heavy jet storyline.

And, to my best friend since the 6th grade, the late Joseph Charles Bedsole Jr. who died on February 18, 2019.

And to Joe's wife and my good friend Kathy Maguire Bedsole who died on April 6, 2021 from COVID.

Flight 3911

Chapter 1

New York's JFK airport, one of three major airports serving the New York area, is a gateway for travelers. Tens of thousands of airline passengers move through JFK each day bound for international and domestic destinations. Passengers walk through the terminal's concourses, focusing on travel plans, hoping their flight isn't delayed, luggage lost, or wondering what they forgot to pack.

On this morning not one of those sleepy American passengers was thinking soon their lives would be forever changed.

Earlier that morning, five men of Middle Eastern descent arrived at JFK singularly, deliberately avoiding the appearance of traveling together. They passed through several security gates at different times. Each of the five was surprised how easy it was to clear the scrutiny of screening agents, especially knowing what events were planned and what was concealed in their pockets and carry-on luggage.

BILLY PAUL SMITH

Of the more than 20,000 people scurrying in the airport terminal this fall morning, 48 passengers and a crew of five were making their way to Gate 11 to board Northeast Flight 3911, nonstop to Seattle, Washington. Those needing boarding passes crowded the counter, while those with advance passes gathered near the boarding ramp. To the seasoned traveler, this appeared an unusually light load considering the heavy Boeing 757 could carry 200 people. This flight was usually full, but not today.

The flight crew boarded only minutes before passengers were allowed onboard. The pilot, Hubbell Jenson, 58, was a Vietnam veteran and had flown over 30 combat missions. He'd flown for Northeast Airlines for 20 years during which his wife, Gloria, had raised their four children, three boys and a girl, pretty much on her own.

Traveling as he did, Hubbell missed many birthdays, games, plays and bedtime stories. After every trip, there was something new that had happened while he was flying the skies. How often he had missed a new tooth, an exciting homerun, and the need for bigger shoes. In fact, this had sparked another argument with Gloria that very morning. On the Seattle trip, Hubbell would miss another of his son's games and a dinner party with friends. In two years, Hubbell planned to retire at the government mandated age of 60. In just two years, he could stay home and enjoy family milestones; but not today. Today, he was scheduled to fly to Seattle.

Hubbell's co-pilot, Larry Homer, 56, was a former Air Force pilot and Air Force Academy graduate. Larry had been married for 24 wonderful years and blessed with twin girls, Julie and Jodie. When they were born, Sarah, his wife, kept the hospital wrist bands on the girls' tiny arms to tell them apart. Now at 21, the twins were more different than they were alike. Julie was in college, majoring in biology, and Jodie was "finding herself," whatever that meant.

Between Hubbell and Larry, they had accumulated 50 years flying experience and were the most respected flight crew the small airline boasted. They were good friends and dedicated family men, although Hubbell seemed more to be married to his job. Like Hubbell, being away much of the time took its toll on Larry's marriage. Despite personal obstacles and difficulties both men experienced in their lives, often labeled as occupational hazards, both loved to fly.

Three flight attendants completed the flight crew. The senior flight attendant, Stacy Martin, 38, and Kaitlynn Morrison, 38, newest member of the crew, were best friends. They'd grown up in the same small town just outside Richmond, Virginia, but hadn't seen each other since graduation until meeting at a high school reunion only a few years before. Stacy was married and had a teenage daughter who was in the middle of a raging hormone explosion, bent on showing her independence.

Kaitlynn was newly divorced and had no children. She needed a change in her life, and it was Stacy's urging that encouraged Kaitlynn to become a flight attendant. With Stacy's seniority at Northeast, she was often able to design the schedule to ensure she and Kaitlynn worked flights together.

Suzette Quincy, 29, was the youngest flight attendant and crew member. She preferred to be known as Suzette rather than Suzie. As a child, family and friends always called her Suzie Q, and she detested the nickname. What were her parents thinking when they named her? Suzette considered legally changing her name but could not bring herself to hurt her parents' feelings. Even if she didn't like her name, her parents honored her with it.

Suzette was single and didn't have a significant other in her life. When asked why she wasn't married or why she didn't have a boyfriend, she teased it was because she hadn't met the right man. This was true, in part, because Suzette had only recently realized she preferred female companionship. She was still dealing with this surprising self-discovery and was not ready to come out of the closet but would when she met the right woman.

Brandon Powell, a business executive and part-time author, was flying to Seattle for a book signing for his newly released novel. Brandon, 46, was in excellent physical shape and, if not for the crow's feet accenting his eyes and a touch of gray teasing his temples, looked years younger than his actual age. Brandon, a seasoned pilot himself, preferred traveling in his twin-engine Baron to dealing with boarding passes and checked baggage. However, on long flights, especially coast-to-coast flights, it was more practical to travel on an airline.

After passing through security screening, Brandon headed for the Executive Club. The club was an exclusive enclave where travelers could relax in comfortable and quiet surroundings rather than the cavernous, crowded, noisy boarding gate waiting areas. The Executive Club was the airport's equivalent of a seat in first class.

As Brandon entered the club, the receptionist warmly greeted him. She flashed Brandon her gleaming Barbie smile, the same welcome she offered every traveler entering the club's double doors. "Good morning, sir. Welcome to the Executive Club." Brandon marveled at how cheerful she could be this early in the morning. The Executive Club was open 24/7. Just how long had Barbie been smiling and greeting guests during her current work shift?

Brandon smiled back and greeted her with a friendly "Good morning." Glancing at her name plate announcing she was Jennifer Bailey, he added "Jennifer" to his greeting.

"Where are you traveling today, sir?" she asked.

"Seattle," Brandon replied.

"May I see your boarding pass?" Jennifer made a notation on her pad and returned the pass to Brandon.

"Welcome to the club, Mr. Powell. I'll announce your flight when it's ready for boarding."

Brandon found a place to settle in a leather armchair.

As the crew completed preparations for the coast-to-coast flight, passengers began boarding Flight 3911. The first passengers allowed on board were passengers needing help and those traveling with children, followed by first class passengers, and finally passengers traveling in coach, beginning with the rows situated in the rear of the aircraft.

A short while later, Jennifer announced, "May I have your attention, please. Flight 3911 to Seattle, Washington, is now ready for boarding at Gate 11."

That was Brandon's call.

When Brandon reached the gate, the agent was welcoming first-class passengers to board the flight. Brandon was assigned seat 4A. As he made his way down the jetway, two men behind him were discussing their plans for the weekend. The two took their seats in 6C and 6D directly behind Brandon.

Rylander Brookhaven and John Dawsett had known each other since childhood. Ry, as his friends called him, was the president of StarTrax, a high-tech satellite communications company. Ry was on his way to Seattle to attend a three-day trade show. John had no business in Seattle but had time off and decided to go along with Ry just for the fun of it. At the end of the show, the two planned to take a side trip to Alaska for a little fishing and maybe glimpse a few bears. On their return, they planned to meet their wives in Las Vegas to cap the weekend.

In the gate waiting area, the agent announced passengers in the coach cabin were now allowed to board. Hampton Greene heard the announcement and made his way to the jetway. As Hampton passed through the cabin, he was pleased to see wide-open seating was available. Hampton usually had to buy two tickets because of his enormous girth. Today he would have an entire row of seats to himself! Ignoring his seating assignment, the big man continued to the back of the cabin and seated himself in row 21, seats A, B and C. His 390-pound frame with a 54-inch waistline comfortably spilled into all three seats. Perfect!

The last to board were four of the five Middle Eastern passengers. Abdul Mohatazana entered and took his seat in the first-class cabin, seat 2B. Following were the other three passengers speaking in heavily accented, but otherwise exceptionally good English. They appeared to know each another and were traveling together as they continued past first class aiming for their seats in coach.

The flight attendant announced the cabin door had been closed and the flight was ready for departure. She instructed all passengers to fasten their seat belts securely, place their seats in an upright position and turn off all cell phones and electronic devices.

In the cockpit, the pilots completed pre-flight procedures.

"Ground, this is Northeast 3911, ready to taxi," Hubbell announced to the ground control center.

"Northeast 3911, taxi to Runway 4 via taxiway Bravo," ground control center ordered. "You will be number three for take-off."

At exactly 8:35 am, the 757 pushed back from the jetway. By the time Flight 3911 reached the end of the taxiway, the other two jets had soared into the sky, and Flight 3911 was immediately cleared for takeoff, right on time.

"What a beautiful day it is," Hubbell noted as he and Larry eased the jet's thrusters forward and began the jet's takeoff roll.

"Northeast 3911 is rolling," he advised the tower as the 757 accelerated down the runway. When the jet reached a ground speed of 155 mph, Hubbell eased back on the yoke, and the 757 gently lifted off the runway. Northeast 3911 was airborne. The jet headed in a Northeasterly direction.

As they began their climb, Larry took the controls and turned the 757 to the west. The spectacular Manhattan skyline loomed ahead. At the southern end of the island rose two monolithic skyscrapers, the World Trade Center Towers. The Trade Towers were built during the 1970s and were the most recognizable skyscrapers in New York City, if not the world, overshadowing the Empire State Building. "Look! It's such a cloudless day we can see the towers even from this distance," Larry remarked. "What a beautiful day! We should be playing golf, not going to Seattle."

"Yep, it's a great day alright, actually perfect. Stacy has a great set of legs, did you notice?"

"Of course, I noticed. I'm a pilot, you know." The men chuckled. Small talk continued while confidently maneuvering the Boeing 757 through its ascent. Clearly their collective flying experience was obvious.

The jet continued its climb, passing through 10,000 feet at 240 knots. Air Traffic Control cleared 3911 to the cruising altitude of 37,000 feet. As Larry leveled off, Hubbell called Northeast's flight center for an update of the route's weather forecast. Off the ground for less than 20 minutes, and Hubbell was already bored.

The Boeing 757 provided the latest automatic pilot technology. The jet had the capability of taking off and landing without a pilot to guide the maneuvers. However, pilots do man the controls during takeoff and landing. Once at cruising altitude, the cockpit captains can simply sit back and enjoy the flight until time to descend and make the final approach. During long flights, this idle time can become boring.

"Northeast Dispatch, this is 3911."

"We have you 3911, go ahead."

"Level at 37,000, departure smooth, Seattle looks to be another on time arrival. What's the weather like ahead?"

"Roger 3911, no change in weather since your preflight briefing," the Northeast dispatcher responded. "There's fog on the west coast, but it should burn off before your scheduled arrival."

"Not sure of the significance," the dispatcher added, "but United just issued a directive to all captains to secure the cockpit doors. Not sure if there's a threat or if it's a drill."

"Roger, dispatch, we'll take appropriate precautions, over."

"What do you make of that?" Larry asked.

"Don't know. United might be having a safety drill. Then again, some psycho may have called in a threat," Hubbell said.

"Just so the cockpit recorder notes we took the message seriously, I'll make sure the door is shut and locked," Larry reported before getting up from his seat. Larry asked, "Do you have control of the aircraft?"

Hubbell confirmed. "Yes, I have control of the aircraft." It was procedure before a pilot or co-pilot could leave his seat, even if not leaving the cockpit, to confirm the remaining pilot had control of the aircraft.

Larry did the best he could with what he had, but the door was hardly more secure than what the locks offered. He checked the door's security by wiggling the handle before climbing back into his seat. He shook his head.

"These doors are a joke. If someone wants to get in, we both know it would be a piece of cake.

Hubbell nodded in agreement, as he scanned the instrument panel. He chuckled, then asked, "Do you know what separates flight attendants from the scum of the earth?"

"I haven't a clue, Hubbell. What separates flight attendants from the scum of the earth?"

"Cockpit doors." The two men burst into laughter, enjoying humor made at their expense.

Back in the first-class cabin, Brandon was thinking about his life. He was 46 and the only son in an affluent family. Just 10 years before, life was good until he'd been dealt serious emotional and financial blows.

His father, his mentor and best friend, died unexpectedly from a heart attack. He was only 55 years old. At 36, Brandon was forced to step into his father's shoes and take over the family business. With the responsibilities that went with his new role, he was barely able to mourn his father's passing. Then, just a year after his father died, Brandon's marriage ended. Brandon met Maureen during high school, and they were married shortly after graduation. Their union produced two sons. Brandon believed their marriage would last until death parted them. How wrong he was. To his dismay, the ending of their 17-year marriage was more dramatic than he could have imagined.

After the dust settled, the couple shared custody of their children, and the Powell family still had control of the company.

Things seemed to turn around for Brandon. He met Carmen, who he thought was the ideal woman. His relationship with Carmen remained great until additional financial difficulties forced Brandon to make major cutbacks to preserve his estate. Eventually he had no choice but to file bankruptcy. He lost everything, including Carmen. He believed his relationship with Carmen was solid, but she bolted for the door at the first hint of the bankruptcy. So much for relationships made in heaven.

The bankruptcy educated Brandon to abuses in the legal system perpetrated by lawyers. The abuses he encountered became the basis for his just released novel and the reason for traveling to Seattle.

It had been six years since his latest financial disaster. Brandon rebounded nicely and started a software company supplying global tracking solutions for small to mid-size trucking companies. He recently started a spin-off second company for his children and welcomed a new woman into his life, Grace Morrison.

Brandon and Grace had been dating for almost a year. For Brandon, it was love at first sight. Grace had the beauty every man desired. When she walked into a room every eye, men and women alike, noticed. With her 5'8" frame always accented with sexy high heels, she reached the same height as Brandon. Her glowing blonde hair hung loosely just below her shoulders. She wore the classiest clothes, usually featuring a blouse that showed just enough cleavage, but not too much. It was just enough to let everybody know she had great breasts. Her toned flat belly was just shy of six-pack abs. Her long perfectly shaped ballet designed legs rounded out a toned, well-shaped body, one any model would die for.

Their relationship ended suddenly a month before when he refused to share his financial situation with his lady love. Her questions about his financial status and net worth made him uneasy. It reminded him of Carmen who left abruptly when financial hardships surfaced. Carmen's actions had wounded Brandon so deeply that he swore he would find a woman who wanted him for the good man he was and not for what was in his bank account. He thought he had found that woman in Grace, but he was no longer sure.

Events may have changed that; he wondered if he had misjudged Grace.

He daydreamed about his relationship with this remarkable woman. The two had been inseparable since meeting. Their first major argument over his reluctance to share information about his finances ended the relationship, and Brandon had been miserable without her for the last month.

When Grace learned of the book signing and media reception in New York, she surprised him by flying from Atlanta unannounced. He had no idea she knew about the signing and was shocked when she entered the room. She was stunning in a one-piece black knee length dress with four-inch heels showing her excellent legs. When she entered the room, all eyes followed her which made Brandon swell with pride.

"How did you find out about this?" he asked with surprise. "Oh, it doesn't matter. I'm so glad to see you," he said as he hugged and kissed her gently.

"I received an invitation. I wasn't sure you would want to see me, so I waffled back and forth about going. I didn't decide until last night. I was able to get a flight on short notice, but I have no place to stay."

"You do now. I've missed you so much." Brandon's heart swelled and he felt a kaleidoscope of butterflies swirling in his stomach.

"Oh, I'm so happy to hear you say that. I would hate to feel I was the only one who was miserable. I've missed you too. I'm so proud of you. This book signing is so important, I had to be here for you," Grace admitted.

"Does this mean you want to spend the rest of your life with me for richer or poorer?" he asked.

"I prefer richer," Grace responded causing Brandon to flinch initially but then eased on hearing the rest of her answer. "But yes, I have faith in you and that's what I should have told you in the first place."

"Thanks for coming. Will you help me work the room and meet the press?" Brandon asked.

"Okay, mingle now, talk later, and we do have a lot to talk about," she admitted.

He wanted to stay with her, but the purpose of the cocktail party was to meet the press and get the word out about his book. He would be alone with Grace soon enough.

Reality interrupted his thoughts when a passenger laughed loudly while saying something to a fellow passenger seated next to him about revenge, of all things!

As John Dawsett passed Brandon's seat, it became clear by his haste this man needed the restroom fast. Montezuma's Revenge! Unfortunately for John, it was occupied. He turned and ran toward the back of the cabin for an open lavatory in the coach section.

As he rushed down the aisle, John noticed the three Middle Eastern men. Their heads were bowed, but they sat separately spaced throughout the cabin. How odd, John thought. The three seemed to be traveling together when they boarded the flight. All the empty seats and they were not sitting close together to chat; all appeared to be in prayer. John, an ex-Army Ranger with elite military training, was probably the only one on the aircraft who would make such an observation. *Allah Akbar, God is great!* John thought to himself. He continued to the lavatory, passing by unnoticed.

Back in first class, Stacy woke Brandon out of another Grace inspired daydream to take his order for breakfast. "I'd like some orange juice and maybe a bagel."

"Yes, sir," she said moving to the next occupied seat.

Rylander asked her to come back shortly because his friend was in the lavatory.

Brandon returned to daydreaming. After the author's reception last night, he and Grace left in a taxi to enjoy a late dinner. It was as if the past month of separation had not happened. Things were great, he was on top of the world again, a complete reversal of fortune. The couple made up over dinner and promised a separation would never happen again. Both had early flights in the morning, Brandon to Seattle and Grace returning to Atlanta. They would turn in after their late dinner and continue any discussion when he returned to Atlanta on Wednesday night.

Chapter 2

Seated in 2B, Abdul Mohatazana had sinister things running through his mind. He calculated this flight was right on schedule; however, he knew his fellow comrades on other flights were behind in their schedules. He had talked to Atta as he was boarding his flight in Boston. Atta's flight was bound for San Francisco, but his flight was thirty minutes behind schedule.

Abdul's stomach was churning. He was extremely upset. Abdul calculated he would delay their plan for at least another ten minutes. He knew the other three men positioned in the coach cabin were watching him because, if not for his delay, their attack would have already begun.

Abdul came from a different world. No one knew for sure where he was born. It was known he grew up in the Becca Valley of Lebanon. There was turmoil, terror, and unrest in a country about to enter a civil war. A Muslim, he ended up in school somewhere in Europe where he met Mohamed Atta who would eventually become the leader of their terrorist group.

Atta wanted to attack the White House. However, because Atta's flight was late, Abdul would be closer to the White House and he would need to take it. Atta should arrive in New York for Abdul's target about the time Abdul arrived in Washington. Had Atta's flight been on time, Atta would be in Washington, bearing down to destroy the White House. Abdul would be circling back and bearing down on the North Tower of the World Trade Center.

He checked his watch. Better wait another few minutes.

Abdul and Atta were members of a group known as Al-Qaeda, a Muslim extremist group operating in small groups known as cells. The leader and financial backer of Al-Qaida was Osama bin Laden. Bin Laden was also known as the mastermind behind the World Trade Center bombing that occurred in February 1993. Despite all the United States' intelligence and military resources, bin Laden stayed elusive and at large.

Abdul recalled Al-Qaida's efforts to assemble elite teams to receive flight training so they could commandeer planes and fly them into buildings as an act of destruction. Al-Qaida leaders selected Abdul and Atta to each lead a team of five.

The other five members of Abdul's team included, Imad Bashour, Hashem Moustapha, Said Ebrahim, Daniel Raphia, and Zacarias Moussaoui. Little was known about Imad. He might have been born in Samarra north of Baghdad in 1971. He joined the insurgency erupting in the aftermath of Iraq's invasion of Kuwait after the United States retaliated. It was known Imad had an intense hatred for anything involving the US. He was one of the first recruited and trained for this mission on American soil. Imad disliked Daniel and objected strongly when he was added to the team. But he was overruled since Daniel's features resembled a Westerner. That would be helpful. Just looking like a Westerner was enough to send Imad into a rage.

Hashem, the weakest link in the team, had been a follower and went along with the crowd. He was from Bagdad and the son of prominent Muslim parents. He believed his parents approved of his radical beliefs. Hell, this was the reason he joined the team, to please his father.

Said Ebrahim, also from Bagdad, was the wild card on the team. He spent time studying at a Boston college. He was the only one with a real taste of what it was like to be an American. He was in Boston when the United States invaded Iraq in 1991. He watched his homeland being bombed on late night television.

Daniel would be of little use in the attack because his assignment was to blend in with the passengers as a sleeper. In fact, he had boarded earlier than the other four team members. His mother was British, so his skin color and facial features blended with Caucasians more than that of his fellow jihadists. Looking like a Westerner would be his advantage. Daniel had been incarcerated before being radicalized and most, over a quarter, who spent time in prison were radicalized behind bars. Daniel grew up getting into trouble and spending his formative years in British jails. After his last release, he moved to Syria where he fully transformed into the Muslim community, though he often longed for his childhood spent in London. He often wondered how his life might have been different had he stayed in London. His move to Syria formed his deep-rooted Islamic views.

However, today Abdul's team had only a total of five members, because Zacarias Moussaoui, Abdul's friend for ten years, was arrested on August 16, 2001 for immigration violations. Abdul wondered if the FBI had become aware of their plot because they arrested Zacarias over a month before. There had been no word from his friend since his arrest but, despite detention, Abdul assumed his friend had not told anyone of their plans to attack. If the FBI knew, certainly Abdul and his team would not be on this flight today ready to carry out jihad against the infidels. Jihad is the Islamic term for holy war against the infidels. The most memorable holy war being the Crusades.

Abdul prayed Zacarias' absence would not handicap their efforts. The plan required six men to guarantee success. He prayed they would be successful this day. Allah Akbar!

It was funny what goes through a man's mind at a time like this, Abdul thought. These infidels, they are such fools. They are such easy prey. Hani Hanjour got his flight training in Arizona, Abdul Mohatazana in Florida, as did Mohammad Atta.

For a while, the team thought Hanjour might be found out. Someone from the FAA contacted him as the result of a complaint filed. They never knew for certain but thought his flight instructor suspected something. There was a minor investigation, but when the official learned he could speak broken English he dropped the matter. The FAA supplied an interpreter so Hanjour could take the pilot's exam, even though a requirement was proficiency in the English language. The exam typically took about two hours, but with the help of the interpreter, Hanjour completed the exam in eight.

Atta and Abdul may have been reckless and called unnecessary attention to themselves. But looking back with hindsight, the infidels were not smart enough to catch on. The Muslims blended in at flight schools all over the United States.

Atta left a small trainer airplane on the tarmac blocking a taxiway during his early days of training for his commercial license. The FAA reprimanded the flight school for the misadventure, but the infidels never questioned Atta. All completed their training and left flight schools qualified to fly an airliner, flying a plane into any chosen high-rise building.

Abdul finally decided he had waited long enough to begin the plan. He stood up and calmly made his way back to the curtain separating first class and coach. He stopped just before the curtain. The curtain was open before take-off, but flight attendants closed it shortly after reaching cruising altitude. The reason for this was lost on Abdul. No curtain was going to come between him and his destiny. He peered through the curtain and made eye contact with the four passengers scattered throughout coach.

There was a scream, so shrill that it broke Brandon's reverie. Abdul grabbed Stacy from the back and put a box cutter to her neck. She tried to scream but, before she could call for help, Abdul slit her throat from ear to ear. As she fell to the floor in a pool of her blood, Brandon, without thinking, sprang from his seat and rushed at the man who just slashed and killed the flight attendant. Before he could make it to the aisle, Imad hit him across the head and knocked him to the cabin floor. Rylander, momentarily stunned, started to come to Brandon's aid. He hadn't noticed Stacy lying dead in the aisle with blood gushing from the deep gash in her neck. When he finally saw her, the shock of the carnage caused him to vomit on the seatback in front of him.

"I have bomb, I will explode this plane!" shouted Said who appeared from the rear of the cabin.

"Everyone move to back of cabin at once," he screamed.

While the passengers were moving as ordered, Abdul and Imad were breaking into the cockpit. The cockpit door offered no resistance. It happened so quickly that Abdul was able to overpower Larry and repeat the professional ear-to-ear cut killing him instantly. Imad grabbed Hubbell and beat him unmercifully to the point of death.

The bodies of the pilots and Stacy were removed and tossed haphazardly onto the floor of the first-class galley.

Abdul assumed the captain's seat and took over the controls. He entered coordinates into the 757's autopilot and the jet immediately banked to the left, heading south to Washington DC toward his chosen target, the White House.

Imad started to get into the copilot's seat, but Abdul stopped him. Because they were only five and not six, he would have to fly the plane alone. Three were needed to guard and control the passengers, while Daniel, their fifth, would continue to observe as the sleeper. Since they had destroyed the cockpit door, only a curtain between first class and coach cabins separated Abdul from the passengers. If Imad stayed in the cockpit with him, the passengers might overpower them and regain control of the plane. Imad protested, but Abdul was the leader and Imad was forced to obey his orders. As he left the cockpit to join his comrades, he heard Abdul contacting the infidels on the ground.

"Control, this is the Captain," Abdul said into the radio.

"This is New York Center, identify yourself," demanded Paul Stamps who received the call.

Abdul realized he made a mistake. He should have identified the flight first. He needed to gain control and think clearly. He could not afford any more mistakes.

"We have an emergency on-board. Number four engine is on fire. We are changing course for Washington," Abdul said, realizing almost instantly he had just made another costly mistake. A 757 does not have four engines. Even with limited flying experience, he knew he raised alarms because no pilot would request an airport 200 miles away if there was an emergency. He panicked and turned the communications and transponders off. Another mistake. The infidels on the ground would surely know he was not the real captain. Abdul hoped he had not alerted them too soon to give ground time to react. Things were clearly not going according to plan.

Abdul's stomach was churning. He was especially angry with Zacarias. He would not be in such a vulnerable position if his friend had not been arrested by the authorities. If they failed, it would be because of Zacarias.

Said pointed to the red straps around their waists and again reminded, "We have bombs."

The passengers scurried to the back of the cabin. Brandon was the last to follow the order. Forty-eight passengers and the two surviving crew members moved into the rows in the rear of the airliner.

"Now that we have your attention," the leader said with a sneer, "we have bombs. We can explode plane. Keep quiet, keep seat. You will be freed when we get demands. No one is hurt."

In the New York Air Traffic Control Center, Paul Stamps notified his supervisor Jeff Nichols of the unusual radio transmission he received from Northeast Flight 3911. Paul had been on the job only three weeks but was rated among the best in his training class. He heard mumbling among his fellow controllers but wasn't aware of any major developments in the making, although sensing something big was happening. Paul and Jeff were unaware two other similar changes in course actions were issued, one by an American flight and one by a United. Neither flight called in an emergency because, just like Northeast 3911, the pilots had been overpowered and killed before they could declare an emergency.

Jeff Nichols, the supervisor on duty, suddenly learned three aircraft had gone silent at the same time. Paul's contact with Northeast 3911 meant four aircraft went silent within minutes of each other. Jeff's intuition based on 30 years on the job realized this morning was going to be different. On his first day on the job at Teterboro at 29 years old, Jeff put two jets on final for the same runway at the same time. Disaster was avoided by an alert supervisor observing the new guy on the job. It was a lesson Jeff never forgot and believed it ultimately made him a better controller. It could have cost him his job but thanks to his supervisor, he was able to go on to become one of the best in the area. Jeff put a watchful eye over Paul since he reported for work three weeks before.

"This is BS, what other contact have you had?" asked Jeff.

"No contact sir, other than Flight 3911 declared an emergency. He stated number four engine was on fire."

"Yeah, well, a 757 only has two engines," said Nichols.

"That's what I mean."

"This is too suspicious! Try to contact them again. Try reaching them on the emergency frequency," Nichols directed the young controller.

Stamps turned to his control panel and tried to make contact. "Northeast 3911, this is New York," he repeated over and over, but he never received a response.

Meanwhile, Jeff opened the direct line to the North American Aerospace Defense Command better known as NORAD. General Oliver Hopkins was on the other end of the line. He was already aware of the missing airliners and had ordered F18s to turn toward the north east quadrant of the United States. For a moment, General Hopkins thought his staff might be playing a joke. After all, this was the most unusual day of his 35-year career. Today was to be his last day as a working general, his retirement was to begin at 1600 hours. His staff had a retirement reception planned during the lunch hour. Refreshments were already being set up. So much for it being a surprise, and so much for this being a joke.

"General Hopkins here, report?"

"Sir, this is Jeff Echols, supervisor in charge in New York Center. We have four airliners…

"Good God. Look toward Manhattan! There is an explosion in one of the Trade Center Towers," Paul exclaimed.

"General Hopkins, our situation just turned serious. I am confident we have four hijacked airliners and I'm sure one just hit the World Trade Center Towers," explained Jeff.

"Network news just broke in and confirmed, there is an explosion, we are monitoring the situation. Let's keep this line open," General Hopkins ordered. "This is real world." There would be no retirement party today.

In the back of the coach cabin, John opened the door to the lavatory. Imad, unaware a passenger was occupying it, slammed the door back in John's face knocking him partially back into the lavatory, splitting open his forehead just above his eyebrow. Blood spattered everywhere.

"Get up! Take a seat or die now!" the hijacker commanded.

Dazed, John staggered up the aisle looking for the first empty seat he could find, blood dripping from his head. He slipped into the seat next to Brandon. He noticed his seat mate also appeared injured, blood flowing from his nose and mouth. Rylander was behind them along with Hampton Green, who now was taking up only two seats.

Brandon and Rylander were the only passengers who had witnessed death. Those seated in coach had no idea the flight attendant, pilot, and first officer were murdered, and a hijacker was flying the jet.

Imad stood guard in the rear cabin while Said and Hashem remained next to Brandon and John who were sitting in the front row of passengers. They were speaking in Arabic when Hashem, who appeared in charge, straddled two seats to tower above everyone. He called for their attention.

"We are well armed," he began in perfect, but thick English, "You will not be harmed if you keep seated and stay quiet. We are heading to Washington DC and they have agreed to meet our terms. We will release you in Washington in less than one hour after they meet our demands. We have weapons and bombs. Do not talk, do not move, and do not get out of your seats."

Hashem, Said, and Imad walked forward to first class but stopped at the curtain. They each turned as if standing guard but had left no one in the rear of the plane guarding the passengers.

Despite the surreal series of events, Brandon carefully glanced around and pulled out his seat phone. He dialed Grace. There was no answer. She must be on her flight he thought. Then he tried to call his mother, again no answer.

Then he dialed 911.

"911, what's your emergency?"

"I am on Northeast Flight 3911. We have been hijacked!" he whispered.

"I can't hear you, sir, speak up, I can't hear you over the background noise."

He noticed a hijacker staring in his direction and hid the phone under his leg.

Hampton used his cell phone to call his wife and noticed the hijacker staring at them.

"Hello."

"Oh, my God!" Hampton first said loudly, toning it down to continue. "Call the FBI, tell 'em Flight 3911 has been hijacked. They told us we are headed to Washington. Best I can tell, we turned south. I don't know what's going to happen, but always know I love you and the children. If I can, I'll call back in a couple minutes." He stared at the screen on his cell phone displaying his home telephone, reluctant to press End. He hoped beyond all hope he would be alive to make that call in minutes.

"My wife just told me two airliners hit the World Trade Center Towers; both buildings are in flames," he announced to everyone close enough to hear.

Rylander grabbed the seat phone to place a call to his wife on her cell phone. He believed she was at home but was certain she would have her cell phone nearby and would answer regardless of where she was.

The phone rang once, and he heard her voice. "Hello," he heard her say. The greeting sounded more like a question than a greeting.

"Ann, it's me. We…"

"God, thank God you're safe," Ann interrupted with a sigh of relief upon hearing Ry's voice. "I thought it might be your flight. The World Trade Center has been hit by an airliner and…"

"Ann," Ry exclaimed, cutting her off. "We have been hijacked, get the FBI on the other line, I'll keep this line open."

"Oh God! Hijacked? Are you alright? What's going on? Ry, please tell me they haven't hurt you. Oh, I pray they haven't hurt you," Ann rambled, panic filling her voice.

"We're okay right now, but I'm a witness to the pilots' murders. I don't have time to explain everything. These guys are serious and dangerous. I need you to get the FBI on the phone. Tell them we have been hijacked and need help. We need their help. Now, Ann. We need help NOW."

Ann froze with panic. The phrase "Be careful what you pray for" passed through her mind. She prayed her husband was alive and he would call her. God answered her prayer. Ry was alive for now. It never occurred to her she would need to do more than pray. Now she needed to act, and act swiftly, to save Ry, her Ry.

Ann always prided herself on her abilities and capabilities as the perfect homemaker. She made sure her family and her home were priorities. She was highly organized and planned well in advance, anticipating every reasonable need and contingency. Never in her wildest dreams did it occur to her she would need to know how to contact the FBI on a moment's notice. A moment that could mean life or death for her husband. Her Ry.

"Get the FBI on the line," Ry instructed her. Fine, she could make a phone call. She would need to look up the number. Is the FBI listed under the white pages or yellow pages, she wondered? Where was the FBI office? Was there a local office or did she need to call Washington DC? Could she call 911 and ask them to connect her? Yes, she thought, that's exactly what she would do.

She used her cell phone and put Ry on hold, then dialed 911.

John and Brandon seated in front of Rylander and Hampton overheard Rylander's conversation. Although they knew the crew was dead, it was only now John and Hampton realized this was more serious than just a hijacking.

A muffle of whispers was heard as passengers began using seat phones and cell phones to call loved ones.

"It's not the World Trade Centers, it's the Pentagon, my wife has it on the TV."

"No, it's the Pentagon and the World Trade Center Towers" claimed another.

Brandon tried to reach Grace. No answer. This might be his last chance, so he called her home number to leave a voicemail.

"We have been hijacked. I've witnessed the killing of three people. We've got to do something," Brandon said loud enough for those around him to hear.

"How many are there?" asked John.

"I think there are three," whispered Rylander.

"There are four. One is flying the plane, one is guarding the cockpit door, and there are two watching us. That's at least four."

"Yeah, and two keep going back and forth between our cabin and the cockpit door," reported Hampton.

"They are guarding the cockpit," mused John. "They don't seem to be too concerned about us. They must know everybody is on their phones. They have to hear the mumbling."

"They're not worried about us because they got bombs strapped around their waists," said a lady sitting somewhere behind them.

"That's what they want us to think. I'm an ex-Army Ranger. I know explosives. That was not a bomb around the leader's waist. I saw it. I'd bet my life, it's nothing more than small pieces of wood block painted red with strings connecting them."

"That makes sense, how else could they have gotten past security?" Hampton asked no one in particular.

"That may be so, but I know they have knives; they cut the throats of two of the crew. So, they have weapons," said Brandon.

"Yeah, and they beat the pilot to death; they mean business and won't hesitate to kill again," Hampton feared.

"Seems I remember seeing the cockpit doors busted wide open before I was knocked out," added Brandon.

He turned toward Rylander. Remarkably he was able to reach an FBI office. He was on the phone with an FBI agent.

"Yes, best we can tell there are maybe four hijackers. They look Iranian, or Arabic, or something."

"If we're really going to Washington, we better do something fast. We will be there soon," called Brandon.

"But what can we do?" cried someone from the other side of the cabin.

"We have to fight, and we have to do it fast!" declared John.

"So, if we take out the guards, there's still the one flying the plane. You said the pilots are dead." said Hampton.

"We'll be killed if we move, they said so. They will blow us up, we will all die," cried the lady across the aisle as she started to sob.

"We're going to die anyway," Rylander said as he waited on the line. "They're telling me the Pentagon and World Trade Center crashes appear to have been deliberate. This is no coincidence. We will certainly be next!"

"We only have a few minutes to agree on an attack plan and go for it. All or nothing!" urged John.

Brandon contemplated for a moment and then spoke up. "I'm a pilot, I can fly this thing if we can take them out."

"John, you are the ex-military expert, make a plan fast, tell us what to do," Rylander begged.

He returned to the FBI on the open phone.

"We decided to fight back. There's a passenger with us who says he's a pilot."

"I need to speak with him. Can you make it happen?" asked the agent.

"Not sure, I am on a seat phone, the cord may not be long enough," he said as he tapped Brandon on the shoulder. "FBI wants to talk to you."

"How?"

"Here, see if you can get the phone without them seeing."

Brandon reached his hand between the seats as Rylander stretched the phone cord to its limits. It reached far enough, and he sank low in his seat.

"This is Brandon Powell."

"This is Special Agent Brown and patched in is NORAD Commander General Hopkins. You have a serious problem and I understand you are a pilot. Please don't tell me you're a model airplane pilot! What's your experience?"

"Nothing this big, but I can handle this one with ground help."

"We have a 757 pilot ready to talk you through."

"Mr. Powell, this is General Hopkins, can you hear me?"

"Yes, sir."

"You will have to carry this burden alone. I would not say anything to anyone else to keep panic to a minimum. We have reason to believe the hijackers are heading for a target in Washington. Sir, we cannot let that happen.

"Two fighter jets will intercept you in less than ten minutes. If you people are successful in taking over the aircraft, we must have a way to verify it is you at the controls. Use code word Sampson if you get command of the aircraft. If we do not hear that code word in 15 minutes, we will have no choice but to shoot your airliner down."

As Brandon's life flashed before him, he realized he was about to die.

"I understand, but I've never seen the cockpit of an airliner. I don't know anything about the communications package, what channel, what switches. Are the hijackers in contact with you by radio as we speak?"

"No, sir, we have had no contact by radio in over 20 minutes."

"We'll do our best, but if I get in that seat, I don't want to become target practice for your fighters. Here's what I'll do. If your fighters see me begin a steady climb to increase my altitude by 2500 feet, you'll know it's me."

"Very well, but immediately bring your course to 2-7-0 degrees."

"Okay, let me get this straight, we overtake four armed hijackers. Then get control, climb 2500 feet while coming to 2-7-0, right?"

"Sounds simple enough, and our prayers are with you."

Brandon put the phone down and began to inform the others within hearing range.

"We have about ten minutes. We need to storm the front of the cabin and do it fast."

"Everyone get behind me I'm the biggest. It will be like a football play. I'll run interference, everybody and I mean everybody, get behind me and push," Hampton volunteered.

"I'll be right behind you. Give me your belt, Hampton. I'll use it to snare the pilot so he can't put us in a dive, if we get that far," added John.

"I have to be in front. I have to get to the controls fast," said Brandon.

"But you're the only one who can fly this bird, we have to protect you at all costs, stay at least fifth in line," John reminded Brandon.

You could sense and smell the fear among the passengers. By now it was clear the nation was under a terrorist attack. Word spread terrorists used three airliners as bombs. All knew their airliner was clearly hijacked for the same purpose and they would be next. Many were on phones saying goodbyes to loved ones, others were crying, others praying. A few planned to take a part in the charge to stop the hijackers.

"We go in one minute. Everybody prepare to charge down the aisle behind Hampton. We must take out the ones guarding the door fast. I'll work my way into the cockpit and take care of the guy flying the plane. Be fast and be silent," ordered John.

"If there is a way, subdue rather than kill. I'm sure the FBI will want to talk to them. Let's all say the Lord's Prayer and then go on amen," said Brandon.

Chapter 3

Williiam Branson Cauldwell squatted on a rocky promontory and studied the bleak, boulder-strewn landscape. His ruggedly chiseled face bore the look of intense dissatisfaction. His fierce blue eyes peered through the thin column of smoke steadily wafting upward from the thick cigar firmly clenched between strong, white teeth.

The object of his gaze was a group of Afghan tribesmen 100-yards distant and 50-feet below, who were trying to execute immediate reaction drills under the direction of four American Army Rangers. The drills were designed to enable the Afghan militia members to survive and beat back any Taliban ambushes they were sure to encounter upon deployment in the field. This group apparently wasn't comprised of the sharpest tools in the shed.

As Cauldwell watched the hesitant, ineffectual maneuvering of the hapless group of new trainees, he began to think back about the series of events that conspired to bring him to this forsaken spot, 7,000 feet up in the Hindu Kush, 200 miles Northeast of Kabul and hard upon the Pakistan border.

W. B. Cauldwell ("Wild Bill" behind his back, but never to his face), was born and raised in the coalfields of Harlan County, Kentucky. He had been a bruising, 210-pound All American fullback in high school and heavily recruited by a multitude of Division I-A universities. He signed a letter of intent to accept a full scholarship at the University of Kentucky and both his immediate and extended families rejoiced, as he would become the first of any in the family to enter the realm of higher education.

Then his father died in a mine explosion and for 18-year-old Bill Cauldwell, the appeal of academia and college football disappeared with irrevocable finality.

He enlisted in the Marine Corps in August 1982 and was meritoriously promoted to private first class upon graduation from boot camp. His performance as an infantry rifleman in the Second Marine Division was so outstanding that, after successive meritorious promotions to lance corporal, corporal and sergeant, he was persuaded by his superiors to apply for Officer Candidate School (OCS), at Quantico, Virginia. To his very great surprise he was accepted and reported in on 2 January 1983.

As a second lieutenant he attended Basic School at Quantico, then reported to the 1st Marine Division at Camp Pendleton, California on 3 September 1983. He was assigned as a rifle platoon commander with Company A, 1st Battalion, Fifth Marine Regiment. Cauldwell's rise was then nothing if not meteoric. As a first lieutenant, and again as a captain and company commander in 1986, he was promoted ahead of his contemporaries. In 1990 he found himself in the Middle East as a 26-year-old major and the only battalion commander in the 1st Marine Division who was not a lieutenant colonel.

In the crushing rout of the Iraqi forces that freed Kuwait, one of Cauldwell's rifle companies captured a five-man cell of Iraqi irregulars and a marine interpreter whom the captives did not realize could speak Farsi. The interpreter overheard the five praising Allah and indicating the entire 1000-man marine battalion would shortly be annihilated.

Not willing to trust in the rapidity of prisoner processing likely to accrue sending the five to regimental headquarters, Cauldwell told the company commander to have three of his best NCOs, sergeant or above, escort the Iraqis to the most secluded venue that could be found in the immediate vicinity.

Within minutes, the captain returned to report that the mission had been carried out and led his battalion commander to an underground bunker the enemy had constructed to house tank ammunition and rocket rounds.

Cauldwell paused just inside the bunker entrance to allow his eyes to adjust from the brutal glare of a merciless sun to the semi-darkness of the interior. He then saw three marines standing with their weapons trained on the five prisoners. The Iraqis sat on the dirt deck of the bunker, backs against a row of heavy crates, hands secured to the rear and with their ankles lashed together.

"Captain have your three marines stand by outside and keep all hands at least 100 feet away from the entrance. Find our interpreter who heard this motley crew yappin' about killing us and get him in here. Tell him to leave his weapon outside."

"Aye, aye, sir. Okay, men, follow me." The captain exited the bunker followed by his NCOs.

Less than a minute later a young marine corporal appeared in the hatch.

"Corporal Devane reporting as ordered, sir."

"Awright, Corporal Devane, get in here."

The marine stepped forward hesitantly, squinting hard to pierce the gloom. Cauldwell then swung the massive, eight-foot steel door, which closed with a heavy resounding clang.

Producing a flashlight, Cauldwell switched it on and placed it on top of a crate to the left of the hatch so the beam fell upon the five captives.

"Now then corporal, since these assholes are about to kill us, I am gonna learn the when, how, and where of it. These scumbags will talk. Your only function will be to speak to these maggots in rag head talk and tell me what they say. You got that?"

"Sir. Yes, sir."

"Right. Let's start with the shit head in the middle so his four friends can see the show. Ask him what they have in the works that is going to kill my marines."

The corporal approached the dirty, heavy-set Iraqi, kicked the bottom of his right foot and spoke in Farsi. When the corporal finished there was a moment of silence, then snarling teeth flashed amid the recesses of a thick, black beard as a torrent of words erupted. When the tirade ceased, Cauldwell grunted.

"I take it from the tone of his voice that our friend doesn't want to cooperate."

"No sir, he doesn't. He says Americans are camel dung and that in less than an hour all of us will be dead. He says the arms of Allah will embrace him as he watches thousands of American infidels burn amid the fires of hell."

"Yeah? Well we will see if we can't give 'em a little taste of hell before we go."

From a leather sheath on his belt, Cauldwell removed a stainless-steel Leatherman combination tool and opened it to expose the heavy, needle-nosed pliers. Bringing out his Ka-Bar fighting knife, he bent down, sliced the laces on the man's left boot and jerked the footwear free. A powerful stench caused an involuntary recoil.

"Christ on a crutch! Don't these sonsabitches ever wash?"

Not wanting to touch the stinking sock now exposed, Cauldwell worked the garment free of the foot with the point of the Ka-Bar, then pressed his left combat boot down hard on the bare ankle. Bending at the waist, he forced the lower jaw of the pliers up under the nail of the big toe to a depth of half an inch, then closed the jaws in an iron grip. The Iraqi roared in pain.

"Hell, he ain't felt nothin' yet! Ask him again, corporal."

Devane spoke and the captive answered.

"Sir, he says you are a sodomizer of goats and camels, he hates you to the depths of his soul, and you will never make him talk."

Without a word, Cauldwell imparted a sudden, violent twisting and pulling motion to the pliers. The entire toenail tore free and the man screamed.

"Ask him how he likes me now. See if he has any answers to our original questions."

Amid groans of pain the man replied to the interpreter.

"Major, he still won't talk and says Allah will give him the strength to endure anything you can do to him."

"Tell 'em he better have Allah send him strength right quick." Cauldwell reached down with the pliers and tore off the nail on the little toe. The Iraqi emitted a high-pitched, piercing scream but Devane's next inquiry produced only another stream of outburst.

Cauldwell started to feel grudging admiration for the man's toughness and was about to escalate the severity of his method when he noticed the captive at the end of the line to the right was showing great distress. Unlike the other three who had remained stoic in manner and expression while their comrade was suffering at the major's hands, this one was sweating profusely, his breathing short and shallow and great fear showed in his eyes.

Moving swiftly, Cauldwell knelt beside the terrified prisoner and pressed the tip of his fighting knife into the skin beneath the man's left eye.

"Corporal, tell this scum-suckin' pig that he better tell me what I want to know, or I'll scoop out his fuckin' eye, mangle it, then hold it out and show it to the good eye."

Devane began to speak and Cauldwell pressed a little harder with the point of the razor-sharp weapon. Intermittently gasping for air, the diminutive Iraqi spoke fluently for several seconds, then was interrupted by a burst of words from Toes.

"Hey sir, this guy says it's some kind of bomb and he'll show us where it is. The one you were working on must be the boss and he says he's going to cut this one to pieces one inch at a time."

Cauldwell jumped to his feet, took two strides, bent down slightly, and rendered Toes immediately unconscious with a crushing right cross. Moving to the door, he jerked it open and let it swing until it hit the wall. Retrieving his flashlight, he turned to Devane.

"Okay, corporal, help me get 'I'll Spill My Guts' on his damn feet."

"Aye, aye, sir."

The two marines pulled the captive upright and Cauldwell slashed the rope binding the man's ankles. The major seized the man by the back of his shirt and propelled him through the hatch up the narrow wooden stairs with Devane trailing close behind. On the surface, he addressed the nearest of the marines standing guard.

"Sergeant get a corpsman up here. One of 'em stubbed his toes. Then get a vehicle and transport all four back to regiment."

"Aye, aye, sir."

"Captain Akers!" Cauldwell bellowed.

"Yes, sir!" The company commander hustled across the sand.

"Get a radio and accompany me. This puke says there's a bomb around here an' he's gonna show us where."

"Aye, aye, sir. RADIO MAN UP!" A marine with a radio strapped to his back plowed through the dunes. "Follow me and the battalion commander, lance corporal."

"Aye, aye, sir."

26

Cauldwell turned to Devane. "Okay, corporal tell this numb nut to lead the way. Tell him he better not be bullshittin' me, or I'll cut off his damn dick an' make 'im eat it!"

"Aye, aye, sir." The interpreter spoke to the prisoner who nodded repeatedly and then moved off with short, rapid steps to the right on an oblique angle.

In less than three minutes the Iraqi stopped, balanced on his left foot, pointed with the toe of his right foot, and said something to Devane.

"Sir. He says the bomb is right here, sir."

Cauldwell eyed the ground and saw evidence the sand had recently been disturbed.

"Ask him if the damn thing is booby trapped. Will it blow if we try to uncover it?"

The corporal and the captive conversed briefly.

"Sir, he says they didn't have time to emplace booby traps. Says the thing is on a timer and set to go at twelve hundred."

Cauldwell glanced at his watch. Eleven eighteen. They had forty-two minutes.

"Captain Akers, get on the horn an' get EOD up here, right now!"

"Aye, aye, sir." The company commander seized the radio handset and spoke rapidly. Nine minutes later, five explosive ordnance disposal personnel roared up in a HUMV producing a rooster tail of swirling sand.

As soon as the team leader dismounted, Cauldwell spoke.

"Okay, men, there's some kind of serious damn bomb right here beneath my feet. It's on a timer an' set to go in thirty minutes, so get at it."

"Aye, aye, sir."

The EOD marines went to work with practiced efficiency as the five marines and their nervous prisoner looked on.

"Sir, shouldn't we clear the area?" Captain Akers sounded concerned.

"What the hell for, skipper? If this thing is as bad as those assholes say, it'll eat us up anyway."

The EOD team defused the bomb with six minutes to spare.

"Well, men, I guess that's all the entertainment for today." Cauldwell began to retrace his steps and the others followed.

Once back in the vicinity of the bunker, Cauldwell addressed his company commander. "Skipper, Corporal Devane did a hell of a fine job. I'd like to see a meritorious promotion to the sergeant on my desk in the near future."

"Roger that, sir."

"Now then, have somebody take this poor soul back to regiment. Make sure that the people in S-2 know he showed us the bomb and that they have to keep him away from the other prisoners."

"Aye, aye, sir."

Cauldwell's eyes suddenly fixed on a small group standing about 40 yards off. "Say Skipper, who's your company corpsman talkin' to over there?"

"His name's Saunders, sir. He's imbedded press corps with AP, sir."

"Well, I guess the defecation is about to make contact with the whirling blades of a very large fan."

"Sir?"

"Nothing, skipper. Carry on."

"Aye, aye, sir."

Cauldwell walked away knowing the life he had known and loved was about to end.

The story of Cauldwell's interrogation tactics aired two days later. No mention of the fact the bomb had proved a sophisticated and deadly combination with a nuclear core, surrounded with chemical and biological agents that would have assuredly caused a massive loss of life.

Three weeks after the incident resulting in a court martial ended, Cauldwell's regimental commander said good-bye with tears in his eyes and Cauldwell found himself a civilian passenger on an aircraft bound for Washington, DC. He had been requested to pay a visit to a specific office at the Pentagon and agreed to do so.

Two hours after landing at Reagan International the disgraced Cauldwell entered the Pentagon. No longer in possession of a military ID card, security held him for twelve minutes until an escort arrived to get him.

He had expected a bureaucratic ass chewing for his actions in Kuwait and was greatly surprised when he was offered a job as a covert advisor to provide military training to tribesmen in Afghanistan.

He had accepted immediately and landed in Kabul two days later. He had been in the armpit of the world for more than 11 years living in a tent that was stifling in summer and freezing in winter. He hadn't tasted real coffee in four months and his only cooking implement was a small microwave that emitted sounds of serious electronic distress when used, which wasn't often because the diesel-powered generator suffered from a variety of internal ailments that were defiant of cure at the hands of their only mechanic.

Still, Cauldwell was glad to be doing something he believed was furthering the cause of freedom. He had developed both a liking and respect for the Afghans under his charge.

The high-country tribe members were strong, tough and possessed great character. They trained hard and when giving their word it could be relied upon absolutely. In a firefight they were, to a man, stalwart, unflinching and ferocious, something the Taliban had learned at great cost. Those he trained revered Cauldwell, rendered unto him a fierce loyalty, and called him "The Major," a name he did not discourage for he still spit-shined his combat boots and wore his marine corps camouflage utilities, albeit without rank insignia. Wild Bill still considered himself a marine and bore no grudge toward the organization that had not wanted to court martial him, but which in the glare of publicity was offered no other choice.

He thought briefly and with distaste about those proceedings, then grunted and muttered, "Ah well a small price to pay for having been one of the world's finest and for saving my marines."

So here he was surrounded by splendid desolation. It was Tuesday, 11 September 2001, a day marking 11 years.

Cauldwell stood up, removed the cigar from his mouth and said to himself, "Better get on down there and see if I can bring some order to that damn Chinese fire drill."

Replacing the cigar between his teeth, he took two vigorous pulls, then started downhill through a wreath of swirling blue smoke.

Chapter 4

Everyone began to pray. Fifty heads bowed.

"Our Father, who art in heaven, hallowed be Thy name."

A few whimpered and sniffled back tears, but there was an unusual sense of serenity filling the cabin, considering they could all be dead in less than five minutes. They all knew it.

"Deliver us from evil."

The hijackers stood at the entrance to the first-class cabin seemingly unconcerned.

"Forever and ever, Amen."

"God be with us!" Hampton got up and began a fast, almost running pace toward the front of the cabin. John and Rylander came next with Brandon following from the rear.

Imad screamed in Arabic to warn the others and then braced for the advancing assault. Those joining the assault behind Brandon hurled plates and unopened soft drink cans over Hampton's head toward the hijackers as if pitching a barrage of grenades. The hijackers stood firm at the entrance to first class. They brandished what appeared to be box cutters but did not make overt gestures to reach the supposed bombs around their waists. Hampton, closing in for face-to-face combat, prepared for the worse, but prayed there would be no attempt by the hijackers to set off a bomb.

Like a sumo wrestler, Hampton's almost 400-pound body with his log-sized arms stretched wide, dove into the three hijackers protecting the cockpit. A razor-sharp blade pierced his chest, making a cut down to his navel. Hampton's blood spattered over John as he ran up the big man's back like a fullback trying to score a touchdown at the goal line over the biggest lineman ever produced. John jumped over the scuffle and raced toward the cockpit.

Imad retreated to the open cockpit door, ready to pull the cord on the red waistband bomb hoping to scare off any further advance. Adrenaline and anger now in control, John bore down on the only obstacle between him and the pilot. John wasn't sure if the hijacker had a bomb but didn't have the balls to obey orders and detonate it. He was sure this low-life piece of worthless crap would be no match for this ex, scratch that, this retired but determined army ranger.

Imad could see darkness in the infidel's eyes. The man's eyes were dark with purpose, but without emotion. Unprepared for retaliation by the infidels, he stood his ground and prepared to defend the cockpit without the aid of his fake bomb, but with the use of a plastic box cutter showing a one-inch razor blade. He extended the box cutter at the infidel, more in defense rather than offense.

John's former combat skills were still sharp. Imad was inexperienced; John grabbed the terrorist's arm, easily avoiding the blade flying toward him, shattering it as he did. A direct blow to the head knocked out the hijacker. John wanted to twist him around and snap his neck but remembered Brandon's instructions to subdue the hijackers and avoid killing them. As he reluctantly released the unconscious body, he felt a sharp, hot searing pain in his back. He'd been stabbed.

Said had been able to escape the pandemonium at the first-class entrance and retreated to help defend the cockpit. He was desperate to help his comrade who was knocked unconscious by the infidel.

In hot pursuit, Rylander jumped on the hijacker and began beating him about the head with his fists, trying to defend his longtime friend who had been stabbed in the back.

At that same time, John turned to face the hijacker who had just stabbed him. Utilizing every bit of his close quarter combat skills, he grabbed the hijacker by his head. His anger was so intense he was unable to control himself and snapped his neck like a twig, killing him, and watched him fall to the floor. Said Ebrahim lay dead, the first death inflicted by the angry and outraged passengers.

As soon as he released the dead hijacker, John realized he had not only subdued, but he had also killed. His inability to control his anger made him unable to think straight. The fight was far from over and he needed to gather himself and keep going.

Don't stop! Go through them. Keep moving. Think! Think!

During his attack, Hampton, although badly bleeding, managed to pin the hijacker still flailing his box cutter. Two passengers risked a slashing to grab the arm and pin it down behind a seat. Hashem, the lone remaining guard in first class, had already killed two passengers with his deadly blade. Several passengers cornered him; he was not getting away.

John, also badly bleeding, turned toward the cockpit just as the pilot put the plane into a deep dive. John sailed through the air with the belt ready to cuff the hijacker to the chair. He stunned the terrorist, hitting the SOB on the side of the head. He wrapped the belt over the shoulders of the counterfeit pilot and cinched it tight, pulling his arms away from the flight control wheel. Abdul squirmed, but was unable to free himself as the jet automatically returned to level flight.

"I've got him! I've got him!" yelled John as he hit the terrorist pilot on the back of his head. He beat the man until he slumped in his seat, unconscious, keeping full pressure on the cinched belt. He continued his assault, each blow landing on target.

Rylander entered the cockpit.

"Don't kill him, John, don't do it!" Ry exclaimed.

"Sorry, got carried away," John apologized to his friend. "I'm hurt, I'm bleeding really bad, and I got to take another crap."

"Brandon, get in here!" screamed Rylander heading back to the cabin.

Brandon made his way out of the fracas, leaving passengers to detain the two hijackers still alive.

"Get him outta here fast!" ordered Brandon, "I've got to make contact. I've got to signal Air Control now!"

John gave the cinched belt to Rylander to keep tight as he reached over and pulled the unconscious drooling pilot from the seat. Brandon moved into position and scanned the control panel to get familiar with it. He couldn't find the radio, but he did find the autopilot. He hoped everything worked the way it was labeled. The autopilot was off, so he pulled back on the control yoke to begin an abrupt climb.

"Altimeter—37,000. Must get 2500 feet fast and hold." Brandon said to himself. "Ease to 39,500. They will know we did it; they won't shoot us down. Turning to 2-7-0 degrees."

An F18 fighter pulled alongside the 757. Brandon waved to the fighter but still could not make radio contact. He had never seen so many switches in an airplane. Find the right one, turn it on, and hope they are on the frequency. Yeah, he'd flown small airplanes, but this? Insane!

"Acclimate yourself to this aircraft. Scan the instruments, scan the instruments! Blue side up! Blue side up!" he said aloud, mimicking the instructions of his first flight instruction some 20 years earlier. Funny the things you think about in a situation like this.

Brandon found the transponder first. It was the first thing he recognized. It was off. Turn it on; squawk 7700, the emergency code. Ident! That'll tell them we are in control, but where are the radios?

"Look at that fighter off to the left. Looks like he's showing us he's armed," noted Rylander as the jet rocked to show missiles noticeably stashed under the wings.

"Find a paper and pen and write in big letters the word SAMPSON!"

"What?" Rylander asked, not understanding Brandon's instructions.

"Do it now. It's the code showing we have control. They're gonna shoot us down if we can't confirm we've taken control. If I can't figure out the radio, they are gonna shoot us down!" Brandon explained quickly.

Rylander tore through a flight bag behind the copilot's seat and found a legal pad and pen. He quickly scribbled the code word and held it to the window. He hoped the fighter pilot could see the message and not blow them out of the sky. How ironic, he thought, if it was the US military that exploded their plane to bits and not the hijackers.

Captain Mark Martin in his F18 fighter eased up alongside the Boeing 757. Code name, Markle, he was a career military man. He couldn't remember a day when the thought of climbing into his jet and flying high didn't thrill him. Flying was his passion. Protecting America and its air space and borders was his duty. It never occurred to him he would be ordered to shoot down a commercial airliner with innocent Americans on board. As conflicted as he was, he knew he would never disobey an order from a superior officer, especially his commander in chief.

He pulled alongside the 757 and tipped his wings to show the weapons he was carrying on the underside of his jet. He hoped this show of force would intimidate the hijackers if they were still in control. What they did not know was the arms beneath the wings were dummies. He happened to be on a routine training exercise when he was ordered to intercept the 757. During exercises, his jet carried dummy arms.

This was no exercise. This was the real world. When he received instructions to intercept the airliner, he also received the rules of engagement. The President of the United States authorized deadly force. If the passengers were not able to regain control of the aircraft, his orders were to destroy the 757. If he were carrying live weapons, he could fire a missile and shoot down the plane. However, with no munitions he would need to ram the 757. He was not expected to die when he rammed the plane. He would eject himself from his fighter moments before.

Markle noticed a piece of paper plastered on the cockpit window. A message. He eased the jet closer to the airliner trying to decipher the message. Then he saw it. "NORAD, this is Angel Leader. We have Sampson! I repeat, we have Sampson! We have Sampson!"

"Roger, Angel Leader. Advise Sampson to continue 2-7-0 heading and escort Sampson to the west. Will advise destination shortly," replied NORAD.

"Roger, NORAD. No radio contact with Sampson. It's busted or maybe he can't figure it out, but we will attempt to have him follow us."

"Roger, Angel Leader. Our flyboy has limited experience. None in heavy jets."

"Roger, NORAD. Copy that."

Markle nudged his F18 forward, dipping his wings and making a shallow turn to the south then back west.

Brandon saw the F18 dip its wings. He understood the pilot's signal to follow him and intended to do just that. He felt relieved; they had done it, defeated the hijackers and saved themselves. But Brandon soon realized his biggest challenge lay ahead; he had to land this thing.

Brandon engaged the autopilot and hoped it worked as advertised. Now he could scan the instruments and familiarize himself with the panel. He would have to learn a lot more between now and time to land the big jet.

The passengers secured the three hijackers who were still alive, not realizing they just captured the first POWs of the War on Terror. They used at least five belts each to bind their hands and feet. Then John, injured but still moving and helping secure the hijackers in seats, slumped to the floor.

Rylander began taking care of the wounded while a passenger claiming to be a doctor attended to John.

Two passengers died in the assault. Hampton was the most seriously injured but would survive. His wound was a razor cut from his upper chest to his navel. Because of his enormous girth and the relatively small size of the box cutter, the cut to Hampton's body was only half-inch deep. John had a similar cut down his back which was bleeding badly. They would survive, but both needed immediate medical attention.

Rylander organized those willing to survey the destruction created during the assault. He helped the injured to seats in first class while others returned to the back cabin. They were unable to move Hampton because of his size so he stayed on the floor with a lady attending him. The dead were moved to the rear of the cabin. Rylander placed blankets over them as he bowed his head.

"Somebody help me!" Brandon screamed from the cockpit.

Rylander turned and ran to the front of the jet.

"What's wrong?" he asked entering the cockpit like a sprinter.

"I can't figure out this radio. They busted it or took out a fuse or something. I don't know, but I can't make contact," cried Brandon.

"What can I do?" Rylander asked.

"See if you can find a manual or placard. Something that shows approach speeds, stall speeds, power settings; anything that shows me what to do."

Rylander searched, not knowing exactly what he was looking for. He tore open cabinets, the closet, and finally a compartment to the left of the cockpit door where he found the operations manual, all six inches of it.

"There won't be enough time to read this; I hope he knows what to look for," Rylander mumbled under his breath.

"Here," he said pushing the manual toward Brandon. "Is this what you're looking for?"

"I was hoping for an abbreviated version of the basics, but it's a place to start. See if there's anything with landing speeds or flaps or anything like that. Check the index."

Just as Rylander began to look through the thick book, Brandon spotted something.

"Hey, there it is, the radio controller." He turned it on and started to tune the radio to 121.5, the international emergency channel. Then thought better of it, the radio was left on a good channel when the hijacker turned it off. He put on the headset and toggled the communications switch on the control yoke.

"MAYDAY! MAYDAY! Does anyone read me?"

"Identify yourself. It is imperative you use the proper code words."

"Roger, this is Sampson."

"This is New York Center, switch to frequency 127.95."

"Roger, New York switching to 127.95," Brandon said and changed channels. "Sampson on 127.95, New York do you read me?"

"This is NORAD, we have been expecting you, Sampson! What are the conditions on the aircraft?"

"All seems stable. The two pilots are dead. A flight attendant is dead. Two or three passengers are dead. At least one hijacker is dead. The remaining hijackers, two or three have been captured alive. Several passengers are seriously injured, the rest of us are still shaking."

"Confirm, did I understand two hijackers are alive?"

"Affirmative, it's still very confusing here, but confirm that two, maybe three, hijackers are alive. The one who took over the cockpit and was flying this plane is injured. One or two in the back are okay."

"Roger that, we need to go over a few things. Have you calmed down and are you ready to help us make decisions?" NORAD asked.

"Yes, sir. I am going to need help getting this jet down. Definitely need help."

"We have a chief pilot familiar with the 757. He'll talk you down. He should be patched in any minute now, but for the time being, are you having any problem with straight and level and following the fighter in front of you?"

"No sir. We are stable, we are fine."

"Great, we'll be with you shortly. Captain Martin is just off your wing tip, just stay with him. He is monitoring this communication. We must consider options. May take a few minutes but will be back to you shortly."

"Sampson, this is Captain Martin. Sir, I am in the F18 to your left. You are doing a fantastic job. NORAD is deciding where we should take you. I am going to stay just off your left wing. Keep it steady on heading 2-7-0."

"Roger," answered Brandon.

At NORAD, General Hopkins called an emergency meeting with his staff. Live hijackers in custody are an intelligence gold mine. He instructed his staff to consider options and come up with a plan to get the 757 down safely. Suddenly the need to capture the hijackers became top priority. He instructed his staff to have a plan ready in ten minutes. He then instructed his aide to call the president.

President George Walker had been in office eight months. He learned of the attack minutes after the first plane hit the World Trade Center. He took the attack personally and immediately vowed to destroy those responsible, whatever it would take.

"Sir, President Walker is on the line," another aide announced. "He has been briefed on the latest update, including news both World Trade Center Towers have been hit as well as the Pentagon. Flight 93 has been downed and the word is Flight 3911 might have been bound for the White House."

General Hopkins grabbed the phone. "Hello, Mr. President."

"General Hopkins, it's a sad day for our country. Do I understand you are in contact with American civilians on Flight 3911, the flight that saved the White House, America's house and my house?"

"Yes, sir. The passengers fought back, some lost their lives in the process, but they got the job done. A small private plane pilot happened to be on board, and he's now at the controls. I don't have much information about his experience yet, but we do have a 757 chief pilot ready to talk him down."

"Thank God. I'm going to want to thank those passengers personally, so you get them down safely," ordered the president.

"Yes sir. Sir, there are at least two hijackers alive. This could be an intelligence bonanza for us."

"I agree. Now you have two more reasons to get them down safely. The FBI will be talking with you in the next few minutes. I want you to cooperate with them and coordinate plans for the transfer of the prisoners. They will need to take the hijackers into custody as soon as the plane lands."

"Yes sir, Mr. President."

"General Hopkins, the joint chiefs have been hastily putting together a plan to deal with the event you have code named Sampson. It is important you make every effort to complete the plan they have in mind. For now, proceed as you just outlined."

"We will, sir. Goodbye, Mr. President."

As General Hopkins hung up the phone, a dozen FBI agents entered the room. In charge of this committee was Special Agent Bobby Barnes who immediately assigned agents to cover all doors. No one in and no one out was the order.

Special Agent Barnes had seventeen years on the job. His claim to fame in the agency was he had worked major cases with the CIA and knew most of the key decision makers. His experience could be helpful to build an interagency alliance. He might even be able to head a joint agency task force. His ambition was well known throughout the agency. Some believed he was on track to head the FBI someday.

Everyone in NORAD understood the new and increasing sense of urgency.

"Sir, what if we let the world believe the hijackers are dead? Whoever is behind this attack might think there was no link back to them," offered a senior aide.

"Get me Render in Ohio. They have a drone training unit there," ordered General Hopkins.

"General, give me the details," Barnes directed.

General Hopkins briefed Barnes without hesitation or small talk.

"I requested the National Security Agency director join us and he will be available by teleconference," Barnes informed those in the room. "In the meantime, we need to continue to put together a plan to safely bring the airliner down."

"General," Barnes continued, "I'm sure you will agree we need to get that airliner to a secure military installation, while following proper emergency procedures. We must not only do everything possible to increase survivability for the passengers in a crash landing, but we must also take those hijackers alive. I repeat, the hijackers must be taken alive!" Barnes implored emphatically. There was no need to question why.

General Hopkins' senior aide was the first to respond to Special Agent Barnes' comments. "We believe the best place for the plane to land is about an hour away for them. It's Wright-Patterson Air Force base. Because of the length of the runway and the wide-open spaces surrounding it, there's a greater chance of surviving a crash landing there."

"They are being routed to Wright-Patterson as we speak," General Hopkins' aide advised. All precautions are in place. ETA is approximately 50 minutes."

"General, I believe the 757 has four hours of fuel remaining. It is also our understanding the guy flying it is inexperienced, but he is capable of straight and level flight. There is no immediate need to get the plane on the ground, is that correct?" Barnes asked.

"Correct, except there are injured civilians aboard. We don't know the extent of those injuries, but we have been assured medical assistance is needed immediately," General Hopkins responded.

"Now is not the time to assume anything. We need to know the time we have. We don't want that plane down yet. Washington is working on something. Our orders are to maintain on course, we will have further instructions shortly," Barnes advised.

"General Hopkins," another senior aide chimed in. "We keep going back to the idea of letting the world believe this plane has crashed, just as Flight 93 did. We believe Flight 93 must have had a similar passenger uprising but failed. It went down in Pennsylvania. The press has already gotten wind of the crash and we've only known for ten minutes. They are reporting all are dead."

"What if we crash a drone in the general area, tell the press it was Flight 3911 and the 757 met a similar fate as Flight 93. All aboard are dead, including the hijackers. Then, if we are successful in getting the 757 down, we will have our intelligence bonanza, at least for a few hours or days, maybe longer. The organizers of this attack on America might enjoy a false sense of security for a while, just long enough for us to neutralize the bastards," suggested Barnes.

"That's exactly the plan we've been working on, Agent Barnes. We have it ready to carry out on General Hopkins' command. A remote controlled C130 aircraft is currently in the air over Ohio, circling a cornfield. Upon its crash, there will be no chance of any recognizable parts surviving. To the press, to the public, it will be another unfortunate but heroic effort by passengers to thwart an attack on our country," General Hopkins explained.

"Outstanding, General Hopkins, I like it," Barnes applauded verbally.

"Put the contingency plan in effect but wait on my orders. Things are happening fast, wait on my orders," the general commanded as he left the room to confer with the president.

Barnes heard from the CIA that had already been in touch with President Walker.

"The attacks on the United States had to be a well-planned and financed operation. Intelligence suggests involvement by the Al-Qaeda organization headed by Osama bin Laden. The FAA ordered all aircraft flying over the country to land at once at the closest airport. Any aircraft not on the ground in one hour will be shot down. The concern is there may be other airliners hijacked we are not aware of at this time. The country is in a full state of emergency. We are under attack and we are at war with somebody. The damage assessment so far has been two airliners at the World Trade Center, one hitting the Pentagon, one crashed in Pennsylvania, and one hijacking thwarted by civilian passengers. Fighters are on alert and ordered to shoot down any aircraft that looks suspicious and does not comply with our orders."

Barnes motioned to General Hopkins as he returned in the room; he was ready to lay out the plan.

"This comes from the highest authority. We must take the 757 to a secure base. At the same time, an old cargo jet will be crashed in the West Virginia mountains," Barnes said.

"Agent Barnes, if I may interrupt," General Hopkins countered. "We've been thinking the same thing. I've just been in touch with the president's staff and others in my planning department. We have a remote controlled C130 in place over a cornfield in Ohio. The area will be secured in 50 minutes with smoldering wreckage. We have a secure base in mind to divert the 757. All cellular telecommunications have been jammed to and from the 757. No one can call out with seat phones or their personal cell phones. No calls can get in either. With everything happening today, the country is ready to believe, not only one, but two flights were downed by passenger uprisings."

"Perfect, let's get the C130 in the cornfield once 3911 lands. If it crashes, there's no need to crash the C130. If the C130 goes into the cornfield, I want the area secured at once. Do not let the press within five miles of the site. Understood?" Barnes demanded.

All heads nodded in understanding.

"Commence Operation Bonanza!" General Hopkins barked.

"Yes, sir, operation code name Bonanza commencing," an aide responded, acknowledging the general's orders.

Chapter 5

Barnes called the meeting to order.

"Gentlemen, is there anything else requiring our immediate attention?" Barnes asked the assembled group.

"We need to concentrate on Sampson," General Hopkins replied, somewhat befuddled at Barnes' question.

"What?" asked Barnes.

"Sampson, sir. Code name for the 757," an aide explained.

Barnes, realizing his shortsightedness exclaimed, "Absolutely. Our main goal now is saving Sampson!"

General Hopkins, to help Barnes save face, instructed his aides. "Give us an update on the status of Sampson."

"Harold MacLuskey, a chief flight instructor for the 757, just arrived at Wright-Patterson. His orders are to contact Sampson," an aide advised the group. "MacLuskey stands ready whenever you want to talk to him."

General Hopkins got MacLuskey on the line immediately to discuss the top-secret mission privately. It was MacLuskey's responsibility to make sure the civilian pilot flying Sampson could learn to land the 757 and that MacLuskey could teach him this skill in less than one hour. As planned, the plane would be diverted to Wright-Patterson. MacLuskey advised General Hopkins ground crews had begun procedures for a crash landing and were preparing for the worst.

General Hopkins' heart sank hearing the worst-case scenario. As a military strategist and soldier, casualties were a consequence and an accepted liability of war. However, collateral damage, the undesirable and unavoidable loss of civilian life, left a bitter taste on his tongue.

"Johnson," barked General Hopkins to his top aide, "You are to provide MacLuskey with all information first."

"Yes, sir," Johnson acknowledged.

"Make sure MacLuskey receives an update on everything that happens or could possibly happen. Anticipate everything and be surprised by nothing."

"Yes, sir," Johnson acknowledged again, completely understanding the general's anguish.

Most of the mission would be handled by the ground crew. Too much information given to the novice pilot or those aboard the 757 could only alarm or scare them further. Emergency crews on the ground at Wright-Patterson took MacLuskey to a communication van. MacLuskey wanted to be stationed as close to the end of the runway as possible. This job called for being on site for a visual inside a remote office. MacLuskey insisted on being outside, much like the landing officer on the deck of an aircraft carrier does making the call as his fighters returned to the mother ship.

"Sampson, this is NORAD, I am Harold MacLuskey. I am a chief flight instructor for 757s and I'm here to talk you down safely."

"My name is Brandon Powell and really glad to hear from you," replied Brandon trying to keep his fright to a minimum.

"Brandon, I am in a van at the end of the runway. I will be watching and helping from here. Do not change the frequency on the radio. We do not want to lose communication. When you need me, call me by name, Mac, so I'll know you are speaking to me. NORAD is also on this channel."

"Thanks, it sounds simple enough, Mac," Brandon replied. His knuckles were locked around the flight yoke. He knew he had to calm down. He had to lower his heartbeat from its frantic pace. The crackle over the headset broke his fear, at least for the time being.

"Brandon, tell me about yourself, what is your flying experience?"

"Couple of thousand hours, mostly in a Cessna 182 and a Beech Sundowner. Limited time in a Lear, a Citation, and King Air. Just recently bought a Baron, got around a hundred hours in it. All those hours, but I am not instrument rated." Talking about his flying experience gave Brandon confidence.

"That's alright. Your hours of experience will make up for anything you lack. You have the experience to pull this off, and I am going to help you do it. The 757 is an easy plane to fly. First, we need information about the conditions on board."

Brandon briefed MacLuskey on everything he remembered. Two passengers were dead, three crewmembers dead, one hijacker dead. Six passengers injured, two seriously, but not life threatening. Three hijackers tied up in seats, five of the biggest passengers guarding them. Blood everywhere. But, given the circumstances, the situation was under control. Over the next ten minutes, MacLuskey outlined the controls, radios, and general game plan. MacLuskey owned a calming voice and the more he explained the controls, the more Brandon settled down.

"Brandon, the F18 is about to begin a decent to 25,000 feet. In a moment, I want you to release the autopilot and push forward ever so slightly to begin a gradual decent. Whatever you are comfortable with. Don't hurry, we have plenty of time. Do you understand?"

"Yes, that shouldn't be a problem."

"Okay, turn off the auto pilot and start a gradual decent at your discretion. The fighter is leading you to Wright-Patterson AFB. We are going to take this nice and easy. We will configure the aircraft for landing about 40 miles out to give you plenty of time to get the feel of the plane as it readies for landing."

Brandon released the autopilot and took command. He pushed forward on the control stick and began a descent of a thousand feet per minute. He figured he should be at flight level 25,000 feet in about ten minutes. So far, so good. The 757 was lot bigger than his Baron, but up is up and down is down regardless of the size of an aircraft he figured.

Rylander entered the cockpit.

"Brandon, we have been trying to call our families from cell phones and seat phones, they're all dead. Can you ask them what happened to the signal?"

"NORAD, passengers are trying to call from cell phones and seat phones. They don't seem to be working," repeated Brandon.

"Roger, Brandon, it is pandemonium down here. Everybody in the country is trying to contact loved ones. Lines are jammed all over," replied NORAD.

"Roger, NORAD. I'll relay the message to the other passengers."

Rylander returned to the cabin to make the announcement.

"NORAD, what's the plan, where are we going?" Brandon asked.

"As I explained before, we are taking you to Wright-Patterson AFB. It's in Ohio, about 45 minutes away. The base has wide-open spaces around it and 14,000 feet of runway. There are emergency crews preparing for you now. Medical teams are standing by."

"Tell us, NORAD, what the hell has happened? We understand the World Trade Center Towers were hit."

"Still too early to say, details aren't in, but yes, both towers have collapsed. Another airliner crashed into the Pentagon. A United flight like the one you're on crashed. That's all we know at this time."

NORAD confirmed what those aboard Flight 3911 already knew. They were in the middle of a war on America.

In the surreal environment of the cockpit of the 757, Brandon considered the heavy responsibility on his shoulders. A half mile ahead of him was a jet fighter leading the way to a military base. He could see fighters just off each wing. The fighter pilots provided occasional words of encouragement over the radio, but most communications were between him, NORAD, and Mac.

Brandon allowed himself to think of Grace. Was she safe? Could she have been on one of the other downed flights? They had come so far in their relationship to see it crash and burn. There were hard times, but the fact Grace had surprised him by attending his author's reception the night before seemed to start things fresh. If they both made it through this ordeal, they were going to get married right away, he planned.

"Brandon," called McCluskey bringing him back to reality, "We need you to come to heading 2-4-0. Descend at your discretion to 10,000 feet. In about 15 minutes, we are going to begin setting up a landing configuration."

"Roger, descending to 10,000 and coming around to 2-4-0."

"Brandon, it's time to talk to the passengers. Tell them what's going on and what to expect over the next 30 minutes or so. We don't want to do too many things at once, so when you have your descent stable, let me know."

"Roger, I have a thousand feet per minute descent set up. That should put me at 10,000 feet in about 15 minutes. How do I make an announcement to the cabin?"

"In the middle of the panel, you will find the communication package."

"Got it." Brandon acknowledged.

"Push down on the one marked CABIN and you can speak into your headset microphone."

"Okay, got it, what do I tell them?" Brandon asked.

"First, reassure everyone everything is under control and you are fully capable of landing the airplane. Tell them it may be a hard landing, but you are going to get them down safely. Then tell them you will make a few more announcements over the next twenty minutes to keep them informed."

"Okay." Brandon's stomach was in knots.

Brandon spoke to the passengers reassuring them and explaining his flying experience. He told everyone to stay seated and asked for a member of the flight crew to come forward. Kaitlynn came forward and introduced herself.

"Hi, I'm Kaitlynn. Suzette, the other flight attendant, is helping with the injured and other passengers trying to keep things in order. I am new at this. I've only been flying for three months."

"I'm Brandon Powell. We need to prepare the passengers for a rough landing. I think we should be landing in about thirty minutes. I have no doubts about getting us down, but I've never landed anything this big. It could be rough. Everyone has to be prepared."

"Yes, sir. Brandon, I would like you to know what all of you did was so brave. God bless you. God bless all of us."

"Thanks. It was a team effort. Every passenger and crewmember played a vital role. We're all in this together."

Kaitlynn squeezed Brandon's shoulder and gave a reassuring smile before leaving the cockpit.

Kaitlynn's smile reminded Brandon of the gleaming Barbie smile he received from another Northeast airline employee only a little while earlier. It was hard to believe this nightmare began only a few short hours ago, it felt like a lifetime. He hoped he'd be able to see that smile again soon.

General Hopkins and his aides reconvened to discuss how to handle the hijackers. The president instructed him to coordinate the transfer of custody to the FBI. But what about the interrogation of the prisoners? If any intelligence was going to be obtained from the hijackers, there must be a plan. What branch of intelligence will oversee interrogation? Every agency will want to be involved. CIA. FBI. Military intelligence units. Which organization should handle the interrogation of the terrorist prisoners? Who was going to handle the situation to keep control of not only the prisoners, but the intelligence agencies as well?

After some discussion among General Hopkins and his advisors, it was determined due to the complexity and interplay among the various intelligence agencies, an executive decision would be prudent. General Hopkins ordered a meeting in the situation room and put in a request that the president join via video conference. A team in the Pentagon started working out the procedures and protocol.

"Mr. President, we understand you want the FBI to take charge of the hijackers upon getting them down safely. However, sir, it's unclear which agency should oversee Operation Bonanza. I felt we should discuss this and get your input. All this is coming together quickly, and we don't want to waste time over turf wars," General Hopkins suggested.

"As I see it, we have several options which agency will head the operation. What are your recommendations, general?" asked the president.

"Sir, between the CIA, FBI, and our military branches, we have many options to handle Operation Bonanza. Frankly, sir, I would prefer to handle this totally off the record and without having to worry about how our mission is carried out. Our plan is to get information from the hijackers and, if necessary, it could involve extreme measures."

"Whichever agency takes charge, perhaps we should immediately get them on forcign soil for the interrogation," suggested one of the staffers.

"The CIA is best equipped for such covert operations, Mr. President," offered a member of the CIA staff.

"However, today's events are federal crimes committed on US soil. The CIA has no authority, and the FBI should have complete autonomy over this matter," suggested Special Agent Barnes.

"Gentlemen, please," the president interjected into the interagency cat fight. "This is the precise situation we are attempting to avoid. If we cannot agree on who is going to handle the interrogation, we have already lost. I agree with General Hopkins. We need an independent agency formed immediately. Not to keep ourselves at arm's length from criticism, but rather to keep our arms around the matter and keep control."

"I may have a suggestion. I recall there was an army, or maybe a marine officer, who was demoted some time back due to his interrogation tactics. His name was Major or Colonel Cauldwell. Does this ring a bell with you, general?" the president asked.

"You are referring to Major William Cauldwell. He obtained information from a terrorist by, ahem, scaring the hell out of him." General Hopkins responded.

"Yes, general. That's him. The information he obtained by doing what he believed he had to do saved his entire unit. That's the kind of man we need to question these terrorists."

"But, Mr. President, Cauldwell is retired. He is currently in Afghanistan for private industry as an advisor."

"General, he's the type of man we need to get information from the hijackers. I want Cauldwell on a jet within the hour headed for Washington. Assuming Northeast 3911 lands safely and the hijackers survive, I want Cauldwell in the Oval Office tomorrow afternoon. I will explain his mission to him personally. Gentlemen, Cauldwell will be in command of Operation Bonanza with full authority of the White House, and I want him to have all the resources he needs to complete his mission. As your Commander in Chief, I take full responsibility for this decision. Although Cauldwell was demoted for how he handled that incident, I admire he had the determination to do what needed to be done. I wasn't president at the time; but had I been, I'd have promoted him. If he carries out this mission, I will restore his rank and maybe promote him to position of general."

It was clear to all Cauldwell was being called back to active duty if Brandon was able to land the big 757.

"Brandon, we show you closing in on 10,000, confirm," MacLuskey ordered.

"I am level at 10,000."

"Alright, change heading to 2-9-0."

"Roger, coming to 2-9-0."

"We have you on a straight on course for runway two-niner at Wright-Patterson AFB. We have about 20 minutes to get everything set up for landing. We've got plenty of time. Are you ready to get started?" MacLuskey asked.

"Ready as I'm ever going to be, Mac. Under different circumstances, this would be quite an adventure."

"Well, under different circumstances, I would agree. Right now, you and I have an important job to do. I want you to reduce your power to 60 percent and pull the nose up just slightly, then start bleeding off some speed. You should be at about 300 knots; we need to slow you to about 250. This should put you at a 500-foot per minute descent."

"Roger. It's no different at this point than my Baron. Nose up to slow, nose down to gain speed."

"You are doing good, but drifting left, keep it on 2-9-0. The more we set things up at this altitude, the less we will have to worry about on final approach.

When you're half mile out, I don't want you thinking about anything but landing on the stripes, just like in your Baron."

"Mac, now I know why you are a chief flight instructor. I really think I can do this."

"I am sure you can, Brandon. What is your airspeed?"

"Airspeed, 290.

"What is your altitude?"

"Coming through 8,000."

"Great, everything is looking good. You're doing fine. Reduce power setting to 50 percent."

"Roger, power down to 50 percent. Are the brakes the top of the rudders, just like the smaller planes?" Brandon asks.

"Yes. Don't worry about brakes; you have an auto brake switch located below and next to the gear handle. Find it and rotate the switch to the number three. When it's time for brakes, just remember you have a long runway. If you need more, the end has been cleared of everything except the fence. There is another mile of open field beyond the runway. With the brake setting on three, you won't have to touch the brakes. Once on the ground, auto control will take over and bring the aircraft to a complete stop. Take your time, and remember, do not touch the brakes. Let the auto brakes work for you."

"Okay, I can do this."

"Roger, you are looking good. Speed?"

"290."

"Altitude?"

"Coming up on 5,000."

"Okay, but we're not losing speed fast enough. Pull the nose up just a little, maybe two degrees."

"Roger, just went through 5,000 at 270 knots."

"That's more like it. Now just like the Baron, I want you to maintain attitude and speed using 50 percent setting on power. You should maintain 250 knots with fifty percent power. This will get you in the proper approach attitude. Touch down speed is 150, but if you are a little fast don't worry, just keep pulling that stick and bleeding the speed once you have the runway under you."

"Roger, I think I can see the runway now, maybe twenty miles straight ahead."

"Good. One more thing, Brandon. Instruct the passengers to stay seated when you come to a stop. No one is to get out of their seats. This is important. Do you understand?"

"I understand, but I can't see these people sitting still if there's a problem."

"We are going to think positive. You are going to safely land and bring that 757 to a controlled stop. When it rolls to a stop, instruct a flight attendant to open the front door and get out of the way. An Army Ranger SWAT team will board and secure the hijackers. No one moves until the hijackers are off the plane, understand? Now make that announcement to the passengers. And please make sure they understand; no one leaves their seats until instructed to do so."

Brandon pushed the cabin button.

"Folks, this is Brandon Powell. The runway is in sight. This is going to be easy, but it may be a hard landing. It is important that everyone, and I mean everyone, stay seated when we come to a stop. All are to remain seated until we receive further instructions. Flight attendants are to immediately open the front doors. A SWAT team will board the plane to take the hijackers off, and then we can move. Let's not make it any more confusing for them than necessary. God be with us all."

Chapter 6

The big jet handles great, Brandon thought. Of course, this was a much larger airplane than his Baron.

"Seems a little high and fast on final to me," Brandon remarked.

I know I can do this; I just know I can.

"MacLuskey, if I pull this off, Northeast should fly me on my honeymoon anywhere I want to go. Do you think you can arrange that?"

"So, you're getting married, are you?"

"I think so. She just doesn't know it yet."

"I am sure Northeast will accommodate. You are right on centerline; looking great!"

"Roger, it's almost like the plane is flying itself."

"You're doing great. Are you sure you've never flown a 757?"

"No, sir."

"Amazing!" commented MacLuskey. "You are exactly twenty miles out, straight in. It's time for the landing gear. Do you see them?"

"Roger, landing gear going down. I now have three green locked lights."

"Okay, give me 30-degree flaps. The plane is going to try to float on you, steady down pressure on the stick. Trim as necessary so the jet is almost flying itself."

"Airspeed is about 180. Is that too fast?"

"Don't worry. When you get over the runway, just keep holding it up and let it settle, just like the Baron. Try to touch down at about 140. Remember, there's plenty of room."

"If it doesn't feel right, just go around." Those were the same words Brandon's first flight instructor often used.

"Just add full power and go around until you feel right about the landing," he would say. There was something about the approach that didn't feel right. It was too fast; they were too high. "Something is just not right," Brandon mumbled to himself.

At 1,500 feet from the runway, MacLuskey offered words of encouragement. Brandon didn't like it, he knew he could do better and increase the chances of a successful landing. Add a little power, maintain this altitude. Go around! Level off!

"I don't like this! We are going around!" he shouted in the headset to MacLuskey.

"Okay, but you were fine. Just line it up the same way again."

"Roger."

The jet rose effortlessly. Brandon told the passengers not to be alarmed. It was just a practice run, he told them. The next approach would be touch down. He now had the feel of the aircraft. Though he had only been at the controls an hour or less, he felt he could successfully land the 757. This time, he would make the approach, the way he wanted, the way he knew was right. As the jet rose, he leveled off at 3,000 feet and put it in a gradual left turn. A bigger airplane, a faster airplane, but he figured the basics would be the same. As he turned on the downwind leg, he kept the runway in sight just off the tip of the left wing. He was a bit higher and farther from the runway than in the Baron, but it was a much larger aircraft, he reasoned. Let's stretch the downwind leg so we can make a long straight in final, he thought. Now we should have a ten-mile final. That ought to be enough time. He came left and continued the turn until he lined up with the runway.

"MacLuskey, I feel better about it this time."

"Great, you are looking good. How's the speed?"

"180, stall is 120, right?"

"Stall is not a factor. We'll keep your speed well above Vs. Just stay above 140 until you are over the runway."

"Roger."

"Your glide slope looks great."

Brandon felt at ease considering the enormous responsibility fate had placed on him. Any other time and he would be the luckiest general aviation pilot around, flying a 757. Four miles straight in and looking good. I'm going to do this. It's going to be all right, Brandon continued to tell himself. This time at 100 feet, things looked perfect. He eased back on the throttles as he crossed the end of the runway. With little power to push the big jet forward, he gently raised the nose to bleed off the speed until it stalled and settled gently on the runway. That was not so bad he thought. Now with no power and about two miles to stop the big jet, he had the presence of mind to let the auto brakes slow the 757, then gently applied the brakes keeping right on the centerline as if landing a 757 was something he did every day. He then remembered to shut off the fuel switches to the engines and everything became quiet.

Emergency vehicles, ambulances, fire trucks, and rescue units lined both sides of the runway and began to follow the 757 as it rolled by. As Brandon brought the jet to a safe stop, he saw the SWAT team driving up in a ladder truck. Kaitlynn opened the door and within seconds the cabin was filled with members of the SWAT team wearing tactical gear and carrying Colt Commando weapons. Three of the four hijackers were alive and in good condition save for a broken arm, cuts and a few scrapes. They untied each one, taking several minutes considering the number of belts the passengers had used. Once they were loose, the SWAT team placed the prisoners in handcuffs and leg chains and hustled them out the door and down the aircraft steps. They were placed in an armored vehicle and taken to a secure area of the base for questioning.

Medical teams boarded to care for the injured. Hampton and John were transported to the base hospital. Two guards were positioned inside each of their rooms and given instructions not to let either man out of sight or allow contact with anyone. Those less injured received treatment before exiting the plane and boarded a bus to the hospital. Guards with the same orders were placed on the transport buses. The remaining passengers were escorted from the jet through the back door to a waiting bus under armed guarded escort. After all passengers exited the jet, military personnel had the grim task of removing the dead and declaring the jet an official crime scene. Hopefully, there would be clues on board to help figure out who was behind the terror that rained on America.

***

General Hopkins returned to the situation room to start Operation Bonanza.

"Let's get the C130 in that cornfield," he ordered.

Spotter aircraft circled the area one last time to make sure the cornfield was empty. The last thing they needed were more casualties.

Meanwhile, in the control center at the National Guard Armory outside Cleveland, Captain Johnson banked the C130 from his computer as he watched the onboard camera confirming the airplane to be in a steep, but controlled dive to the ground. The airplane, rigged with explosives, would cause a big explosion simulating full fuel tanks.

National Guard troops were already heading for the crash site, even before the C130 completed its dive to destruction. Their orders were to seal the area as a crash site. Keep the media far enough away to give the impression an unknown airliner had crashed. No other information was to be released. No flight numbers, no names, nothing.

Thirty-five minutes after United Flight 93 crashed in Pennsylvania, and eight minutes after Brandon landed the 757, a phantom airliner, yet to be identified, crashed in a cornfield, just outside Athens, Ohio. Operation Bonanza was underway.

The crash site was horrific. Nothing about the wreckage was recognizable. Local authorities and area farmers began converging on the scene as soon as the plane was spotted falling from the sky. The National Guard, who just happened to be in the area on a training mission, quickly secured the site and gave strict orders to curiosity seekers to stay well out of range of the crash site. Witnesses not from the area, but shipped in as a part of Operation Bonanza, were awaiting television crews. Locals quickly convened a prayer service for the dead, no one could have survived this devastation. Operation Bonanza, only fifteen minutes old, appeared to be going according to plan. News crews would arrive on the scene shortly. Witnesses were ready and waiting for them to share their fabricated stories.

A local deputy sheriff was upset with the soldiers when he was refused access to the crash site. Captain Jordan, a member of the National Guard, pulled him aside and explained this was a terrorist crime scene. He explained this might be the crash site of an airliner believed hijacked by a terrorist. To appease the deputy, Captain Jordan placed the deputy in charge of activities outside the five-mile limit.

Television networks broke into regular programming to announce yet another airliner was down in Ohio, under suspicious conditions.

Within twenty minutes of the C130 crash, news crews arrived and began videotaping from the perimeter set up by the National Guard. The best vantage point gave a clear view for a long-range telephoto lens. Activity at the crash site appeared almost non-existent. Rumors spread quickly, there were no survivors. Although some said this was possibly a military cargo plane.

A news crew arranged interviews with several eyewitnesses.

"Sir, can you tell us what you saw?" asked a CNN reporter.

"Sure, I can," boasted one of the assigned military witnesses. "We were driving along the road when we saw this airliner begin a steady dive from high up in the sky. It looked just like one of those kamikazes in the old war movies. For a while, it looked like it was diving straight for my truck. But then it took an even steeper dive and hit the ground over there with a boom. Then it exploded!"

"Did it go straight into the ground?"

"Well, sorta, it was at kind of an angle."

"Could you tell what kind of airplane it was?"

"No, but it was a big airliner, I know that much. It had the red tail with the Northeast Airline emblem."

"So, you are sure it was Northeast?"

"No doubt!"

Another witness from behind stepped forward.

"Yeah, I saw it too, it was Northeast, for sure Northeast! We see them overhead almost every day."

A local ABC television affiliate arrived and began videotaping and interviewing the National Guard and the fake witnesses.

"Yeah, we saw it, came in almost straight down in the final moments."

"No way anyone could survive that crash," another added.

"I'm sure, one of those big airliners with the red Northeast tail on it, definitely a Northeast airliner, no doubt," another said on camera.

***

For the survivors of Flight 3911, the shock was beginning to wear off. Those not requiring medical treatment were taken to dignitary quarters. The base activated the contingency quarters used for handling and protecting government officials and senior politicians during national emergencies.

Passengers would undergo debriefing, but that wouldn't start until the next morning. No one could make calls to families, and many were extremely upset by this, especially the terrorist sleeper, Daniel Raphia. Someone wearing a military uniform stepped forward and told the passengers a meeting has been planned for later in the day with the President of the United States who would personally explain the duty that now fell on each one.

A bittersweet day for sure. Passengers of Flight 3911, snatched from death, could not call their families, but were preparing to meet with the President of the United States. Something big was going on and yet they knew little about the events of the day. Were their families okay? Their homes secure? Had the United States been invaded? Could this be the start of war?

Chapter 7

Cauldwell was in his tent trying to take advantage of a functioning generator by making instant soup in his small microwave. The machine gave out with a shrill beep and he removed the bowl carefully cradling his precious chicken noodle soup. He sat down on a rickety lawn chair and began to eat with relish.

At that moment, a voice sounded from the darkness beyond the closed canvas flap.

"Sir! Request permission to speak to the major."

Without turning from his task, Cauldwell barked, "Enter!" and heard the rasp of a body forcing aside the coarse canvas sheet. Carefully placing what promised to be his first hot chow in three days, he sat the bowl on a footlocker beside the chair and turned to find the camp's army communications specialist standing at attention.

"At ease, soldier. Whatchya got?"

"Sir, we just received a report that an aircraft flew into the World Trade Center in New York, and I thought you would want to know."

"Damn right! Excellent job, soldier. Do we know what type aircraft?"

"No sir, that's all I got."

"Okay, go on back to the radio shack and let me know if and when you get more details."

"Yes, sir." The soldier came briefly to attention, executed an about face and departed. Cauldwell gave a low growl that signified displeasure. He had never become accustomed to the army's protocol whereby "Yes, sir" was rendered in response to a command. In the Marine Corps, "Yes, sir" was an affirmative response to a yes or no question while "Aye, aye, sir" was the reply indicating an order was understood and would be carried out. The army reply grated on his nerves every time, but he never made a comment as he accepted his young soldiers were following what they had been taught.

Shortly thereafter his thoughts were again interrupted.

"Request permission to speak to the major, sir!"

"Enter!"

The specialist charged through the flap. "Jesus, sir! The damn thing was an airliner! It hit one tower and now another one flew into the second tower!"

"Son of a bitch!" Cauldwell jumped to his feet spilling his precious soup and slammed the bowl down on the microwave table, spilling more. "Okay, that's no damn accident. Somebody's attacking the country. Awright, soldier, go back and monitor events. Keep me apprised. I don't give a screamin' shit what time of night it is. I'm bettin' this ain't all the assholes have planned."

"Yes, sir!"

The soldier retreated and Cauldwell glanced at his watch, 2040, so that would make it 1110 in New York.

Son of a wicked bitch! Some worthless scumbags are attacking my country and I'm stuck here in this godforsaken hellhole where I can't do a damn thing about it!

Cauldwell looked at his soup and saw vapor still rising above the rim, but he no longer felt like eating. Wrapping himself in a poncho liner, he snapped out the light and stretched out on his canvas cot to stare into the darkness and think about what was going on.

He had just fallen into a fitful sleep when a voice hailed from without. "Sir, I need to speak with the major."

Instantly awake, Cauldwell swung his still booted feet over the side of the rack and stood up.

"Wait one." He flipped on the light switch without positive result.

Bloody hell! Generator's dead again!

With a practiced hand he found kitchen matches and lit his hurricane lantern. "Enter!"

A younger communicator came through the tent flap to stand at attention bathed in the pale glow of the kerosene-fired flame.

"What's up, soldier?"

"Sir, Spec-5 Armstrong sent me to tell the major. We have somebody on the horn from Washington who is demanding to speak to the major, sir."

"Well, who the hell is it?"

"I didn't get the name sir, but he says he's a special assistant to the president."

"Huh! He better be who he says he is! Okay, let's go. Lead off there, soldier."

Cauldwell followed his guide across the broken, rock-strewn ground and into the communications shack. Specialist E-5 Armstrong pointed to the KY-38, a radio that provided encrypted voice communication. "We have him standing by on the other end, sir."

"Right. Thanks." Cauldwell seated himself at the table, picked up the handset and squeezed the transmission trigger. "This is Cauldwell. Over."

"Major, my name is Rick Davis. I am a special assistant to President Walker. Got that? Over."

"Got it. Over."

"Okay, the president wants to see you. A CH53 is inbound to your position and will take you to Kabul. A C17 is standing by in Kabul to bring you to Reagan International where you will be met and escorted. Got all that? Over."

"I got it. What's this all about? Over."

"You'll be told more on the ground in DC. Over."

"Roger that. Over."

"See you Thursday. Davis out."

"Roger, Cauldwell out."

As he replaced the handset Cauldwell heard the loud beat of an incoming helicopter.

Holy shit! These guys don't fool around, even a little.

"Specialist Armstrong."

"Sir?"

"Send somebody to hold reveille on Sergeant First Class Downs and have him report to my tent, ASAP."

"Yes, sir!"

Cauldwell left the shack and retraced his steps. Reaching his tent, he stood ruefully regarding the now congealed remains of his chicken noodle soup while he gathered his thoughts. After several seconds of reflection, he grabbed a black, zippered canvas bag and began to fill it with selected items. Two pairs of wool socks, two sets of skivvies, his personal 9mm Glock pistol, four full magazines, a lensatic compass, and an acetate covered map of the one-hundred-square kilometers surrounding the camp. He paused and looked around the dimly lit confines. Suddenly he grunted and swiftly added two small, hardcover books to the contents of the bag, S.G. Brady's Caesar's *Gallic Campaigns*, and *Battle Studies* by Ardant du Picq. Satisfied, he pulled the zipper closed.

"Sir! Sergeant First Class Downs reporting as ordered, sir."

"Enter!"

A tall, blonde, broad-shouldered soldier forced his way past the canvas sheeting and stood at attention.

"At ease, Sergeant Downs. Okay, here's the deal. I've been called to Washington. I don't know how long I'll be gone but in the interim, you will be in command here. Continue with the training, but you will not accompany any of the Afghan patrols. You will leave that to your sergeant instructors. Got it?"

"Yes, sir."

"Right. Well, you've been with me long enough to know how I want things done. However militarily inept these people were when they came to us, they are good men with great hearts and stalwart characters. I know that training, especially in the early going, can be frustrating as hell, but I want you to ride close herd on your sergeants. They will treat these tribesmen with dignity and respect at all times, okay?"

"Yes, sir."

"Right. Well then, you have the con and I better get out to the pad before that friggin' chopper shakes itself to pieces. See ya when I get back."

"Yes sir, and sir?"

"What?"

"Don't worry about a damn thing here, sir. I'll handle it all just like you were here, but we do need the major back, sir."

"Don't concern yourself there, soldier. As MacArthur said, 'I shall return.'" With that, Cauldwell seized his bag, left the tent and headed toward the sound of helicopter rotors. He boarded and immediately headed toward Kabul.

As the big helicopter descended toward the airport Northeast of the city center, the cold blush of dawn bathed the land below. To the east a burnished copper glare behind the unbroken chain of snow-covered mountain peaks heralded the advance of a rising sun. Below, Cauldwell discerned the stately meanderings of the Kabul River and the gathering spread of the capital, which lay 6000 feet above sea level. As they entered final approach, he picked out the arrow-straight line of Airport Road, which from prior experience, knew led right past the US Embassy.

Before the chopper settled in the tarmac, Cauldwell saw the US Air Force C17 Globemaster standing by about 40 meters off. Heat waves roiling through the cold mountain air told him all four of the jet's engines were turning.

Cauldwell grabbed his bag and headed toward the open hatch on the port side of the cargo jet where an Air Force staff sergeant awaited his arrival. As he neared the hatch, the sergeant saluted smartly.

"Good morning, sir. Should I take your bag?"

"Good morning, sergeant, and no, I have it."

"Very well, sir. After you."

Cauldwell clambered aboard and took a seat aft of the portside wing. Both sides of the aircraft interior were lined with continuous, orange canvas benches, individual seating spaces being defined by the many pairs of seat belts. He was the only passenger.

"Sir, our flying time to Reagan International will be approximately 16 hours. We will be refueling over the North Sea and the weather report calls for clear skies all the way."

Cauldwell groaned inwardly, but replied, "That's great, sergeant, thanks."

As soon as he fastened his seat belt the sergeant faced forward and gave a thumbs up to the co-pilot who was looking rearward over his left shoulder through the open cockpit door. Immediately the aircraft lumbered into motion. Cauldwell glanced at his watch, it was 0130.

That means it's 1600 DC time, so we'll be landing somewhere around 1000 tomorrow morning in the land of the free and home of the brave.

As soon as they were airborne Cauldwell freed himself from the black nylon restraints, stretched out at full length and was instantly asleep.

Chapter 8

There was a knock at the door of Mrs. Rylander Brookhaven's home. After her phone went dead talking with her husband and the FBI, she heard nothing after the first airliner hit the World Trade Center. She watched as CNN News broadcast information on a flight that went down in Pennsylvania under suspicious circumstances. This could not be the flight her husband was on. In fact, she was certain of it, because the news of the fallen flight came while she was on the telephone with Ry. Another news report told of an airliner down in Ohio, but details were slow to reach news outlets.

A sudden knocking at the front door broke her concentration. Hating to leave the television even for a second, she pulled herself away and walked toward the knocking. Through the glass of the storm door, she could see two men in dark suits, both standing with serious looks covering their faces. One was holding a badge of some sort, so she unlatched the door. He flashed the badge at her, FBI. It took a few seconds for it to sink in, FBI. This could not be good. She momentarily froze, and then opened the door.

"Mrs. Rylander Brookhaven?" asked FBI Agent Bobby Noland.

"Yes, I'm Virginia Brookhaven," she answered as she began trembling, anticipating his next words.

"Mrs. Brookhaven, you were on the telephone earlier today with your husband and also with Agent Brown from the FBI."

"Yes. But how did…"

"Mrs. Brookhaven, I have been instructed by Agent Brown and the Director of the FBI to ask you to come with me immediately. A government jet is waiting for us and we must leave now."

"What's this about, I can't just leave; I need to wait to hear from my husband."

"I am authorized to place you in protective custody if necessary. Please come with me. We are asking for your cooperation."

"But why, what has happened?" she pleaded. The agents became a blur through her tears.

"I am authorized to tell you a government official will be aboard the aircraft to explain and try to answer all your questions. The government understands your husband is a concern to you, so I will break rules and tell you he is safe. You will be taken to him, however, you cannot call anyone."

Relief swept over her face. "Thank God! Please tell me the truth, is he really safe?"

"Yes. Now, we must leave immediately."

"I only need five minutes to pack a bag. I'll…"

"Your needs will be met, there is no time. Please, we must leave now."

"I'll get my purse."

They rushed to a waiting jet and immediately departed for Wright-Patterson.

A similar series of events were taking place with family members of eight other passengers on Flight 3911. These families had also received calls or messages from passengers aboard the flight. These included Mrs. Clara Greene, who like Virginia Brookhaven, was already in route. Unlike Virginia's husband, who was resting comfortably at The Guest House, the diplomatic facility on base, they took Mrs. Greene's husband, Hampton, via Medevac helicopter to Central Medical Center. He required emergency surgery to stop the bleeding caused by the hijacker's box cutter. After surgery, he would be in intensive care, but would recover. She would learn of his condition upon arrival at Wright-Patterson.

Code name Operation Round-up, was complete. Fortunately for the CIA and FBI, only nine calls were completed from the flight. Anyone who talked to or got a message from a passenger or crewmember on Flight 3911 was to be at Wright-Patterson AFB by the time the president arrived later in the evening. This phase of the operation went much easier than the FBI initially expected. They found most family members at home, praying against lost hope that the telephone would ring and the voice they so desperately needed to hear was on the other end.

Within an hour of the start of Operation Round-up, all family members were in government jets heading for Wright-Patterson. Aboard each jet, a government official began to explain the jet that went down in Ohio was not Flight 3911. Every passenger on each of the planes sat quietly as this unbelievable story was explained to them. As unbelievable as it was, it was true, and there was more. That evening the President of the United States was going to meet with them, the passengers and crew of Flight 3911 personally. He would explain what happened and what a significant role each of them would play. The president cleared his schedule to handle this matter himself.

By 5:00 pm, all family members had arrived and were taken to a holding area to wait for a meeting with the Director of the CIA. Words like duty and responsibility were tossed around like a ball in play. It was becoming clear people here were to take a major role, but no one told them yet what that part would be.

One of those arriving, Mrs. Ann Watson and her teenage son, Jim, were escorted to a side room that was a reception area to a private office. Walter

Clayton, the government liaison assigned to the Watson family, explained details were still unclear; her husband, Stuart Watson was in seat 17A. He had died heroically during the passenger take over. Mrs. Watson began rummaging through her purse frantically. She located her rosary beads and began to sob. A priest had been called in to pray and console her and her son. They were promised more details as they were made available. Mrs. Watson spoke with her husband moments before the takeover. She could already feel deep sorrow filling her heart, but also felt pride knowing her husband died a hero. Jim, only four days short of his eighteenth birthday, knew he would have to be strong for his mother. She would need him. He also knew their lives would never be the same again.

Jason Pearce, another assigned government liaison, escorted Mrs. Kathy Mason to a similar room. Her fiancé, Bobby Harper, filled seat 22B. He also died in the takeover. Like Mrs. Watson, Kathy had her last conversation with Bobby moments before he died. Since background yielded her religion as Baptist, a Baptist minister met her in the room to offer comfort as she heard the news of Bobby's death. She was also promised more details once they were available.

In another part of the facility, happier reunions took place. Rylander and Virginia Brookhaven were reunited and taken to the hospital to be with John Dawsett. Clara Greene was led a room further down the hall where medical personnel were waiting for her. She was given the news of her husband, Hampton. A true hero, and although seriously injured, would survive. She could see him as soon as he was out of surgery in an hour or so.

Chapter 9

Mystery surrounded the remaining passengers of Flight 3911. There was the subtle sign of being under a watchful eye, being guarded like prisoners. Daniel did his best to blend in with the rest, but he was desperate to find a way out. There were no phones available, and no one could place calls to friends or relatives. No one could call in; no one knew where they were. Their every need was met, but information was zero. No television, no radio. These passengers were likely to be the only people in the world who did not know the full extent of what was going on. When someone became irritated and pressed for answers, the standard response was, "The president wants to fill you in personally and bring you up to date with the events of this day," or "Please be patient. The president will be here between 6:00 and 7:00 this evening."

Air Force One lifted off from an undisclosed military base bound to Wright-Patterson in Ohio. In flight, President Walker met with his military advisors, the NSC director and FBI top brass to discuss the latest intelligence and assess damage. The top item on the agenda, the passengers on Flight 3911.

"I don't know what to say," admitted the president. "The White House was certainly the target. These passengers saved the White House."

NSC laid out the plan to handle the passengers and the hijackers. Total secrecy would be necessary. It would be the responsibility of the president to listen to the story of each remaining passenger and to learn more about the individuals who gave their lives for the country.

On arriving at Wright-Patterson, the president met with the families of the fallen passengers and crewmembers first. After comforting them, he asked them to join him along with the other passengers in the next room. He needed to talk to them as a united group. They entered the large conference room where everyone was waiting. The president spoke with each passenger briefly as he mingled in the crowd as if it were a solemn gathering of some kind. After 30 minutes of greetings, he asked everyone to take a seat. He made his way to the front of the room to a podium holding a microphone. A closed-circuit television had been set up in a private room just outside the hospital ICU unit for Hampton's wife to watch and another in John's private room. The hospital was on the other side of the base. Both men were out of surgery, but only John was fully aware of what was going on. Hampton would have to be told the story when the sedation wore off.

"Ladies and gentlemen, your country owes you a great debt of gratitude. What you did today is unimaginable. I want you to know I'm here this evening to bring you up to date on the events that have taken place today. It is possible we will be interrupted on occasion as events unfold. Please be patient. My time with you will not be cut short. I may need to be involved in making decisions and may leave for a few minutes. But it is my intention to be here with you, all night if necessary, to keep you informed about what is going on.

"First, I will begin with a timeline of today's events. About twelve or thirteen hours ago at 8:46 this morning, American Airlines Flight 11 crashed into the North Tower of the World Trade Center. This Tower is known as Tower I. At 9:02, United Flight 175 struck the South Tower of the World Trade Center, this is Tower II.

"At 9:38, United Flight 77 crashed into the Pentagon. Then at 10:06, United Airlines Flight 93 crashed in a field in Pennsylvania. At this time, there is reason to believe Flight 93 may have been heading to Washington. We believe passengers may have struggled with the hijackers, forcing the plane to crash. There are no survivors."

The shock registered on the faces of the passengers.

"This brings us to your flight, Flight 3911. At 8:50 this morning, air traffic control received a message from which we assumed to be from the terrorist flying your aircraft. Someone with a thick foreign accent declared an emergency and requested routing to Washington, then all communications ceased.

Ten minutes later, after the WTC was attacked, the FBI received a call from Mrs. Virginia Brookhaven."

Virginia grabbed Rylander's hand.

"We learned her husband was aboard Flight 3911. We also learned passengers were planning to overtake the hijackers. To put things in perspective, by then it was about 9:45; both towers were destroyed, and the Pentagon had been attacked. Radar indicated your flight and United Flight 93 were under the control of terrorists, and if so, had not yet located their target. We now believe the brave passengers aboard Flight 93 attempted the same heroic feat as you did. Unfortunately, they were not successful; fortunately, you were. Flight 93 as I said crashed in Pennsylvania. A short time later, an unmanned military plane flown by remote control intentionally crashed in a cornfield in Ohio. More about that in just a moment.

66

"About the time you were taking over your aircraft, the FAA ordered all aircraft flying over the USA on the ground immediately. Within one hour, there was not a plane in the sky above the United States. One of the last to land was in fact your flight, here at Wright-Patterson AFB. As we speak, there are passengers all over the country at airports who are unable to get home. Many are unable to reach family members. Phone lines are jammed all over the country with people trying to check on loved ones. In one sense, you are like anyone on any other airliner that was diverted. The difference is, you are here at a military base; they are sitting on tarmacs and sleeping on airport floors tonight.

"This brings us to why you and I are here tonight. The news has been speculating that two airliners crashed. Information has just confirmed the flight numbers and the information released is that both 93 and 3911 crashed with no hope of survivors."

Bewildered looks, muffled voices and sounds of shuffling feet swept over the crowd of survivors. The president held his hand up.

"Please bear with me, I'm sure you will understand when I am finished. Ladies and gentlemen, we live in a free country so what I am asking of you is your patriotism. You have captured the first POWs of this war. To find out who is behind this act of terror, we need the world to believe the three terrorists you captured are dead. The only way to do that is to let the world believe your flight crashed. We realize the truth is going to leak out, but we plan to keep exposure to a minimum. What I am proposing is each of you agree to keep this to yourself for now. Give us time to gain the intelligence we can from your captured POWs.

"Here is what I see happening over the next three or four months. Beginning tomorrow, each of you will undergo debriefing. As you finish with our intelligence people, you will begin to contact your family and loved ones. Tell them you were switched to another flight at the last minute; that you were not on Flight 3911. Tell them you are at a military base and should be on the next available flight home. None of you will mention this meeting to anyone. Collectively, forty-eight passengers missing the same flight is unbelievable. Singularly, people miss flights all the time and each family will be assured only their loved one missed that flight. We only need this quiet long enough to gather intelligence and find those responsible for this terrorist attack. We know it will be a much easier task if those behind this attack believe the terrorists are in fact dead.

"The world deserves to know of your heroic actions. As your president, I want the honor to be the one to make the announcement. Therefore, I am calling on each of you to cooperate. You, as a group, will be invited to the State of the Union address in January. I will introduce you to the nation and tell the story myself. I am committing the full resources of this country to bringing those responsible for this tragic day to justice. Your cooperation will help ensure our chances of completing this in short order.

"This about concludes my remarks. I need to be involved in a brief meeting with my staff for a few minutes now. This will ensure I have relayed to you every piece of information, information you surely deserve. I would like each of you to absorb what I have just told you. When I return, it would be my pleasure to discuss this further and answer any questions you may have."

The president left the room. Everyone remained strangely quiet, each allowing this information to be absorbed, each shocked to learn what had happened. No one knew what to say, what could they say? After a minute or so, Brandon rose from his seat and walked to the podium.

"Folks, may I have your attention? My name is Brandon Powell. Most of us do not even know each other's names, but we now have a common bond that binds us together. We have a duty to cooperate with President Walker. I for one understand the need for keeping this quiet. I thought this out as he was speaking. I see no problem calling my family tomorrow and simply saying I was on a different flight and that I am safe. All they want to know, all they need to know, is that I am safe. If each of us repeats that same story, our families are going to be more relieved we are safe than trying to analyze the matter any further. If keeping our story quiet for the time being can help our government in getting those responsible, I am all for it. I personally saw two members of the crew get their throats cut. I have never seen anything like that before. If the hijackers even have a remote chance of providing information that may lead to their leaders, we have to help."

"My husband was killed taking over that airplane," added Mrs. Watson as she stood to face the passengers. "I don't have the full details of how he died yet. But if he could speak to us now, he would support our president. I support him."

Rylander stood. "Is there anyone here who has a problem with this plan?"

The room came alive. Heads began to nod.

"Hell, no! This is a lie, it's wrong!" Came a shout from the back.

"I want no part of it!" shouted another.

"I am proud our president came to us personally, I support him," claimed another.

A phone rang and one of the aides put the call over the intercom.

"This is Clara Greene calling from the hospital. My husband, Hampton, was seriously injured during the overtaking by you fine people. He is out of surgery but is still heavily sedated. They say he will survive. John Dawsett and I have been watching by closed circuit TV. We support the president and urge everyone to do the same."

Silence once again fell over the room.

From the podium, Brandon broke the silence. "I am urging every one of you to consider what is at stake here. The people, these hijackers, tried to take away our freedom, our way of life. Should we, can we, let them get away with this? Can we let them win?"

Brandon stepped away from the podium. A moment of ponderous silence gave way to a sense of cooperation. He noticed a few passengers began to mingle and introduce themselves to each other. Real bonding had begun. The few who seemed unsure stood flat backed against the wall. One small group of four gathered and were talking intensely. One lonely passenger sat at the back of the room, surveying the scene. Daniel needed to get the word out. No one knew he was the fifth hijacker, the sleeper team member assigned to observe and intervene only if required to ensure success. It was obvious there was nothing he could do to help during the takeover. But if he could now alert his leaders? He must wait for the right time to escape or be released by these infidels. These few fellow passengers unhappy with being held like prisoners were all he needed, all it would take. His plan was underway. He still had a chance to escape, to warn those in control. He would not let everything that they had worked so hard for so many months end this way. He would escape, he would! All Daniel needed were a few unwilling fools and the help of an unsuspecting government official. Which one would he choose?

Brandon had been elevated to the group's spokesperson. "I am asking everyone stand and say the Pledge of Allegiance when the president asks for our comments. This will show our support for this important operation."

Most nodded that they understood what he was asking of them. President Walker returned to the room and everyone took their seats. He made his way to the podium.

"I am interested in discussing your concerns regarding the plan I have asked you to participate in."

Everyone stood and began reciting the Pledge of Allegiance. The president joined in.

"One nation, under God, indivisible, with liberty and justice for all."

Everyone except Brandon took their seats.

"Mr. President, you can depend on us," assured Brandon.

"I take that as a yes!" the president exclaimed.

"Yes sir, Mr. President," they said together.

"Excellent! We are preparing to help each of you in every way possible to help you deal with what has happened. You will be assigned a government liaison. You may voice your concerns and express your needs to this person. I would like to explain what is going to happen from this point on. Beginning immediately, debriefing sessions will start. We realize each of you need to get the facts straight in your minds. Some of you may wish to sleep on it overnight and begin tomorrow morning. Please take your time, but remember, the sooner we get the information together, the sooner we can discover who is behind this. When you are ready, please proceed to the debriefing area down the hall to the left. The rooms are clearly marked, and someone will be there to help you each step of the way. Once the debriefing is complete, you are free to make calls and then meet with the counselors assigned to each of you. I encourage you to stay here for a few days. Meet with your counselors and prepare for the next several months with our staff. You must learn to resist the need to tell anyone about what happened to you today. We know rumors will get out, but we need to keep them to a minimum. If asked by anyone, just keep it simple, you missed your flight and were assigned another flight at the last minute."

Brandon raised his hand and stood. The president nodded.

"Mr. President, my name is Brandon Powell. We have been asked to stay for several days to learn to cope with what has happened. Some of us may and some of us may not feel the need to do so. Some have expressed concerns regarding their jobs and livelihoods."

"Mr. Powell, you people are national heroes. Your needs will be met. Let me repeat, your needs will be met. Your liaison is going to be your best friend. Get to know them on a personal level. If any of you need anything, you are to let your liaison know. In addition, it is my intention to seek funding from Congress to aid each of you."

The president lowered his head as he searched for the words he needed. His face began to reveal what an emotional and trying day this had been. When he felt he could hold his composure, he spoke. "Ladies and gentlemen, we have reason to believe the hijackers who took control of your flight were heading for the White House. Had your reclaiming efforts not been successful, the White House would lay in ruin. It is also believed Flight 93 was aimed at the Capitol. This country owes these two landmarks to everyday American citizen heroes. I don't know if you realize how much your lives will change after we release the true story of Flight 3911. Your country will forever be indebted to you, and your country is going to take care of each of you. I would like to add something on a personal level. I was observing in a classroom in Florida this morning when the attacks began. The first lady and my daughter, Cynthia, were in the White House private quarters. Need I say more? I need to make my way to Air Force One now and prepare to return to Washington. Seated behind me is General Carl Echols. General Echols is overseeing this operation. From here, he will direct the activities setting this operation in motion. In the morning, he will go into greater detail about what I am asking from each of you. The general will be responsible for your well-being and will report directly to me. The first thing I need is a minute-by-minute account of what happened on Flight 3911. When the time comes, I want the country to know what you did."

Applause erupted from the passengers and their families. The president was escorted from the room and the group resumed chattering.

General Echols took the podium and announced his staff would begin debriefing for anyone who wanted to get started. For those who did not, their assigned liaison would escort them to their rooms where earlier in the evening their luggage and personal belongings had been placed. Most wanted to tell their version of the story right away. The others returned to their assigned rooms. Daniel, the lonely passenger, the fifth hijacker, stood and watched.

Brandon began his debriefing immediately. After about an hour, the events began to take shape for those investigating. John Dawsett, though in a hospital bed, felt well enough to be interviewed. Hampton was still too sedated; his debriefing would have to wait until the next morning. By midnight more than half the passengers were debriefed. All those directly involved in the overtaking, except for Hampton, told their stories.

Once debriefed, the passengers were allowed in the television lounge. For the first time they watched news accounts on television. It became clear the entire country was in mourning. Patriotism soared to an all-time high. American flags were being bought and displayed by the thousands. Churches were overflowing. People were connecting on new levels. The country was bonding like never before.

After Brandon returned to his assigned room, he tried to reach Grace. There was no answer. Since her trip to New York had been a surprise, he did not know what flight or even what airline she would have flown on from New York. After several attempts, he left a voice message; she might have heard about Flight 3911 going down. She knew where he was going, she knew his flight number. Based on the reports from his liaison, he felt sure she was safe somewhere.

***

Imad Bashour, Hashem Moustapha, and Abdul Mohatazana were from Afghanistan. During the night, under extraordinary security, armed guards took them to an undisclosed location controlled by the CIA. Intelligence officer, Special Agent Larry Cameron, a 20-year CIA special purpose expert, was placed in charge. He was to hold the prisoners until receiving further orders. Something at the highest level was in the making but he was not yet in the loop. Although the United States was known as a humane country and human rights were important, this was terrorism and Larry knew we were headed for war. The word, both spoken and unspoken, was to find who was behind this massacre. Find out how to get to them, and when and where to plan a retaliatory strike.

Interrogation began immediately upon removing the terrorists from the plane. Though roughed up, bleeding, bruised, and beaten by the passengers, they were in decent shape. The CIA had already started a file on the suspected terrorists they gleaned from the flight manifest, but after examining the detailed file it appeared one might still be missing. Special Agent Cameron had given orders the prisoners were to be kept awake for the next 36 hours while the final mission was planned. This would give him time to review the dossier on each captive. Most useful information is derived during the first couple days. The terrorists received nothing more than first aid as far as medical attention was concerned so the next 36 hours would be extremely uncomfortable for them.

***

The passengers of Flight 3911 began their day at 7:00 am. Those who had not endured debriefing the day before went first. The others started with an orientation and then resumed individual debriefing sessions. The government staff worked through the night planning the next couple days. Assembling individual transition teams for each of the passengers had to be a well-orchestrated exercise. Each member of each transition team, liaisons, grief counselors, therapists, and financial advisors all had to be brought up to speed on Operation Chameleon. By daybreak, transition packets were assembled, and hand delivered to each passenger.

The first meeting following breakfast was with the liaisons. Financial advisors were brought in to help the passengers with compensation packages. The government wanted these "national treasures" to have everything they needed and wanted. Therapists were to help anyone, anytime, with problems related to the hijacking or events occurring over the next few months. Grief counselors were to help with the trauma of the hijacking. With the nightmare of the flight, bloodshed, and deaths witnessed, it would take more than a bottle of whisky or a friendly ear to deal with the events of 9/11. For the next few months, the liaisons were to be each passenger's guide.

A meeting was scheduled for noon and everyone involved had been asked to attend. Hampton and John would watch on a closed-circuit television. Both Hampton and John rested well overnight and woke in good spirits. Hampton needed seventy-eight stitches to close his chest. John needed 34 to close his back. Both were long clean cuts, and the surgeries were routine and uneventful. Both men were fortunate if luck had anything to do with it. The meeting's agenda was to keep everyone well informed.

Brandon sat at the window with a steaming cup of the best coffee he ever tasted and after reading an old magazine article suggesting a sure-fire way to handle anger was to count to ten, he started on his transition packet. Brandon completed his debriefing the night before. Even while reliving the terror, it seemed unreal. But it was real. It was very real. He wanted to speak with Grace last night; he needed to speak to her, desperately. He called her once an hour since sleep was not an option for him. He finally gave up at 6:00 am. She was nowhere to be found. Brandon felt a sinking feeling in his chest. He couldn't explain it; it was just there. This was not the first time he had experienced this. Not the first time in his life; not the first time with Grace. It hit him often and hard. He had to shake off the dreary mood he was headed for. His first appointment was at 0900 with his liaison, Captain Ronnie Harold.

The captain had been handling special project assignments for ten years and as a rule, liked his job. It was something different each day. His previous assignment was acting as an escort and guide to dignitaries' families from around the world when they were in the US for extended periods. Captain Harold was resourceful and had more than enough connections at his disposal. The captain knocked on Brandon's door at 0915.

"Mr. Powell, I'm Captain Harold, your liaison. I'm sorry I'm late. I had to speak with General Hopkins concerning the noon meeting and it took a little longer than I expected."

"No problem, Captain Harold, and please call me Brandon."

"Okay, Brandon, if you need anything or want anything, I'm the man who can make it happen." The two men made their way to the captain's office. The captain appeared to be about Brandon's age and like Brandon, had two sons. He seemed down to earth and devoted to his wife of 18 years.

"Brandon, please excuse me for a minute. Have a seat and make yourself comfortable."

Brandon took a seat in the office and waited for the captain to return. His office was in the corner of the building and was substantially nicer than the temporary makeshift offices of the other liaisons who were called in especially for this project. The office was beautifully decorated with custom oak furniture and the desk was covered with personal items and pictures of Captain Harold's family.

"Sorry to keep you waiting," the captain apologized as he entered the room.

"No problem."

"Please, call me Ronnie. I hope we'll get to know each another well over the next several months so I would prefer to be on a first name basis."

"That's fine with me," Brandon agreed. "So, what happens now?"

"First, I want you to understand our mission. Primarily we have been instructed to keep the fact that three terrorists are still alive for the short term. Short term being defined as no later than January 20, the date for the State of the Union speech. We will try to do this by working with those of you aboard the flight who were personally responsible for apprehending the prisoners. We plan to manipulate the media to ensure a plausible story. For the record, we will not attempt to control your lives. Obviously, we cannot force you to cooperate. We hope patriotism will secure your cooperation, not to mention the financial need of every passenger will be met.

"I was present when the president referred to all of you passengers as 'National Treasures' which will not be taken lightly. We need you to keep a low profile, going about your daily lives as much as possible until the State of the Union address. The president has made a commitment to get those responsible and make the announcement of what really happened on Flight 3911 in that annual speech. He intends to introduce each passenger at that time. Brandon, believe me when the truth is revealed, your lives will forever change."

"Yeah, the president said that same thing last night. It's just now beginning to sink in."

"You all are real American heroes, and that will take some time to get used to. You and your fellow passengers risked your lives and took on trained killers and you were successful, remarkably successful. Although there were many heroes involved, it is my opinion your life will be the most affected. Brandon, you need to prepare yourself. As the passenger who took the controls and landed a 757 without any jet training, I expect talk shows, book deals and overall media attention are likely going to focus on you. The president is extending an invitation to you, Rylander Brookhaven, John Dawsett, and Hampton Greene to meet with him at the White House. He is anxious to meet with each of you, but he understands the injuries sustained by Mr. Greene and Mr. Dawsett need more time to heal. He is willing to wait, but he is anxious for you all to be his guests at the White House."

"Why just us?"

"Initial accounts clearly indicate the four of you were the driving force in the takeover. He wants to personally thank you and simply to get to know you. Imagine that, the President of the United States simply wants to be your friend. Make no mistake, the entire group of passengers is near and dear to his heart. In the coming months, all passengers will receive invitations to the White House, but the four of you will be first."

"So, what do we do now?"

"Brandon, I need you to treat me like your long-lost friend. You must be very honest with me. To start with, I want to know each and everything that is of concern in your life. This can be anything from being behind on car payments to your kids being in trouble. From business problems to drug problems. I do mean everything. Because of the important position you will be placed in, we cannot afford a scandal, no surprises. If you have problems, we'll make them go away. If you have issues, we can produce a solution. Do you understand what I am asking of you?"

Brandon sat thunder struck; the impact was just realized. His life was never going to be the same again. After a few minutes, he simply nodded his head.

"Good." Ronnie continued, "Now, right off the top of your head, what is your biggest concern? What is bothering you the..."

"I can't find out anything about the special person in my life. She should have been on a flight leaving New York for Atlanta about the same time my flight took off. I don't know if she's okay or not."

"I will need her name and anything else that may help me track her down."

"Grace Morrison. Home is Alpharetta, Georgia. Address is 1801 Hannover Drive, but I don't know a Social Security number or anything like that. She was on an early afternoon flight that left Atlanta day before yesterday bound for New York. Her return flight to Atlanta likely left New York yesterday morning around the same time my flight left for Seattle."

"That's more than enough." The liaison pressed the intercom button on his telephone. "Marsha, will you step in here, please?"

Almost immediately, an attractive woman in her late twenties entered his office. She held a stenographer's pad.

"Marsha, please locate this person ASAP," he said as he handed her a slip of paper containing the information Brandon had given him. "This is her name, address, and some notes that might help. Use the airline database of passengers. Focus on round trips between Atlanta to New York. The return flight is in the same period as Tuesday's events. Let me know as soon as you find out something."

"No problem," Marsha answered as she turned and hurriedly left the office.

"That simple? You can find her just like that?" Brandon asked.

"If she was on a flight, any flight, Marsha will have an answer in less than 30 minutes."

"I'm impressed."

"That's the first concern? She must be important to you."

"She is. We've had our problems, but who hasn't? First impression when I met her was she would be the one. Love at first sight, knocked my socks off. Then we split up. After a month of no calls, no e-mails, no nothing, she surprised me and showed up at a literary media reception Monday night. I was so surprised. I think it may just work out after all."

"We will call that the second concern. You'll be meeting with Dr. Carley Hollace later today. She is a staff relationship therapist. Maybe she can help with sorting out any issues you and Grace may need to resolve."

"Will she resolve it in less than thirty minutes too?" Brandon asked with a smile.

"That one may take a little longer. What are your other concerns?"

"Things are going pretty well for me. Nothing comes to mind right now. Oh yeah, I did miss a book signing in Seattle. Struggling authors always need help, but then that's probably one thing you can't do anything about."

"Don't be so sure about that, what's the name of the book?"

"Abuse of Process, it's a legal story, good boy exposes bad lawyers."

"I'll see what I can do," he said as a knock came at the door.

Marsha entered, smiling. Good news, Brandon thought to himself.

"Captain, Grace Morrison is still aboard a Delta flight that was forced to land in Durham, North Carolina. They expect to be able to release those passengers within the next hour or so."

"What the hell is she doing still on an airliner?" Brandon said.

"It's happening all over the country. All flights were ordered down within minutes of the Pentagon hit. They were ordered to land at the closest airport. For security reasons, some passengers have been sitting on tarmacs ever since."

At least she's safe, Brandon thought.

"Would it be too much to ask? I mean can someone tell her I'm okay?"

"Marsha, please get word to Ms. Morrison that Brandon is safe and well."

Marsha answered with her usual, "No problem" and exited the office as quickly and as quietly as she had entered.

"Brandon, I want to meet with you again after the noon luncheon with General Echols."

"No problem," replied Brandon.

Having time before he needed to report to General Echols' meeting room, Brandon decided to pass the time by taking a walk around the facility. He passed several small groups of people huddled together. Although, the faces were different, conversations were all the same. No one could believe what had happened. No one thought it could happen, not to the United States. Brandon stopped at a lobby area where a television was tuned to CNN. A little over twenty-four hours had passed since the ordeal and there was still much confusion. More questions than answers. Devastation!

For the first time the enormity of the situation hit him, and Brandon felt as if he would collapse. The World Trade Center Towers were reduced to rubble and still on fire. The Pentagon was still smoldering. The Flight 93 crash site in Pennsylvania produced thirty-eight dead. Then he saw it, his own flight and the crash site in Athens, Ohio of Flight 3911, forty-eight passengers and crew of five totaling fifty-three dead. The reporter was saying passengers may have forced both flights into the ground. Brandon paused and prayed for those who died. The country may have been glued to the television since the day before, but passengers of Flight 3911 were just now seeing it.

The meeting started promptly at noon. Lunch consisted of sandwiches, fruit, and canned drinks. General Carl Echols entered a bit late and approached the podium.

"Please continue eating and allow me to make a few comments. My name is General Carl Echols and as the president told you yesterday, I have been placed in charge of this operation. I will direct the activities that will help you in the coming months. Today you can begin calling your families.

"Here is the scenario. Each of you missed your original flight, which was Flight 3911. Tell them you simply missed the flight, caught an earlier flight or needed a later flight for business reasons. Thank God, you had to take another flight. Tell them you are at a military base where you were forced to land. Because it's a military base, you were not able to get to a phone quickly. Folks, I need everyone to stick to this story. There are people all over the country at airports unable to reach loved ones. Feel free to start making those calls immediately following lunch.

"We will begin arranging for you to go home or continue your flight when the FAA reopens airports. This could be several more days. So, you, like passengers all over the country, are stranded. The only exception is you are not cramped in some jet on a tarmac or lying on the floor in an airport. As the president said yesterday, I am responsible for your well-being. I will report directly to him with updates. We want to thank you for your debriefing reports. I am near completion of a minute-by-minute account of what happened on Flight 3911. I will be sending this report to the president. He will have it by the end of this week. I urge each of you to get to know your liaison over the next couple days. Address any questions or needs to him or her. We will meet again at lunch tomorrow at which time I plan to answer all questions you wish to ask. Thank you and have a good day."

General Echols left the podium and exited the room. Meetings resumed for some while others gathered at the television. Brandon took a seat in front of one of the sets when an aide spotted him and approached.

"Mr. Powell, you have a phone call, please come with me." She took him to a private office and closed the door behind her as she left.

"Hello," said Brandon.

"Thank God you're alright!"

"Grace! Is it really you, thank God! Please tell me you're okay. I've been trying to get you since late yesterday."

"When the government issued orders for all planes to land, we were forced to land at a small airport in North Carolina. They would not let us off the plane until just an hour ago. Two hundred passengers trapped on that plane for twenty-four hours, it was terrible. I just saw the news. Can you believe what's going on?"

"No, I can't, it's like a bad dream. I just saw the first of it a little while ago, reality is starting to set in. I was shocked to see the towers fall. All that smoke, those poor people. I can't wait to see you, everything would seem better if you were here with me. When do you expect to get back to Atlanta?"

"I don't know. They're saying it could be a couple days before airports open again. Some of us on the plane are trying to rent cars and drive back, but there are no cars available."

"Grace, I'd be worried about you taking such a long drive with perfect strangers."

"Me too, but I've got to get home. This is scary. Where are you?"

"We landed at a military base in Ohio. We are in dignitary quarters."

There was a long pause.

"Grace?"

"Brandon, I need to go, others are waiting for the phone."

"Okay, but keep this number, it may be easier for you to reach me until we both get home. Grace, I love you."

A longer pause.

"Okay, we'll talk later. Bye."

Brandon heard the telephone disconnect but he couldn't quite believe it. He stood there stunned, a look of dismay on his face. No I love you too? Just okay? What did that mean? What was she trying to tell him? They hadn't talked for a month, she flew to New York to his party to surprise him, they spent the night together and promised to continue in Atlanta, and after a near death experience and hours of separation and worry, Grace greeted his "I love you" with a flat "Okay?" Brandon hung up the telephone receiver. He misread her intentions. Something was just not right with this relationship. Then maybe it was just the events of the past couple days affecting them.

Brandon returned to the lounge to watch the rest of the CNN special broadcast on the television. This activity quickly became the way everyone passed their time. If there was nothing else going on, they stayed glued to nonstop coverage. The staff brought in more chairs to accommodate everyone. Occasionally a staff member would enter and call out a name when they needed to meet with an advisor, therapist, liaison, or other government official. Brandon intently watched the update concerning the two downed flights presumed to be heading to Washington but managed to catch his name being called by a staff member at the door. He raised his hand in acknowledgment.

"Sir, Dr. Hollace would like to see you, would you please come with me?"

"Okay," he answered and stood to follow. Dr. Hollace's office was in the next building with a connecting covered walkway. The aide opened the door and held it for Brandon to walk through. It was a beautiful, clear day, the sun was shining so brightly that Brandon had to cover his eyes with his hand. It was then he realized he had not been outside since he arrived at the base the day before.

Dr. Hollace was expecting him and greeted him warmly as he walked in. She was beautifully exquisite with long black hair and piercing blue eyes, a small frame and was dressed to kill. She held out her hand to greet him.

"Hello, Mr. Powell, my name is Carley Hollace."

He returned the handshake and was shocked to feel the warmth and tenderness with which she shook hands. "Hello, it's nice to meet you, but please call me Brandon."

"Alright, Brandon. I understand that you're quite a fellow. I've heard of your actions on that flight. I just want to say how brave that was of you."

"Thanks. The danger of what we did is just now beginning to sink in. While it was happening, there was no time to think, it was just the thing to do. It all happened so fast, the instinct for survival took over."

"Those instincts saved a lot of lives. Please, have a seat. Anyway, you are a brave bunch of people and I wanted to see if there is anything I can do to help you. Ronnie tells me one of your concerns may be a relationship you are currently involved in. Would you like to talk about it?"

"Yes, I would. I have been thinking about seeing a therapist. Maybe try to sort out some issues."

"I'd like to be the one to help if I can. Why don't you start by telling me a little about...?"

"Grace," he said as he sat further back in the chair and crossed his foot over his knee.

"Grace. What's Grace like?"

Her voice was so reassuring, so soft. She had the prettiest blue eyes he had ever seen.

"She is everything I've always wanted in a woman. We've been dating for about eight months or so. There was talk of being married by Christmas. Things were going great. Then a month ago it ended. It was just over. No calls, no contact, nothing. Monday, she showed up at a media party for me in New York. You can't imagine how shocked I was when I looked up and there Grace stood. She flew up without telling me and just walked in. We had a good evening together but did not have much time to discuss the reason for her being there or the future of our relationship. I took it as possibly being a new beginning. I had to leave for Seattle, she to Atlanta, and then this terrorist thing happened. I hoped we could continue the discussion and start all over again when we were both back in Atlanta."

"Tell me, if things were so good, what caused the break-up?"

"Grace has some sharing issues. Privacy is what she thinks it is. Grace likes to go out often with her girlfriends. She's always vague about where they're going as though she doesn't want me to know her whereabouts. She refuses to call me when she gets home, like she's hiding something. Well, it happened again about a month ago. We had dinner plans, but at the last minute she broke our date saying she needed to spend some time with her friends. It has happened too many times. I would never break a date with her at the last minute. The following morning, I called her. She would not discuss the night before. She told me it was not my business and she did not like me checking up on her. I knew there was no point in going on. No point in trying to discuss this, so I ended the relationship right there over the phone."

"Why?"

"Well, as I said this was not the first time this had happened. We were in a one-on-one relationship, we made a commitment to the relationship and to each other. We had a wonderful life, we seemed to fit like a hand in a glove. The intimacy we shared was beyond description; it was wonderful. Everything, and I mean everything, was perfect. We never argued, except when it came to her group's occasional little outings. Those nights out were always so vague, almost secret. She would describe it as going out to dinner with my friends. Yet, there was only one time it was going to dinner. Every other time without exception, the real purpose of those girlfriend outings was to go clubbing. They would be out until well after midnight, sometimes two or three in the morning."

"And this bothered you?"

"Yes, it did and does upset me. In a committed relationship you don't need to be going to night clubs with the girls. Dinner is fine and I don't have a problem with that. But have dinner and return home at a respectable hour. Call me when you get home. Include me occasionally. Ask me to join you for drinks afterward, but don't take the position you are going out without accountability to the man you are committed to."

"I understand. Is this weekly thing?"

"No, not every week, maybe twice a month. Regardless, it's just a courtesy to let someone who cares about you and who you are supposed to care about know where you are and what time you'll be home. If you refuse to share the fun with your mate, it seems to me perhaps there might be a reason."

"For instance?"

"I don't know, but for God's sake, it's her group of single friends." The temperature in the room seemed to rise. "She is the only one involved in a committed relationship."

"So, you asked her to marry you?"

"Well, no! But she still has an obligation to me in some respects. Their nights out are in nightclubs. Not once has she said, 'We're going to a movie' or 'We're going shopping and I'll be home in a couple hours.' It is always a nightclub and it's always out until after midnight. I want to be with a woman who wants to be with me."

"Is the problem with her going out with the girls, not informing you of her whereabouts, or do you have a problem with her staying out so late?"

"First, I have no problem with Grace occasionally having dinner with the girls. But sometimes, ask me to join her afterwards for a drink. Inform me of the plans and be home at a respectable hour. The split up a month ago was the result of repeated events in which I was out of the loop. Her dinners with friends were nights out on the town and I was told it was none of my business where they were or what they were doing. Any questions on my part were an invasion of her privacy. I had enough and ended it."

"Yet she still surprised you and showed up at your reception. Why do you suppose she did that?"

"I took it as she reconsidered what she was doing, maybe felt badly for what she had said and decided she was wrong. We were going to talk about it when we returned to Atlanta."

"Well, you've given me quite a few things to think over. I would like you to think over the last few weeks you spent with Grace. Consider the things you did together, things you said to each other. How she made you feel. Take a sheet of paper and write down the good and bad. Bring this with you tonight. Can you come in again at seven this evening?"

"Yes."

"I'll see you at seven. Oh, and before I forget, Ronnie asked me to have you meet him in his office when we finished. He's expecting you."

"That's fine, I'm on my way."

Brandon left for the short walk back to the dignitary complex and Ronnie's office. He wondered if he might be making more of the past problems with Grace than he needed to. She did fly to New York for his reception. It couldn't hurt to talk to Dr. Hollace while he was there. It was a good diversion, and if he could learn anything that would help with the relationship, he was all for it. As he walked past the picture window of the TV lounge, he saw it was packed. When Brandon arrived, Ronnie was giving Marsha instructions. Brandon waited to hear Marsha's "No problem," then knocked on the open door.

"Brandon. Come on in."

"Ronnie." Brandon said as he jumped out of the way as Marsha charged back to her desk.

"How did it go with Carley?" Ronnie asked with a smile.

"Carley? Oh, you mean Dr. Hollace? Fine, but she didn't solve anything in thirty minutes like you promised," Brandon teased returning the smile.

"But we did find Grace in less than 30 minutes."

"Yes, you did, and as I said, I'm most impressed."

"Quite a looker, wouldn't you say?"

"Who?"

"Carley Hollace," replied Ronnie, a little miffed.

"Oh yeah, she's fantastic and she's gorgeous. She's the ultimate description of eye candy. Has one of the prettiest smiles I've ever seen."

"She just got engaged to an international airline pilot. They travel the world together when he's not on duty. But when he is, he's gone for weeks at a time. Everyone around here has been trying to date her. That rock on her finger put a stop to that."

"Too bad."

"That's the consensus. Okay, now back to you. How are things going?"

"Fine, we're all being treated very well."

"Well, actually, I was talking more specifically about you. Let's continue with problems and concerns. You mentioned your book. Unknown writers rarely get shelf space from what I understand. However, in your case, your book will be in bookstores nationwide within thirty days. Each of the major bookstores will be in touch to arrange book signings. How is that for service?"

Brandon could have been knocked over with a feather. "That's, that's…fantastic, but impossible. How did you do it?"

"Not impossible, just a little challenging. There are very few things this office cannot do. I'll expect a copy of Abuse of Process, autographed and hand delivered by the author.

"You bet!" Brandon exclaimed.

Ronnie continued. "Earlier I asked you to think of other matters of concern. What about financial or business matters?"

"Things are going well right now with the business ventures. My consulting business is doing well. Money is coming in and going out; fortunately, more is coming in than going out for a change. A businessman always wants more business, but things are moving along."

"What kind of consulting do you do?"

"Trucking industry, international shipping."

"Make a list of the companies you do business with and what you do for each, maybe there's something I can do in the government arena to land you more contracts. What about the two new business ventures, tell me about them."

"We developed a GPS tracking system and software designed to help small trucking companies monitor their shipments. The technology is like that used by FedEx or UPS when you track a package. We made it affordable for smaller companies, so now a business doesn't have to be a giant company to afford the technology.

"The other venture is a spin-off of that which is targeting individuals. Now you can track your kids, your boat, or whatever else you want right from your home computer. You know the old saying, 'Get between your kids and drugs anyway you can.' Well, we are going to give parents that choice."

"Sounds interesting. Timing may be perfect. I'll be putting together a list of government leads, people who do business with the government that I think might benefit from your service. They will be expecting you to call."

"Thanks. You really are serious, aren't you?"

"I've told you, the president is one hundred percent behind this operation. My job is to help you in any way possible. Your life has changed and any time now you are going to believe it."

"I don't doubt it. I'm just a little more than slightly overwhelmed."

The meeting ended and Brandon returned to the television lounge. Death toll was now in the thousands, still counting but expected to be extremely high. Patriotism continued to climb to an all-time high. Everyone was flying flags on their cars, houses, and businesses. People in New York were helping each other. The nation was in mourning.

Brandon's meeting with Dr. Hollace began a little bit before 7:00. She was in her office and ready to begin. She reviewed the earlier session in which Brandon expressed concern over Grace's nights out with the girls. She decided to explore the significance behind this.

"Tell me," she began, "why do you think it's important you're 'in the loop' as you put it?"

"For one thing, Grace asked for the committed one-on-one relationship. Secondly, I question why a woman, an attached woman, would feel the need to be running around in bars at such hours. It's one thing to have dinner with your friends and be home at a respectable hour, but it's quite different when your need is to be in a singles' club mingling with lounge lizards at midnight. If you're in a committed relationship, there should be no need or desire to be visiting a night club, unless you are with your partner."

"So, Brandon, what does that tell you?"

"That Grace is…"

"Not her. What does this tell you about yourself?"

Brandon thought hard.

"Let's talk about something else. Give me some background about you and your past relationships," she asked, changing the subject.

"One of my girlfriends had several relationships while with me. I learned later 'going to the post office' meant she was meeting a lover for a short romp while I watched her kids.

"In my next relationship, though never serious, going to a play out of town with friends, meant she was meeting a man at the Hilton for the weekend. For this one, I was gullible enough that I believed the story and even kept her cat while she was gone. Never would have known if the cat had not gotten sick and I had to call to ask her the vet's name. She was not at the friend's house but called back when she learned there was a problem. This was when caller ID was new, and she was not aware I had it added to our number. The number she called from was the Hilton in Atlanta. Should I continue?"

"Sure, if there's more," the therapist encouraged.

"Okay, then there was Becca. Her previous boyfriend was in drug rehab at Menninger Clinic in Kansas. His family asked her to come to Kansas to help with his treatment. He was having problems dealing with the loss of their relationship. It was important, according to the therapist, that he heard directly from her that their relationship was over. Gullible me, I kept her kid while she was gone for three days at the old boyfriend's family's expense. A week after she returned, my hairdresser let it slip that they had been in Las Vegas with Becca and the old boyfriend. It was all a lie. You want more?" he asked.

"Yes, I think you should get it all out."

"Then there was Carmen. We were close to marriage; this was the most committed relationship since being married. After a year of thinking she was the perfect woman, we ran into her old boyfriend at dinner one night. I trusted her one hundred percent, so I excused myself and went to the men's room to allow them to chat for a couple minutes. It took a lot for me to do that, but like I said, I trusted her. The next morning, she told me she needed to stay in bed the rest of the day with a migraine. I gave her space. The next week she left for the mountains with the old boyfriend. Gullible me.

"But wait, there's still another. Grace and her friends are next. After one evening, she left the group and met an old boyfriend for drinks. She did call me when she got home at midnight. She told me the girls stayed afterwards to talk. At first, the girls unusually headed home between 8:30 and 9:00. Long talk, but I believed her, after all, I loved her.

"Two weeks later, she was boasting what better cell phone service she had than I did. She showed me the bill and I noticed a telephone call at 12:15 in the morning. I didn't say anything but made a note of the number, did a reverse number look up on the Internet and learned the number belonged to her previous boyfriend. The call was dated that night. I asked her about it and only after I told her what I knew, she admitted to meeting the old boyfriend for drinks. Gullible me. That's about all that comes to mind now."

"Would you say you have a problem with trust as it relates to women?"

"Doctor, I resent that. Did you hear what I've been saying? Sure, I have reasons to distrust. However, in each example, I trusted the women I was seeing. Remember, I watched her small children while their mother went to the post office. I kept the cat while the girlfriend went to a play. I kept the kid while another girlfriend went to Las Vegas. I slept while Carmen set up a reunion with an old boyfriend. I accepted Grace staying out late with her friends when actually she was meeting an old boyfriend."

Brandon was sitting on the edge of his chair. One more shuffle and he would find himself on the floor.

"In each of the instances, Doctor, I trusted these women were doing what they said they were doing. They violated that trust."

"I hear you and I understand what you're saying. Why don't we call it a session? Let me digest this information and we'll get together again in the morning."

"Fine." Brandon slammed his back against his seat.

"What's good for you?"

"I'm an early riser, I can be here anytime."

"Shall we say 9:00 tomorrow morning?"

"Fine by me, good evening," Brandon called as he turned and left the office.

Dr. Carley Hollace had a strong one here; hurt, but strong. This will be a challenge. She needed a good challenge she thought to herself and smiled.

Brandon made his way back to the dignitary quarters. Dr. Hollace hit sensitive buttons and he was trying hard to contain himself. The look on a few of the faces he passed confirmed he was doing a bad job of it. He needed to shake the session off. He closed his eyes.

"Ten, nine, eight, seven…"

"Brandon!" a familiar voice interrupted.

"Ronnie!"

"Can we meet for a few minutes?"

"Sure. I was just on my way back to my room."

They walked to Ronnie's office and along the way compared notes on Dr. Hollace. In the office, they sat down as Ronnie pulled a file from the messy stack of papers.

"Brandon, I have your medical records. I would like you to tell me about your health."

"How did you get those records?" Brandon asked. He was not at all pleased with this invasion of his privacy.

"I have access to anything I want. Your wellbeing is my job for the next few months. So, tell me about the condition you have with your liver."

"No one knows, no one. Do you understand?" Brandon felt his bad mood rushing back. This time, it would take more than counting to calm him down.

"Brandon, I will repeat this one more time, I am here to help you. It's my job to help you and I am going to do just that. Do you understand?" Ronnie was almost yelling.

Brandon took a breath, nodded, and began.

"About a year ago, routine blood work yielded high enzymes. No reason, no explanation at first but then the issue was traced back to a blood transfusion when I was five years old. Back then screening blood was not as sophisticated as it is today. Anyway, turned out that transfusion may have been contaminated with hepatitis. Hepatitis stays in the blood and slowly damages the liver. I am on a liver transplant list as a precaution."

"We can't have that" Ronnie said. "I can help you, send you to as many specialists as necessary to find the problem. Do I have your permission to transfer your records?"

"So, you're gonna fix this too?"

"I intend to see what I can do."

Brandon signed the forms and Ronnie put the process in motion to get Brandon the best medical care available. The president certainly would not want anything to happen to Brandon.

Brandon returned to the TV lounge but found he couldn't take any more of the news for the day. He returned to his room to lie down. He was asleep before his head hit the pillow. Exhaustion claimed him.

Brandon rose early and after a warm shower and change of clothes set out by military aides, he walked to the TV lounge hoping to get alone time outside his room and catch up on the latest news. When he got there, he found he was not the only early riser. Rylander was there, already having a cup of coffee, reading a newspaper and watching CNN. When they first landed, Rylander was taken to meet his wife. Then meetings with the various government people began so Rylander and Brandon had not been able to talk about what had happened. They could talk now. Their paths had taken different courses the day before with Rylander spending a lot of his free time at the hospital visiting John.

"Brandon, how the hell are you?" Rylander asked as he stood to shake Brandon's hand. "Have a cup of coffee and join me. We have a lot to talk about."

"Fine, I'm doing fine. Let me see if I can find any juice, I'll be right back." He found several pitchers of juice, picked up a couple donuts sat down with his new friend.

"Can you believe what we got caught up in?" exclaimed Rylander.

"I still think I'll be waking up any minute. That it was just a dream. I still see that pretty flight attendant stunned as that guy cut her throat. It was horrible. I've never witnessed death. I never knew that blood could…well, I just never knew. Her blood gushed like a fountain, and then she fell lifeless to the floor. Someone or something hit me from behind. I wonder why they didn't just kill me."

"We are all having similar dreams. I didn't see her die. I saw you jump up and get hit from behind and at that same instant another one busted through the cockpit door. I witnessed the pilot having his throat cut then the co-pilot getting beaten to death. Then when we took over, one of the passengers right next to me got cut across his inner leg with a razor that must have cut an artery because he fell into a seat and was dead before I could beat back the one who did it. I've never seen so much blood."

"How are John Dawsett and that other guy, the big man, doing?" asked Brandon.

"His name is Hampton Greene, and both are doing fine. They have a lot of stitches, but both are going to be okay. They are up and walking the halls in the hospital. They've become good friends. I think they will be in good enough condition to be released from the hospital today, at least that's what I hear. They will be able to spend time here with us."

"That's great. I would like the four of us to get together to know each other before we leave here."

"That's a great idea. If we don't get to do it here, maybe we can at Camp David," Rylander said with smile.

"Camp David? What are you talking about?"

"I heard the president will be inviting those who led the attack to spend an afternoon with him at Camp David or the White House as soon as John and Hampton are up to doing it."

"Are you serious?" asked Brandon.

"It seems reliable. The president holds a great debt of gratitude for what happened. I hear he called General Echols several times already, simply to check on us."

"I'll say one thing for sure, these people have really gone out of their way to treat us well. I'm overwhelmed at the direction this has taken."

"Yeah, me too. There have been a few rotten apples in this group. Can you believe the complaining that has been going on by the people who froze in place and would not budge when the attack started? You know the ones."

"I was sitting far up front as everything was going down. I heard mumbling and discord from several passengers in the back, but I couldn't see their faces. I don't know what was happening behind me and then John took out the Muslim pilot. I had no idea what was going on back there."

"There are those who are the ambulance chaser types. They're going to bleed this to get everything they can out of it. What gets me is those are the same people who didn't lift a finger to help. They stayed seated with their seat belts tight around their bellies. Now some of those people are having their homes paid off by the government."

"Rylander, how do you feel about our situation, I mean, being here then returning home and keeping this to ourselves?" Brandon wondered.

"I don't have a problem with it at all, it's our duty. My wife is here, and she's involved. With all they are giving us, it's the least we can do. It's the least the ambulance chasers can do. But you, on the other hand, are divorced, seriously involved with someone you will marry. I think it will be harder on someone like you who has to decide to tell your lady or keep it quiet."

"I know it's our duty, but Grace and I are going to be working through some issues. What if I decide not to tell her? Will she understand when the news finally breaks, or will she think I didn't trust her enough to share things with her? I'd like to think we'll be married by the end of the year, but we're having some serious problems right now. I don't know whether to tell her or not. What if it doesn't work out and she decides to tell someone else? Maybe I'll discuss it with Dr. Hollace."

"At least it's your choice and I'm sure you'll make the right decision. Virginia and I decided not to tell anyone. I've been hearing about this Dr. Hollace, she's supposed to be a fantastic doctor. Great looking too is the word around."

"Yeah, she is beautiful and very taken, engaged I hear. She's a relationship specialist. Ronnie set me up with her to sort through issues since we have to be here a few days," explained Brandon.

"Is Ronnie your liaison?"

"Yeah, that guy can do anything. It's unbelievable the resources he has. He could make a fortune in the business world. He found Grace in just thirty minutes. Then he obtained my medical records. Now he wants my files transferred to a specialist who is better equipped to handle a medical problem I have. He got my financial records and wants to repair a few minor scars. They want to make sure we aren't having any financial problems."

"Yeah," Rylander nodded. "I've experienced the same thing. My liaison is Joe Watson. He's the same way. Not that I need financial aid, but they're insisting on paying off everything, both business and personal debts. They want to make sure we all present well once the news breaks."

"That's got to have something to do with it. It's been great talking to you, but I have a meeting at 9:00. Please tell John and Hampton I'm looking forward to getting together soon and doing the male bonding thing."

"Great, maybe we'll see you around later today."

Brandon left the lounge and made his way to Dr. Hollace's office. He wondered if he would recognize John and Hampton if he had come across them. In fact, he didn't even know the big guy's name until Rylander told him. He promised himself he would go to the hospital after meeting with the doctor. These guys were injured making room for him in the cockpit. It was time to get to know them. Waiting for a trip to Camp David was not an option, he would spend time with them later this morning and if he had a problem making it happen, he would get Ronnie to handle it.

Almost immediately his thoughts shifted to the two passengers who died in the fight. He wanted to get with their families to offer comfort as well as for himself. Guilt started to seep in. Why was his life spared and other lives taken? How would Grace have reacted if she received news of his death? Brandon walked straight past Dr. Hollace and did not even see her waiting for him in the doorway of her office.

"Brandon," she called almost yelling. Brandon was jolted back to reality.

"I'm sorry Brandon, I didn't mean to scare you, but you were a million miles away. A penny for your thoughts," she said smiling. The two walked into her office together. Brandon noticed again how stunning she looked, dressed in a blue knee length dress with a pullover sweater. The sweater and dress showed off her well defined, perfectly shaped body.

"How are things going?" she asked.

"Alright, I guess. I met with Ronnie after I left here last night. Then I tried to watch the news reports. I'm still in shock over what has happened."

"Brandon, you have been through a terrible ordeal and it's going to take time for you to come to grips with it. Please give yourself that time. Shall we continue with cram therapy?"

"Sure." She did understand; he felt better already.

Dr. Hollace spent the next twenty minutes trying to understand the relationship between Brandon and Grace. He had forgiven her for seeing the old boyfriend and according to Brandon, all other areas of the relationship were perfect, except nights out with the girls. Brandon felt respectable women, especially ones in a committed relationship, had no business in nightclubs. If anything destroyed his relationship with Grace, it would be her need to maintain privacy, secrecy or whatever it was and to exclude Brandon from these nights out. When the session was over, the doctor scheduled another appointment for

1:00 that afternoon. Ronnie asked to see him between sessions, so he hurried off to meet with him.

When he arrived at his next appointment, he had only one thing on his mind. "Ronnie, before we get started, I want to go to the hospital to see John and Hampton before my early afternoon session with Dr. Hollace. Can you arrange for me to get a ride?" Brandon asked.

"What time are you meeting with Dr. Hollace?"

"One o'clock"

"Sure, that won't be a problem. Did you want to leave right now?"

"Thanks, but no, let's talk first."

"Brandon, I received additional information this morning. I need you to be totally open with me so I can help you."

"What do you mean?" Brandon asked. He was puzzled.

"I can't seem to determine your current financial situation. I can't find any assets, but I understand you own a Baron, homes and investment properties. On the other hand, I found several large loans in your name. A balance sheet would look like you are heavily in debt."

"My attorney and financial planner suggested a few major asset shifts when I learned about my liver issue. I moved my assets to a trust fund for my family when I learned I might need a transplant. I still control the trust so it helps me as I see fit, but if I die, my family will not lose everything to estate taxes. They will not have to deal with my business affairs. In addition, I manage family investment properties that are held in another trust name. My sisters and I own that, but it's in a trust account and not in my name. The loans are business and stand-alone. Insurance and the business will handle that debt load if I die."

"I understand and that makes perfectly good business sense. Sounds like you need a wife you can fully trust."

"Yes, it does."

"But if you don't mind, I'm going to issue instructions to pay off those loans. I want you debt free. The same scenario is being repeated for the other passengers," Ronnie explained.

"Ronnie, I don't know what to say, that's over a million dollars. There are people that need that kind of government assistance more than I do."

"That's not the point, you are likely going to become a goodwill ambassador for the country. I predict you won't need any outside worries after the president announces what you did. Consider this your country's payment of gratitude."

"Well, thanks."

"No, Brandon, thank you. That is all that I need to know at this time. Do you have any more concerns?"

"Not that I can think of, but I'm sure you'd let me know," Brandon joked.

"Like I told you before. I'm here to serve you and my resources are unlimited."

"Now, if you can arrange a ride, I'd like to go to the hospital."

"By the time you get to the door, there will be a van waiting, use it as you wish. Oh, and one other thing, we still don't know when flights will resume. It could be another couple days, maybe longer."

"Thanks for the update, see you later," Brandon said as he left. He went to the front door and sure enough, a van was waiting for him. The ride to the hospital took about fifteen minutes. During the ride, he noticed not a cloud in the sky, but more noticeable was the lack of contrails streaming from high flying jets. Not a plane in the sky. Brandon wondered about the long-term effect of the terrorist acts. How would it change the way Americans live? Life as we knew it would not be the same, he thought as the van pulled in front of the hospital.

"Sir, I'll be here when you are ready, so take your time," the driver acknowledged.

"Thank you, I have a meeting at 1:00, so I'll be ready by 12:30," Brandon instructed as he exited the van. He made his way to the nurse's station.

"Excuse me?"

"Yes?" answered the cherub face nurse sitting behind the desk.

"Can you please direct me to John Dawsett and Hampton Greene?"

"They're over there." Her chubby finger pointed to two men in wheelchairs watching the news. Brandon walked over to introduce himself.

"Gentlemen, we have never actually been introduced. You, I know are John and you," extending his hand toward the big guy, "must be Hampton."

"That's right and I'm guessing, you must be the pilot."

"Yes, I'm Brandon Powell. Everything was so tense and happened so fast."

"That's right and when we charged the cockpit, you were behind me and I never saw your face."

The three moved to another room and compared notes on their treatment, the fight and its aftermath, and current events. It quickly became an emotional meeting. Saving that plane could not have happened had it not been for the separate, but collective, efforts of each of the three men. John hastily put the plan together and took out two hijackers; Hampton became a human shield charging down the aisle throwing his large body on the hijackers, and Brandon flew an unknown entity landing the big jet safely. Lifelong friendships were forming in the small waiting room. The three began talking about their experiences on the base.

John was not in need of financial aid, but like Brandon was thankful for what the government was doing for them. Hampton, on the other hand, was having serious financial problems. He was overwhelmed with relief and guilt. Relief that his financial problems were over; guilt that two passengers died within inches of his face during the attack. Hampton was a big, emotional man who had a heart that was pure as gold.

"I hate so many people died." Hampton held back tears.

"Me too," agreed Brandon. "But think about how many more lives you saved."

The reunion went on much longer than expected, right through lunch. Brandon hated to leave but had to excuse himself to get back to see Dr. Hollace. They agreed to get together again later in the day or the next morning. As Brandon boarded the van, he felt as if he was leaving apart of himself behind. Two new friends he had only just met, but their lives were interwoven more deeply than anyone would ever understand. He asked the driver to drop him off in front of Dr. Hollace's office, and then closed his eyes to rest for the rest of the ride.

Chapter 10

The government car was waiting with the engine running. The driver opened the rear passenger-side door as the big marine approached. Cauldwell climbed in and the driver climbed behind the wheel. The vehicle continued to idle and after several seconds, the driver spoke. "Seat belt please, sir."

"Oh yeah, right. Sorry." As soon as the click of the buckle sounded, the car pulled out on the thoroughfare heading southeast.

As they approached 17th Street, Cauldwell was surprised to see heavy concrete barriers had been placed to deny vehicular access to Pennsylvania Avenue between the White House to his right and Lafayette Square to the left. "Blocked the damn road, eh?"

"Yes, sir. Same thing at 15th Street where Pennsylvania hits New York Avenue."

"Makes sense. If the assholes can steal planes, they can sure as hell steal trucks and cars."

"Yes, sir."

The light changed and reaching the intersection the driver turned right and went ahead down 17th Street past the Old Executive Office Building on their left. At the intersection of 17th and an E Street spur was a huge iron gate staffed by marines barring access to the eastbound continuation of the spur.

While one armed marine sergeant watched closely, a corporal approached the driver who handed the sentry a plastic card. The marine scanned the card, bent over at the waist to peer into the back seat, then returned the card, straightened and rendered a hand salute. Cauldwell returned the salute as the massive gates slid open and the vehicle continued east along the north side of the State Place gardens. After about 100 yards, the driver turned left on Executive Avenue, which formed a horseshoe around the White House with two ends anchored on Pennsylvania Avenue. As they traveled north, Cauldwell spoke. "Marines on the gates, huh? I thought the uniformed Secret Service did that."

"That was true before the attack, sir, but this president is a big believer in marines, and he's got 'em everywhere," explained the driver.

"Well, good for him, by God!" Cauldwell exclaimed.

After 250 yards the vehicle swung right around the front of the White House. As they pulled up, Cauldwell noticed several more marines in strategic locations noting they were armed and were covering all entrances to the West Wing. As the driver opened his door for Cauldwell, Rick Davis stood ready to meet him.

"You're looking good, major. That uniform suits you well," said Davis.

"Yeah," was all the big man could think to say.

Davis handed him a laminated security pass affixed to a long chain loop. Cauldwell had a deep aversion to adding anything to his uniform, he especially hated name tags, so he carried the pass in his hand as he followed Davis through a set of double doors, opened by two marines leading into the West Wing. Davis led the way to a small office, which Cauldwell surmised to belong to a secretary.

"You have about 20 minutes before your appointment with President Walker. Wait here for a bit and I'll come back to get you. Have a seat."

"No, thanks. Riding in that damn car was bad enough. I have no need to be addin' wrinkles to this uniform. I don't want to be standin' tall before the Commander in Chief lookin' like Rumple-damn-stiltskin."

"Suit yourself." Davis said as he left.

For some moments, Cauldwell stood trying to recall what he knew of the recently elected president. He remembered the former governor as a steadfast Republican and a stalwart defender of traditional American values as derived from Judeo-Christian heritage. He recalled he had always liked the man, invariably agreed with his position on a myriad of issues and respected and admired the many manifestations of character he had evinced dealing with controversial matters. Cauldwell seemed to recall having read or heard something about the governor voicing strong disapproval of Cauldwell's court martial.

As Cauldwell moved to examine books shelved along the back wall behind the desk, he heard someone enter the office behind him. Turning, he saw the most beautiful woman he had ever seen. Her flexible, well-endowed body was topped by green eyes and auburn hair that shone as if lit from within.

"Uh, hello." She was obviously surprised to find him there.

"Hi, ma'am. I'm Major Cauldwell, Bill." He held out his hand.

"Mary O'Hara." She smiled displaying perfectly brilliant white teeth. As she shook his hand Cauldwell felt electricity flash through his body.

"Glad to meet you, ma'am. Is this your office?"

"That it is. I'm a secretary to the chief of staff."

"And Irish too, huh?"

"That I am."

"Well, I'm about to have a fierce fit of envy and jealousy with regard to your boss."

"Ah now, and why would that be?"

"Have you seen yourself in a mirror anytime lately? How can you even ask that question with that beautiful face, those eyes and that glorious mane of hair?"

"I see. So are ye not after likin' me body at all?"

"Well, I, uh, that is..." Cauldwell was completely unmanned.

She smiled, obviously enjoying his discomfort. "Now then boyo, calm yerself. Yer by far bein' the best-lookin' man in this bloody great buildin' and I'd very much like to be knowin' ye better."

"Well, I guess that would be number one on my wish list too."

"Alright then, let's get on with it. Why are ye here?"

"Flew in from Afghanistan today for an appointment with the president."

"So how long d'ye think ye'll be in town?" Mary asked.

"Don't really know, but I suspect it'll be several days."

"Where are ye stayin' then?" she asked.

"At the Melrose."

"Sure, an' that's too grand a place fer the likes of' me."

"For me too, but Uncle Sam is paying the tab."

"I see. So, what are ye gonna be on about doin' when the president is done with ye?"

Not sure, but I expect I'll be returning to my room, number 714."

"Alright then, Sergeant Friday's badge number. I'll be rememberin' that" she said with a smile and a wink.

Cauldwell was surprised one so young would refer to the television show Dragnet, an offering from thirty years before. "Ma'am, I sure do hope you will remember it and that you'll find a way to put that knowledge to good use."

"Well now, I just might do that, boyo. I just might do that very thing."

"Major Cauldwell?" Their bantering was interrupted when Davis entered the room.

"Yo," Cauldwell said never taking his eyes off Mary.

"Have I interrupted something here?" Davis asked while sensing something electric filling the room.

"Sir, no sir," responded Cauldwell while snapping to attention.

"The president will see you now. Please follow me."

Davis moved off and as he followed, Cauldwell turned for one last look at the beautiful creature he had just met. He was rewarded with a mischievous smile and a blown kiss.

Davis led the way down a thickly carpeted hallway at the end of which an oak paneled door stood slightly ajar. The special assistant stepped through and announced, "Major Cauldwell, Mister President."

From within a voice sounded, "Very good, Rick. Have him come on in."

Davis stood aside and Cauldwell marched in, halted at attention in front of a ponderous desk, and saluted.

"Major Cauldwell reporting as ordered, sir."

The president rose and returned the salute. "At ease, major. Let's find a seat over here." The president moved from behind his desk toward the center of the Oval Office, stopping before a green armchair and pointing to a small couch which faced the chair across an antique coffee table.

"Please be seated, Major Cauldwell."

"Aye, aye, sir." Cauldwell sat down on the couch which was far too low to accommodate his big frame and long legs. He glanced down at the beige, blue-bordered rug emblazoned with the Presidential Seal.

Wonder how much that thing cost?

"Now then, major, let me begin with two things. First, all that passes between the two of us today is classified at the highest level. You will discuss the contents of our conversation with no one other than myself. Do you understand?"

"Sir! Yes, sir, Mister President."

"Secondly, I want you to know I took great umbrage at the political motivations and addendum that led to your court martial. It was, in my view, a travesty of the highest order. We should have given you a damn medal for what you did."

"Sir. Thank you, sir."

"Now then, I take it you are aware of the attacks that took place two days ago."

"Sir. Yes, sir."

"Right. So, you and the rest of the world heard about the five airliners that were involved. What nobody except a very few are aware of, is that the fifth plane that was hijacked did not actually crash leaving no survivors as was reported by the news media. The passengers were able to subdue the four terrorists on board, one of whom died in the struggle. The aircraft landed at Wright-Patterson in Ohio safely, so security and secrecy were never a problem.

"At any rate, the three surviving terrorists were taken into custody by federal agents and are being held at an undisclosed location. They have been interrogated, but all we have been able to learn is that their boss is somewhere in the Middle East and while he was not the mastermind of the attack, he is closely allied with whoever orchestrated the thing. Moreover, it seems this individual is involved in planning and implementing an even more devastating evolution that is supposed to take place early in the new year somewhere on American soil.

"Our problem is, in view of congressional mandates as well as two separate presidential findings, we are precluded from employing interrogation techniques that would likely produce information we need to avert another disaster of possibly much greater magnitude than the one we currently have on our hands.

"What I am now proposing for your consideration is as follows. You come to work directly for me. You take charge of the three captives and get them out of the country, anywhere you wish, short of any of the four communist countries.

You then do whatever you have to do to extract the required information and report it to me. Should you do all of this, I will personally reinstate your commission in the Marine Corps with the rank of colonel. What say you, major?"

"Sir. I'll do it, sir, and I don't need any special compensation or consideration. I'll be doing it for my country and that will be reward enough for me, sir."

"I thought your response would be precisely that; I knew I picked the right man for the job. As for the reward, you must allow your Commander in Chief to engender his own, personal satisfaction."

"Sir. Aye, aye, sir."

"Right then, it's settled. One thing more, I would very much like to have everything finished and done, including the capture or elimination of the mastermind by 20 January when I deliver the State of the Union address. Also, I must maintain absolute deniability in all this, so you will not disclose the nature of your mission to anyone!"

"Sir. Aye, aye, sir."

"If you are somehow compromised and your mission becomes known, this administration will deny all knowledge of you and your activities."

"I understand, Mister President."

"Now then, do you have any questions or comments for me?"

"Well, sir, first I need to know if anyone besides you knows about this."

"No one does."

"How about Davis, sir?"

"All he knows is you will be performing a special mission for me. His mandate is to get and give you whatever you need, no questions asked."

"Very well, sir. I know where I can best operate. I'll need to get back to Afghanistan to set it up and I'd like to have the prisoners sent to me when I'm ready for them, rather than escort them myself."

"Done. This time we'll see if we can't find you something a little better to fly on. When do you want to leave?"

"Sir. I need two..." The image of Mary O'Hara flashed into his mind. "... three days, sir. I'll need to do heavy duty coordinating to put together a team. I'll need an interpreter, preferably one who is trilingual in Dari, Uzbek, and Turkmen."

"Very good, Major Cauldwell. Deal with Rick Davis for all the logistical support you need."

The president stood up and held out his hand. Cauldwell shook his commander's hand, then came to attention and saluted.

"Good luck, major, and thank you."

"Thank you, Mister President." Cauldwell turned and moved to the door through which he had entered. Davis was waiting for him in the hall.

"So, how did it go, major?"

"Just great, he's one hell of a fine man."

"That he is. What do you need from me right now?"

"Just transport back to the Melrose. I have some planning to do but then I'll need to do a radio-relay with my camp in Afghanistan at 0600 on Sunday morning. Also, I'll need interpreters, just one if he's trilingual in Dari, Uzbek, and Turkmen."

"Consider it done. I'll set things up in the Situation Room. We have a lady who speaks several of the Afghan dialects."

"That won't do. It must be a man, it's a cultural thing."

"Okay, I'll take care of it and send a car for you at five-fifteen."

"Thanks. I'll be flying back to Kabul on Monday, and the president said something about a better ride than a damn C130."

"Yeah, he already mentioned that to me. What time do you want to go wheels up?"

Cauldwell thought for a minute. Let's see. If I leave Washington at 1230, it'll be 2200 in Kabul, so I'd land about 1400 Afghan time. That leaves plenty of daylight to get back to the mountains and get organized.

"Twelve thirty."

"At night?"

"No, that would be zero, zero, thirty. I mean thirty minutes past noon. I'll need a chopper standing by on the other end to take me back to the hills."

"Okay, I'll see to it. Your car is standing by. Call me if you need anything else."

"Roger that, and thanks."

As he followed Davis, Cauldwell paused to glance into Mary O'Hara's office and felt a sharp twinge of disappointment finding her absent.

Back at the hotel, Cauldwell took off the uniform and hung it in a closet with a rueful look at the wrinkles in the backs of the trouser knees. Clad only in a white t-shirt and boxer briefs, he pulled on one of the thick hotel bathrobes with the Melrose crest stitched colorfully on the breast pocket. Laying on the huge bed, he used the remote to turn on the television.

The news was on all the major network channels. There was nothing besides continuous coverage of the World Trade Center disaster. Cauldwell felt a sense of overpowering sadness as he viewed the endless throng of New Yorkers with stricken faces, holding up photographs of loved ones in the forlorn hope someone might recognize the person and be able to tell the holder something about them.

The news was interrupted by a knock at the door. Dressed now in sweats and almost ready for bed, he opened the door to find the most beautiful woman he'd ever seen. His jaw dropped wide as he was rendered speechless.

"Well, you did tell me to act on Sergeant Friday's badge number, right?" asked Mary O'Hara.

"Well, ah, oh, yes, I did, but I can't believe you're here," he stammered.

"I am, are you going to invite me in or am I expected to stand in the hallway?"

"Sure, come in, Mary O'Hara," Cauldwell invited, beaming from ear to ear.

She entered the room and offered a seat on the couch while he returned to the suite bedroom to put on a better shirt and pull himself together. He became quite disheveled. He needed time to compose himself. No one especially, Mary O'Hara, should see a marine in such a vulnerable condition.

He returned and said, "Mary, I never expected you to show up here. But I must admit I was disappointed when I left and did not see you sitting in your office. It was disheartening."

"When you said I should act on the information about your room number, I knew I had to blow your socks off. So, I was in the area and thought I would show up and let you buy me a drink in the lobby downstairs. What do you say, marine?"

"That is the second best offer I've had today."

"So, marine, what was the first best offer all about?" she asked.

"Sorry, Missy, but that's classified and if I told you I'd have to kill you," he laughed.

"Yes," she said. "You met with the president today. I should have known. Why don't I go to the bar and get a table while you change into something more presentable than grubby sweats."

"You bet, I'll be there in fifteen minutes he assured, walking her to the door."

She smiled and winked, "Don't take too long," she called over her shoulder as she sauntered down the hall.

Cauldwell was amazed she came to his room, it never occurred to him she might have showed up. He hurried to change clothes and put on a dab of the hotel supplied cologne.

Cauldwell entered the crowded hotel bar and saw Mary at a table in the middle of the room.

My lucky day. Seated in the middle of the room where everyone can see the beautiful lady with me, he thought to himself.

He joined Mary at the table, and both ordered a glass of wine, then sat smiling at each another for what seemed like an eternity, at least for Cauldwell.

She finally broke the silence. "I was in the area and thought you might like to join me for a drink. I would love to get to know you better."

Major Cauldwell remembered the chemistry he felt when he first saw this woman. He knew time was not on his side since he was leaving in a couple days to go back to Afghanistan. He wanted to make the most of the time they would have together.

"What a great suggestion," Cauldwell exclaimed.

When they met in the White House, she could not take her eyes off him and kept thinking about how strikingly handsome this man was. That might have played a part in flirting so openly with him. Cauldwell felt the same way. All he could think about was how she tossed her hair when she talked, her beautiful green eyes and her well-endowed body. During that short meeting it was obvious they were equally attracted to each other.

A server broke the trance as she served their glasses of wine. He reached to hand her a glass as she did the same. Their hands touched causing both to experience the electricity crackling between them. He touched her hand again handing her the glass of wine. He couldn't contain himself. How was he ever going to walk away from such a beauty? The chemistry was overwhelming between them and before he knew it, he grabbed her hand as he raised his glass.

"To the most beautiful lady I've ever met. Here's to you, Mary O'Hara."

She smiled. "To me!" as they laughed together.

"Mary, there's something different from earlier today, something about you I can't quite figure out. What's different?" he asked.

"Oh, ye must be a talkin' about me Irish accent," she said returning to her Irish roots.

"That's it, so what happened to the Irish?"

"Oh, nothing, I was flirting and went into character. I'm from Missouri. My dad is Irish. He moved to this country and married my mom. He's full Irish and still wears a kilt on special occasions. So, Marine, I know a lot about the Irish, ya know what I mean, boyo?"

They had two more glasses of wine and continued to talk until they realized it was almost midnight. The sexual tension between them was overwhelming. Cauldwell remembered when he first met her in her office that she was a bit of a tease. She gave him a goodbye wink and blew him a kiss. Obviously, she was confident and loved to make men squirm.

At midnight, they agreed the night had to end. Both had a busy day ahead. He walked her to the front door to hail a cab and while waiting, he told her he'd be at the White House the next day but didn't know what plans lay ahead.

"I may not be able to see you tomorrow. I may ship out right away, but I will be in touch."

"I hope so," she said, disappointed the evening was over.

He looked into her eyes. "Would you be offended if I kissed you?"

"Marine, I'd be offended if you did not kiss me. I need something to remember you. So, kiss me, marine," she ordered.

They embraced in a kiss that both would remember for a long time, then the cab pulled up to the curb.

He opened the door, helped her in and leaned into the cab for one more kiss. He knew he had to make sure he saw her again. He returned to his room and drifted into a dreamless sleep.

***

Special Agent Cameron decided to move the captives to separate facilities. They were too important to have all at one location. They were moved in military aircraft at different times. They moved Abdul Mohatazana to Fort Benning, Georgia. Hashem Moustapha was sent to Fort McCoy in Wisconsin. And the third, who had not yet been identified, was transferred to Fort Carson in Colorado. If word got out about Flight 3911, one lucky strike could eliminate the best intelligence sources behind the attacks. A top-secret plan was in the making, but no one knew who would handle the mission. Meantime, it was top priority to protect the lives of the hijackers. Special Agent Cameron continued to investigate the possibility of a fourth hijacker as well. All his instincts pointed to the possibility that one of the other passengers was also a terrorist.

* * *

The phone shocked Major Cauldwell back to wakefulness.

What the hell?

He rolled off the bed and when the phone sounded a second time, he answered.

"Good morning, major. This is Rick Davis. I have you all set up for your radio communication and I found a guy who speaks the three dialects plus something called Pashto."

"Yeah, well, he won't be needin' that one. Anyway, I'll be waiting at zero five-fifteen."

"You sound seriously out of breath. Everything okay?"

"Yeah, just waking up."

"Right. Well, good luck with the radio communication. Again, if you need anything just call me."

"Thanks, I will." He hung up the phone.

He showered and dressed in the cavernous master bathroom then left the room.

Though he reached the lobby exit at 0505, his car and the driver who had carted him around on Thursday were already waiting.

At the main White House entrance, a marine saluted smartly and presented a plastic security pass as Cauldwell emerged from the vehicle. This time in civilian clothes, Cauldwell had no trouble hanging the card chain around his neck. He followed the sergeant down two flights of stairs and along a corridor to a set of oak-paneled double doors where two marine corporals stood guard. Both saluted and one opened the right side door for Cauldwell to enter. As he did, a young man rose from a nearby chair and approached.

"Sir," said the sergeant, "this is Mister Hamid Taniwal, your interpreter. Mister Taniwal, this is Major Cauldwell." The two shook hands and the sergeant continued. "The radio phone is already connected to the switchboard with an

101

operator standing by. I will leave now, and the hatch will be secured behind me. When you wish to leave, just knock. One of my sentries will open for you and immediately page me, whereupon I will escort you back to your vehicle. Is there anything else the major needs, sir?"

"Not unless you guys have coffee stashed around here somewhere."

The sergeant pointed to a table behind Cauldwell. "Right there, sir. With all the fixings, plus a mess of doughnuts fresh from the White House kitchen."

"Outstanding, marine! I've got everything I need now."

"Very well, sir." The sergeant saluted and left as the heavy door closed behind him.

Cauldwell filled a blue and white porcelain mug displaying the presidential seal and placed four doughnuts on a china plate. "How about you, Hamid. Coffee?"

"No thank you, sir, I'm good but I would just like to say it is an honor to meet the major. You are a famous man in my country, and we are grateful for all you've done for us helping to fight the hated Taliban."

"Thanks, and for my part I am honored to work with such brave men of high character. Okay, here's the deal. I need to contact my camp in Afghanistan and have them get Zabi Zamani, the district chieftain on the horn. I chose this time to call because it's 1800 over there and I know he will be free of duties and obligations until 2100 when he holds his weekly bitch session so folks from far and wide can lay their problems before him. Still, his village is a way off from the camp and there may be something of a delay."

"No problem, sir."

"Fine. What I need you to do is translate what I have written here." Cauldwell handed a single sheet of handwritten paragraphs. "Make sure he understands exactly what I am asking for. When he agrees completely with my request, you will convey that to me."

"I am asking for a secure building and location under his protection to undertake a particular and extremely urgent mission, the nature of which I may not disclose to anyone. You got that?"

Taniwal had been scanning the sheet as Cauldwell spoke. "Yes, sir. I've got a good handle on what is needed."

"All right then, let's get to it."

Cauldwell picked up the handset and read the contact instructions. Three minutes later he heard, "Camp Subat here."

"Hey, Armstrong, this is Major Cauldwell. I need you to get Sergeant Downs on the horn asap!"

"Yes, sir!"

A few minutes later the radio again came alive. "Sergeant First Class Downs speaking, sir."

"Sergeant Downs, I need you to haul ass up to the village and bring Zamani down to talk to me."

"Roger that, sir. I'm on the way."

Seventeen minutes later, a heavily accented voice broke the silence. "Zabi Zamani is now talking."

"Hey, chief, this is Major Cauldwell."

"Hallo, majah, you are good, yes?"

"I'm fine, chief. I need to ask you a big favor."

"Whatevah Zamani can do for majah, he will do."

"Okay then, chief, I have someone from your country standing by to ask for what I need in your language, so you will understand clearly."

"So, I will most gladly speak to this man."

"Right, chief, here he is, Mister Hamid Taniwal." Cauldwell handed the receiver to the interpreter.

The conversation lasted for several minutes and as Cauldwell anticipated all three dialects were employed so any concept difficult to express in one could be presented in another. Finally, Taniwal removed the handset from his ear. "Sir, Chief Zamani understands the request and says, 'Whatever the major wants that is in Zamani's power to provide, that he shall have.' He also said he believes he has a place that would be ideally suited for your purpose."

"Outstanding! Let me talk to him." Taniwal handed over the phone. "Hey, chief, thank you very much! I'll see you on Tuesday."

"Very good, majah. I shall be here."

"Roger that. Goodbye, sir."

"Goodbye, majah."

Cauldwell asked his White House guide to take him to Mary O'Hara's office. It was Sunday so she's probably not working today, he thought. But it was worth the effort, besides, he had no contact information to call her. As they turned the corner to the hallway, he saw her. She was delighted to see him. The White House aide stood by the door as Cauldwell entered Mary's office.

"I leave to go overseas for an unknown amount of time. I leave in the morning. Can you stop by when you get off?" he asked.

"I am off on Sunday," she answered.

"So, what are you doing here today?

"You mentioned you'd be in today, and I saw your name on Sunday's visitor list so I thought I would be here and hopefully see you. My hunch worked!"

"I am going back to the Melrose to complete planning and logistics. I should finish in a few hours. I leave on government transport tomorrow morning. What say you, shall we make the best of my remaining time?"

"Tell me a time, I know where you live, ya know," she said, unable to contain her excitement.

"Four o'clock?"

She smiled, "I can be there by four."

"Fantastic, I can't wait, will you come to the badge number?"

"Of course."

Cauldwell returned to his suite to complete planning for his return to Afghanistan the next day. After things were set, he took a shower, shaved and took a nap while he waited for the 4:00 knock on the door.

At exactly 4:00 Mary knocked. Caldwell rushed to answer. She was surprised to see him in a bathrobe, but he quickly explained that he had settled down for a nap.

"Time slipped away and here I am answering the door to such a beautiful sight. Would you like to come in?"

"That is why I came, right?" she said teasing him.

"What say you, want to go out and get something to eat?" he asked.

"One would think a place like the Melrose would have great room service," she said taking control of the situation. "Why don't we order in and not waste our time outside this room."

"Works for me, how about a glass of wine?" he offered.

"Yes, but I may be a bit over dressed. You're in a bathrobe, one would think a place like the Melrose, would have a matching robe hanging in the closet. I'll check and get a little more comfortable," she said heading toward the bedroom.

Cauldwell watched as she entered the bedroom. He watched from the couch and had a clear view as she checked the closet and found the matching robe. He continued to watch as she laid it on the bed and began slowly and deliberately undressing. She removed her clothes and briefly stood still. He held his gaze as she stood naked. Her body was even more perfect and beautiful than he imagined. She leaned over to get the robe from the bed and slipped it on. She turned and started toward the sitting room where Cauldwell sat speechless.

In addition to the robe, she wore a mischievous Mona Lisa smile as she approached him. She sat down and as she took her seat, deliberately sat at an angle so the slight fold in her robe opened just enough to reveal her breasts.

Cauldwell was the consummate military man on duty, but with Mary, he now understood what it might be like for his soldiers because she had full command of the situation. She was in charge.

He poured glasses of the hotel's finest wine. He touched her hand as he handed her the wine. He could hardly contain himself. How was he ever going to walk away from such a beautiful creature? They tried to talk, but the sexual tension between them was overwhelming. Chemistry took over and before he knew it, he gently kissed her. Mary stayed the night and they made love over and over again.

Chapter 11

Word spread fast that General Echols called a meeting for 6:00 that evening. It would be held in the dining room and was not expected to last but thirty minutes. Meanwhile, all debriefings had been completed, and the passengers were beginning to get restless. They experienced similar feelings as other passengers stranded around the country. Many, like Brandon, were making use of counseling to pass the time. The TV lounge was the primary social gathering place and there was someone there 24/7. The lounge was usually filled this time of day, and as Brandon approached he found it to be no exception. The only difference was the addition of two wheelchairs, John and Hampton had joined them.

"I'm glad to see you guys out," Brandon said to John and Hampton.

"Thanks, they asked us to have dinner with the group because there's a meeting with General Echols," John explained.

"I don't see Rylander, anyone know where he is?" asked Brandon.

"Yeah, something came up back home, he had to go. He and Virginia left after eating breakfast this morning. Rumor has it they got a ride on a military jet," John shared.

"Anyone know what this meeting is about?" asked Hampton.

Everyone shook their heads. They all wondered the same thing. People huddled in separate groups listening to the news and talking. At 6:00 they lined up for dinner while aides began setting up the podium for General Echols. The word spread he'd be a few minutes late but expected to be there by 6:15. As the last person went through the line and took a seat, General Echols arrived and walked around the room starting small talk at each table. The questions were the same, how are things going? How are they treating you? Is there anything we can do to make your stay more comfortable? As the general finished, he stepped behind the podium.

"Ladies and gentlemen, I just wanted to give you an update on things. First, the FAA announced today, airspace is now open and some flights have already taken off. However, for many of those stranded around the country, this will not immediately offer relief. We expect it to be several days before flight service as we know it is fully resumed. The priority is to reposition airplanes in the right locations. This will require ferrying planes around the country before passenger service can continue.

"Limited passenger service has begun simply because being in the right place at the right time works. Most can expect to get home or to their destinations over the next couple days. As for you, to fit in with the country, we will begin arranging flights within the same periods as the others. Your liaisons will be coordinating this for you. Those who want could possibly get out of here beginning tomorrow. However, I will be having a meeting at this same time tomorrow when I return from Washington. I hope each of you will be here when I return.

"Next, with your cooperation, we have completed all debriefings. I've completed the minute-by-minute summary of events that took place aboard Flight 3911 on September 11. I just spoke with the president about this, that's why I was late arriving. He asked me to bring the summary report to Washington to meet with him and the joint chiefs in the morning. I'll be leaving shortly. He sends his best wishes to each of you. We still have more to do with you, and I know many of you want to get home right away. We will not stop you if you want to find alternative ways of travel, but please be patient and wait until I return tomorrow evening. The president has information he will want me to pass on to you. It's information about what he plans to do to help you. It will be much easier if we can handle this as a group before too many disperse to your homes throughout the country. Please be patient and let us take care of you."

The meeting ended a few minutes after it began. General Echols left for Washington aboard a private government jet, one of only a handful in the air. The passengers mingled around the dining room and TV lounge for most of the evening. Many were burned out hearing the repeated news. Names of the dead aboard Flight 93 and Flight 3911 were released. The only correct names for Flight 3911 were those, by agreement with their families, killed aboard the flight. The remaining names were phantom names that could not be traced. Detailed accounts of both flights were similar. Both had passengers calling families telling of plans to take over the flight. Silence followed by "Let's roll" on Flight 93 and "Amen, God be with us" on Flight 3911.

There was still no way to come up with a death toll in New York. It had been a few days and was still just as confusing as the day the attack happened. There were so many heart-breaking stories being aired.

General Echols met with the president at 5:15 in the morning, fifteen minutes before the joint chiefs' meeting. General Echols was escorted through the gate for his first visit to the Oval Office. The president was waiting.

"How are our people doing, general?" asked President Walker.

"They're doing great. The cooperation is what I would expect of my own men, sir."

"How are they taking to anonymity?"

"It's fine with them, sir. They are a great bunch of Americans. It's like they joined the military and are doing their duty."

"What problems do you anticipate carrying out this mission successfully?"

"Mr. President, I'm sure there will be rumors about the plane crashing in Ohio being a military cargo plane. But sir, that's all we could round up on such short notice. We will just have to downplay those reports when they come in. Personally, over the next months, I believe the media will have more important things to do than launch an investigative report on a rumor over what kind of plane it was. Another thing, sir, we will likely hear someone claiming to know a passenger on the flight, a relative or something. Keeping the secret for four months with fifty people involved is not going to be easy. But most of the passengers are not going to tell family members, except for those who feel they should share it with their spouses."

"Great, what kind of concerns are they raising?"

"Surprisingly enough, very few. We're paying off about $21 million in debt. This includes mortgages, various outstanding loans and credit cards. None of them were expecting it, but all are grateful. Before the end of the week, all these people will be debt free. They are a great bunch of folks. Just going with the flow as we say."

"I'm glad to hear we have their full cooperation. Please let them know I am thinking of them. I'll be in touch with each personally by phone in the coming weeks. Thanks for this report. I'll get to it later this morning. We have a meeting to get to, shall we go?"

"Mr. President," General Echols interrupted. "There is one issue to bring to your attention. There is one passenger we find suspicious. We have full control and are investigating his background. He has not called any relatives; he's called no one to report on his well-being. He's acted suspiciously from the beginning. We intend to keep an eye on this individual until we can find out about his background."

"Fine, keep me informed," instructed the president.

In the dignitary quarters, early risers were beginning to gather in the TV lounge for breakfast and the latest news. Brandon was among them. The cameras captured people making signs and cards asking loved ones to call them. He thanked God none of his family had to look for him. He spoke with his kids the day before, but Grace had not called. He didn't know if she was still in Durham or if she rented a car with other passengers and drove to Atlanta. She had his number and he thought he asked her to call back. He realized it was early but decided to call her anyway. There was no answer at home or on her cell phone. He left messages on both. It was only 6:00 and there was nothing to do until 9:00, so Brandon watched the news along with others as they arrived.

At 9:00, Brandon again met with Dr. Hollace.

"This morning, I want to stray away from what we have been talking about to see if there are hidden issues. Ronnie shared you have a life-threatening liver problem," said Dr. Hollace.

"That's right. I'm on a liver transplant waiting list. The issue could have life threatening consequences. But since the liver regenerates, the problem could be handled with drugs. That is the best case/worst case scenario. I'm told removing a quarter of my liver might be a solution. At this time, I'm hopeful meds will clear up the high enzymes and existing liver damage. Even if the transplant becomes necessary, full recovery is 85 percent, so the odds are with me. Based on what I've seen of Ronnie, he is going to make it happen, he's moving my medical records to a specialist in a research center."

"Brandon, I'm sorry to hear that. Have you accepted the possibility of death?"

"Yes, I have all the precautions in place. Financial planning is done for the family, lawyers are in place if needed and I have a cemetery plot near where my dad is buried. I am not planning to die. There will be a solution for this, I know it. My doctor is optimistic we caught it in time to give me plenty of opportunity to find a donor or cure it with medication. Those who die from this condition are the ones already in the shutdown phase and there is no time to receive a transplant. Fortunately, we found my problem early during a routine physical."

Dr. Hollace had always been professional. Today she interjected a personal bit of information that gave Brandon insight into her relationship with her fiancé. What a lucky man he must be to be engaged to a lady as beautiful and loyal as Dr. Hollace.

"We covered enough for now. I've learned when we must use cram therapy, it's best to do it in short sessions. Why don't we stay on the same schedule as yesterday and meet again at 1:00? If you're up to it, maybe add a late afternoon or early evening session."

"That sounds fine to me. I enjoy our time together. I hope I leave here with the tools I need when Grace and I finally talk this over. You have already given me insight into the widow aspect I had not thought about it. I've been thinking about survival and not considered Grace may be thinking I'm dying."

He left the office and returned to his room to call Grace. This time when he dialed her number, she answered.

"Hello," She said, obviously groggy from sleep.

"Morning, it's me," Brandon answered.

"Good morning seems like I just got to sleep. I didn't get in until 5:00 this morning."

"Why on earth so late?" he asked.

"Three of us rented a car and drove home last night. They told us it could be another few days before the airports opened. We had to get home, so we drove."

"I'm glad you're home and safe. We have so much to talk about and it's looking like I won't get home for another couple days. How are you otherwise?"

"I'm fine. Can we talk later? I'm so tired. Call me tonight, okay?"

"Sure, get back to sleep, miss you."

"Me too, bye."

Brandon sat back in the chair overlooking the pool outside his room and decided to go to the lounge to be around other people. Many were, as usual, keeping up with the news. Others were telling of plans to leave the next morning. Most wanted to wait for General Echols to return and see what he had to say in the meeting. Those who wanted to leave were persuaded to wait until the next day; General Echols may have an important message from the president.

The mood remained somber, but many were beginning to see they would be going their separate ways soon. Friendships had been formed and most agreed to keep in touch. Brandon kept to himself. Now that airports were beginning to open, he was going to get with Ronnie and arrange to get home and spend the weekend with Grace. There were issues that needed to be resolved. He had accepted the loss of the relationship, although Grace showing up at the reception may have confused things. Was she at the event as support for the man she wanted back in her life? He went to a phone and called, by now she must be up. There was no answer so he left a message saying he was going to try to be home for the weekend so they can spend it together. He ate lunch with the others, and then went to his afternoon session with Dr. Hollace.

"Brandon," Dr. Hollace began. "I want you to think for a minute and search your mind for anything else you may have overlooked about your relationship with Grace that may be bothering her. Put yourself in her shoes for a moment. Why would she appear to be keeping her options open if the relationship was as great as you say it was?"

"I'm not really sure, but I intend to deal with it when I see her. It may be time to end it for the final time. I will wait and see how it goes when I get back to Atlanta. You've given me plenty of tools to use and insight to deal with the situation."

"Have you heard the term 'equally yoked?'" she asked.

"Sure, comes from the Bible. Generally thought of as a husband and wife having similar or equal faith."

"What about your faith as compared to hers?"

"We attend church regularly, but we still haven't found our church home. I'm more traditional in my worship. Grace is more contemporary. We are both devout

Christians. We worship a little differently, but I don't see our differences as a conflict."

"Okay, like you said earlier, maybe you might consider equal yoking as it relates in other areas of your life as well, like as it relates to finances. For example, relationships may work better for you if you did find someone who has her own wealth."

"Okay, but I'm a traditionalist, I feel more like the man should be the provider. It's my job and desire to take care of my family."

"Hmmm. We should stop for the day. Rumor has it many of you may be leaving tonight or tomorrow. In the last packet Ronnie will give you has all my numbers, which includes my pager and voice mail. I will be available by phone to continue our sessions if you'd like. I want you to feel free to contact me for anything, anytime. Also, anytime you want to come back for a visit, these facilities will be available for you."

"Thanks for your time and it has been a pleasure. I will be keeping in touch." As he began to leave, she stepped forward and hugged him. As he returned her hug, Brandon squeezed a little harder and inhaled the subtle fragrance of Dr. Hollace's hair.

On his way to the dignitary quarters, Brandon stopped by Ronnie's office. He was not in, so he left a message with Marsha that he wanted to see him. He then went to the TV lounge to mix with those watching the news. The television had been tuned to CNN nonstop since they arrived on Tuesday night.

Chapter 12

At 10:30 Rick Davis riding in a chauffeured government sedan appeared at the Melrose loading zone. Davis smiled when he saw Cauldwell with his black bag and his own assistant, Mary O'Hara waiting at the curb.

"Good morning, Mary," Davis greeted, although perplexed.

"Morning, Davis, I thought we could give Mary a ride, I hope you don't mind," Cauldwell said.

"Not at all, major, the president told me to support you in any way needed, no questions asked, those are my orders," Davis replied as they all laughed.

"Your transport is waiting at Joint Base Andrews, rather than Reagan. We'll drop you off and Mary can accompany me back to the White House."

"Thank you, Davis, I appreciate your support and discretion," Cauldwell crisply stated as he would a usual military command.

"Everything you requested from this side is aboard the transport. Wheels up immediately after you are buckled in. Everything on the other end is set and will be awaiting your arrival."

Mary was used to seeing important people. Dealing with dignitaries was a daily happening in her position, but this situation was a bit unusual for her. Her newfound romantic interest was a marine, one that had been court martialed. Here she was in a government limo with her boss and her new lover, and everyone was cool with the situation. She had never been to Andrews, but here she was hand in hand with Cauldwell and her boss entering security at one of the country's most secure bases. They passed security and the limo pulled up to the bottom of the stairs leading to a jet she recognized as the vice president's jumbo jet. For the first time since meeting Cauldwell, she was unable to speak. Why in the world did this marine rate personal use of the VP's airplane?

As the limo came to a stop Davis announced, "Major Cauldwell, I'll leave you two alone. I'll board the aircraft, assemble the communications team and arrange introductions. You will be the only passenger on the trip and will have full use of the space you need. Crew has been briefed and are ready for departure. We can cover the classified discussion on board." They all understood there were topics that could not be discussed in front of Mary O'Hara.

"Outstanding, Davis, I'll be with you in five," Cauldwell said as Davis exited the limo and closed the door behind him.

"A marine and personal use of the vice president's jet, Wow! I'm missing something here, must be well above my pay grade!" Mary teased.

"I could tell you but…"

"I'd have to kill you," they said in harmony laughing.

"Mary, you are fantastic, I'm glad I met you. I want to see you again when I return."

"When will that be?"

"Not sure, a week, a month, a year, no way to tell. But yours is the first face I want to see when I return to US soil."

"Count on it," Mary said as he opened the door and hiked up the jet's stairway.

At 1232 Cauldwell was aboard the jumbo jet designated as Air Force Two. He and Davis completed a few last-minute details and as Davis was ready to leave the plane Cauldwell said, "Davis, Mary is special. I'll request confidential communication time on occasions. Obviously, she knows nothing about my mission."

"Understood. Major Cauldwell, no problem with me. She is a well-respected member of the White House staff and reports directly to me, so this will not be an issue."

Davis left the plane and got back into the limo. Mary asked to wait to see the jumbo jet become airborne. At 1239 Cauldwell was in the air.

For some time after takeoff he wandered about the lavish interior, marveling at the interior design that accommodated both administrative functionality and bodily comfort. He slipped in and out of daydreams about Mary before settling into a plush, leather recliner to read a chapter of Battle Studies, then fell into a deep sleep.

When he awoke eight hours later the communications officer was touching him on his arm and sounding his name.

"Major, the captain asked me to inform you we are currently in German airspace with an ETA in Kabul of 1200 local time."

Cauldwell glanced at his watch. It was 2230 Eastern Standard Time, 0800 in Kabul so, fourteen hours flying time for the trip.

"Damn! This kite is a hell of a lot faster than the rattletraps I'm used to."

The officer grinned, "I'm sure it is, sir. In addition, we've had an excellent tailwind for much of the time."

"Yeah, I guess that happens when you're following the rotation of the planet."

"Exactly, sir. In any case we'll be touching down in four hours or less."

"Thanks very much. I need the time to get my thoughts in order."

112

"Very good, sir. Enjoy the rest of the flight." The officer disappeared forward and Cauldwell rummaged through his black bag, extracting a wire-bound notebook and a ballpoint pen.

Chapter 13

Word spread through the dignitary center that General Echols was back from Washington earlier than expected. The group of passengers gathered in the large conference room in hopes of being served dinner early. The general would be on time today. Most enjoyed dinner and almost finished when the military man stepped to the podium.

"Ladies and gentlemen, the president sends his regards to each of you. I met with him privately early this morning, then joined him in a meeting with the Joint Chiefs of Staff. He wants me to tell you the country will not forget the service you performed or are about to perform.

"First, the FAA opened airports today and we can begin processing departures for you tomorrow. It could be another day or so before you get home, but the process can start tomorrow. Your liaisons will be working with you right away to make any arrangements. We will begin what amounts to out processing for you in the morning.

Daniel was pleased he was about to be released. He blended with the rest long enough and now it was time to get to a secure phone so he could alert his leaders.

General Echols continued, "I am pleased to report the president has named each of you honorary ambassadors. With this appointment, you are now on the General Services Administration's payroll commonly known as GSA, at an annual salary of $92,000 for life. This makes each of you available for government retirement pensions and insurance. In addition, during out processing, you will be given a GSA credit card to use within a profile of your life patterns. This profile was put together during your debriefing and meetings with your liaisons. These profiles vary a great deal from passenger to passenger. Your liaisons will explain this to you in detail when you get your cards.

"Finally, the president has requested funding from Congress for unspecified needs to deal with terrorism. Portions of those funds are going to you. We don't know what that will be yet, but each will receive a lump sum payment sometime between now and the State of the Union address in January. All your outstanding mortgages and bills have been paid by GSA. When you leave here, you will leave debt free. When you leave, you will leave on the GSA payroll, you are now government employees. Your only job is to keep quiet about the events of Flight 3911 until after the State of the Union address. After that, you are free to do as you please, but your pension will stay with you for life.

"The last few days have been trying times for all of us. I hope we made you as comfortable as possible and that under the circumstances you might even say you have enjoyed your time here with us. We apologize if at times you may have felt like prisoners. I admit that due to national security we have been watching your every move. We have done so as discretely as possible, but it has been necessary. We are entering a time when each of us will have to look at the one standing next to us differently."

Daniel began having second thoughts. Since no one knew about him, the offerings of the United States government sounded great. Maybe blending in as an American might not be so bad after all. The promise of $92,000 for life, a government credit card, a lump sum bundle of money, and being an American hero might not be so bad. There was no one for him back home. Maybe simply taking the bribe and keeping quiet would pay big dividends for future attacks.

"Now in closing. This facility will be open to you anytime between now and the speech in January. The ID card you will receive when you check out will give access to the base anytime. If you feel the need to get away from your everyday life for any reason and need peace and solitude, your room will be available. Make use of this facility and its resources. That is all. Good luck, and Godspeed to each of you."

Brandon returned to his room and began to think about all that had happened. Adding $92,000 a year for life to his already handsome income of $100,000 a year from his business, plus the other $105,000 a year from family assets and investment properties came close to $300,000 a year. Selling his business interest might be an option now and he could begin to think about early retirement. Maybe author another book about this adventure? Would he go stir crazy in retirement at age 50? Travel and seeing the world was taking on new meaning now. He worked hard all his life, most of the time putting in sixty-hour weeks. It was time to cut back. Life was going to be hectic after January. He realized he was going to be one of the most sought-after guests on every TV show in the country, possibly the world.

At 9:00 Brandon called Grace, this time she answered.

"Hi, it's me, how are you doing?" he asked.

"Fine, but I'm still so tired. I'm just now getting over the shock of last Tuesday."

"Yeah, me too. Things have been hectic around here, but from the news, I guess we've been better off than some. At least we've been put up in military housing on a base."

"We had to stay on the airplane all night, there was something about security and the police needed to check everyone's background before they would let us off," she said.

"It looks like flights may be going out tomorrow, so I may be home in the late afternoon."

"Great, maybe we can get together and talk for a while."

"I think that's a good idea, I was so glad to see you in New York, but we had so little time to talk. After nothing for a month, then you show up unexpectedly. It's confusing and I didn't want to ruin the moment, so what's going on?"

"I've just been thinking. We have too much going on to throw this all away. Going out with my girlfriends is not worth losing you over. We do so much together. We have so much fun. We can talk when you get back. I've missed you so much, hurry home!" she pleaded.

"I'll let you know as soon as they schedule my flight. In the meantime, you have the number here and you can call anytime," Brandon assured her.

"What have you been doing all this time?" Grace asked.

Brandon froze. He knew he would have to tell her something, but should he tell her the truth?

"We'll talk when I get home. Miss you, see you tomorrow."

"Okay, I miss you too, goodnight," she answered.

Brandon immediately went to bed, and for the first time since Tuesday, rested well all night.

Chapter 14

At 1202 Afghanistan time, the huge aircraft rolled to a stop in the charter/private air section of the Kabul airport. Through a portside window Cauldwell could see a CH53 standing by with rotors turning. As he deplaned, he saw the usual contingent of heavily armed government militia watching the proceedings from just beyond the nine-foot chain link fence that cordoned off this little used section from the rest of the airport runways and outbuildings.

For the umpteenth time Cauldwell thought it was still a damn mystery why the friggin' Taliban allowed him to come and go without interference. He heard once from a guy that it was the result of a deep cover agreement whereby the US keeps the Russians off their ass. Still, they must know what he does. Ah well, just as long as they don't know where I do it.

Cauldwell boarded the big helicopter, buckled up and was immediately airborne. An hour and twenty minutes later the familiar peaks, ridges and valleys that surrounded Camp Subat came into view and seven minutes after that he was on the ground.

"Welcome back, sir!" Sergeant First Class Downs shouted over the roar of engines as the chopper lifted off to head for its clandestine base just inside the Pakistan border.

Cauldwell waited for the noise to diminish. "Thanks, sergeant. Everything okay around here?"

"Hell ya, sir. Almost as good as if the major had been here all the time."

"Great. Walk with me." Cauldwell headed for his tent and Downs fell in step beside him. "Any more news from Zamani?"

"Yes, sir. He sent a runner down about 0900 this morning to say he made all your required preparations, and he would be standing by to meet with the major at your convenience, sir."

"Outstanding." Cauldwell pushed through the tent flap as Downs followed in trace. He threw his bag on to the cot and dragged a wooden folding chair away from the small, spindle-legged table that served as his desk. "Have a seat, Sergeant Downs."

"Yes, sir."

Cauldwell sat down on his lawn chair. "Now then, here's the deal. You are going to have to run the training program yourself for a while longer. I've been assigned a mission that no one will be privy to. Chief Zamani is providing a place for me to work so I can conduct my business outside this camp and away from you guys. It's for the welfare of all our own people that I will absolutely preclude everyone from any knowledge of or any association with the enterprise to which I have been assigned. Is that clear?"

"Yes, sir."

"Right. Now then, in a couple days three prisoners will be brought in by one of our Pakistan based choppers under cover of darkness. When that happens, and except for you and Sergeant Allen, all hands will be confined to barracks or the Com Shack. No one else will bear witness to the arrival and processing of these three individuals. You or Sergeant Allen will then transport me and the three captives to the end of the road where the trail up to Zamani's village begins. You will deposit the four of us at the foot of the trail and return to camp. Neither of you will ever speak of this evolution again, even to each other. In the future, should anyone ask you anything about this action, you will both deny all knowledge of it. You with me so far?"

"Yes, sir."

"Right. Now you must understand and make sure Allen also understands the measures I am implementing are designed solely for the purpose of protecting the two of you and the rest of our people here. You got that?"

"I've got it, sir."

"Alright then. From time to time I may send one of Zamani's men down here or I may appear in person to request certain items. I want absolutely no questions or oral speculation to accrue to those requests. You understand?"

"I understand, sir."

"Okay then, Sergeant Downs, carry on and send Sergeant Allen to me now. I need him to drive me up to the trail right away."

"Yes, sir." Downs stood and left the tent.

Within minutes Sergeant Allen's voice sounded from outside the tent. "Sir. Sergeant Allen reporting as ordered, sir."

"Enter."

The tough young ranger entered and snapped to attention.

"At ease, Sergeant Allen. As Sergeant Downs told you, I want you to drive me to the foot of the trail up to Zamani's village."

"Yes sir, he did."

"Fine, so let's get to it. When you return, report at once to Sergeant First Class Downs for a briefing."

"Yes, sir."

Cauldwell led the way to an M-151 Jeep and climbed into the front passenger seat. Allen got behind the wheel and fired the engine to life. He selected a low gear and the vehicle lurched forward, climbing the rock strewn, 1200-yard road Chief Zamani's people had hewn from the mountainside some eight years before.

The road ended in a wide semi-circle with a well-worn, steep foot trail leading off to the left. Allen swung the vehicle through 180 degrees and came to a stop. Cauldwell stepped down at the spot where trail and road joined. "Okay. Thanks, sergeant. Carry on."

"Yes, sir." Allen let out the clutch and the Jeep started back down the road. Cauldwell was left alone in a silence so powerful it seemed tangible. For a time Cauldwell stood staring east where a huge valley spread some five hundred feet below.

> *I have stood in some mighty-mouthed hollow.*
> *That's plumb-full of hush to the brim.*
> *I've watched the big, husky sun wallow.*
> *In crimson and gold and grow dim...*

The words of poet Robert W. Service describing the Yukon came to mind and he couldn't help thinking that Service would have liked this country too, especially the great reaches high up where the snows never left.

The major turned and began to climb. The trail followed a twisting, turning fissure that had been a watercourse sometime in the dim and distant past. The footing was treacherous; the steepness of the grade demanded considerable exertion. By the time Cauldwell had climbed through 300 feet, he was breathing hard and welcomed the upward angle decreased by twenty degrees as he left the fissure and began traversing a narrow valley that ran straight before him for 200 yards with a succession of low, rounded hills defined by crevasses on both sides.

At the far end of the valley the trail climbed sharply between two massive granite walls. He labored through another 100 feet of elevation and suddenly entered an almost level ground on the floor of a grass covered valley that stretched a thousand yards to the west and spread 200 yards to his left and right.

About 800 yards ahead he could see the cluster of huts that formed a village and at this distance was readily able to discern the largest and most solidly constructed of these, which he knew to be Chief Zamani's dwelling.

About 300 yards away and to his left front, two young lads were supervising the foraging of a small herd of goats as they pushed steadily through the knee-high grass, now turned brown and brittle with the approach of winter.

As he neared the herd, one of the boys broke away and ran with amazing speed across the field, then down the trail in the direction of the village.

Cauldwell followed the boy's course all the way to the biggest structure and smiled to himself.

So, the lad gets to report the approach of the major and for a few moments bask in the glow of the chief's favor.

Within a short time Cauldwell saw a small knot of men emerge from the dwelling and stand in front of it, obviously awaiting his arrival. As he drew nearer, he identified Zamani and saw four men, members of the village council, had accompanied the tribal chief.

When Cauldwell drew to within ten yards of the group, Zamani stepped forward smiling and came to greet him with outstretched arms. "Welcome, Majah Cauldwell. Welcome to my village." The two embraced in a fierce bear hug and not for the first time, Cauldwell felt the tremendous physical power of the man.

At six-foot-two, the 44-year-old chief was two inches shorter than Cauldwell and weighed 210 pounds, at least 20 pounds lighter. Still, Cauldwell thought him to be the strongest man he had ever known.

"Thank you, chief. I am honored you have taken the time to meet with me."

"Zamani has always time for majah with heart of lion."

"You give me too much credit, chief."

"Not so! Zamani remembers early times when majah teach my people, lead patrols and kill many Taliban and maybe some Russians."

"Well, in those days we had to get things done in a hurry."

"Yes, big hurry. Still, other advisors in my country never go where bullets fly."

"I was just doing what I thought was necessary to help the fine men that Chief Zamani was sending me."

"Exactly so! That is why all high-country tribe members say majah is great warrior!"

"Then they do me honor for they too are warriors."

"Not all. Only some. Most be just soldiers. I remember majah teach Zamani warriors be separate from soldiers and that we find very few warriors."

Cauldwell laughed. "Yeah, Chief Zamani, you are right about that."

"Ok. Then Zamani say majah is great warrior."

"Thanks, chief. You do me a great honor for Zamani himself is a true warrior."

The tribal leader bowed slightly from the waist. "Now I show majah place he can work."

The group of tribe members turned and moved toward the house where five Kalashnikov rifles leaned against an exterior wall. The men armed themselves and all but Zamani slung ammunition belts across their bodies.

"Okay, we go now." The chief gestured and two of his men led off down the valley to the west, while the remaining two fell in behind Cauldwell and his host.

The path ran arrow straight through the grassland to a point at the base of the mountains that marked the end of the meadow. As they neared the sheer granite walls, Cauldwell could see the path continued west in the form of a narrow fissure that cut sharply up and into the mountains.

As the men entered the ravine they were forced into a single file as the climb became arduous. Several times Cauldwell turned his body and side stepped to effect passage around jagged stone outcroppings, all while marveling at the apparent ease with which the Afghans negotiated the precipitous trail.

After thirty minutes of hard labor and gaining three hundred feet of additional altitude, the pathway suddenly leveled for ten yards then emerged from the defile.

They were now at the eastern end of a bowl-shaped valley about half the size of the one below where the village was situated. The grass covered clearing was completely encircled by an unbroken ring of saw-toothed peaks that rose a thousand feet or more. About 200 yards to the west and just south of the trail lay the remnants, mostly crude foundations, of what had once been a cluster of huts. Now, only three retained walls and just two had roofing.

Closer, and on the north side of the trail, a large stone building stood by itself. Chief Zamani led the way toward the structure and, when ten feet from the walls, stopped and pointed. "Zamani thinks this be what majah needs."

"Looks good to me, chief." Cauldwell ran his eyes over the stout walls and the sturdy, intact roof.

Zamani approached a heavy wooden door hung on, massive, wrought-iron hinges. He seized the large ringbolt latch and twisted hard to the right. Putting his shoulder to the door, he forced it open and stepped inside. Cauldwell followed and found himself in a dimly lit, earthen floored space 60 by 40 feet. Ten feet above his head were huge, hand created beams extending from wall to wall at regular intervals.

Daylight filtered through a series of narrow apertures, five in each wall that looked like firing slits. Peering through the closest of these, Cauldwell saw the walls of neatly fitted, hand-hewn granite were more than four feet thick. The slits were about four inches wide at the exterior but tapered toward the interior so the stock of a shoulder weapon could be moved a considerable distance to the left or right thereby greatly increasing the arc of fire.

"Hey, chief, your people sure as hell built this thing to last."

"Exactly so, majah. We build for two purpose. When part of village still be here in high valley, we store food here. Also, if Russians or Taliban come to low valley, whole village come here. Attackers have hard job to come up narrow trail and if attackers get into high valley, we give them bad time from inside stone house."

"Good planning, chief. I can't see anybody having much of a chance coming up the ravine. Two men with good weapons could hold off a damn army."

"Exactly so, majah."

"Tell you what, chief, this will be ideally suited to my purpose. I'll need to get a few things brought up here, communications gear, medical supplies, and some other stuff." Cauldwell consulted his watch "It's too late to do much today, but first thing in the morning I'll have my soldiers start packing in what I need."

"Very good, majah. Zamani will send men down to camp to help."

"That's good of you, chief, but I don't want to trouble your people any further."

"What we do for majah never be trouble, only big honor. My men go down in morning."

"Well, okay, chief, and thank you."

"You welcome, majah."

"Now then, chief, in a couple days I will be bringing three very bad men up here to stay with me in the stone house."

"That fine, majah. These bad men be prisoners?"

"That's right, chief. I'll bring 'em up in handcuffs and try to herd them through the ravine."

"Zamani's men will help with that. They are exceptionally good at getting bad man to go when bad man become reluctant."

"Reluctant? Damn, chief, you're getting really good with English!"

The tribal leader's handsome face broke into a pleased grin. "Exactly so, majah. Zamani everyday study crazy language."

Cauldwell laughed. "Yeah, it is a crazy language, but you're doing great there, chief."

"Thank you, majah."

"Another thing, chief. No one must ever speak of this or mention I brought three bad men up here. No one must ever know that they were here."

"There not be needed to say this, majah. Zamani and all his people will have no memory of these three assholes."

"Huh? Yeah, right. Okay then, chief, I had better get back to camp and start getting things organized."

"Very good, majah. We go now."

Shortly after 1800 Cauldwell entered the Communications Shack at Camp Subat. "Spec-5 Armstrong."

"Yes, sir?"

"I'm going to need some com gear to take up into the hills, whatever will let me contact you down here. If we can spare crypto gear, I'll take it. If not, I'll make do with whatever you can spare."

"Well, sir, six months ago a logistical genius sent us three more KY-38s that are still in the shipping boxes. I can give the major one of those, sir."

"Outstanding, Armstrong! Now, get hold of Sergeant First Class Downs and have him report to my personal palace."

"Roger that, sir."

Cauldwell walked into his now freezing tent. He put a match to his hurricane lantern and fell wearily into his lawn chair. He leaned back and closed his eyes, thinking hard.

"Sir! Sergeant First Class Downs reporting as ordered, sir."

Cauldwell sat up. "Enter!"

Downs pushed through the door flap and came to attention.

"At ease, sergeant. Have a seat."

"Yes, sir." Downs pulled the desk chair around to face his superior and sat.

Cauldwell rose, stepped to his desk and picked up a small pad and a pen, both he handed to the sergeant before reseating himself. "You're gonna need to take notes. Here's where I am so far. Chief Zamani has taken care of me on his end. In a few minutes it'll be coming up on zero-nine hundred in DC, and I'll be putting in a call to have our three visitors sent over. Before they arrive, I'll need to pack a bunch of trash up into the hills like com gear, medical stuff, and so forth. Armstrong is seeing about the radio and I need you to get with Doc Adams and have him make me up a medical kit with basic crap like bandages and adhesive tape, but also three heavy duty syringes and a bunch of needles with various lengths and calibers.

"Find our ace diesel mechanic and tell him I need a cordless drill with extra batteries and a charger. Have him give you a half dozen of the smallest caliber drill bits he has. Pliers, both needle-nose and straight-jaw. The smallest gas-powered generator we have, plus a jerry can of gas. I also want two heavy duty, 30-foot extension cords. Next, get him to supply the biggest portable floodlight he can find, along with an extra bulb. Tell him I want three, three-foot pieces of steel which are two inches thick and six inches wide with heavy U-bolts welded dead center on the wide side. I'll also need six big padlocks like the ones we have on the ammunition locker. Finally, have him supply six rolls of duct tape and a hundred feet of stripped com wire.

"I want you to have Sergeant Allen round up a half dozen water cans, leave 'em empty as there's a stream through the high valley I can use to fill them. Also, have him break out six cases of MREs. I'll need a resupply of those in due course. Tell him to find three galvanized wash buckets so our visitors can have a place to defecate. Better get me a case of ass wipe too and three sets of leg shackles.

"I'm also going to need that big-ass wooden chair from the recreation tent as well as one of the six-foot tables in there. You guys will have to break those sonsabitches down into the smallest pieces possible or I'll never get 'em up that friggin' trail.

"Last thing. Scrounge around and see if you can find somebody willing to lend me their boom box. The bigger an' louder, the better. I will also need a couple tapes or CDs with the most aggravating excuses for music. Rap would be fine, gangsta rap would be even better. Here's a short list of items that occurred to me after the fact." Cauldwell handed over a sheet of note pad paper.

"Any questions?"

"No, sir. I have everything written down."

"Very good, sergeant. Thanks, and carry on."

Downs got to his feet and came briefly to attention. "Yes, sir."

The young sergeant left and Cauldwell was alone in the pale, flickering light of the lantern. He raised his right arm and turned his watch face toward the light. 1827, almost 0900 in DC. It was time to make the call. Emitting a low groan born of weariness, he dragged himself from the chair, left the tent and headed through the swiftly gathering gloom toward the Com Shack.

"Specialist Armstrong, I need to get on the radio phone to DC. Here's the number." Cauldwell pushed a note pad page across the counter.

"Right away, sir." Armstrong took the paper and seated himself before the apparatus. In less than two minutes Cauldwell heard, "Yes, sir. Please stand by for Major Cauldwell."

The specialist stood as Cauldwell approached and seized the proffered headset. Adjusting the headset, Cauldwell triggered the transmitter. "Cauldwell here, over."

"Hey Major! Rick Davis here. What can I do for you? Over."

"I'm pretty well organized on my end and now I need you to send the tourists. Over."

"Roger. I'll get right on it. Over."

"When can I expect to see them? Over."

"I'll call you when I have an ETA at your position. Over."

"How long you figure it'll take for you to come up with that? Over."

"About five minutes. Over."

"Roger. I'll be standing by. Cauldwell out."

"Davis out."

Keeping the headset on Cauldwell folded his arms on the table and put his forehead on them. Seven minutes later the low-pitched hum of an incoming call sounded in his ears. Raising his head, he depressed and released the transmitter trigger to complete the connection. "Cauldwell here. Over."

"Davis again, major. Your tourists will arrive in Kabul at 11:30 am the day after tomorrow. We will have a helo standing by to bring them to you, over."

"That won't do. Have the chopper swing by here first. I want to be on the ground in Kabul to receive them. Over."

Several seconds of dead air followed. Finally, "Roger that, major. Helo will come to your position at 10:00 am, okay? Over."

"Roger. I'll be standing by here at ten hundred Thursday. Over."

"Right. See that our tourists enjoy their stay. Over."

"I'll do my best. One question, do these hammerheads speak English? Over."

"They sometimes try to pretend otherwise, but they were part of a sleeper cell and lived in the States for nine years, so they actually understand and speak the language well. Over."

"That's all I need to know. Cauldwell out."

"Davis out."

By 1000 the next day Cauldwell's cache of required items was staged at one corner of the camp's concrete helo pad with ten tribe members Zamani dispatched serving as porters standing by. Cauldwell eyed the paraphernalia dubiously, remembering the torturous trail through the ravine. Suddenly, he struck his forehead a resounding smack with the palm of his right hand and marched purposely into the Communications Shack.

Specialist Armstrong get on the horn with aviation support and tell them I need something to helo lift a load of gear to a meadow in the hills. Probably about an hour's time on this end, and they'll be on the way home."

"Roger that, sir."

Cauldwell retraced his steps to the helo pad with notebook and pen in hand to begin checking the piled items to ensure that nothing had been forgotten. Four minutes passed before Specialist-5 Armstrong appeared.

"Sir. We'll have a CH46 inbound shortly. They say they'll be airborne in ten and here in about 50 minutes."

"Outstanding, Armstrong! Thank you."

"No sweat, sir."

Fifty-seven minutes later the steady beat of the helicopter's twin rotors could be heard as the aircraft approached from the Northeast, flying low through the valley before climbing sharply to reach Camp Subat's altitude. The chopper settled on the pad and the rear cargo ramp came down smoothly.

Cauldwell indicated to the leader of the tribal working party the material filling the pad should be loaded aboard the aircraft.

As the helo engines were still running and the blades turning, the first three or four tribe members approaching the ramp with burdens, did so with hesitancy and apprehension. As soon as it was obvious they had nothing to fear from the machine, all ten bent to their task with a will and within 15 minutes Cauldwell's requisitions were stowed and secured.

Cauldwell approached the lead Afghani. "You speak English?"

"Little bit English, majah."

"You want to bring your men on the helicopter up to the high valley?"

The man did not immediately understand Cauldwell's meaning, but with a few more words and a series of gestures, the American finally made himself understood. The Afghani turned and said something to his nine-man detail. Immediately great smiling and nodding of heads broke forth. The man turned to Cauldwell. "Okay, majah. We go."

"Guess a chopper ride's gonna be a big thrill for those guys huh, sir?"

127

"Damn straight, Sergeant Allen. Not only that, but it will also give them special status in the village for quite a while. Come with me and help show them how to strap in."

"Yes, sir."

Leading the way through the cargo hatch, Cauldwell encountered the helicopter's crew chief. "Either one of the two up front know where we're headed?"

"Yes, sir. Your com guy briefed us. Northwest to the valley above the village."

"Outstanding!"

Once the tribe members become acquainted with the intricacies of seat belt buckles, Cauldwell and Sergeant Allen found seats for themselves and Cauldwell gave a thumbs up to the crew chief. The aircraft lifted off accompanied by smiles, gestures, and excited conversations of the Afghans who all twisted and turned their bodies to glimpse the world below through the portals.

After six minutes, the chopper began to descend and Cauldwell signaled the crew chief to approach.

"Yes, sir?"

"Tell the pilot to set down near the large stone building."

"Roger, sir." The crewman moved away, speaking into his flight helmet microphone.

The aircraft flared, then settled gently into the brown, knee-high grass. Glancing through a starboard portal, Cauldwell could see they were about 30 yards south of the stone structure and nodded with satisfaction.

The whine of hydraulic systems filled the air, and the ramp went down. All hands disembarked and Cauldwell stepped quickly to the building's large door and swung it open. He beckoned the Afghani detail leader.

"We put everything in here at the east end," he pointed.

"Ok majah, we put all here." The man walked back to the aircraft and spoke rapidly to his assembled group.

Zamani's men were models of discipline and efficiency. In less than twelve minutes the entire load was artfully arranged, centered, and positioned ten feet from the east wall.

Cauldwell walked back to the helo and spoke to the crew chief. "Ask your pilot if he would do me one final favor and lift my working party back to the village."

"Roger, sir." The airman pulled his helmet mike down in front of his mouth, keyed the switch on the com cord that trailed behind him and spoke quickly. He listened to the response then addressed Cauldwell. "Pilot says no problem, sir. Just load 'em up.'"

"Great! Tell him I said thanks very much."

"Roger, sir. Will do."

Cauldwell turned to the Afghan group leader. "Chopper will take you and your men back down to the village."

The man gave a huge toothy smile and his eyes sparkled with delight. "Ah! Thank you, majah. Thank you!" He spoke rapidly to his men and the tribe members began to file aboard. Both Cauldwell and the crew chief watched the strapping in process closely, but none of the men needed further instruction in the use of belts and buckles.

"Thank you for your help. Please tell Chief Zamani the major said thank you."

"No problem. We have always help for majah. I will tell Zamani what majah say."

Cauldwell walked down the ramp, which immediately began to rise. Eleven seconds later the aircraft was airborne and heading east. When the engine noise receded, Sergeant Allen spoke. "Guess those guys were really happy not having to walk down through that friggin' trail, huh, major?"

"That wasn't it at all, sergeant. Having the whole damn village bear witness to them emerging from that bird, that's the big deal. That's far better than just telling about the experience." Cauldwell turned toward the building. "Okay, let's get this crap organized."

Once inside, Cauldwell considered the vast pile for several seconds. "Sergeant Allen, break out that toolbox and see if you can put that big chair back together and get the legs back on that table."

"Yes, sir."

As Allen bent to his tasks, Cauldwell extricated three lengths of chain and dragged them to the far end of the building with its five firing slits. He passed the ends of the chains through the first, third, and fifth of the slits, allowing several feet of heavy links to land along the exterior wall. He returned to the pile and extracted three flat sections of two-by-six-inch steel and three padlocks. These he carried outside and around to the western wall. Each of the three-foot steel pieces had a U-bolt welded to the center of one of its six-inch wide sides. He connected each of the steel sections to one of the chains by passing a padlock shackle through both the last link and the U-bolt.

Returning to the equipment dump, he collected the three sets of leg shackles and the remaining three padlocks. Carrying these, he moved back to the west interior wall and using the three padlocks, fastened a set of leg irons to each of the three chains. After completing this operation, he seized the irons and pulled hard on the chain, stepping backward as he did so. He threaded several feet before he was jerked to a halt when the outside steel section came hard against the exterior wall at the bottom of the aperture. Cauldwell grunted with satisfaction. Since the exterior dimensions of the firing slits were 4-by-24 inches and the steel plates were 6-by-36, there was no way they could be manipulated to pass through the apertures and grant any freedom to anyone shackled to the interior end of the chains. He dropped the irons, which immediately retreated about four feet back toward the wall.

Cauldwell reflected. Guess I made those plates a bit heavy. Ah well, if any of the assholes want to move another four feet, they'll have to work for it.

As Cauldwell moved back he was pleased to note Sergeant Allen had finished with the chair and was attaching the last of the legs to the heavy table, which lay upside down on the earthen floor. "Good work there, Sergeant Allen. When you're done, come help me get the generator and floodlight into position."

"Yes, sir. Be right there."

Cauldwell carefully moved the cardboard box containing a spare bulb off to one side, then picked up the tripod mounted floodlight and carried it to a center position about twenty feet from the west wall. Allen moved to join him and together they carried the five-kilowatt Honda generator to a spot ten feet north, or right of the floodlight. Cauldwell retreated to his stack of goods and after rummaging briefly, returned with two heavy-duty extension cables. "Sergeant Allen, see if you can find that damn boom box and bring me the gas jerry can."

"Yes, sir."

Cauldwell plugged the extensions into the generator outlets and attached one of them to the floodlight. After finishing, Allen returned carrying the boom box in one hand and lugging the heavy jerry can with the other. Cauldwell plugged the music machine into the remaining cord and removed the gas cap from the generator. Sergeant Allen filled the tank and replaced the cap. Cauldwell pulled hard on the starter cord and was immediately rewarded when the engine roared to life. He pushed the switch on the floodlight and was satisfied with the brilliant, blinding glare that suddenly bounced from the gray stone wall. "Now let's see what we get from that damn boom box. Turn the volume all the way up."

"Roger that, sir." Allen bent down, fiddled with the volume knob and pushed the Play button. Raucous, ear-splitting sounds bent the air with a shrill male voice screaming words accompanied by the reverberating thunder of a drum.

"Okay, OKAY, SERGEANT ALLEN!" The sound ceased. "Gawdamighty! I can't stand that crap!"

"I know what ya mean, sir. It drives me friggin' crazy too."

"Well, I sure as hell hope it'll bother my guests a whole lot. Awright, shut down the generator and help me move the table and chair up here."

Together they hauled the heavy wooden armchair next to the floodlight.

"Okay, let's turn this bitch around so it faces the end wall."

"Roger, sir. Is the major going to use it to observe his guests, sir?"

"No, sergeant, the chair's not for me. When one of the assholes is in it, I want the other two to be able to see his face clearly just in case it happens to register a certain amount of pain. That way they might grow a bit apprehensive knowing their turns are coming. Now then, help me with the table."

With one man on each end, they carried the sturdily built table to a point midway between the chair and the generator.

"Thanks, sergeant. I can handle it from here if you need to get down the mountain."

"Is the major not coming back to camp, sir?"

"Not right now. I have a few more things to do first. I may come down later tonight or maybe at first light in the morning."

"Jesus, sir! How's the major gonna sleep up here? All we loaded were three of those skinny, Afghan sleeping mats and three summertime blankets."

"Not to worry there, sergeant. I have my sleeping bag and an isopor mat somewhere in that damn pile. However, before you go, how 'bout firing up that KY-38 an' doing a radio check with Armstrong so I know the damn thing works."

"Yes, sir."

As Allen went about unpacking the radio, Cauldwell selected various small items from the heap of supplies and arranged them on the table.

"Radio works fine, sir."

"Alright then, Sergeant Allen. Thanks for your help. Carry on."

"Okay, sir. I'll be on my way."

Left alone, Cauldwell continued to prepare and position the gear. At 1830 hours with night beginning to fall and a deepening gloom creeping over the stone walls, he found both a kerosene and a hurricane lantern. Lighting the lantern, Cauldwell set it in the middle of the table and continued to work in the feeble light it afforded.

At 2000 hours he ceased his labors, cut the steel bands securing the six cases of MREs, pulled out a random meal and set it on the table. Seizing a water can, he exited the building, walked around the western end, and headed for the small mountain stream some forty yards to the north. After filling the rugged plastic container, he returned to the table, filled a canteen cup, picked up his meal and sank wearily into the armchair. He ate methodically without enjoyment. Once finished, he lit a cigar and leaned back in the chair, puffing contentedly. Within minutes he was sound asleep and dreaming of Mary O'Hara.

Chapter 15

Brandon was one of the first up on Saturday morning, but the TV lounge quickly began filling. Many thought out processing and meetings with liaisons would take too long. A few were eating breakfast, some were watching the news, and others were exchanging addresses and phone numbers. It was like the end of a convention when everyone was preparing to leave and saying their goodbyes.

The group had been through an experience that would bind them forever. Except for a few troublemakers in the passenger group, most were down to earth examples of good, patriotic citizens. Most realized their semi-detainment was for the national good and besides, they were paid handsomely for any inconvenience.

An announcement came at 7:00 that interrupted breakfast for many. It was General Echols advising of an important meeting in the dining room in thirty minutes. He asked everyone to be there. Those in the TV lounge and those still in their rooms began wandering into the dining room in anticipation. Just before 7:30, General Echols entered the dining room looking grim.

"Ladies and gentlemen," he began, "we have been informed of a problem that might delay your departures."

Everyone looked around to find Brandon. He had become the unofficial spokesman for the group. The room filled with low level murmur.

"Please, let me have your attention. This is only a minor delay. We will immediately begin processing and by the time this operation wraps up, we should be back on schedule."

"General, what is the purpose of the delay?" Brandon asked on behalf of the passengers.

"I'm sorry, but I'm not at liberty to discuss it at this time," General Echols said, not mentioning the possibility one of them might be a terrorist. "However, continue as though everything is fine. Even with the delay, I am confident we can get most of you who want to leave on a flight later today."

As soon as General Echols finished his remarks, the puzzled passengers separated into several distinct groups, many beginning to feel as though they were prisoners.

Five new faces went unnoticed on a security detail. Daniel had been under scrutiny since he arrived. He never made calls to family and distinctively stayed apart from the others. Special Agent Cameron's cross check of his ID confirmed Daniel Raphia was one of the terrorist hijackers. He had eluded detection because of his British family and British passport. The security detail waited until Daniel was alone and away from the others, then took him into custody. He was immediately removed from the facility and handed off to Intelligence Officer, Special Agent Larry Cameron to be secured separately from the other surviving terrorist POWs; now there were four. Special Agent Cameron's instincts paid off. The new POW would be kept secure so the other POWs would not know he had been detained.

Brandon went to Ronnie's office in hopes of beginning processing and learning more about what was going on. As usual, Ronnie was in his office as if waiting for his charge to arrive. Ronnie told Brandon he wasn't sure what General Echols meant or what the delay might be. His orders were to begin processing and ensure all liaisons were getting their people ready to leave.

"Okay, what does "processing" mean and what do we do?" asked Brandon.

"First is issuing your government ID. This will enable you the liberties much like a retired military person to use the PX on bases as well as return here anytime you want. Your room will be yours and you may consider this base as your home away from home. Come back when you feel the need for counseling or simply to get away."

"Sounds good, what else?" Brandon asked.

"Next is issuing a GSA credit card. The limits on these cards vary among passengers. In your instance, it's intended for use such as air travel, car rental, and dining when traveling. Based on your previous travel profile, and a little extra I arranged, your card is virtually bottomless," Ronnie said with a smile.

"What do you mean?" asked Brandon.

"Your previous travel history indicated you generally fly in your own airplane and airline travel is secondary. Anytime you do need to fly commercial, charge it. The magnetic strip has your profile encoded for first class travel as you see fit. I have added this because I know you may be traveling more in connection with your book. I made arrangements for it to be carried nationwide, as I expect you will need it to travel to book signings."

"That's fantastic!" Brandon exclaimed. His mind returned to his thoughts last night about retiring. He had not considered the income from book sales.

"You are an ambassador for this country. Please be aware this card and ID must be returned when you join us for the State of the Union address. This will be a coming out party in your honor at which time you will be expected to return the card and ID. In the meantime, please do not abuse this privilege, but feel free to use it, as necessary."

"I understand, so what else is there to out processing?" Brandon asked.

"Previously you indicated you did not intend to inform any one about Flight 3911. Has that changed?"

"I'm not sure. That depends on my relationship with Grace. I will make that decision after talking to her."

"That's fine, but please let me know if you decide to let her in on it. On another subject, I'll call you when Hampton and John are ready to travel. The president is going to invite you to Camp David for an afternoon. You can bring your spouse or significant other with you. As far as long-term planning, you will be included on a White House guest list for a function in the next few months that will also be an invitation to include your spouse or significant other."

"I'll be looking forward to it. I expect to be seeing you in the coming weeks. I want to take advantage of the resources here and return for follow up with Dr. Hollace. I may even want to bring Grace. We talked about pre-marital counseling, but never did anything about it."

"Fine, I'll have a shuttle to take you to hop on a government jet going to Atlanta. It will leave in an hour, so be back here so I can see you off."

"Sure, but General Echols..."

"I am aware of the delay, but you've been cleared to leave. I can't go into details, but you are clear. See you in less than an hour."

Brandon wandered through the halls and lounge looking for anyone to say goodbye to. The place was a ghost town compared to previous days. The makeshift office liaisons were closing the few files left on their desks. The boxes of information gathered from their assigned passengers lined the halls awaiting pick-up. There were only a few people in the lounge reading, a contrast from the zombies hovering in front of the TV watching nonstop CNN. Most passengers were busy packing and waiting for the go ahead from their liaison.

After gathering his things, Brandon returned to the lounge and announced to his fellow passengers he was cleared to leave. Some were excited for him, others were jealous. Everyone shook his hand and after hugs and well wishes, Brandon returned to Ronnie's office. The two also shook hands and Ronnie walked his charge to the front door where a military car and driver waited. Ronnie helped load up and told the driver to rush to the flight line to connect with the jet heading for Atlanta.

"Ronnie, thanks for everything. I will definitely keep in touch," Brandon assured his liaison and now friend as he slid into the car.

"Remember, if you need anything, don't hesitate to call."

Brandon said goodbye and left to board the jet. He expected it to be a military cargo plane, but it was a Gulf Stream IV and there was no one else onboard. Ronnie privately ordered the jet to return Brandon to Atlanta. The flight took a

135

little more than an hour and when they landed a car waited to take Brandon to his house. He had taken MARTA to the airport the Sunday before and couldn't remember telling Ronnie he would need a ride home. But then again, Ronnie was a resourceful man who could find out anything he wanted. Everything looked the same, yet so different. There was little traffic on GA 400 as they made their way north of the city. There was an eerie calm over Atlanta. Not one car was speeding, no hustle and bustle. Just silent and slow. When he reached home, he dumped his things inside the front door and called Grace to let her know he was on his way.

"Stop and pick up a bottle of wine and we'll just chill out here. It's late and we don't need to be going out, I'll get some cheese and crackers ready," she suggested.

"Sounds fine to me," Brandon said.

"I'm getting in the shower, just come on in when you get here."

"Okay, see you in a few minutes."

Brandon stopped for the bottle of wine. He decided to take the scenic route to Grace's house. He needed a little time to work things out in his head. Should he tell what happened? It was going to be a tough secret to keep. She was going to have to know soon. How else would he explain their afternoon at Camp David or the White House invitations? He could possibly propose to her in the Lincoln Bedroom. Grace had always joked that she wanted a bigger engagement ring than her daughter's. He would give her that and more. Brandon's lifestyle after his divorce and bankruptcy took a more conservative side once he rebounded. He stayed away from the pompous self-indulgent lifestyle he once led. But he decided right then he would go all out and find the most beautiful engagement ring money could buy for his lady love. This was the woman he deeply cared for and if she enjoyed grandeur, then grandeur he would give her. It occurred to him he needed to find out her ring size. He would enlist the help of her daughters and hold them to secrecy. Brandon wanted his proposal to be a surprise. He started planning in his mind.

Note to self, stop by Holliman Brothers Jewelers on Monday. He needed to hurry this plan. He wanted to make sure he had the ring when he went to visit Camp David or the White House.

Grace finished her shower and greeted Brandon at the door in silk pajamas. He grabbed her tight and held her close. After his ordeal on Tuesday, he just wanted this moment to last. He kissed her and then stepped back to take a long look at his woman.

Grace was gorgeous. As often happened in their relationship, after a disagreement they wouldn't discuss anything right away. They just enjoyed each other's company and got reacquainted. After opening the wine, they toasted to life and rebuilding, said a prayer for those lost in the attacks, nibbled cheese and crackers, and drank wine. Little was said that night, though they stayed in each other's arms. At times, the couple didn't make a sound for what seemed like hours. They fell asleep without making love and both slept until the Sunday morning alarm went off signaling time to get ready for church. After the service, they enjoyed lunch before returning home, knowing the afternoon would inevitably end with openly discussing their relationship, past and future.

Brandon and Grace took seats on the couch in the den, their go-to place for frank conversations. Most times the couch worked magic encouraging common ground. Brandon hoped for the same outcome this time.

"Grace," he began, "I was so proud when you walked into the New York reception. I had given up on any chance of a relationship with you, but then you appeared out of nowhere. The night was fantastic, but we never had time to resolve the differences that caused us to split up a month ago. Tell me what you have in mind. Do you want to begin finding solutions that will lead to a loving and stable relationship?"

"Yes, and I mean it. I don't know what's wrong with me. My own kids tell me I seem to self-destruct when it comes to relationships. I know I love you. The things you do for me; the places we go. Over the last month I realized I do not want to lose you."

"I love you too," Brandon said as he leaned over and kissed her cheek. "But we have to deal with the issue that keeps coming between us. The issue has come up six or seven times in the past year and the results are always the same. You insist on being vague and going out 'til all hours without any accountability to me. That would be fine if you were not in a committed relationship, but we are and you asked for it."

"I know. I do want a committed relationship, but I also need you to trust me. I would never do anything to hurt you."

"But your girls' nights out do hurt me."

"I know and I'm sorry. I talked to Angie about it and her husband would not stand for it either. Angie said she wants him to know where she is. I am coming around, just be patient with me. I love you."

"That's all I need to hear. I don't have a problem with you having dinner with your friends, just be home at a decent hour. Include me in occasionally, I could meet you later."

"Okay. But, Brandon, you need to learn to trust me."

"Teach me how to trust you."

"Looks like I have work to do!"

"Honey, there are other things I want to talk about. We hinted at being married and spending our first Christmas together this year. I had all but given up on that notion. We need to begin thinking about it and talking about it. After all, we're not getting any younger."

"I know," she agreed.

"While stranded this week, there was a marriage counselor on my flight. We got to know one another pretty well with all the time on our hands," Brandon began. He thought this out on the flight home. He wanted to discuss issues Dr. Hollace raised, but he did not want to tell her the real story yet. This way, he reasoned, he could talk about his cram counseling without going into details.

"Oh, you did. Male or female?" Grace asked, showing signs of jealousy never seen before.

"I will not lie, she was great looking."

"I didn't ask if she was great looking. I guess I can deduce the answer to my question. Female."

"Don't get jealous. I am in love with an even better looking woman. The counselor helped me sort through things I hope will bring us closer together. Besides, she's engaged to an airline pilot and madly in love."

"Okay. What issues did she help you with?" Grace asked, lightening up.

"Since she was a total stranger, I felt free to open up to her. She was professional and overall, I got a couple thousands of dollars of counseling for free. It was interesting the things she helped me understand."

"Like what?"

"Well, there were several things. First, your faith and values contradict your need to belly up to a bar in a singles' nightclub, so the question becomes why? Are you unsure of us and looking? Are you wanting out and purposefully doing destructive things to sabotage our relationship?"

"The answer to both questions is no," Grace assured him.

"Is there a concern on your part you may become a widow if you marry me?"

"Are you talking about the liver problem?"

"Yes, is it a concern to you I could die from this?"

"Sure, I am concerned about you dying, but I would not leave you. You should know I'm not that kind of person. That's not an issue."

"Okay then, what are your concerns about our relationship?" Brandon asked.

"Money! I don't know anything about your finances. I know you were bankrupt ten years ago, but I don't know anything about how you stand right now."

"That issue bothers me because it seems money is more important to you than a good man. But let me say this. When we get serious about discussing a wedding date, I will tell you anything you want to know. But for now, it's important for you to know the lifestyle we shared for the past year is a good indicator of what kind of lifestyle we will have as a married couple. You met my family and my great circle of friends. We've gotten to know each other well. I would think after this past year, you met enough people who know me and you should be comfortable with me."

"I understand. But how can I decide about marrying you if I don't know about your finances? Don't you trust me enough to share that information with me?"

"The only thing you need to know to make your decision is do I love you. And I've already given you that information. Grace, when I learned I might be dying, I put all my assets in a trust for my family. Technically, I don't have any assets in my name, that would be foolish. That's why I have been encouraging you to consider interior design work, real estate, or buying rental properties. I don't want anything in my name. It was a way for me to help build security for you after I'm gone if that happens. Building businesses and investments is what I do. I need a wife I can trust because if I'm not going to put anything in my name, it will need to be in yours. I want to build our marital assets in your name only."

"I understand, and I don't mean to pry, but I need to know these things."

"I understand, it's just the way you put it makes it sound as if the stock market fails and everything is lost, you'd be searching for greener pastures."

"Brandon, I love you," Grace said. "Let's not talk about this anymore."

"Grace, I don't want you to worry. We will be comfortable, amazingly comfortable," Brandon assured her. Grace leaned over and kissed him. The couch was having the desired effect. When differences were resolved, the couple ended up in each other's arms making love. This was not an exception.

***

John and Hampton were the last of the passengers to leave the base. Special arrangements were made for them. Instead of going home, they were being transferred to separate hospitals. The best care for them was waiting when their planes touched down. Their full recovery was imperative. Anything less was unacceptable. How would they explain to these men who survived a terrorist attack, only to be mistreated later by the government? They were being well taken care of. The president himself saw to it.

Chapter 16

Cauldwell woke with a start. He was cold and shivering. The cigar was still balanced between the fingers of his right hand and he could see the large burn mark it had made on the arm of the chair before going out. He got up, set the cigar carefully on the table, picked up the lantern and walked back to the supply dump. He found his sleeping bag and mat, spread both on the ground where he stood and tore off a cardboard flap from one of the boxes. He placed the cardboard on the earthen deck by the head of his bag and set his pistol on it. Removing his boots, Cauldwell crawled into the bag, pulled the zipper halfway up, blew out the lantern, and laid back.

He tried to concentrate on the required actions of the day to come, but Mary's face kept swimming into his consciousness. After a time, he gave up attempts at planning for the morrow and let himself drift into sleep.

At 0642 on 20 September, Cauldwell ambled down the makeshift road and through the camp gate, returning the rifle salute rendered by the sentry.

He went straight to his tent, leaving the door flap open to admit the dawn's early light. He broke out his notebook and began to make notes. At 0925 he was still alternatively thinking and writing.

"Sir! Request permission to speak to the major, sir."

"Enter!"

A young corporal stepped in and stood at attention.

"At ease there, Corporal Dawes. Whatchya got?"

"Sir, Spec-5 Armstrong asked me to tell the major the helo is inbound with an ETA of 25 minutes, sir."

"Okay. Thanks, corporal. Tell Sergeant Allen to stand by at the pad. Carry on."

"Yes, sir." Dawes came to attention, executed an about face and marched out.

Cauldwell shaved using a basin of cold water while standing before a grimy small mirror. He cut himself four times in the process. He put on a clean pair of spit-shined boots and arrived at the landing pad just as the CH53 was flaring to set down.

Specialist Armstrong rushed from the Com Shack and raced toward the pad, slamming to a halt three feet from Cauldwell.

"Hey, sir! We just got the word. The US launched a damn invasion of Afghanistan an' we are flat kickin' some Taliban ass!"

"That's outstanding, Armstrong! Thanks for letting me know."

"Yes, sir."

Cauldwell climbed aboard, took a seat next to Sergeant Allen, strapped in and immediately found himself airborne, heading southwest.

As they landed behind the high fence within the non-commercial section of the Kabul airport, Cauldwell saw security was now being provided by a company of marines. He grinned to himself.

Guarandamntee ya there ain't gonna be any problem gettin' my three assholes in an' outta here now!

At 1148 a U.S. Air Force C141 landed and taxied to within thirty yards of the big helicopter. The rear cargo hatch opened, the ramp dropped and four US Army Military Police herded three men in orange jumpsuits down the ramp and on to the tarmac. The group made slow progress toward the waiting helo as they were restrained by handcuffs, waist chains, and leg irons.

Hey! That's all right! Never thought they'd send 'em in irons. Hell, I bet I can find a use or two for that gear.

As the seven men drew close, Cauldwell could see each prisoner wore laminated tags attached to neck chains. When the group was ten feet away, Cauldwell held up a hand and both prisoners and guards came to a halt. One of the MPs stepped forward. "Sir, I am Captain Charles Oliver. Would you be Major Cauldwell, sir?"

"That I would, captain. Were you not shown my picture before being dispatched on this mission?"

"No, sir."

"Well, you damn well should have been. However, that's a mistake not of your doing."

"Sir, I have a classified document for your eyes only," Captain Oliver reported. "The message instructs you to read it in my presence, then return the missive to me."

Oliver handed the classified envelope to Cauldwell and stood by as he opened and carefully read the message:

> *Your eyes only:*
>
> *Read, fold and insert this message in the enclosed return classified envelope. Seal and return to Captain Oliver for destruction.*
>
> *A fourth prisoner, Daniel Raphia was apprehended. He was embedded as a sleeper on Flight 3911 and was one of the terrorist hijackers. He has eluded detection because of his British family and having a British passport. Special Agent Larry Cameron secured him separately from the other POWs. The POWs being handed over to you do NOT know about this capture. The new POW will be kept secure where none of the other POWs would know he had been detained. CIA will handle the interrogation of Daniel Raphia in Guantanamo.*

Cauldwell acknowledged the message, folded it, and sealed it in the return envelope. As he handed it to Captain Oliver, he added, "Good job, Captain Oliver. I acknowledge receipt and understanding of the message. It is yours now."

"Thank you, sir, now for the transfer of the tourists."

"What are those cards around their necks?" Cauldwell asked.

"ID cards, sir. Names in Aramaic and English on one side, head-shot pictures on the other."

"I see. Okay, let's get 'em loaded on the chopper." Cauldwell led off toward the cargo ramp of the CH53.

The MPs hustled the captives forward as quickly as the leg chains would allow and prodded and pushed the three men up the ramp and onto the bench seats. As they shuffled in, Cauldwell noticed the jump suits had built-in trap doors in the rear like old fashioned long johns. Swiftly, the soldiers snapped seat belts in place then exited the helo. Captain Oliver approached Cauldwell and held out a clipboard and a pen. "Would the major please sign for receipt of the prisoners?"

"What in hell is going on here? They'll be playing ice hockey in hell before I do anything of the sort! Let me ask you, captain. What was your mission here today?"

"I don't understand, sir. What mission? Also, we are not here, never have been here, and never will come here."

"Very good, captain. So, if there was no mission and you were never here, how in God's name could I have signed for anything?"

"Right, sir. It didn't seem right to me, but those were my orders."

"Yeah, well, whoever gave that order is as screwed up as Hogan's goat. If anybody gives you grief about it when you get back, get on the horn to Camp Subat and leave word for me. I guarandamntee I'll fix that in a big hurry."

"Roger that, sir." The soldier saluted, faced about and began to leave.

"Hey, Captain Oliver!"

"Yes, sir?"

"Better let me have that worthless piece of ass-wipe ya got on that clipboard."

The MP removed the document and handed it to Cauldwell.

"Right. Thanks. Carry on."

"Yes, sir." The soldier saluted again and moved toward the C141, signaling his detail to follow.

Cauldwell crumpled the paper and stuffed it into a trouser pocket. He boarded the helicopter where Sergeant Allen was sitting directly across from the captives and holding a wary eye on all three.

"Come with me, sergeant. We're gonna move forward a bit where we can watch those assholes but where none of 'em is gonna be tempted to make a play for our weapons."

"Yes, sir."

Cauldwell beckoned the crew chief. "Staff sergeant, let me borrow your headset, I need to speak with the pilot." The airman handed it over and Cauldwell triggered the intercom switch. "Hey, skipper, Cauldwell here. Please radio ahead to the camp. Tell them I need to have word sent to Chief Zamani I'm bringing tourists up to see his village and I'd like a couple guides standing by when we land."

"Roger, I'll take care of it as soon as we're in the sky."

When they landed, four tribal members were waiting and the man in charge was the one who headed up the working party the previous day.

"What's your name, my man?" Cauldwell inquired.

"My name Hakim, majah. Hakim Wordak."

"Okay, Hakim, I've got three tourists to take up the mountain. I don't want to make it easy for them, so we will walk the whole way. They may not want to go all the way up to the high valley, but we must get them there."

"No problem, majah. If they do not want to go, me and my men change their minds pretty quick."

"That's good, Hakim. Okay, Sergeant Allen, bring 'em on out."

Slowly the three orange jumpsuits appeared and shuffled down the cargo ramp to the helo pad. The ramp retracted and Cauldwell walked forward to give the pilot a thumbs up. The hand signal was returned along with a grin, and the aircraft lifted off.

"Awright you three, get goin'!" Cauldwell pointed and the prisoners shuffled off toward the north gate of the camp.

By 1535 they were through the village valley and approaching the ravine. To this point the captives had been cooperative and quiet, but the difficulty of the fissure trail almost immediately brought a change in attitude. Cauldwell was leading with Hakim behind him, followed by the first of the terrorists. Thereafter, Hakim's men were interspersed between the jumpsuits, so each prisoner had a tribe member in front of and behind him. After five minutes of climbing, the lead captive suddenly stopped and cried out. "The hell with this! I need a rest."

Cauldwell turned and bellowed. "Get on with it, asshole! You'll get plenty of rest when we get to where we're goin'.."

The man bowed his head and stood unmoving in silence. Hakim said something and the tribe member behind the recalcitrant terrorist stepped forward and smashed the man between the shoulder blades with the butt of his AK47. With a sharp groan of pain, the prisoner lurched forward and fell to his knees. Then, after being vigorously jabbed and prodded with the barrel of the rifle, he struggled to his feet and staggered forward.

Despite the enthusiastic physical encouragement rendered by tribe members with considerable frequency, it took them more than an hour to reach the high valley.

Cauldwell went immediately to the door of the stone building, opened it and stood by as Hakim and his people brought the terrorists across the winter killed meadow and through the entrance.

Cauldwell pointed. "Okay, Hakim, we need these assholes down at the west end. Put each one in front of a set of the leg irons."

This was soon done and the three stood with their backs to Cauldwell.

"Awright, scumbags, turn around and face me." He waited until the shuffling ceased. "Now then, on your backs, lie down on those mats and extend your legs."

There was universal compliance and Cauldwell moved from one to the other locking his pre-positioned leg irons above those they already wore.

"Awright, ragheads, on yer feet!"

With a three-foot standoff, Cauldwell went from one to the other, peering at the laminated name cards. The top part of each card bore something in Aramaic while below, the man's name appeared in black block lettering. From left to right as he faced them, Cauldwell reviewed their CIA dossier, they were. Imad Bashour, Hashem Moustapha, and Abdul Mohatazana.

Bashour was the biggest, almost six feet and about 190 pounds; he had an open, square-jawed face, short black hair and a neatly trimmed beard.

Moustapha was about five-eight and 150. His black hair was longer than Bashour's and beneath a full beard, a perpetual sneer gave him a mean and vicious look.

Abdul Mohatazana was diminutive. It was expected he might be the leader. He stood barely five-six and weighed 140. His thin, hawkish face, beaked nose and beady eyes gave the impression of implacable, malevolent evil. Long, lank, unkempt hair the color of dirty rust and a scraggly beard accentuated the satanic nature of his appearance.

Cauldwell turned. "Hakim, I thank you and your men for your help today. Please return to your village and thank Chief Zamani for his great generosity."

"If it is your wish, majah, it will be so." Wordak led the way, his three men followed, and the party left the building.

Cauldwell turned back to contemplate his three charges. For several minutes he studied each in turn. "Right, first off I have neither the time nor the inclination to remember your damn camel-jockey names, much less try to pronounce 'em, so I will now bestow your new names. Bashour, you are Lard Ass; Moustapha, your name is Shit Head; and Mohatazana, you are now Pig Face. Any questions?"

Silence.

"Okay, then. You all had better get it straight and you will answer up to the names I have given you. From my left to right, give me your new names so I know you have 'em fixed in those feeble brains of yours. Begin!"

"Lard Ass."

"Shit Head."

Unintelligible mumble.

"Speak up, Fruit Loop! Give me your damn name so I can hear it. Now!"

Silence and a baleful glare of defiance.

Cauldwell strode rapidly to his right front and centered himself before Mohatazana. Without a word and with cobra-like swiftness, Cauldwell knuckle-punched the man in the throat. Mohatazana went down heavily on to his back, gasping for air, and trying to reach his throat with his hands, something the waist chain affixed to the handcuffs would not allow.

"On yer feet asshole! Get yer ass up! Right friggin' now!"

The hapless captive struggled to his feet, still gagging and fighting to breathe.

"Now then camel turd, what's yer damn name?"

"Pig Face."

The response was barely audible but Cauldwell felt he made his point. "Awright, let's clear the decks so we understand each other. First off, I consider people like you to be the absolute scum of the earth and unfit to live. I will have no trouble killing any or all of you because in doing so I will have made the world a better place.

"I know you work for another fucked up raghead sonofabitch and before I'm done one of you is gonna tell me who and where that worthless asshole is. You may have noticed you arc no longer on US soil. You may safely assume the interrogation protocols that prevented massive damage to your filthy, disgusting bodies are no longer in place.

"No one knows where you are, and no one knows about me or about the havoc I am about to bring upon you. I guarandamntee eventually you will tell me what I want to know. It may take a while, but I have nothing better to do so all resistance by you three dung eating dogs costs me not a damn thing. Your cost, on the other hand will be the experiencing of pain that right now is beyond anything your pea sized brains can fathom. I am free to employ whatever methods I may find to be sufficient unto the task at hand and I will use 'em all, plus those my fertile imagination has not yet fastened on.

"Those mats behind you are for sleeping. At the head of the mat you will find a blanket. When reveille sounds each day, those blankets will be neatly folded and placed in the positions you see now.

"To your rear, against the wall you will see a bucket for each of you, with a roll of ass wipe alongside. The buckets will be used to defecate and to urinate. Each day, one at a time, you will be taken forth to empty your own bucket into a pit the three of you, one at a time, will dig.

"You will be given one MRE, that's Meals Ready to Eat, per day. It's American chow and some meals may contain pork, that's the flesh of the pig for you dimwits, and you may not wish to eat it. That's your choice. You will receive one canteen per day, containing one quart, thirty-two fluid ounces of water. Don't spill or waste it because that's all you'll get.

"Another thing, if you choose to act like the despicable, degenerate assholes you are and you piss me off, then either food, water or both will be curtailed.

"You can see from a cursory examination your chains and shackles have been arranged so you cannot get within ten feet of each another so don't bother trying. When Taps is sounded at night, you will lie down on your mats and remain silent. If I hear any talking, I will immediately sound reveille and fix things, so you are either no longer able, or no longer desirous of oral communications. Any questions?"

Silence.

"Right. Well, being the benevolent man I am, I am now going to free the left wrist of each of you camel turds, so you'll be able to operate the back hatch of your jump suits an' wipe yer asses, assuming you ascribe to that function of personal hygiene. Lie down and roll onto your right side, all of you, NOW!'

The operations were completed without incident and Cauldwell again centered himself and addressed the terrorists. "Leave the cuffs I have just removed open. Now, before I leave, I have a question for you. Does any one of you want to save himself from the excruciating torment I will inflict by telling me who your boss is, where he is, and how he's planning to attack America?"

A long silence.

"Yeah, that's what I thought." Cauldwell grinned. "Well, ladies, that works for me 'cause I'm gonna enjoy this shit."

It was 1827 and dusk was beginning to settle. Cauldwell moved to the generator and fired it up. He switched on the floodlight and was gratified by the sudden squinting of eyes and turning of heads.

Okay, four hours running time. Got it. Say, the fumes from this thing ought to help the cause. Not enough to kill the assholes but might be enough to make 'em sick.

Next, Cauldwell picked up the boom box and studied the control panel by the reflected glare.

Good stuff! Plays the damn tape forward and back.

"Now then, girls, for your nighttime enjoyment I give you this. Enjoy." He cranked the volume full up and pushed Continuous Play. He walked away heading to his supply pile. As the aggravating shrieks and sounds of rap music began to reverberate, he quickened his pace. Swiftly he gathered his sleeping bag and mat, pulled out an MRE, seized a water can, and hustled through the door, closing it behind him.

He angled southwest across the meadow toward the dilapidated remnants of the tribal dwellings. He found a structure with three standing walls and roofing still in place over one corner and laid his mat and bag beneath this protection. After eating part of the MRE and drinking ten ounces of water, he shoved his booted feet into the sleeping bag and lay back contentedly. The sounds emanating from the stone building were distant and muffled. They would not in the least disturb his sleep.

***

Brandon called and caught Grace just as she was leaving to spend time at his house.

"Sure. What do we have planned for the weekend," Grace asked?

"Anything you want. I thought we might go downtown for dinner, but I would be just as happy doing anything else you have in mind." He was sure it would be something extravagant.

"I really want to just chill this weekend, maybe rent a couple movies and just stay in," she suggested. Brandon was shocked.

"That's fine with me, we'll talk about it when you get here, love. See you soon."

"Okay"

"Love you…"

She hung up the phone before Brandon had a chance to finish the conversation. As he hung up the phone, he thought, that was strange. She was the one who always wanted to have a busy weekend. Maybe Grace was beginning to settle into just being happy to spend time with him. The past few weeks must have really put something in perspective for her. He knew it did for him. She was passing his test with flying colors. He was startled back to reality by the ringing phone still in his hand. Grace was calling back to tell him she loved him too.

"Yes, darling," he said.

"This is the president, is this Brandon Powell?" President Walker chuckled.

"Oh, Mr. President, I'm sorry, I was just talking to a special friend, I thought she had forgotten something," Brandon apologized.

"That's fine, I understand, but let's not let the press know you called me darling," the president laughed.

"I agree, sir. I can't believe I'm actually having a telephone conversation with the President of the United States."

"I am honored to be talking to you, Mr. Powell. We were unable to talk at Wright-Patterson privately, but I have since read the reports. I am amazed at the role you played, and I wanted to personally tell you how much I appreciate your heroic acts."

"Thank you, but all I did was fly the plane. It was Hampton who put his body in the lead of the attack. He's the real hero, as were the rest of them. They insisted on protecting my life at the risk of theirs."

"I've read the reports, and all seem to point to one thing, it was a group effort with the four of you leading the way. I am proud to know you and I want to get to know you better."

"I'd be honored."

"Here's what I have in mind. I'm inviting those who led the attack to Camp David to spend the day on Saturday, November 3. Arrive at 9:00 spend the day and leave after dinner, say 8:00 or so that evening. Can you make it?" asked the president.

"Sure."

"Great, then get with your liaison right away to make travel arrangements. A government jet will pick you up and return you as you please."

"Thank you, Mr. President."

"Thank you. I'm looking forward to spending one on one time with each of you. I am so proud to be your president and I want to get to know you."

"Great, I'll see you on November third," Brandon said. He hung up the phone and fell on the couch. The President of the United States just invited him to Camp David! He pinched his leg to make sure it wasn't a dream. It wasn't.

When Grace arrived, he could hardly contain the excitement, but he was determined to be patient and find the right time to tell her about the invitation. They kissed at the door and he helped get her weekend bag from the car. He suggested one of their favorite restaurants for dinner, but she said she preferred carry-out, bottle of wine and a movie in the bedroom. He had never seen this side of Grace before and he liked it. He seemed even more comfortable with his decision to share his secret and his future with her. He opened the wine and ordered a pizza. Since he had a library of recent movies, there was no need to leave the house. Grace took a shower while he waited for the pizza. It had been a while since they shared real intimacy, something that was once the highlight of their time together. There was something vastly different about her on this night.

He couldn't quite put his finger on it, but he liked it. She was finally beginning to settle down. They crashed on the bed to watch the movie over dinner and wine; it was certainly not the type evening they were used to, but romantic because he loved her so much. He held Grace close and relaxed. She spoke little but drank the whole bottle of wine and passed out before the end of the movie. Not exactly what Brandon had in mind when it started. He tucked her in, and they went to sleep without so much as a good night kiss. The rest of the weekend was just as uneventful. Sunday, they went to church and came back home. They usually laid around in bed, made love and napped for the afternoon, but this Sunday she decided she needed to go home early to clean the house.

"Grace, what's going on?"

"What do you mean?"

"I mean this weekend. You haven't been yourself."

"I've been who you want me to be. You don't want me to go out, so fine. I won't go out. You don't want to share your life with me. Fine, keep it to yourself."

"What are you talking about?"

"Do you think I'm stupid, Brandon? You're keeping something from me? Is this retaliation for my girls' nights out? Brandon, if you can't trust me..."

"I do trust you."

"Tell me about your finances."

Brandon stood in silence. Was she giving him an ultimatum? This was not the right time to share Flight 3911 or the presidential invitation. He was beginning to question if Grace was the right person to share the news with anyway.

"Look, Brandon, I need to go."

"To clean your house."

"Yes, to clean my house. "

The argument ended as abruptly as it started. The loud bang as she slammed the door signaled the beginning of silence. Brandon spent the rest of the afternoon thinking about the relationship. There was something wrong and one night on the couch wasn't going to fix it. It was time to go their separate ways.

After a sleepless night, Brandon called Ronnie on Monday morning to work out the details for the Camp David trip. Brandon would be coming alone. Ronnie would arrange for a government jet to pick him up in Atlanta on Thursday, November 1 to head for Wright-Patterson. Then Saturday, November 3 he would meet the rest of the group at Andrews AFB for a helicopter ride to Camp David. He called Dr. Hollace and set aside some time to meet with her during the long weekend. She was glad to hear from him because they had not talked since he left. She readily agreed to make herself available.

Chapter 17

Cauldwell woke in predawn darkness. Muted sounds from the boom box was all that kept the valley from being one of absolute silence. He grunted in acknowledgement, pleased his two generator fuel replenishments (at 2200 and again at 0200) proved sufficient to the task of supplying continuous light and sound throughout the night.

He performed a rapid toilet, ate the rest of his MRE and drank half a canteen of water, slowly to keep the ice-cold liquid from causing stomach cramps. At 0532 as the first, timid tendrils of dawn inched above the far-off peaks to the east, he pushed through the door of his private interrogation facility. Being careful to betray no evidence of his distaste for the blaring music, Cauldwell approached his captives. All three men sat up and glowered at the sound of his coming, but he remained invisible to them behind the glare of the floodlight. He was satisfied to see they appeared worn, haggard, red-eyed, and wretched.

So, no sleep to be had, huh, boys? Tough shit!

Cauldwell flicked off the boom box but allowed the floodlight to continue burning. "Reveille, scumbags! Reveille! No more sleeping to the dulcet tones of Guy Lombardo and his Royal Canadians. Now, relock those free cuffs over your left wrist."

Bashour and Moustapha complied immediately, but Mohatazana remained motionless.

"What's yer damn problem there, Pig Face? Somethin' in what I said you didn't understand?"

Stepping closer, Cauldwell saw the problem. "Oh, I see! Ya closed the fuckin' thing in contravention of my direct order. Awright, lie back an' roll on yer right side." Cauldwell moved to Mohatazana, bent down, unlocked the cuff and closed it on the man's left wrist with all the grip strength he could muster. "Sit up, Pig Face."

151

Mohatazana rolled on his back and sat up. Without warning, Cauldwell swung his right arm in a vicious arc catching the terrorist flush on the left ear with his open hand. There was a resounding smack, the man uttered a sharp cry and pitched sideways. For some moments he stayed in a fetal position, his face registering shock, pain and surprise.

"Sit up, asshole! Sit back up! Right, now get this goatfucker, when I give you an order, you had better by GOD comply with that order. You got that?"

"Yes."

"Yes, what shit-for-brains?"

"Yes, sir."

Cauldwell walked away. "Now, we'll hold roll call. From my left to right sound off with your name and say 'Present, sir.' Ready...begin!"

"Ima...Lard Ass, present, sir."

"Shit Head, present, sir."

"Pig Face, present, sir."

"Good, we still have everybody. Now then, I'm beginning to detect a certain disagreeable stench, over and above the foul odors emanating from your disgusting bodies. Thus, the first of the day's activities here at Camp Tell-the-Truth will be a group excavation. I use the term 'group' loosely since, while you will all participate, you will do so one at a time. When you have completed this task, we will have a six by six-foot hole that is four feet deep. All the earth accruing to the manufacture of this hole will be neatly piled.

"First off, Lard Ass, get that damn blanket folded and placed as you were instructed, then lie back and roll over on your face."

The man complied and Cauldwell stepped forward, bent down and unlocked the leg shackles affixed to the long window chain. Stepping back, he ordered, "Awright, Lard Ass, on yer feet!"

Bashour came first to his knees then stood, fighting to maintain his balance as he rose.

"Right, now get your slop bucket, then turn around and walk to the door in front of me."

Shuffle, clank, scrape.

"To the left of the door you will see a long-handled spade. Pick up the spade and precede me through the hatch. Don't be having any grand ideas about using the spade as a weapon to force me to shoot you so you can escape the pain I have in store for you. That will never work. First, I will always maintain a standoff that exceeds the range of the spade; and second, while I will shoot you, I will only blow off a kneecap."

Cauldwell drew his pistol, pulled and released the slide to chamber a round and followed Bashour at a distance of four feet. The prisoner had some difficulty securing the spade since he was already carrying the bucket and his wrists were cuffed together. Finally, he succeeded and shuffled through the door.

"Turn right there, Lard Ass."

When they passed the western end of the granite-walled building, Cauldwell barked, "Turn right, Lard Ass. Your OTHER right, asshole!"

They proceeded north for 40 yards. "Awright, Lard Ass, stop! Put down the pail an' get down on yer back. Roll on to one side." Cauldwell stood over the prostrate form, unlocked the handcuffs and stepped back. "Okay, stand up, get yer spade, an' start diggin.' We should still be far enough from the stream so even your infested filth can't contaminate it."

With Cauldwell supervising from 12 feet away, Bashour began digging into the heavy sod and soon struck light, sandy soil that served to accelerate his progress.

At 0610, the sound of the generator ceased. Cauldwell glanced at his watch and shrugged.

At 0715 Cauldwell spoke. "That's enough there, Lard Ass. Dump yer bucket at the deep end and start back. Leave the spade."

The process was repeated with Moustapha and at 0835 the two reentered the building. "Awright, Shit Head, shuffle off to yer mat an' lie down on yer face." The captive obeyed and Cauldwell moved up to refasten the leg shackles.

"Now then, Pig Face. It's your turn."

As Cauldwell started in his direction, the sitting Mohatazana raised his manacled hands and with his right closed as if around the butt of a pistol, turned it toward the American and motioned with his forefinger to simulate pulling a trigger.

"Someday I will shoot you, big man."

"Think so huh, ya ignorant little prick? Well, today ain't gonna be that day. I already harbor a deep and abiding hatred of that porcine face of yers, so ya might want to keep that molar-filled anus you call a mouth shut at all times when not answering one of my questions."

When Cauldwell and Mohatazana arrived at the partially dug pit, the parameters had been marked out by Moustapha under Cauldwell's supervision, it was obvious more than half the digging had yet to be done. If Mohatazana noticed he was being given more than a one-third share of the labor, he said nothing.

It was 1112 before Cauldwell declared the project complete. Mohatazana had been working steadily for almost three hours. He was sweating profusely despite the chilly mountain air. As he replaced the handcuffs, Cauldwell was pleased to see many blisters on the prisoner's palms and fingers.

For all this guy's hardass belligerence, I think he's fundamentally flawed, a coward without any real strength of character. I'm guessin' he won't wear like a pig's nose...won't stand up to the grind over time. I'll have to be careful I don't accidentally kill the little prick.

At 1127 Caldwell put Bashour in the heavy armchair facing his compatriots. He passed one end of a chain over the man's right wrist, under his left, beneath the seat of the chair, then pulled it tight and fastened it with a snap link. Another piece of chain was used to anchor Bashour's ankles to the front chair legs. He then passed three turns of duct tape across the captive's forehead and around the center slat of the chair, fixing his head firmly to the backrest.

Cauldwell ordered Bashour to open his mouth, then inserted the center portion of a length of half-inch cord. He passed the cord ends beneath each of the man's arm pits and brought them forward over his shoulders. Using a slipknot, he jerked the cord tight, pulling Bashour's jaw down. He locked the slipknot so that it pressed hard on the terrorist's throat.

"Now then, ladies, before I begin to dispense discomfort in ever increasing amounts, does anyone want to tell me who and where your asshole boss is?"

Silence.

"How 'bout you there, Lard Ass?"

"Uh-uh."

"Very well then, let the games begin."

Cauldwell moved to the table, picked up a cordless drill, selected a one-sixteenths bit and tightened it into the chuck. Returning to the chair he knelt at Bashour's feet to give the other two hijackers an unobstructed view. Reaching up and out, Cauldwell placed the drill point on the man's left front incisor just below the gum line.

"Now then Lard Ass, don't move. Oh, I forgot, you can't move."

Cauldwell pulled the trigger and the drill bit began to eat into the tooth. For several seconds Bashour's face registered only fear and discomfort, then suddenly he roared with pain. Cauldwell stopped the drill. "Oh dear, guess we struck a nerve. You wanna tell me about your boss?"

"Uhhh-uh."

"Okay, then." The drill whirred again. This time Bashour's roar quickly turned into a scream. Several seconds of whirring and screaming ensued before Bashour's body went limp.

"Ain't this a bitch? The man went to sleep on me. Well then, Shit Head, now that Lard Ass has dozed off, looks like it's your turn."

Cauldwell unhooked Bashour, dragged the inert body back to its place, and reattached the leg shackles. He brought Moustapha forward and secured him to the chair. This time he took a turn with the cord around the man's neck and tied it to the leg iron chain so that the hijacker's back was bent forward slightly.

"Relax there, Shit Head. Before we start proceedings on you, we have to awaken ol' Lard Ass over there. I know he won't want to miss the show."

At the table Cauldwell removed a vial of ammonia from the first aid kit. Moving to

Bashour's unconscious body, he bent, broke the vial between his fingers and held it beneath the man's nose.

"Ahh! Uuugh! Ohhhh!" The terrorist regained consciousness then became aware of his pain.

"Hey, Lard Ass! Good to have ya with us again. Sit up an' watch. We've got a new performer in the chair."

Bashour kept his mouth open and instinctively tried to reach his throbbing tooth with his hands. When the waist chain jerked the handcuffs short of his mark, he moaned and shook his head.

"Guess when ya eat, you'll have to bypass that tooth for a while, huh? Now, watch and learn."

Cauldwell walked past the chair to the table and selected a four-inch hypodermic needle with a large caliber. He then chose a six-inch syringe with a three-quarter inch diameter. From a dark colored bottle he sucked three inches of iodine into the syringe, then turned and approached his victim. Because Cauldwell's actions at the table had been masked by his body, Moustapha had seen nothing of the hypodermic and as he stepped to the chair, Cauldwell kept the instrument hidden from view.

Standing slightly to the prisoner's rear, Cauldwell reached out with his left hand and laid hold of the man's right, posterior shoulder. He began to push and prod in an exploratory manner.

"So, what do ya think there, Shit Head? The nerve bundle should be right below this spot, am I right?"

No response.

"Ah well, one of the great perks of being in charge is if I miss, I can always try again." With that, Cauldwell suddenly brought his right hand forward and stabbed hard with the needle, burying the length of it in the terrorist's back.

Moustapha's body convulsed as he screamed in agony.

"Well now, looks like I got it right the first time. Who's yer boss an' where is he?"

"I do not tell." Moustapha replied through clenched teeth amid constant moaning.

"Maybe you have just forgotten. Allow me to try and kick start your failing memory." With that, Cauldwell tilted the syringe and moved his fist through a 100-degree arc. This time the man shrieked and began to dry heave.

"You ain't pregnant are ya, Shit Head? Reason I ask is that ya sound like a damn female giving' birth. Damn good thing I haven't fed ya since ya been here, otherwise you'd have puked all over yourself. Now then, one more time, who and where is the scum suckin' pig you work for?"

Moustapha, moaning with pain and fighting for air amid his retching, could only shake his head.

"That's fine, 'cause I've always wanted to see how this next maneuver would work." Slowly and steadily Cauldwell depressed the plunger, forcing the iodine into the captive's body. The pain increased in direct proportion to the infusion as his screams became a series of inhuman shrieks which suddenly ceased in mid-career.

"Well, kiss my sister's black cat ass! What's up with you people? A little physical discomfort and ya pass the hell out? Damn it all, you girls are about as tough as a cotton swab."

Cauldwell removed the hypodermic with its now-empty syringe, unfastened Moustapha from the chair, dragged him back to his mat, and secured the leg shackles. Another ammonia vial served to return the man to consciousness; he immediately began to writhe and moan.

"Damn, Shit Head, after all the work I did you could at least stay awake and enjoy the pain. From now on this passin' out crap ain't gonna get it. I'm just gonna wake ya the hell up an' keep on goin' from where I left off when ya dozed off.

"Before I set to work on you, Pig Face…" Cauldwell thought he saw fear in the man's eyes. "I have a few questions. I take it from your rag head names you three ambulatory sacks of defecation are all from Syria. That right?" He stared at Bashour.

"Yes, sir."

Cauldwell turned his gaze upon Moustapha who nodded while continuing to moan softly. He turned to Mohatazana.

"Yes, sir."

"Okay, from my left to right, sound off with your hometown."

"Aleppo, sir." Bashour answered.

"Yeah, on the banks of the Euphrates. You assholes call it Halab, correct?"

"Yes, sir."

"Hims, sir." Moustapha managed to find his voice.

"Right. Just south of Hamah, yes?"

"Yes, sir."

"Dimashq, sir." Mohatazana said with a note of defiance in his voice.

"Don't screw with me ya little ass wipe, or I'll come over there an' beat yer ugly face to a pulp before I put ya in the chair."

"Damascus, sir."

"Yeah, no shit! That's what the rest of the world has called it for centuries. It's only you murdering scumbags that want to name it according to yer illiterate, ignorant, stone-age, language. Okay, wise ass, your turn in the chair."

After Cauldwell secured Mohatazana to the armchair, he approached with another, shorter and finer hypodermic. The syringe was again filled with iodine. As Cauldwell took a knee to the right of the chair he looked the terrorist in the eyes. Despite the sneer of defiance, he knew he saw fear cloud Mohatazana's snake-like eyes.

"Now then, Pig Face, before I begin to hurt you, you wanna take this opportunity to tell me who your boss is and where he's hiding?"

"I will tell you nothing, American fornicator." Mohatazana's voice lacked the conviction Bashour and Moustapha had shown.

"Gee, that's too bad, for you, I mean." With his left hand, Caldwell briefly explored the man's right knee, positioned the needle and drove it hard and at an upward angle into the soft tissue immediately below and out from the kneecap.

Mohatazana's eyes opened wide in shock, gave a strangled cry and the man strained at his bonds with every muscle and sinew in his body.

"So, how do you like me now there, Pig Face?"

Other than a guttural moan, the man made no reply.

"Listen up, ladies, while it would deprive me of a great deal of pleasure, you all could save yourselves a whole bunch of pain and torment if you'd just give me your boss's name and tell me where he is and what he's planning. No one is ever going to know you gave him up and once you've come clean with me, you'll be taken to any country you wish and set free to live there as you please. However, lest any of you get the idea you can feed me a load of bullshit, let me tell you I have myriad of awesome assets at my disposal that will allow me to quickly ascertain the veracity of your statements. For the slow witted among you, that means the truth of what you tell me. You will not be set free until I have verified your story and, if I find you've lied to me, you will not believe what will happen next. So, do I have any takers? Anyone want to tell me what I want to know?"

Silence from Bashour and Moustapha, low moans and a head shake from Mohatazana.

"Suit yourselves, assholes." Cauldwell gripped the syringe and began to depress the plunger. Mohatazana screamed and his body jerked convulsively. Cauldwell let up on the plunger and the hijacker's screams diminished to a series of choking moans.

"Hell, Pig Face, I'm only half done. There's lots more pain where that came from, or do you want to answer my questions?"

A shaking of the head as groans emanated from between clenched teeth.

"Right. Get ready. On the count of three...one...two...three!" Cauldwell pushed the plunger down swiftly, emptying the syringe. Fighting his restraints, Mohatazana turned his face up and howled at the rafters while thrashing his head from side to side.

Cauldwell stood up and began to clap his hands. "Well done, Pig Face! Great show! You win today's theatrical performance award. Now get your slimy little body under control an' I'll free ya up from the chair. Oh ya, almost forgot. Guess I better take that needle outta yer knee, huh?" Cauldwell seized the syringe and moved it from side to side several times before pulling it free. Mohatazana screamed and thrashed violently.

Cauldwell released the chair chains and hauled Mohatazana to his feet. "Get yer digustin' ass back to yer mat!"

Mohatazana shuffled off and promptly fell, full length on his face.

"What's the matter, Pig Face? Got a problem with one of your wheels? Well, I ain't helpin' ya, maggot. Get back to yer mat there, turd!"

Breathing heavily and groaning with pain the terrorist began crawling, using his manacled hands and left knee.

After he had secured Mohatazana, Cauldwell took a seat in the armchair and broke out a cigar, which he lit with considerable flourish. Billowing clouds of blue-gray smoke filled the air.

"Now then, peckerheads, all of you sit up, remain silent and stay awake. If I see anybody dozing off, I will be forced to render assistance by producing into that person's body, a throbbing and lasting pain that will preclude any possibility of sleep."

Cauldwell took up Caesar's *Gallic Campaigns* and began reading the chapter, 'The Siege of Avaricum – 52 B.C.'

At 1900 hours he got up, placed his book on the table and walked back to his supply pile. Returning, he tossed each prisoner one MRE and a canteen of water.

"I don't really want to feed and water you mangy animals, but I have to keep you alive so I can put some more hurt on ya."

He then filled the generator with gasoline, fired it up, and turned on both the floodlight and boom box. Grabbing another MRE as he went, Cauldwell made a hasty exit and retired to his corner amid the ruins.

Chapter 18

Later in the evening Brandon called Grace to sort through things and find a peaceful way to end the relationship. He thought it best to go to her house to talk rather than end it over the phone. When he told her he'd like to talk and preferred to see her, she said she had plans for dinner with a friend from Bible study, so rather than make an issue over it, he let it go.

"Just call me when you get home," Brandon asked.

"Bye," she coolly responded.

Brandon accepted the fact the relationship was doomed. She was not going to change, and he was tired of covering the same old problems. He felt like a broken record. He was loved but there had to be something else in the mix for her to continue to blatantly disregard his feelings. At 12:05 Brandon checked the clock. Grace hadn't called. She was drunk in a club as usual. He picked up the phone and dialed her cell phone. After the first ring he hung up. It wasn't worth it. It was best to wait until he could end it in person. He fell asleep with the phone still in his hand.

The next morning, he called her. "Why didn't you call me when you got home last night?" he asked.

"I don't like you checking up on me and besides, I was at home by 11:00."

"Why didn't you call me, I asked you to call when you got home."

"I saw your number on my caller ID. If you weren't checking up on me, what were you doing?"

"Never mind, but you were supposed to call me, I had no idea when you would be getting home. I need to talk, it's important."

"I was out, okay," she said determined not to tell him where.

"Fine, but we need to talk about some things. Do you want to come over now or do you want me to come over tonight?

"Can't it wait until the weekend? You are spending the weekend here aren't you?" she questioned.

"Okay, I really wanted to talk in person, but to hell with it. No, it will not wait for the weekend. I am not coming. I have reached my limit. I do not want to see you anymore. This is over. So, let's just give each other space and deal with this in our own separate ways."

Chapter 19

When Cauldwell held reveille for his captives at 0530 the next morning he was confronted by haggard, listless creatures who reacted to roll call and latrine duty like zombies.

For Bashour and Moustapha he reversed the procedures of the previous day, then freed Mohatazana from the wall chain and ushered him outside. With Cauldwell providing directions, the terrorist shuffled to the far western end of the ruins behind the remains of a five-foot, mud brick wall. Here, about three feet off the ground, a stout wooden pole rested transversely upon two stone pillars. Cauldwell put Mohatazana on his knees, freed the wrist manacles from the waist chain and unlocked the right handcuff. He then ordered the captive to put his free hand over the pole and then refastened the cuff.

Taking wire and a one-inch-thick wooden dowel from his pocket, Cauldwell securely fastened both wire ends to the center of the dowel creating a three-inch loop. He passed the loop over Mohatazana 's right index finger past the second knuckle and twisted the dowel clockwise until the wire was pulled tight around the finger.

"So, you're gonna shoot me huh, turd? Well, you're gonna have to learn to shoot left-handed, 'cause yer about to lose yer fuckin' trigger finger."

Cauldwell twisted the dowel and the wire cut into the flesh producing both blood and pain. Mohatazana grimaced, then cried out.

"Anything ya wanna tell me, asshole?"

There was a significant hesitation before the terrorist shook his head.

"Okay then, kiss yer friggin' finger goodbye." The dowel twisted and the wire cut deeply, generating a flow of crimson. Mohatazana alternatively sucked air and shrieked in rapid succession.

"Stop! Stop! I will tell you."

"Okay, let's hear it. I'll just leave the wire where it is, so I don't have to start over in case I think you're bullshitting me."

"Okay! Okay! The name you seek is Hassan Sharaf. He is in Damascus. On a map, I can show you where. Loosen the wire!"

"Not yet there, camel breath. What is the attack he is planning?"

"He has acquired a suitcase nuke from the Iranians and this he intends to detonate in Washington when the Prime Minister of Israel addresses a joint session of Congress in March next year. Your president will be in attendance."

"Who is he gonna entrust with that life-changing mission?"

"He will do it himself for he knows Allah will receive him with open arms and his reward in heaven will be very great."

"Yeah, right. More like an express, one-way ticket to hell."

Cauldwell released the wire and from a pocket produced a spray can of iodine and a small roll of gauze. He sprayed the wound while Mohatazana howled, then bound it perfunctorily with gauze.

"You stay here, Pig Face. Relax and enjoy the day. I'll be back after I've checked out your story. If you've lied to me, that finger's comin' off, along with a couple more."

"I no lie. I speak the truth. When you learn it is truth, we can go free?"

"Yeah, sure."

Cauldwell walked away heading to the stone building.

Cauldwell got the feeling the worthless little asshole was telling the truth. He was going to find out in a big damn hurry. His two shit for brains partners better be telling the same story.

As he passed the east end of the abandoned village, Cauldwell turned aside and tore free two three-by-eight planks, each about eight feet in length. These he carried back to his interrogation facility.

Once inside he placed one end of each plank on the seat of the armchair so that they angled sharply downward in the direction of the two remaining hijackers. He then moved the ground ends apart to create an inverted V.

"Awright, here's the deal. Pig Face is dead, and I've lost my patience. So, you two maggots are either gonna tell me what I want to know, or you're gonna die right quick so I can get the hell out of this asshole place."

"Allah will provide us the strength to resist." This came from Bashour.

"Think so, huh? Tell ya what there, Lard Ass. I don't give a flyin' fuck what kind of deal you think you have with Allah, but I'm sure as hell gonna arrange the meeting so y'all can work it out together."

One at a time Cauldwell brought the terrorists and chained them, feet elevated to the planks. He moved to the east end of the room and returned with a water can and an eighteen-inch-wide roll of cellophane.

He wrapped each prisoner's head and face with the cellophane and in turn began dousing each with water, moving from one to the other in rapid succession. The gag reflex set in immediately, eyes bulged in fear and the cellophane was sucked in cutting off their air. Moustapha broke first, nodding his head violently to show his willingness to cooperate. Cauldwell tore away the cellophane and, as the man gasped for air, poured more water over Bashour who then began to emulate the actions of his fellow criminal. Cauldwell pulled the cellophane free and the man heaved air into his lungs.

"Fourteen seconds there, Lard Ass. That's damn good. Most of you worthless rag heads don't make it to ten. Now then, I'll ask each of you specific questions, which you will immediately answer. The one not being spoken to will remain silent.

"I'll start with you, Shit Head. What is your boss's first name?"

"Hassan, sir."

"Ok, Lard Ass. What's his last name?"

"Sharaf, sir."

"Now then Shit Head, where is he?"

"He is in Damascus, sir."

"Okay. What's he planning, Lard Ass?"

"He will detonate a nuclear device, sir."

"What sort of device, Shit Head?"

"A small one called a suitcase bomb, sir."

"Where'd he get it, Lard Ass?"

"From Iran, sir."

"Where's he gonna blow it, Shit Head?"

"In Washington, sir."

"Awright, Lard Ass, who's gonna do it?"

"He will do this thing himself, sir."

"Now then Shit Head, when is this to take place?"

"He intends to destroy your Capitol when your president accompanies the Israeli Prime Minister to speak before your House and Senate."

"Very good, ladies. Now, to show you my heart's in the right place, here's another MRE for each of you and more water." Cauldwell tossed each man a box and canteen. "Relax and enjoy the rest of your day."

Cauldwell moved to the other end of the room and hauled the KY-38 outside. He set the radio against a small boulder and headed for the ruins.

When Mohatazana shuffled through the door ahead of Cauldwell, he was greeted by looks of great surprise on the faces of his fellow hijackers. Cauldwell furnished the diminutive Syrian with food and water, then headed for the door.

"Ah sir, excuse me."

Cauldwell stopped and turned at the sound of Bashour's voice.

"What, Lard Ass?"

"You will now soon set us free?"

"Yeah, I'll get y'all outta here directly, soon as I check out yer story."

Cauldwell returned to the radio and keyed the handset. "Subat Four, Subat Four, this is Subat Six. Over."

"Six, this is Four. Over."

"Listen up, Armstrong. Write down what I'm about to give you, then get hold of Davis in DC and tell him I need verification ASAP. Over."

"Roger that, sir. I'm ready to copy. Over."

Cauldwell gave him the information supplied by the terrorists, minus any mention of the bomb. He asked the full name and location of the fourth terrorist in Guantanamo. I think his name is Daniel. Find any confirmation possible. "Their tactics aren't as good as ours, but any confirmation would be good to know. You got all that? Over."

"Roger, sir. Have a solid copy. Will call DC at once. Over."

"Roger. When Davis calls ya back, see if ya can patch him through to me. Over."

"Will do, sir. Over."

"Okay, Six out."

"Four out."

Cauldwell leaned back against the boulder, tipped the brim of his Marine Corps utility cover over his eyes and let his thoughts dwell on Mary O'Hara.

Three hours and twenty minutes later he was jerked awake by the radio. "Subat Six, Subat Six, this is Subat Four. Over."

"This is Six. Over."

"Stand by for Mister Davis. Over."

"Standing by. Over."

"Major Cauldwell? Rick Davis here. Over."

"Yeah, Cauldwell here. What have we got? Over."

"The info on Sharaf checks out. He was in Tehran five weeks ago for purposes unknown. The man is a major Al Qaeda player. He's on our watch list but we have no photograph. As of now we believe he's somewhere in Damascus. Over."

"Okay. Good work, Davis."

"One more interesting fact, Major. The name was used in Guantanamo. It's obvious our guy there knows the name. He also knows he hangs out in Damascus."

"That's not a coincidence, we have the confirmation we need. Can you put me through to the president? Over."

"Hold on and I'll try. Over."

Seven minutes passed before Cauldwell heard, "Great work, major! What do you need? Over."

"Mister President, you should know this Sharaf obtained a suitcase nuke from the Iranians and he's planning to blow himself and the Capitol away in March. We don't know what the rag head looks like, so we've got to put the kabash on him in Syria. We can't take the chance of him getting into the country. Over."

"Sounds right to me, Major. I'll get Delta Force folks moving on this. Over."

"Mister President, I respectfully submit we would be best served if I conduct the operation. I have friends, assets and resources at my disposal that will be

164

indispensable for the mission's success. If I could have four Delta Force people, preferably marines, I believe I can get this guy. Over."

Several seconds of dead air followed.

"Okay, major, I'll pass you back to Rick and you can tell him what you need. Godspeed, my man."

"Thank you, Mister President. Over."

"Hey Major, Rick Davis again. Tell me what you want. Over."

"I need four marines, corporal rank and above from Delta Force, and all need to be HALO qualified. See if you can find one who speaks Arabic, two would be better. Also, no white guys. Dark skins will be more suited to the task of overt infiltration. Have them start growing beards immediately upon selection. They will be sent to me here. I'll pick 'em up in Kabul if you will lay on the transport. You with me so far? Over."

"Yes, but what's HALO? Over."

"Jump qualified for high altitude, low opening. Over."

"Jump qualified? Over."

Cauldwell hid his exasperation. "Parachute trained. Over."

"Okay. Continue. Over."

"Right. All hands should bring their standard breach-and-clear gear, including automatic weapons and side arms. Have them arrive with half a dozen laminated, large scale street maps of Damascus covering a radius of 10,000 meters from the city center. Whoever back there will oversee reacting to my demands, should have a copy of that map. I will fax you a list of other items that will be needed.

"It will take three or four weeks for us to train and effect insertion, and likely another three in country before we go operational. Code name for target will be Sidewinder. Phrase which will signify mission accomplishment, 'The ship has sailed.' Phrase will signify mission failure, 'Ship has sunk.'

"For logistical planning, be advised we will require fighter escort for insertion aircraft. Also, for extraction the code phrase will be, 'Weigh anchor' and this will require either chopper or VSTOL with gunship escort. Got all that? Over."

"Got it. What's VSTOL? Over."

"Vertical or short takeoff and landing, like a helicopter or the Osprey. Over."

"Okay, but what about insertion and extraction coordinates? Over."

God save me from dumb ass civilians!

"I'll let you know well in advance after I've planned all that out. Over."

"Roger. Anything else? Over."

"Would you please get a message to Mary O'Hara?"

"I'll be happy to pass along your message, major," Davis replied.

"Please tell her I'm safe and simply wanted to say hello. Tell her I'll be back in Washington in a couple months and I want to see her," Cauldwell said.

"I'll get your message to her right way, major. Over."

"Thanks, that's it for now. Stand by for my fax in about three hours. I'll be back at Subat by then so contact me there. Cauldwell out."

"Okay. Davis out."

Cauldwell heaved himself to his feet and reentered his interrogation facility. He picked up his copies of Battle Studies and Caesar's Gallic Campaigns, dropped them in a long-strapped canvas bag, slung the bag over a shoulder and started to leave.

"Excuse me, sir?"

"What is it, Lard Ass?"

"You have found we spoke the truth?"

"More or less, yeah."

"So now you will set us free?"

"Yeah, you'll be free of this place shortly."

"We have spoken together, and all would like to be taken to Egypt, to Cairo, please."

"Oh, about that any country thing. You need to understand I lied. Good-bye, ladies. Have a nice life."

Cauldwell strolled out, paying no attention to the tirade of complaints and questions voiced by the three hijackers. He made a rapid descent through the ravine and walked rapidly through the valley toward Zabi Zamani's house. His approach was observed and reported, thus the tribal chieftain emerged to greet him while he was yet some distance away.

"Ah, majah! Welcome. You wish to speak with Zamani, yes?"

"Yeah chief, I do. Our tourists in the high valley have been persuaded to tell me what I wanted to know. Now, they are all yours. You may do with them what you wish. I might suggest they would be well suited to performing slave labor on behalf of your people, forever! But, of course, the decision is yours. All I ask is that they never be allowed to leave."

"Majah, Zamani very much likes the idea for always there is hard work to be done here. We will make sure they stay with us until they die. If any were to escape," he swept his hand in a broad arc, "the great mountains would provide their flesh and bones to the wolves."

"Good point, chief. Anyway, you will find them in the great stone house. Inside there is all the gear Hakim Wordak and his men helped unload from the helicopter. You are welcome to all of it, except the radio, which is outside by a rock close to the door. I will send a couple guys from my camp to haul that heavy beast down."

"Thank you for those things, majah. There will be no need for your men to come. I will have Hakim see your radio is returned to you."

"That's exceptionally good of you, chief. I thank you for that."

"No need for majah to thank Zamani. Already my people owe majah more than ever we can pay."

"You don't owe me anything, chief. Your friendship is more than enough payment for anything I might have done."

"Ah! Majah do Zamani great honor by calling him 'friend.'"

"Actually, the honor is mine, chief, for you have been my friend, and a damn good one too."

The tribal leader bowed in acknowledgement, smiling broadly.

"Well, chief, I better be gettin' on down the mountain. You might want to collect those tourists before the sun hides behind the high mountains. I didn't leave them with much to eat or drink."

"Zamani will have Hakim go right away."

"Okay then, Chief Zamani. Good-bye and thank you."

"Good-bye, majah. Live well."

Cauldwell moved rapidly and without pause. Fifty-eight minutes after leaving Zamani, he was saluted by the sentry at Camp Subat's north gate.

Chapter 20

The Camp David trip was closing in fast. Plans were already made for the government jet to pick him up. Brandon decided to keep the travel plans as they were but spend a couple days at the dignitary quarters in Wright-Patterson. Maybe Dr. Hollace could help him deal with the loss of his relationship with Grace. He called Dr. Hollace but learned she couldn't meet with him now. She learned her fiancé was going to have a long weekend lay over in Paris.

She was going to fly over to surprise him for a romantic weekend and would not be returning until Sunday night. Tuesday would be the soonest she could meet with him. They agreed to keep in touch by phone until he could arrange to spend a few days at Wright-Patterson. He would spend the days before Camp David quietly alone in his room at the dignitary quarters. He needed the solitude anyway.

Although the pilot had instructions to fly two passengers, he asked no questions and Brandon offered no explanations. He flew directly to Wright-Patterson. Ronnie met him at the ramp with a van. Ronnie knew Brandon was not doing well for some reason. He was quiet as if he had the weight of the world on his shoulders. Ronnie decided to wait and let him discuss his concerns later. Ronnie's job was to handle concerns and he was good at it. Once settled in, Brandon walked to Ronnie's office. He noticed how few people there were around the base, nothing at all like it was a month ago.

"Come on in and take a seat," Ronnie invited trying to sound upbeat for Brandon's sake. "So, tell me what's going on with you? Tell me of any problems I can help you with."

"Can't really think of anything. Business is doing well, it's great to be debt free, the book is doing well, thanks to you," Brandon said with a smile.

"Great. I have good news. My medical team pulled strings on your liver issue. Strong possibility you may not need the transplant, instead the less risky choice of removing the damaged portion. They received records from your doctor and want to move ahead when things are right. Could be anytime. I have a pager for you to keep with you at all times."

"They haven't even seen me and I'm supposed to let them cut me open when I get paged?"

"Something like that, but your doctor has agreed to assist. I made all the arrangements. We will put things in motion when the specialists are ready. Your doctor is in the loop and is talking with our medical team."

Brandon returned to his room. Too many things were going through his mind to sit still so he decided to take a walk around the base. A good walk would clear his head. The news of the transplant put things back in perspective for him.

"Get things in perspective," he managed to mutter as he walked down the hall. Get a grip on what is important in your life. He would have this same walk and self-reflective talk with himself several times before he left for Camp David.

He met the jet at the ramp at seven on Saturday morning and immediately left for Andrews AFB, alone, no one on the plane except the pilots. When he arrived, the remaining party, Hampton, John, Rylander, and their wives were just arriving. They greeted each other like long lost friends. A military aide escorted them to a holding room to wait for the helicopter. The president insisted on sending Marine One to get them. It would be arriving any minute.

"Good morning," the aide began. "I would first like to tell you how much of an honor it is to meet with you. You are national heroes. Marine One will be here shortly. The trip is going to take 45 minutes. Please take your seats as soon as you board. Once in the air, we will do everything to make you comfortable. When we land, the president wants to speak with you in a relaxed setting in the living room of the main cabin. The president would also like to spend an hour with each of you individually. You will be given tours and are free to walk the trails. Lunch will be served at 12:30. Hamburgers are on the menu. The president likes football, so the afternoon may be centered around the television. Marine One will return you to this base at 20:00. Individual jets will then take you home. Any questions?" Everyone stood in awe. No one said a word. They could not believe this was happening.

"Enjoy your flight."

It all seemed highly organized. Before Marine One arrived, the guests had a few minutes to reminisce and compare what was going on in each other's lives. The secrecy had not been that difficult for any of them. Lifestyles changed, not because of the financial rewards from the government, but because each had a new lease on life with a fresh outlook. The presidential helicopter interrupted their stories as it landed. As they were escorted to the helicopter, Brandon's hand felt cold as he watched his three friends walk hand in hand with their wives.

They lifted off and flew so near the Washington monument they could almost touch it. Brandon figured the circular pattern over Washington was for the benefit of the passengers who were having a once in a lifetime experience with the president. As they turned toward Camp David, the realization of the day's meaning hit Brandon. He was going to spend a day with the President of the United States. The President of the United States of America wanted to spend an hour of one-on-one time just to get to know him. He was going to sit around on the couch watching a football game with the president. No one will believe this. And there was no one he could share it with. Approaching the landing pad at Camp David, all began to light up with excitement, each trying to act as if this was an everyday thing for them. President Walker was waiting to greet them personally.

"Welcome to my retreat," the president said as his guests left the helicopter. He shook each of their hands and called them by name. He gave the wives a big hug.

"Why don't you follow me? We have refreshments in the main cabin."

Brandon looked at the president and felt at that moment, he was just a regular guy. Like the guy who lived down the street, or pumped gas at the same gas station you did. He wore jeans and a t-shirt and was just lounging around. The only difference was this guy happened to be the President of the United States and he didn't hang out at the local bar, he relaxed at Camp David. The only person more in awe of the experience than the passengers was President Walker himself. There was something even he couldn't figure out about these men, but he wanted to know them on a personal level. It was rare for any president to take the kind of time he offered the passengers of Flight 3911. Over the past month, he called them personally just to chat for a few minutes and thank them for their courage. He was amazed, aside from occasional rumors about the military cargo jet, the cover story held up well enough to be considered plausible by the world. The terrorist leaders had no clue three of their own were beginning to break. Much like President Kennedy who promised a man on the moon by the end of the 1960s, this president promised retribution before the State of the Union address. With the help of these men, he may just keep that promise.

"I wanted to spend a little time with each of you. Brandon, would you take a walk with me?" asked the president.

Brandon wasn't prepared to go first but got up and followed the president.

"Make yourselves at home. Let one of the staff know if you need anything."

The president led Brandon out the door and to a trail leading away from the compound. It was cold and the sky was clear. Brandon was taking a stroll with the most powerful man in the world but was distracted as he thought about his situation.

"How are you doing, Brandon?" the president inquired, breaking Brandon's trance.

"Fine, sir," Brandon said.

"I am concerned about you. General Echols tells me you've been put on a priority list for a liver issue. How is your health?"

Brandon felt like his life was becoming an open book.

"I feel no effects and I feel great. We caught this so early I haven't had any sickness or ill effects at all. They tell me the issue might be cured with meds. If that doesn't work removing the diseased part of the liver might be next, and if that doesn't work a liver transplant would be required. Oddly enough, death has not been a real concern to me. I guess I've had a few more distractions."

"Are you referring to your girlfriend?"

"Wright-Patterson does keep you informed," Brandon said smiling at his walking companion. "Yes, it's been a heartbreak for sure. Grace is a great person and I love her, but there are some things I'm not willing to accept."

"Brandon, you cannot change people. I know it hurts you, but it's time to move on. You have a lot on your plate right now. When I'm facing problems, I bury myself in work. You have a lot of work ahead of you. I hope you realize how your life is about to change. When I tell the nation your story, Brandon, you are going to be the most sought after person on this planet. You are the pilot that retook an airliner and landed it safely. In the process, you saved some forty plus lives on that airplane, not to mention the White House and those in it. You know my wife and daughter were in the house. You will get over this heartbreak and if it's meant to be, she will come around. In the meantime, let's get you a new liver and then get ready for the exciting life that lies ahead of you."

"Yes, sir, I understand what you are saying, and I appreciate taking such a special interest in my health. I, as do all the rest of the passengers, appreciate everything the government has done for us."

"Your government is proud of you and so am I. Now Brandon, if you don't mind, I'd like to hear from you exactly what happened that morning."

Brandon gave the president a vivid and detailed account of the events from the instant he realized the flight attendant died to the time the plane came to a safe stop on the runway. At times, the story became emotional for both, the president often putting his hand on Brandon's shoulder showing comfort and support. Brandon noticed the president's eyes glaze with tears. He listened intently, picking from the story things he wanted to include in his speech when he told the nation what happened. The president's pride in these heroes grew even more by the end of the story.

"It's the most heroic thing I have ever heard. Everyday citizens rising to the occasion, facing enormous odds and carrying out what you did. If you think what happened on 9/11 rallied this country's patriotism, wait until the nation hears this story," the president said as the two returned to the cabin.

Before reaching the rustic building, the president stopped and added, "Brandon, during the coming weeks and months things are going to move pretty fast. I want to give you advance notice about an upcoming holiday party at the

White House. Please pencil in the party for December. I will send you details as things materialize. But I want you to plan to attend. I want to put you up in the Lincoln Bedroom. It will be a treat."

"How can I refuse such an invitation from the President of the United States?"

The president took a similar walk with each of the others before lunch. After hamburgers with all the fixings, the group settled in for the football game. Some sat around and watched it with him while others took walks on the grounds. After a lazy, laid back afternoon with the leader of the free world, dinner was served at 6:00 around a country table. Nothing fancy, it was more like an old family gathering.

President Walker blessed the food and offered a prayer for his new friends. During dinner, the president casually shared information about the terrorists. He wanted to tell them more but was not willing to risk the operation. He needed the brave passengers to know he intended to carry out his promise of ending this awful episode come January.

After dinner, the president and his guests sat around the fireplace for last minute goodbyes and well wishes. It was the perfect ending to a fantastic day. When they returned to the helicopter, he hugged the men and kissed the wives. Brandon waited for his turn to say goodbye to his host.

"Would you mind if I call you from time to time to check on you?" the president asked.

"That would be great. I appreciate today and I enjoyed getting to know you, sir. It was a fantastic day."

Brandon didn't feel quite as lonely as he did when he arrived. Rather than going home, Brandon returned to Wright-Patterson to make use of the dignitary quarters. After the flight to the base, a van waited to take him to the quarters. As they turned into the drive, he noticed a light on in Dr. Hollace's office and through the blinds he thought he saw her. How could it be her? She was in Paris. He decided it was a house cleaner tidying up and brushed it off.

Aides met him at the door and helped with the few things he had. Brandon went to the dining room, which was empty, but a staff member put together something to drink and offered fruit. He took it to the lounge to relax. There was nothing good on TV. A walk would be good to clear his head. He made his way outside and noticed the light still on in Dr. Hollace's office. He walked by, but this time he was certain the figure in the office was not a house cleaner, but Dr. Hollace herself. He decided to stop in for a moment to see if she could see him the next day. Her door was open as usual. He tapped on the door to announce himself. As she turned to see who it was, she tried to wipe the tears from her face.

"Sorry to bother you, just got in from Camp David and thought I'd say hi," he said.

"Oh, hello, I'm sorry. This has not been a good day for me."

"I'm sorry to hear that. I'll leave you alone and maybe see you tomorrow if you're here before I leave."

"Oh, no it's alright. I mean I'm okay if you need to talk. That's what I'm here for," she said trying to smile. "Sit down while I get your file."

"Thanks, but I don't want to burden you. It's just that I split up with Grace last week and it's been much harder than I expected. I just wanted to talk to someone."

"I can understand, you really loved her," she said fighting back tears.

"Dr. Hollace, I can see something is bothering you, maybe this is not a good time."

"No, I'm fine. Look, I haven't eaten, would you like to share a late dinner? We can take my car. I know an excellent restaurant not far from here."

Brandon was caught off guard with the invitation and although he had eaten, he accepted her invitation. On the way to the restaurant, she told him of her surprise trip to Paris.

"I arrived in Paris yesterday and knocked on the door of my fiancé's suite. He thought I was room service, so he opened the door with a towel wrapped around him. I'm sure you can imagine the stunned look on his face. There was another woman sitting on the couch. They wore matching towels. I traveled that far to see him, and I was not about to turn around and leave so I walked right in and confronted them both. It turns out he was also engaged to Patrice. She said she knew about me, but he told her he was breaking it off. He had the nerve to ask me to leave and said he would explain when he returned to the States. I told him an explanation wasn't necessary and never contact me again. I immediately returned to the airport and waited four hours for the next flight home. I still can't believe it really happened.

"Well, when I landed, I didn't want to go home, so I went to the office." She finished the story about the time they pulled into the restaurant. It was a late Saturday night and the place was bustling with a large crowd. The hostess informed them of the twenty-minute wait for a table, so they parked themselves in a bar booth. Not knowing anything about her, he decided to be polite and ask if he could get her a drink, perhaps a glass of wine. She accepted the offer.

"To broke hearts," he toasted, handing her the glass.

"An unusual toast, but here's to broken hearts," she said trying to smile.

They shared stories, Brandon filling her in on the breakup with Grace. They both needed someone to talk to, and the fact Dr. Holland was so beautiful made the pain a bit more bearable for Brandon.

"Powell party of two," announced a frail teenage girl.

"Doctor, shall we eat?"

"Great" Dr. Hollace replied. "But don't you think it's time we get on a first name basis?

Please call me Carley."

"Fine and I'm Brandon," he said holding out his hand. He shook her hand gracefully. "It's nice to meet you, Carley."

"It's my pleasure, Brandon," she said on cue with a curtsey, both acting as if they had just met for the first time.

They followed the frail hostess to a table in the middle of the restaurant. Brandon pulled out her chair.

"Thank you," she said again smiling as she sat.

"I'm sorry to hear things didn't go as you planned in Paris," Brandon began. "But better to find out now than later."

"I agree. I'm sorry to hear about you and Grace. In my case, it's infidelity, yours is much more tragic because you really love her and I think she may really love you. You have an impasse on certain issues and values. People in love should be able to compromise to find solutions in behavior related differences. It's a shame to throw away a year rather than reach a compromise and live by that compromise. As I recall, you did reach a compromise at least a half a dozen times and each time she ignored the solution that could have worked."

"Yes, that was her choice and that's what really bugs me. She was willing to throw away what we had over a simple phone call saying, 'I'm home, honey.' Yet she wanted me to open up about my finances. In those half a dozen instances I've mentioned, if she had done that, was just open and honest, we would be married by now and sleeping in the Lincoln Bedroom at the White House in December."

"There was more to it than that, and I only mention this, so you don't get down on yourself. You did mention she drank too much, and she makes poor choices when she has been drinking. That bothered you. You did mention she lied to you and met an old boyfriend for drinks, then pulled the Bill Clinton syndrome to justify it. So, there's more than just a trust issue."

"That's right, but I forgave her for the drinks with the old boyfriend, and as long as she is with me, I can watch out for her drinking. It's the poor choices when drinking and being out with the girls I couldn't handle."

"It's none of my business, but I think you may have made the right choice," the therapist said.

"I agree, and if I may say so, you've made the right choice as well. I'm glad you discovered the truth before you got married."

"As am I. What did you mean about the Lincoln Bedroom?

"The president has invited me to a holiday reception at the White House during the holiday season, supposed to be a Christmas party, with cocktails, dining, and dancing. He invited me to stay in the Lincoln Bedroom as a gift to Grace. At the time, I thought we might even be married by then. I'll be sleeping alone in that historic place."

"You could always patch things up."

"No way, I am finished," he said trying to be positive.

175

"The thought of being at a Christmas party at the White House and spending the night there is exciting."

They ordered dinner and a bottle of the best wine. She let her guard down and became the patient, and Brandon tried hard to listen as she had done with him so many times before. She sounded off on her failed relationship for a while, but then they both put their troubles on hold long enough to get to know each other.

Carley had been a doctor for fifteen years. She graduated from Johns Hopkins University School of Medicine. Her dad was a retired heart surgeon, her mother died of breast cancer five years ago. She was a private contractor for the Air Force specializing in helping in relationship matters for everything from failing marriages to drug and alcohol abuse. She owned her own home, was forty-four but looked thirty-five and became the widow of an Air Force pilot when he was killed in a tragic crash during the Persian Gulf War. She had not remarried, the airline pilot was as close as she got, and had only two serious relationships since the death of her husband.

Carley certainly didn't need a man in her life for financial security and Brandon liked that. He wouldn't have to worry about her looking at him as a meal ticket. She never had children because of a medical issue that she didn't elaborate on. She passionately believed in burying the past and taking no baggage to the next relationship. As they finished dinner and the wine, another side of Carley began to emerge that Brandon liked. If not both were hurting and vulnerable, this might have been the beginning of something nice. They finished dinner after midnight then returned to the base. As she let him out in front of the dignitary quarters, she squeezed his hand. The night did both a lot of good.

"Would you like to come by the office before you leave tomorrow, I'd be glad to meet you on a Sunday if you'd like," she offered.

"Brunch or an early lunch?

"Brunch sounds great. I go to early church. I'll pick you up right after church unless you want to join me for church."

"I'd love to go with you, what time?"

"I'll be here at 8:30."

For the first time in days, Brandon got a good night's sleep. It was refreshing to spend the evening with Carley sharing and comparing backgrounds. Any other time and he would have considered her as a possible relationship, but neither was ready to think about that now.

The next morning, it was obvious Carley didn't fare as well as Brandon. She seemed depressed when she picked him up but offered a smile when she saw his. After church, they chalked up another similarity, their worship. Both were Methodist and had similar beliefs. After church, she took him to a country club for brunch. They were experiencing similar feelings of the previous evening, neither knowing what to make of it, but the thought of it was heartwarming.

After brunch, Brandon called the pilot's pager and entered a pre-arranged code, rather than a phone number, 1400. Fourteen hundred hours, 2:00 departure time. Carley offered to take him to the ramp to meet the jet. They returned to the dignitary quarters where she went with him to his room to help gather his things. It wasn't much, but alone in the room, often with eye contact, made the walls seem a little closer. It made Carley seem a little closer. Brandon gathered his things.

"Here, let me get that for you," Carley offered.

She grabbed the tie and threw it over his head. Her fingers glided across his neck as she adjusted his collar. As she finagled the knot, he could feel the warm touch of her breath on his face. Another day, another time and things would be different.

"There you go," she said as she ran her hands down his shoulders. The ride to the ramp was quiet. Brandon kept replaying the tie scenario in his head. When they arrived, his jet was waiting. She gave him a departing hug and a compassionate look. He boarded the jet and as the engines began to roar, he looked out the window, she stood leaning on her car like in an old fashion movie, hair blowing in the wind. He waved goodbye. The jet roared down the runway on the take-off roll. He again looked in that direction, she was still leaning on the car, watching his departure.

On Monday morning, the first person he thought to call was Carley.

"Well, I do have a couple of book signings this week. That will give me time away to think."

"Time working and time thinking are not the same things. Go back to the base and spend a few days," Carley said.

"You're right. I'll be flying the Baron this time. I might be able to work in a stop on my way back. Would you like to plan something for Saturday?"

"I would love to go flying."

"Great. Then it's a date."

Brandon couldn't get his date with Carley off his mind. He started to get his things together. He had a long week ahead of him. He was at his office working on his last-minute travel arrangements when the phone rang.

"Hi Brandon, it's President Walker, how are you doing?"

"Fine sir, thanks for asking and how are you?"

"I'm fine, just concerned about you. You seemed very distracted this past Saturday.

"I'm sure things will work out for the best for you. Brandon, I'm calling to invite you to the White House Christmas party and reception. You'll receive an official invitation soon, but the date is Saturday, December 15. I'll send a government jet to get you. I also want to offer you a rare treat. Remember to plan to stay here at the White House in the Lincoln Bedroom."

"Mr. President, I will accept the bedroom offer."

"Great, I'll look forward to seeing you in about a month."

The president really was a nice guy, Brandon thought, not a bad friend to have.

He left Atlanta on a Tuesday, bags packed for any occasion and prepared to be gone for a week. He decided to fly the Baron, since the fare to fly commercially would be outrageous and most of his time would be spent boarding and unboarding. The first stop was in Memphis for a signing that afternoon and evening. He stayed overnight then moved on to Louisville early the next morning for a signing at noon, mid-afternoon, and another in the evening at three different bookstores. Wednesday was Cincinnati for the same routine, then on to Wright-Patterson AFB on Thursday night. Although general aviation aircraft were forbidden in military base air space, Ronnie had arranged for special clearance for 212 Bravo, Brandon's call numbers for the Baron.

"Wright-Patterson Tower, this is Baron 212 Bravo, do you read me?" called Brandon.

"Roger Baron 212 Bravo, we have been expecting you."

"Roger, tower. I am thirty miles southwest at 6500, inbound to land."

"Roger 212 Bravo, please squawk 3232 transponder code, come to 23 degrees and descend to 3500. Active runway is 29 and wind is light, visibility is ten miles."

"Roger, tower." Runway two nine, that was the runway he landed the 757 on just six short weeks ago. It seemed like it was just yesterday, he thought. Memories flashed through his mind of that morning. What an experience it had been and how much it had changed his life.

"212 Bravo, you are now in position for straight in approach on 29, we show you ten miles out, you are clear for final."

"Roger, coming left to 29 degrees."

"212 Bravo, be advised, emergency vehicles along the runways are having emergency drills."

"Roger, 212 Bravo on two-mile final for 29."

"Roger 212 Bravo, you are clear to land. On ground maintain this frequency for ground control, we will take you to the ramp."

"Roger, tower."

Brandon put his Baron on an exact glide slope and touched down for a perfect landing.

"Mr. Powell, welcome to Wright-Patterson AFB sir, please follow the emergency vehicles. They will lead you to a hanger for your aircraft. Follow the hand signals upon approach at the hanger."

"Roger, tower." It looked like a parade with twenty emergency vehicles of every kind surrounding him at safe distances. Red lights were flashing and sirens blasting. He followed them to the hanger and noticed a large crowd of people assembled inside. He looked ahead at the military band set up on a large flatbed truck.

"What's going on?" he wondered aloud. He was directed to park the Baron at the entrance to the hanger then received the signal to cut the engines. As he opened the door to get out, Ronnie stepped up to greet him.

"Welcome, Brandon, General Echols thought it would be great to give you a taste of what your life is going to be like real soon. These people were not told who you were or why we are here, but they just wanted to be involved as a favor to General Echols," Ronnie explained.

"I'm flattered, I have goose bumps and my skin is crawling on my back. What a surprise!" Brandon said enjoying the attention.

Ronnie escorted him to the podium where General Echols stood to present him a symbolic key to the base and Air Force Wings to signify him as an honorary Air Force pilot. The president ordered a military film crew to make a documentary about Brandon; he planned to incorporate footage when he told the story of Flight 3911. Brandon scanned the crowd for a familiar face but found none among the sea of camera lenses and flashes. He was determined to find Carley and let out a sigh when he spotted her standing with Ronnie. She winked at him and he acknowledged her wink with a smile. The welcome party quickly dispersed as a crew pulled his Baron into the hanger. He joined Ronnie and Carley.

"Surprised?" Carley asked Brandon.

"Absolutely, what an incredible feeling!"

Ronnie excused himself with a wink to Brandon; his departure was prearranged.

"I was not expecting to see you until tomorrow. Ronnie told me of your arrival today. When word spread of the welcome reception, I had to be here. Are you free for dinner?" she asked seeming in better spirits than the last time they talked.

"Certainly, I'm free." Brandon grabbed her hand. "Thanks for coming."

Aides loaded his things into her car. Later they returned to the same restaurant they enjoyed the last Saturday night. This time they walked in, she announced her name for reservations and they were immediately seated.

Carley seemed perfect. She was an aggressive but not pushy woman, she asked him to dinner and was confident enough to make reservations ahead of time. A big plus. She was a beautiful woman, truly drop dead gorgeous. Carley was a little shorter than Grace with a great looking athletic body. Long dark hair and blue eyes with fantastic breasts and a perfectly shaped butt. Despite her great looks, the thing that really kept his attention was her ever so slight aggression. Not at all reluctant to be the aggressor to suggest a dinner date. He thought her aggression was sexy and not at all overbearing.

She had just been hurt by a former lover, so they shared a similar pain. They would be more sensitive to each other's emotional needs. His mind raced with the possibilities as he looked into her eyes.

She took charge and ordered that same expensive bottle of wine they had last week. He checked off another quality that he really liked, her assertiveness. This time she raised her glass and toasted.

"To our first date."

"So, this is an official date? Then, to our first date," and they took a sip of wine.

"I was proud to see you coming in today and that's a beautiful airplane you have," she said.

"Thank you. That welcome was such a fantastic feeling. I have never experienced anything like that."

"You better get used to it. That's going to be your lifestyle in a couple months. I expect you will not be able to walk the streets without someone recognizing you."

"I expect I'll get my 15 minutes of fame and then fade away."

"I don't think so."

"Since we're on a date, this is not professional so can I tell you how stunning you look?"

"Well thank you, Mr. Powell," she said trying to mimic his slight southern accent.

"It's only been a week, but you sound as though you're doing much better and accepting what happened in Paris."

"I have, it is over. I had to be honest with myself. Something hasn't been right for a while. I returned his engagement ring with a note. I sent it UPS to his home address. It's over and there is nothing else to say."

"I wish I had that kind of control. Grace called. We met last Sunday for about thirty minutes. She wants to revisit the relationship."

"Well, what do you plan to do?"

"I've heard this line before, and I have no reason to think this time will be any different. I wish I could put it out of my mind like you have."

"I understand, but I will help you through it, professionally speaking of course," she winked.

"Did I tell you the president called me Monday?" he asked.

"No, how exciting!"

"See, even this. It's great to be able to share this experience with someone. I'm glad to be sharing this experience with you."

"So, what did the president say?"

"He wanted to check on me and wish me well. He also invited me to the White House for the Christmas party. He's going to put me up in the Lincoln Bedroom."

"How fantastic!"

"Yeah, but on one hand, it makes me mad and a little depressed to think I may be there alone for such a big event."

"Why would you go alone?" she asked.

"Grace is out of the picture. I am not involved in a relationship. Don't expect to be in one that soon, so I doubt it will be appropriate to ask a certain doctor to spend an overnight in the Lincoln Bedroom."

Carley said nothing but smiled. They finished dinner earlier than the last time. He planned to take her flying the next morning, so they called it a night early. When they returned to the dignitary quarters, as happened the last time, she squeezed his hand and said goodnight. The thought of kissing her goodnight passed his mind, but he just thanked her for a wonderful evening instead.

At seven the next morning, Carley arrived to pick him up and they drove directly to the hanger. They took off and flew around the area without getting more than fifty miles from the base. The early morning weather was perfect for flying. Visibility was unlimited; they could see for miles.

"This is unbelievable. I've always loved being high in the sky," Carley said with excitement.

"Have you ever flown a plane?" he asked.

"No. My husband tried to teach me a long time ago, but I was a nervous wreck."

"Well, I'm a very patient man." He gave her the controls to teach her a few basic flight maneuvers. She was a natural and at home in the air.

"You're a very good student."

"Thank you. I have an excellent teacher."

"Baron 212 Bravo, do you read me?" announced the control tower over the radio.

Brandon returned his attention to his radio and keyed his microphone. "This is Baron 212 Bravo. Over."

"We have a situation, immediately return to base," the tone was stern.

"Roger tower, 212 Bravo returning to base," Brandon said, not understanding why there was such a request but following instructions. He immediately turned toward the base as he looked into Carley's puzzled face.

"What could that be about?" she asked.

"No clue," he answered.

"212 Baron, you are clear to land on 29."

As he entered final approach, Brandon recounted that morning in the 757. She was mesmerized. He landed and taxied to the hanger. As they approached, he noticed a government jet blocking the door. Several people were wandering around the bird and Brandon noticed Ronnie was among them. The ground crew directed Brandon to park next to the jet. He shut down the engines; Ronnie ran to meet them.

"Brandon, come with me," Ronnie ordered.

"What's going on?" Carley asked.

"Brandon, we have to hurry. We have surgery planned for you. We must get you to Emory in Atlanta. Your doctor and our teams are already on their way. We have to hurry."

Bewildered, Brandon followed. Carley ran after them. There was no time to say a proper goodbye, so she squeezed his hand before letting him go. The pilot was already cranking up the engines. Carley offered a compassionate look as Brandon boarded the jet. On board, Ronnie explained they had just received word from the liver specialists at Emory.

"The medical team plans to remove a small portion of your liver," Ronnie explained. "They think this will be the solution with the least number of complications. You should be up and back to your old self in a couple weeks."

"So, what about the transplant?" Brandon asked.

"They have reviewed your records and every health detail in your history. They believe a transplant is not necessary." Ronnie continued. "You should be just fine without the need for a transplant."

By the time they were scheduled to arrive, the medical team was ready with surgery beginning a few hours later. Ronnie's staff was instructed to contact the friends and family members on the list Brandon provided when they first put the transplant request in place. Brandon expected this day, but not this soon. Now that it was happening, he was nervous.

On the flight, he called his mother and sons to let them know that he was alright. They had received a call earlier from one of the government aides and were already on their way to the hospital. The only other person he thought to call was Carley, and she already knew. Brandon was trying to relax but couldn't shake the jitters during the hour long flight to Atlanta. A million things raced through his mind, but he couldn't focus on anything. His will was up to date, assets were designed so the boys could get to them if necessary. His attorneys had their instructions. If anything went wrong, he made all necessary plans to protect his family. There was nothing else to do but pray, and the rest of the flight was spent doing just that.

In Atlanta they landed at Dobbins AFB where an ambulance and police escort were standing by. Brandon was escorted from the jet to the ambulance where a medical team was waiting. When they arrived, they placed their patient on a gurney and immediately took him to his team of doctors who were standing ready. Brandon's personal physician had explained the procedure many times; things seemed to go exactly as planned. They wheeled Brandon into the operating room. He only saw eyes over the mask covered faces. It was hard to figure out who was talking, so he spoke to whichever set of eyes were staring down at him.

"Mr. Powell, just relax."

Relaxing was not a problem, thanks to the sedative. Just two hours before he was flying around with a beautiful lady, now he was going under the knife.

Chapter 21

The arrival of the Delta Force Marines was delayed by more than two weeks as two key members were already deployed on foreign shores in support of a mission considered critical. Sergeant Samir "Sammy" Ayoubi had been born in Syria, leaving at six years of age when his parents emigrated to the United States. Sammy was bilingual in English and Arabic. All four of his promotions had been deemed meritorious. He had been a corps sergeant for only eighteen months when he had been chosen from a 2nd Marine Division rifle company, to undergo the rigorous testing and evaluation process incidental to becoming a Delta Force member. Since that time, after nine months with the force, Sammy had earned two Purple Hearts and a Bronze Star with the combat V for valor.

Sergeant Khaled Fahmi was born in Trenton, New Jersey of Syrian parents who became naturalized US citizens. Both English and Arabic were spoken in the home and Khaled could read, write and speak both languages. He had been with Delta Force for twenty months and had been awarded a Silver Star and Purple Heart.

Sergeants Ayoubi and Fahmi exited a C17 at Kabul and in company with Corporal Juan Gonzales of Los Angeles and Corporal Alfred "Fredo" Garcia, a product of Hell's Kitchen, New York City. Each marine was encumbered with an exceptionally large, top-zippered duffel bag and all wore full combat gear stuffed with automatic weapons and 9mm pistols.

After perfunctory greetings, the four were ushered aboard a CH53 by Sergeant Allen and Major Cauldwell. Once airborne, Sergeant Ayoubi extracted a thick, cord-bound, large envelope from his bag and handed it to Cauldwell.

"Your dossiers?"

"Yes, sir."

"Yeah, heavily redacted no doubt."

"Yes sir, but we can fill the major in verbally."

"You mean, 'orally.'"

"Sir?"

"All word-based communication is verbal, Sergeant, both written and spoken. When spoken, it is delivered orally."

"Makes sense, sir. I never heard it explained before."

"Doesn't surprise me. So, you're the senior man?"

"Yes, sir."

"Okay. I'm not gonna wear my voice out tryin' to overcome the noise from these engines, so sit back an' relax. I'll speak to all of you privately when we hit the deck, which will be in about ninety minutes."

"Aye, aye, sir."

When they landed at Camp Subat, Cauldwell deplaned first and halted at the foot of the cargo ramp. "Thanks, Sergeant Allen. Carry on but stay within shoutin' distance of my tent."

"Yes, sir."

"Right, you four follow me."

Cauldwell led the way into his tent, the interior space now constricted by the addition of four, straight backed wooden chairs.

Cauldwell pulled his desk chair up to his small table, laid down the envelope and sat to face the semi-circle of chairs before him.

"Grab a seat, marines. Now then, I know y'all are familiar with the drill, but for the record this is a black op. Only the five of us will know what we're doing and when we're finished, it never happened, and we were never together anywhere, anytime. Everybody understand?"

"Yes, sir." Four voices replied in unison.

"Now then, I expect most of the gear in those bags is for me?"

"Yes, sir." Sergeant Ayoubi responded.

"Good, then I hope y'all have some maps for me too."

"Yes, sir." Ayoubi quickly jumped to his feet and attacked one of the bags. "Here, sir. Six laminated map sheets."

"Maps of what there, sergeant?"

"The sergeant doesn't know, sir."

"Outstanding. Well, you're all gonna know directly. But first, I want y'all to get squared away with living spaces and have a chance to grab some chow. SARGEANT ALLEN!"

"YES, SIR!" Allen's voice replied from some distance outside the tent and seven seconds later he pushed through the tent flap.

"Sergeant Allen, take these marines to their tent then show 'em where they can chow down."

Yes, sir."

"Okay, marines, take your personal gear outta the bags, get squared away and report back here in one hour."

"Aye, aye, sir." A four-voice chorus sang out.

As soon as the contingent departed, Cauldwell began a systematic inventory of the contents of all four bags. He grunted with satisfaction several times during his search. With that task completed he lined the bags up against the wall at the south end of the tent and returned to the table. Leaving five map sheets on the table, he unfolded the last and hung it on an easel type board to the left rear of his chair. He then turned to the package of dossiers. Cauldwell broke the red wax seal, unwound the cord, opened the flap and pulled out a white envelope marked Cauldwell Eyes Only. Slicing the envelope with his Ka-Bar, he extracted a single sheet, which he scanned quickly before turning to the map.

Fifty-five minutes later, the four marines returned to Cauldwell's tent.

"Get in here, marines. At ease, take a seat. Men, this is a street map of Damascus, Syria. After we are adequately trained, we're going to conduct business in that city. Our business within this thriving metropolis will be to rid the earth of a despicable scumbag who plans to attack our country and who clearly does not deserve to live. This asshole currently resides here."

Cauldwell placed the tip of his fighting knife at a spot on the map. "This is 461 Mu'Awia Street which, as you can see," Cauldwell moved the blade slightly, "is just southwest of the Al'Umawi Mosque."

"The name of this disgusting piece of human excrement is Hassan Sharaf. Unfortunately, we do not have a picture of this prick, so we must proceed slowly and find a way to make a positive ID, probably by having someone point him out to us."

"This brings me to another issue. Do any one of you speak Arabic?"

Simultaneously Fahmi and Ayoubi raised their hands and replied, "Yes, sir."

"Both of you? Holy crap! This is better than I could have hoped for. How about reading the language?"

Again, the two sergeants raised their hands.

"Damn! This is outstanding. Awright then, for a basic overview of the entire operation we will train up here for however many weeks it takes for me to be satisfied. We will make extensive use of the Tire House where we can fire live ammo at pop-up targets, and we will all acquire an intimate knowledge of the southeastern section of the city.

"We will insert by HALO." Cauldwell moved his knife to the countryside east of the urban sprawl. "Here at coordinates three five three nine – three zero seven two."

"To the south you see the International Airport with Airport Road being the only major thoroughfare running southeast out of the city."

"Should we become separated, our rally point will be at the Bab Kissan Church, just north of Dawar Al'Matar Square where Airport Road meets Ibn'Asaker Street. All of you have GPS units?"

"Yes, sir." Four voices sounded in response.

"Outstanding. So, crank in the insertion coordinates, as well as those for the rally point and for Sharaf's hovel. Set 'em up in Quick Search.

"I want each of you to step up to the table and take a copy of the map. I want you to unfold it and hold it so I can clamp one of these medallions into the bottom-right corner. Each medallion is engraved with a number, one through four, and each man will be responsible for the security of the map sheet assigned to him by number. My copy will bear the number five.

"You will not allow these sheets to be out of your possession or view at any time, including eating, sleeping and showering. You will ensure that no one views these sheets other than the five of us in this damn tent. Y'all got that?"

"Yes, sir."

"Right. Now step up in order of seniority."

The marines formed a file led by Sergeants Ayoubi and Fahmi and completed by Corporals Garcia and Gonzales. The process required less than three minutes.

"Awright men, fold 'em up, put 'em away. Get back to yer tent an' start studyin.' At zero seven-thirty we will convene right here, at which time I will administer an oral test to see where you are regarding the memorization of the street grid in and around the Al'Umawi Mosque. Following that we will report to the Tire House for quick-reaction, search-and-clear drills with pop-ups, so we can hone our asshole killin' skills while learning to avoid taking out the innocent, assuming there are innocents in that worthless enclave. That's all. Carry on."

"Aye, aye, sir!"

Chapter 22

Brandon's surgery went exceedingly well. It was determined a transplant was not necessary. Brandon only wore two small incisions. But he did lose eighteen percent of the total mass of his liver. A full recovery was expected.

When Brandon opened his eyes and surveyed the recovery room he saw his sons and his mother sitting in the chairs watching TV. He felt a kiss on his forehead. He struggled to turn his head to see who it was and was surprised to learn it was Grace.

When Brandon first heard he needed the operation, he put her name at the top of his friends and family list. She was the first to arrive and how he wished now he had remembered to update that damn list! For the first 24 hours after the surgery, they kept him under heavy sedation, and he slept most of the time. The next day, the anesthesia began to wear off. During his first few minutes of extended alertness, Brandon realized Grace was there with him. He tried to talk to her, but the medication still made it hard for him to focus and he made no sense. Where was Carley he wondered?

"Shhhhh." Grace said and kissed him. "I'm here. Just…"

She continued her sentence, but he did not understand a word she said and drifted right back to sleep. Carley in the meantime, caught a ride on a military transport plane and went to visit him in the hospital. When she entered his room he was sound asleep, and Grace was sitting next to him. Thinking quickly, Carley introduced herself as a friend, while Grace made sure to call herself Brandon's girlfriend.

"I'll only be in town for a day, so I'll come back later when our patient may be more alert." Carley said.

"Why don't you do that?" Grace replied grabbing Brandon's hand tightly in a show of control.

After lunch, he began to remain in a semi alert state of mind for longer periods. He still didn't make much sense, but Brandon was becoming aware of his surroundings and the people in it. The phone rang and Grace made sure to answer it for him.

"Is this Mr. Brandon Powell's room?" the voice over the phone said.

"Yes, it is," she said.

"May I please speak with him for a moment," the voice asked. Grace thought she recognized the voice but couldn't instantly put a name to it.

"Well, I'll ask him. He's heavily sedated right now. May I ask who is calling?"

"It's the president." Grace's mouth dropped. Why would the President of the United States be calling Brandon she wondered? Grace gently woke him and handed him the phone.

"Brandon. It's President Walker. How are you?"

"Fine, thanks, sir" he said trying to keep his head clear enough to talk.

"Just wanted you to know I was thinking about you. They tell me you're doing great and should be on your feet soon. I know it's not a good time for you, but just wanted to say hello and wish you well. Get your rest."

"Thank you, sir and thanks for calling" the patient said as he faded out again.

"What was that about? Was that really President Walker?" Grace asked in an incredulous voice as she replaced the receiver.

Brandon faded back into a deep sleep as if on cue and gave Grace no response to her question. Thirty minutes later Carley returned to the room to check again to see if Brandon had awakened. She and Grace made small talk for a few minutes and it was somewhat uncomfortable for them both. Grace was very curious who Carley was and how she knew Brandon. Carley was forced to explain she met Brandon on a recent flight that was stranded in Ohio and she is a relationship therapist. This story sounded plausible because Carley remembered Brandon mentioned that's what he told Grace. After a few minutes, Brandon woke up again and saw Carley first, but was totally unaware of Grace still in the room.

"How did you like flying?" he asked without a care in the world feeling medicated and very relaxed.

"It was great, you got away so fast, I am glad things are well. I was just in town and wanted to stop by." As Grace leaned in to eavesdrop on conversation, she assumed they were talking about their stranded flight, but Brandon and Carley both knew they were talking about flying in the Baron just the day before.

Over the next 24 hours Brandon became more alert. The doctors insisted he begin to move around some. Grace still had many questions. Such as why did the president call him? Who was Carley and why would she fly down here to see him? In his recovery condition, it wasn't a good time to get into this so Brandon decided it was much easier to tell Grace they would talk later, possibly when he was feeling better.

Grace couldn't help but feel jealous over Carley coming to Atlanta to see Brandon. What was really going on? How much had Brandon spoken with Carley about their personal relationship? Over the next few days, Brandon recovered faster than expected and he continued to roadblock answering questions Grace threw at him. Ronnie wanted to fly him back to Wright-Patterson to help him escape from Grace and so the staff could help him gain his strength back. Grace relentlessly continued to pry. Brandon resisted and continued to say they could talk when he returned from his recovery time in Ohio.

After Grace pressed him for information to the point of exhaustion, Brandon finally had it. He bluntly told Grace as far as he was concerned, their final split took place weeks ago and she had no right to pry into his life. As they wheeled him out of Emory Hospital for his trip to the base, Grace sat stunned and was silent for the first time since arriving at the hospital.

A military jet returned Brandon to Ohio where he spent the next two weeks gaining a full recovery. Carley came to see him several times a day, every day. Both seemed to be recovering from their failed relationships and enjoying each other's company more and more. Carley at one point mentioned her visit the day after surgery and the uncomfortable meeting with Grace. Brandon was not surprised when he learned Grace introduced herself as his girlfriend. He really didn't remember Carley even being there and detected a hint of jealousy on her part. Grace continued to call numerous times during his recovery stay at Wright-Patterson. He was unclear how she got the number.

Grace wanted to meet and talk things out again. Reluctantly Brandon finally agreed to meet with her after his return to Atlanta. He had no interest in rebuilding their relationship. He only agreed to talk because he had a year invested with Grace and one more discussion couldn't hurt. When it was time to go home, it was too soon after surgery for him to fly the Baron, which still found a home in the hanger. Ronnie arranged for a jet to take Brandon back to Atlanta.

Chapter 23

Over the next four weeks Cauldwell devoted himself exclusively to the rigorous training regimen to which the Delta Force Marines were subject. The training of Afghanis continued at an increased tempo now that coalition forces were engaged in a head on confrontation with Al Qaeda militias and Taliban forces. Apart from daily briefings by Sergeant First Class Downs, Cauldwell played no active role.

He drove himself and his marines relentlessly through fourteen-hour training days that alternated between classroom sessions held in his tent and live fire exercises in the Tire House.

During class time, Cauldwell continually grilled the four young men on their knowledge of the Damascus city center. He would pose and require immediate responses to such questions as, "You are moving west on Al Hamidyeh, what's the next major intersection?" Or "You are proceeding north on Sa'd Zagloul Street, what happens when you pass the intersection with Al Malek Faysal?"

The marine who failed to answer "Sa'd Zagloul Street, sir, and it becomes Ath'Thawra Street, sir, respectively, was treated to an acerbic ass-chewing none of them had enjoyed since boot camp.

The Tire House was a five-room complex Cauldwell built many years before. All interior and exterior walls, including the overhead, were thickly lined with layered strips of rubber from vehicle tires which ensured small arms fire could not travel from room to room or escape to the outside. Throughout the rooms were a great number of hidden pop-up targets. These targets were steel plates painted with various representations ranging from women with children in their arms, unarmed men and enemy figures bearing weapons.

The targets were spring-loaded and would snap into view when an exercise controller touched a button or when a trainee's foot hit a specific spot on the deck. The process demanded both immediate recognition of the target's nature (whether the depicted figure posed a threat), and instantaneous decision-making on whether to open fire. Marines had undergone this type training many times before, but as good as they were, mistakes happened and those generated caustic commentary from Cauldwell such as, "Corporal Gonzales, why would ya wanna blow away that poor woman an' her baby?" or "Damn, marine! Ya just killed a poor ol' sheep-shearer vistin' the big city fer the first time!" or yet again, "Yer dead, marine! Ya hesitated an' ya let that worthless rag head put a whole bunch of holes in ya with his AK-47."

Thanksgiving was celebrated by the rest of the U.S. contingent at Camp Subat but was barely noticed by the big major and his four-man strike team. A week later, on 29 November, Cauldwell was on the radiophone with Rick Davis in Washington.

"Hey, Rick. Cauldwell here. My guys and I are ready to go. I want a HALO drop at twenty-one thirty on Monday 17 December. Over."

"Got it. HAHO, twenty-one thirty on the seventeenth. Over."

Cauldwell did his best to keep exasperation out of his voice. "Not HAHO, that's high altitude, high opening. I need a HALO, low opening. So whatever fixed wing you get to haul us, the wing chutes need to be aboard. Over."

"Okay, I understand HALO, and I'll take care of the chutes. Why the seventeenth? Over."

"It's Eid-al-Fitr, a big feast celebration to mark the end of Ramadan. The rag heads will have been fasting from dawn to dusk for thirty days and should be milling about having a good time with nobody paying too much attention to anything else. Over."

"Makes sense. What are the coordinates for the HALO? Over."

Cauldwell shook his head in disbelief. "I'll give those to the pilot. Over."

"Oh yeah, right. The State of the Union goes at eight pm on Tuesday 22 January. The president needs confirmation of mission success before beginning his address. Over."

"I understand. I see among the gear you sent there was a single frequency satellite phone. I assume you have possession of its twin brother. Over."

"That I do. You can use it to talk to me anytime, especially if we are coming down to the wire on or near the eight pm deadline on Tuesday 22 January. Over."

"Very good. Get ready to write. Over."

"Ready. Over."

"Okay. Team code is Party Favors. Team Leader is Fox. You have copies of the team dossiers? Over."

"I have them. Over."

"Right. After Team Leader and in order of seniority, codes are Star, Trenton, LA, and Apple. Got those? Over."

"I have a copy. Over."

"Roger. Once again, code for mission success is 'The ship has sailed.' Code for mission failure is 'Ship has sunk.' Give those back to me. Over."

"Mission success is 'The ship has sailed.' Failure is 'Ship has sunk.' Over."

"Very good. Call me when you have the air assets laid on."

"I understand, and I gave your last message to Ms. O'Hara. She was incredibly pleased to get the message. Her reply message is to tell you she very much looks forward to your safe return."

"Understood, Cauldwell out."

"Roger. Davis out."

For the next two weeks Cauldwell presided over a much reduced training schedule. The team's daily training consisted of only three hours which was broken into ninety minutes of classroom work at 0900 and another ninety minutes in the Tire House at 1400.

Immediately after their arrival, Cauldwell set out a physical training program for the four Delta Force marines. Twice each day he led them from the camp's north gate to run three, four, or five round-trips up and down the rock-strewn, half-mile road. Now he allowed them to exercise on their own while he did the same.

Cauldwell also began to pay strict attention to their diet with a heavy emphasis on vitamin and protein intake, pastries and other confections were proscribed. In addition, Cauldwell personally sounded Taps and Reveille in the team tent.

On Monday, 11 December he received a call from Rick Davis that the insertion assets were locked on and that a helo would pick them up at 1200 on 17 December to take them to Kabul where a C131 would be standing by for the 1800-mile flight to Damascus.

Immediately upon the conclusion of the call, Cauldwell walked through the gate and made the trek up the mountain to Zabi Zamani's home. He was warmly greeted by the tribal chieftain who was taken aback by the big marine's appearance.

"Ah, majah, Zamani never before see you with beard."

Cauldwell smiled for both he and his four marines had been growing facial hair for six weeks. "Well, chief, I have to make a trip to a very cold place, and I thought the beard might keep my damn face from freezing."

"It will be of help. You almost look like Muslim now except for blonde hair and skin that is white."

"Yeah, chief, an' that's what I came to talk to you about. I need something that will stain my hair and skin, make them dark and keep them that way for a while."

"Ah! We have this. We make from certain tree bark and water we use to color cloth and wool. Women who use this water have very dark hands for many days after."

"That sounds like just what I need. You have any to spare?"

"We always can provide for the majah." Zamani turned to the ever-present Hakim and spoke a few words, after instructions, the lieutenant disappeared.

Cauldwell and the tribal leader spoke about other things for some minutes before Hakim reappeared lugging a plastic water can about half full of liquid.

"Here, majah. You take this and rub on skin and on hair. You will look like large Muslim then."

The marine glanced quickly into Zamani's face to see if the man was signaling a deeper knowledge of Cauldwell's purpose. The chief's expression gave no sign of any hidden meaning.

"That's great, chief. How long will this stuff last?"

"Start to fade in maybe nine days. Stay dark maybe fourteen days if majah no have bath."

"Okay, how much do I have to put on?"

"Very small amount. With what is in this container you can look like Muslim maybe three years."

There it was again. Cauldwell was certain now Zamani had divined the essence of his purpose. "Well, thanks very much, Chief Zamani. I had better be gettin' down the mountain. I'll see you when I return."

"Very good, majah. Zamani think that fine beard keep face of majah all the time warm."

As the two shook hands the chieftain's face remained passive but there was a knowing look in his eyes.

"Good-bye, Chief Zamani."

"Good-bye, Majah Cauldwell. Stay safe. Live strong."

Cauldwell started away with the 25-pound can swinging at his side.

Damn! The man always has been a perceptive sonofabitch.

Chapter 24

Cauldwell issued the contents from two of the canvas bags to his four marines. Each man received a black, ankle-length robe called a thobe, a red and white checkered head cloth known as a shumagh, an embroidered skullcap called takiah, and a headband called the ogal.

"Okay men, I want y'all to take this gear back to your tent and practice putting everything on 'til you get so you can do it in a big hurry and in the dark. We're gonna jump in black gear with all this stuff in a chest pack. When we hit the deck in the farmlands east of the city, we'll have to bury chutes and the black gear and get this crap on in a hurry.

"I want all hands to go through the drill of slinging weapons under these robes so that they do not show like no strange bulges to stir curiosity from the natives. Sergeant Ayoubi, you will supervise."

"Aye, aye, sir."

"Hey, sir?" Corporal Garcia raised a hand.

"Yes, corporal?"

"Sir, I was wonderin' about all the other clothes we brung in them bags." The young marine pointed to the open bags in which items of Arab dress were visible.

"That stuff is of no damn use to us, Garcia. It's all white an' we're in the middle of winter. If we went into town wearin' that crap the homefolks would be on us like a gaggle of friggin' geese on five June bugs. Arabs wear white gear only in summer."

"Oh. Thanks, sir. I didn't know."

"Yeah, you an' somebody else back in DC, who damn well should have known. Now then, for the next couple days we will, among ourselves, use only our code names. See to it, there Star."

"Aye, aye, sir...Fox." Sergeant Ayoubi responded.

"Right, take yer trash to yer tent an' start practicin.' Carry on." The marines left and Cauldwell busied himself with learning to put on the unfamiliar clothing.

The robe presented little problem but the skullcap, head cloth and headband were another story, especially the ogal, which he had to adjust several times so it would effectively secure the other two items of headwear without cutting off circulation.

He then began to experiment with secreting weapons beneath the robe. His 9mm Glock and two Ka-Bar fighting knives were easily dispensed with, but he found the automatic rifle with its silencer to be problematic. He ended up slinging the weapon beneath his left armpit with the pistol grip facing forward. From a shoulder strap passing across his chest he hung a four-inch rayon strap with a quick release buckle. He put the strap through the trigger guard to the rear of the trigger and found that by putting his right hand through the gap between the third and fourth buttons of the four that ran from waist to neck, he could simultaneously seize the pistol grip and free the weapon by pushing the quick release with his thumb. To extract the rifle from beneath the robe he had to undo the third button, but he reasoned, in an operational situation he wouldn't much care about tearing that button off, so the button was in fact not an obstacle to rapid deployment of the weapon. At the same time, he contrived to suspend one of his fighting knives from the shoulder strap, so it too was readily accessible through the same button gap.

On Sunday, the sixteenth at 1400 Cauldwell held a final team briefing.

"Okay men, tomorrow Party Favors goes operational. When we move out of the drop zone, we will advance in two disassociated groups. I want Trenton and Apple with me. Y'all got that?"

"Roger that, Fox," Sergeant Fahmi replied.

"Yes, sir...Fox," said Corporal Garcia.

"Right, so that means Star and LA move together. You two understand?"

"Yes, Fox," came from Sergeant Ayoubi with a "Roger, Fox," from Corporal Gonzales.

"Very good, now listen up. In the city no one can be looked upon as a friend. All we have is each other. Our two groups will stay as close as possible to provide mutual support without appearing to have any intergroup connection.

"Now, all hands know the mission. Find, fix and eliminate Sharaf. Since we don't know what the asshole looks like, we will have to take our time. We need to insinuate ourselves into the general population that lives in or frequents the area surrounding Sharaf's hootch and the Al'Umawi Mosque, of which I'm betting he's a member since it's by far the closest. "No one other than Star and Trenton are to attempt any conversation with anyone. The rest of us will limit ourselves to the 'Allahu Akbar' phrase meaning 'God is great' and we will use it only when it appears necessary.

"All hands need to keep a firm grip on the Syrian currency that was issued to you. You each have 10,246 Syrian pounds, which is 200 US dollars. Remember that they also call these pounds lira, so if you see 'LS' before a price-tag number, they are saying, Lira Syrian, which is the same damn thing as if you saw the

British-looking pound sign. We are going to need this money to rent rooms, eat, and buy a change of clothes. Again Star and Trenton will conduct all required transactions.

"There seems to be any number of rooming houses in the general area and, if possible, our two groups will rent rooms in the same building, preferably adjoining but at the very least on the same floor.

"Once we are situated with a place to stay, we will begin to infiltrate the indigenous population and we will frequent the mosque. Star and Trenton have schooled all hands on the protocols for the prayer service and should any uncertainty be evident, follow their leads.

"We will spend several days attending services, visiting shops and generally mingling with the street folk. Whenever Star or Trenton sees an opportunity to strike up a conversation with a local, they will do so. With any luck they will be able to speak with some of the same people on several different days and reach a point where inquiries about Sharaf will not be viewed with suspicion by any one of those individuals.

"Once we can ID the bastard by sight, we will do a recon of his dwelling place to determine what forces he may have placed against us. When we have a fix on that we will continue as swiftly as possible to affect an assault during the hours of darkness and send the sonofabitch off to talk things over with Allah. We will then get the hell out of the city as fast as we can.

"During the egress after mission completion, we will move as a unit. Should anyone become separated from the group, the rally point remains the Bab Kissan Church. If there is no immediate pursuit to contend with, we will hold at the Rally Point for about twenty minutes before heading Northeast to the extract point.

"If you do become separated and the main body is being pursued or you do not make the rally point within twenty minutes, you're on your own. Should this happen, your best chance is to haul ass to the extraction point and hope you do not see a helo vanishing into the night sky.

"Should you manage to get left behind, your last resort is to get to the US Embassy on Attal'Ayyoubi Street, directly across from the embassies of Greece and Somalia. As you all know from our map studies, this will require negotiating about three klicks worth of highways and byways and will certainly prove problematic if they're looking for us.

"Gaining the embassy will not be the end of your troubles since you will have no identification to offer. Your best bet would be to say that you are an active duty service member on leave, that you were robbed, and ask to speak to the military attaché. This is the only person to whom you may disclose your identity as a Delta Force member but, even with him, stick to your story you are on leave and doing the tourist thing.

"I am the Party Favors leader. Should I be killed, captured or otherwise incapacitated, Star assumes command, followed by Trenton, LA and Apple, in that order. So, if it comes down to the last man, you'll be leadin' yerself, there, Apple. Think you can handle that?"

"Yes, Fox," Corporal Garcia answered with a broad grin.

"Awright then, we all have radio cell phones with ear plugs so if the situation calls for it, we can all go open mic on Channel 9 and talk among ourselves. I have the single satellite phone, which is our only contact with Davis in DC and our call for extract. If I go down somebody better get the damn thing.

"As for aid and logistics, we're gonna have to do the best we can with what the local economy can provide. While we're strolling about with the townsfolk I want Star and Trenton to be on the lookout for a first-aid kit we can buy. We all have our standard pressure bandages, so as a last resort, if kits are not to be had we will need to get heavy gauze rolls and adhesive tape. Y'all have any questions?"

There were none.

"Right, then we'll meet at the helo pad 1130 tomorrow. In the meantime, make sure your gear is squared away and get some good rest. Carry on."

Chapter 25

Three days before the White House Christmas party, Brandon returned to Wright-Patterson for a rest and to see Carley. They had talked every day since Brandon was released from the hospital. He first met with Ronnie, who had last-minute details to go over with him about the Washington trip. A jet would leave the base for Joint Base Andrews on Saturday morning at 9:00. A limousine was scheduled to pick up Brandon and his guest and take them to the White House.

A White House butler would be assigned to him as his personal aide. Anything needed while there should go through the aide. The president would meet with him for an unspecified amount of time, then Brandon would be on his own until the reception started. He would be just one of 250 guests, a businessman and author from Atlanta, and he was expected to introduce himself as such. Sunday morning, a limo would pick him up at 10:00 to take him back to Andrews for a jet back to Wright-Patterson. As usual, Ronnie thought of everything.

Brandon then went to see Carley. They talked for a couple hours in her office. That evening she asked him to her house to grill steaks; she claimed to fix the best twice-baked potatoes on the planet, so he accepted. Carley would pick him up at 6:00 and return him later in the evening rather than arranging for a ride through Ronnie.

Carley lived in a charming home in an exclusive gated community. They pulled into the driveway of the two-story house at the bottom of a cul-de-sac. He followed her up the lighted walkway to the stained glass front door.

"This is a really nice house."

"You haven't seen the inside yet."

"I don't need to see the inside to tell. Besides, I wouldn't expect anything less from you."

Carley blushed profusely as they entered the house. She flipped the light switch in the foyer, took her guest's coat and hung it in the closet. They moved down the hall, past the formal dining room into the kitchen.

"Would you like something to drink?"

"Sure. Water would be fine."

Carley grabbed two glasses and Brandon made his way around the family room. There were so many pictures. Carley by herself, Carley and kids, Carley at the base. There was a picture of Carley and a handsome pilot. He assumed it was her deceased husband. She looked a lot younger, and the picture was faded and torn on one end.

"That's the only picture I have of Michael. We took it only a couple of months after we got married," she said as she handed him the glass.

Brandon quickly scanned the rest of the pictures. Not one of the ex-fiancé pilot. She must really be over him.

"Would you like the grand tour?"

"Lead the way."

The three bedroom, two-and-a-half-bath home was immaculately kept. Custom made window treatments in every room, marble in the bathrooms, hardwood floors throughout.

"I should get the name and number of your interior decorator. This house is beautiful."

"This home is an exclusive Carley Hollace Interiors home," she gushed.

"You might have a second career ahead of you."

They ended up at the bedroom door.

"This is where the magic happens." She tried to keep a straight face, but couldn't hold it in. She started laughing. Her laugh was contagious and before he knew it, they were both giggling. He felt like a high schooler and it felt good. The bedroom was huge. The California King bed sat in the middle of the room. The sitting area was to the right and the master bath to the left.

"There is one more thing I want you to see."

Off the bedroom on a patio deck was a hot tub that connected to a swimming pool.

"Nice bachelorette pad," Brandon said with a wink. He knew he was coming back to life when he thought of things to do in the hot tub with Carley.

Brandon sat back and watched her as she prepared dinner. Being a great cook himself, he always enjoyed puttering in the kitchen, but he enjoyed the change of pace by having a woman cook for him. He opened a bottle of wine and poured a glass, then one more.

"You know my doctor doesn't want me to drink for three months," he said, "but one glass won't hurt."

"Okay, if you're sure," she smiled. "To your new lease on life."

Carley didn't exaggerate her cooking talents. She did a fantastic job and for Brandon to like her twice-baked potatoes better than his own, they had to be fantastic. After dinner, she wouldn't let him help with the dishes. It was getting late, but Brandon had something to talk about.

"Carley, I wonder if you would consider going to the White House Christmas party with me on Saturday."

She looked pleased but said nothing. Rejection so soon Brandon thought. If he knew, he would not have asked.

"Wait a moment," she said as she hopped up and ran to her bedroom. A few minutes later, she returned with the most beautiful red backless cocktail dress on a hanger. "Would this work?" she asked hardly able to contain her excitement.

"I take that as a yes," Brandon said.

"Absolutely, this will be the first time you've asked me on a date, and to the White House no less."

"There is a lot to this, don't you want to know the details first?" he asked.

"I can imagine."

"Here's the tricky part. We're only just getting to know one another aside from professionally. For me this has potential, but timing is wrong for both of us, and I don't want to do anything to ruin what might be. Here's the catch. The president has offered me the Lincoln Bedroom for the night. I don't know how you would feel about us sharing a room."

"Are you kidding, we can put a pillow between us. I wouldn't miss this for the world," she exclaimed.

"Then it's decided. We leave at 9:00 on Saturday morning. You better get me back to my room, I have a long day tomorrow."

"Thanks for asking me. I'm looking forward to being with you."

They agreed they were both vulnerable so they would keep their distance for the time being. Take it slow, easy, and see what happens. Carley returned her guest to the dignitary quarters, took his hand, squeezed it and said good night. Brandon planned to keep busy the next day but decided to do all those things you do before a big bash: haircut, manicure, facial, and just relax. Butterflies in his stomach prevented him from eating all day. Who would he meet? Where would it be? What would he and Carley do after the party was over? Was she feeling the same way about him he was feeling about her? His mind raced all day. When he finished his errands, he called Carley. She had a late hair appointment and lots to do to get ready, so they agreed not to meet that night.

Carley picked Brandon up at 8:00 am the next morning to go the airfield. When they arrived, they parked next to their Falcon Fan Jet. On the hour long flight, they said little but exchanged admiring looks on occasion. The thought of being a guest in the White House for the night was sinking in for both. When they landed at Joint Base Andrews, a limousine pulled alongside the jet as it parked. Staff and crew took charge seating Carley and Brandon in the car as others gathered their baggage and piled it in the trunk.

The limo pulled up to the entrance of the White House. Brandon grabbed Carley's hand and kissed her fingers. She stared out of the window like a little child. This was truly a once in a lifetime experience for them both. They were greeted at the door by Walter, their guide during their stay. He wasn't at all what Brandon expected. He was a much older man, strong and not feeble. He had a pronounced chin and he carried himself with such assurance he commanded attention and respect.

"Good morning, Mr. Powell," he greeted as he shook Brandon's hand. "Good morning, Dr. Hollace."

"Good morning," they replied.

"My name is Walter. I'll be your personal guide. Anything you need, just call for me. I will be on duty for you until you leave tomorrow. I'll be keeping you on a schedule while you're here if you don't mind. The president would like to visit. He wants to welcome you at 12:20 today. If you would follow me, I'll take you to the Lincoln Bedroom."

As they entered the building, it finally hit them. They were spending a part of Christmas at the White House with the President of the United States. The first lady chose "Home for the Holidays" as her Christmas theme and the White House was decorated to the nines. Replicas of the past presidents' homes were on display. Brandon and Carley couldn't help but stop and admire them.

"Brandon, look at this one," she cried. "Can you believe President Lincoln grew up that way?"

Brandon stopped to look.

"Please follow me." Walter said interrupting their sightseeing. "We set time aside in the day for you to take a tour of the White House, but right now, we must stick to the schedule."

"Oh, I'm sorry," Brandon apologized.

Carley and Brandon gave each other sheepish looks and continued following Walter. They walked past the beautifully decorated windows and snow-covered trees in the East Colonnade. As they made their way through the ground floor corridor, Carley and Brandon tried to read the inscriptions under the portraits of the first ladies but didn't dare stop because they didn't want to upset Walter. They had all weekend to go back, they were staying at the White House!

Walter said little on the way through the White House and Brandon asked no questions. He and Carley followed their guide in silence and took in the sights along the way. Walter led them to the second floor and into the Lincoln Bedroom. They stood at the door in awe, almost afraid to enter out of respect for the history the room held.

"This is where you will be staying. Again, if you need anything, dial the extension on the pad by the phone. After you meet with the president, if there is anything you and the missus would like to do, I'll arrange a car or anything else you may need."

"Thank you, Walter. We might want to walk around and do a little sightseeing after we see the president," Brandon suggested.

"Fine, sir, but I can arrange a car and driver if you like."

"Look at the size of that bed, Brandon, it's huge!" Carley said with excitement.

"Yes ma'am. That was President Lincoln's bed. As you may know, he was a very tall man. The bed was specially built for his size. It is eight feet long and six feet wide. You might say he invented the king size bed a long time before it was fashionable," Walter said offering a little humorous history.

Carley grabbed the coveted Christmas invitation and read it. "May happiness be yours during this season of goodwill and may the New Year bring peace on earth."

"Walter, this is a big bed, but Dr. Hollace and I are just friends. Neither of us could resist the invitation to stay here, but it's not appropriate for us to be sleeping in the same bed."

"Say no more, Mr. Powell, I fully understand. I can arrange for another bed to be brought in while you are at the reception tonight. Everything will be set when you return this evening. Now if you will excuse me, I'll leave you two alone. Just call for me if you need anything."

"Thank you," they called in unison as Walter left and closed the door behind him.

Alone at last in the Lincoln Bedroom, they stared at each other in awe. At that moment, Brandon felt something special. He was content. He kissed Carley on her forehead and hugged her tightly. He closed his eyes and listened to her breathe. Time stood still. This was the same floor Lincoln paced at night with the weight of the country on his shoulders. This was the same house Brandon saved in September. He imagined this place would be much different if they had not succeeded that day. Brandon, with Carley in his arms, was glad they had. The knock at the door interrupted his reflection time.

"Come in," Brandon said and gave Carley a squeeze before letting go.

"Good morning and welcome to the White House," greeted President Walker as he entered the room. "You must be Carley?"

"Yes, sir, Mr. President. It is such a pleasure to meet you." Carley responded with excitement.

"No, the pleasure is truly mine. Would you like the ten-cent tour?"

"That would be great," said Brandon.

"Follow me, it will have to be quick. I have a meeting at 1:00," he said leading the way, with staff following him nearby. He led them downstairs and took time to visit rooms not usually seen by the public. When the tour was almost complete, they entered the Oval Office.

"Everyone likes this room the best," he said.

He showed Brandon and Carley to the couch and asked them to be seated. He took his chair at the end of the couch and for a good fifteen minutes they chatted. Carley saw firsthand what Brandon meant when he told her of their talks at Camp David. She didn't feel like she was talking to the most powerful man in the free world. She was laughing and joking with a friend. At 1:00, there was a knock at the door and the president's secretary entered to remind him of a teleconference.

"Please see my guests are taken back upstairs," he said. "Oh, Brandon, Walter will escort you to the family quarters just before 6:00. I'd be honored if the two of you would join me and the first lady for a few minutes before the reception starts. You can walk down with us."

"That would be great, Mr. President, we're looking forward to it."

An aide escorted them back to the Lincoln Bedroom. Brandon and Carley had been to Washington many times before, so there was no need for sightseeing. They decided to take a nap and rest up a bit before the evening started. Carley slept on the Lincoln Bed and he on the couch. After a brief power nap, they dressed for the evening. Carley wore the simple floor length red dress she showed him at her house. She pulled her hair off her face into a chignon and looked even more beautiful and elegant than Brandon imagined. He always knew Carley was beautiful, but on this night, she was exquisite. Brandon had Walter bring wine for them while they waited to meet the president and first lady. They toasted to a wonderful evening as they looked out the window at the arriving crowds. Guests began filling the portico as Brandon and Carley finished their wine.

The White House Christmas reception is the largest of the fifteen parties given during the holiday season. These parties were really to display the president as well as celebrate the holidays, but politics were always at play in DC. Cars snaked through barricades and checkpoints to the East Door of the White House. As they entered, an official social aide greeted them. Unlike Walter who was a butler assigned only to Brandon, these aides were military officers who assisted the president and first lady and their guests. Guests walked down the East Colonnade enjoying the elaborate Christmas decorations finally ending in the East Room.

The East Room is the largest room in the White House, situated on the State Floor. This Christmas event was such a highly sought after party that tables were also set up in the State Dining Room as well as the adjacent Red Room. Each table was set with red damask tablecloths, roses and Santa Claus decorations. Tonight, the famous red and gold Presidential china had been set. The official White House tree was in the Blue Room. This year it was an 18-foot conifer from Pennsylvania, decorated with replicas of historic homes in all fifty states. Just beyond the tree, through the window, guests could see down the south lawn. Tourists' camera flashes illuminated the cold December air like lighting bugs in the distance.

At 20 minutes before 6:00, Walter knocked on the door.

"The president asked me to escort you to his residence."

"Show us the way." Brandon replied eagerly.

Walter led the way and Brandon followed with Carley on his arm. They arrived at the family quarters and were greeted by the Social Secretary who announced them to the president and first lady. The Walkers welcomed them.

"I'm so glad you're here. Let me introduce you to my better half."

The first lady was stunning. She wore a black and white ball gown with hand beading rippling down the back.

"It's so wonderful to meet you. The president has told me a lot about you. I must say, if I were a jealous woman, you would be in trouble. He talks about you all the time, Brandon," declared the first lady.

A butler offered them a glass of wine.

"Attention, everyone," the president began. "I would first like to thank each of you for celebrating the holidays with us. Please enjoy yourselves. My home is your home." He raised his glass. "Here's to a great evening. God bless America."

Cheers rang out in the family suite.

The staff subtly reminded the president it was time to go.

"Brandon, if you and Carley will follow me, we will begin the evening."

"Yes sir, we're ready."

The president broke tradition by entering the party with two unknowns. Since Brandon and Carley entered with the President, they were elevated to royalty status, everyone wondering just who they were. All questions would be answered soon enough. He was setting the tone for the State of the Union address a little over a month away. Unnoticed by most, a discrete camera crew followed Brandon.

The president led them to the East Room for cocktails. Brandon and Carley stood near the first couple. They gazed at the sea of celebrities. The president stopped at the top of the stairs. He pointed to a portrait of George Washington.

"That is the famous portrait of George Washington. Dolly Madison saved it from the fire in 1814 when the British burned the White House."

A voice boomed over the loudspeaker.

"Ladies and gentlemen, please join me in welcoming your President of the United States, his First Lady, and their guests, Mr. Brandon Powell and Dr. Carley Hollace."

"Enjoy the party," the president whispered as they descended the stairs.

Carley looked at Brandon and smiled, both were excited the night was underway. As they reached the bottom of the stairway, several hundred pairs of eyes were on them. The president and first lady took their place in the reception line to welcome their guests, and officially, Brandon and Carley were welcomed first, followed by the guests in line who had been arriving and waiting for over an hour. Once through the line, Brandon and Carley wandered around the ballroom, sipped on wine and took it all in. A short stocky man with a heavy Southern accent smacked Brandon on the back.

"You must be somebody especially important. Let me introduce myself. I'm Roy Alexander, CFP."

Roy Alexander had a round cherub face and parted his gray hair on the right side. When he laughed, his whole face turned bright red, and he wheezed like he spent the last 35 years smoking two packs of Marlboros a day. He was holding two glasses of wine and when he finished one, he placed it on the tray of a passing waiter and started on the other.

"CFP?" Brandon asked.

"Certified Financial Planner. If you have money, and I know you do, or you wouldn't be hanging out with the pres. I'll show you how to make it work for you. What's your name?"

"Brandon Powell. And this is Dr. Hollace."

"Carley." Carley grabbed Roy's hand and shook it.

"So, how do you know the president?"

Brandon knew the question would come up, but he didn't expect it so soon. He hadn't worked out an answer.

"Well, we go way back" Yeah about three months, he thought.

"How far back?"

Carley interrupted. "Honey, they are playing our song."

Brandon looked at Carley. "Oh yes, it is our song. Excuse me Mr. Alexander, but they are playing our song." Brandon took Carley's glass of wine and handed it to Mr. Alexander. "Can you hold that for a minute, we'll be right back."

"No problem," he said. "Any friend of the president is a friend of mine."

Brandon and Carley made their way to the dance floor.

"That was a close one. I love a woman who can think on her feet."

"Well, thank you. I just hope you can keep up."

After cocktails, social aides directed the president and his guests to the head table for dinner. The first lady sat on one side, and Brandon and Carley on the other. Directly across the table were the vice president and his wife. Brandon couldn't believe he was in the presence of such company. Only when he felt Carley's hand on his knee did he realize he was shaking it. Whenever he was nervous, he would shake his knee. It was a habit he picked up as a child, but he learned to control the habit in public. The remaining tables quickly filled with dinner guests.

At the end of the meal, the US Army Strolling Strings entered and played around the tables. The dinner was crowned with frozen dulce de leche topped with tiny chocolate Christmas trees. The president leaned over to Brandon.

"Do you mind if I ask Carley to dance?"

"Of course not, sir," Brandon replied.

Carley looked at the first lady.

"Have fun," she encouraged. Carley and the president made their way to the dance floor. Once they started, the first lady asked Brandon to dance and soon everyone joined in. The next dance, the president switched partners with Brandon.

"Did I tell you how beautiful you look?" Brandon whispered to Carley.

"Yes, you did, but thank you again. Did I mention that you look great in your tuxedo?"

"No, but now you have, thanks."

He held her close.

"Do you get the feeling we're being watched?"

"Absolutely, so don't step on my toes," she chuckled then squeezed him tighter.

They danced nonstop for half a dozen songs before they had to sit for a break. The president took the opportunity to excuse himself to work the room. Brandon sat gazing at Carley. They were both speechless, taking in the enormity of the night. After a rest, they decided to mingle.

"Let's walk the room," he suggested.

"Yeah, lets mingle with the rich and powerful," she replied with a sparkle in her eyes.

Chief Justices were hobnobbing with athletes. Cabinet members schmoozing with movie stars. Brandon and Carley worked the room well and when asked, "What do you do?" Carley was always quick to mention Brandon was a writer.

"Well," she piped in, "he is only the most handsome, brilliant writer in the room."

She gave the name of his book and short bits of information to spark interest since there were a lot of lawyers present. The couple worked the room like professionals.

As they talked, an aide stepped up to Brandon.

"Mr. Powell, the president would like you to join him at the table for a few minutes. Would you please come with me?" he whispered.

"Sure," he said as he took Carley's hand and followed the aide. As they approached the table the president and first lady stood.

"It's past our bedtime so we're going upstairs. You have a good time. Let Walter know if you need anything. I'll see you in the morning for breakfast," the president invited. Then he and the first lady excused themselves for the evening. The orchestra was still playing so Brandon asked Carley to dance again, and they continued until they played the last song. The White House party was over, but the evening was too enchanting to end yet.

Years before, Brandon discovered a great night club called Diversite while in DC on a business trip. Brandon asked Walter how to get there, and true to form, a limo was summoned. They arrived at the club after midnight and found there were only a few people there. They enjoyed another glass of wine and began to dance. They were still euphoric from the White House experience and everything seemed fantastic, but it was lights out for the club at 1:00. Exhausted and deliriously happy, they piled into their limo and returned to the White House to end a perfect evening. Walter met them at the door and escorted them to their room.

"I think you will find everything in order, sir, but if there is anything else you need, I am on duty all night, just call for me," Walter announced as they climbed the stairs to the second floor.

"Thanks for the limo, Walter. We went out for more dancing, it was great."

"You are most welcome, sir. Here we are," he said as he opened the door. "Would you like to check the room to see if everything is in order," Walter continued as he pointed to the extra bed Brandon requested. Brandon made eye contact and nodded with approval.

"That will be all, we've had a long night."

"Great, sir. The president wants you to join him for a private breakfast at 8:30. I'll come for you then, good night," he said as he closed the door.

"I had such an enjoyable time," Carley said as she took off her jewelry.

"Let me help you with that," Brandon said and unhooked her necklace. He could smell the perfume on her shoulder. She turned to face him.

"Thank you for inviting me."

Brandon said nothing. The room was silent and they both enjoyed the company.

"Why don't we change into something more comfortable," she suggested.

"Alright." Brandon searched his bag. There were no pajamas.

"You probably won't believe this, but I didn't bring pajamas. I rarely wear them."

"That presents a problem," she said with a smile.

"It's okay. I'll sleep in a t-shirt and I'll keep my pants on."

"Well, this is the Lincoln Bedroom. I'm not going to insist you sleep in that other bed. This is a big bed and I'm okay with you sleeping in it too if you like.

We can put a pillow between us. We are both grown adults," she said with a devilish smile.

"I will never get the chance to do it again, so I guess I better take you up on it."

"Never get a chance again to sleep in the Lincoln bed or sleep with me?" she laughed.

"I don't know how to answer that one."

"Make sure you answer carefully, Mr. Powell."

She changed into her nightwear and joined Brandon on the large bed; she in pajamas, he in his t-shirt and pants. They sat on the bed, legs crossed, too thrilled to consider sleep, even though it was two o'clock in the morning. For the next hour, they reminisced about the evening, comparing who they met, who they saw and the excitement of being with the president.

"Brandon, I want you to know I had a wonderful time this evening. I also want you to know I was proud to be with you and thanks for asking me," Carley said as she leaned forward and kissed him.

"Thank you. I did too. It was fantastic. I enjoyed being with you. I want to spend more evenings with you in my arms."

"Thank you. Now this is not going to be a therapy session and I may be guilty of breaking confidentiality between my personal side and my professional side. But I want to tell you I've gotten over my failed engagement. Have you gotten over Grace?"

"Yes, I have."

"I think one day she's going to realize the grass is not always greener somewhere else. She is going to realize what a tragic mistake she made. I think someday she may be pounding on your door asking for forgiveness, offering to change if you take her back. Now having made those observations, would you go back?"

"She won't change. I'm moving on with my life. Besides even if she did, if I'm becoming involved with another lady, I wouldn't consider it," Brandon said.

"I've not only enjoyed this night, but I've enjoyed getting to know you before tonight. You were the most compassionate person in my life when I returned from Paris. You helped me through some challenging times. You've been a perfect gentleman. I admire your values. The State of the Union is about a month away and I'm wondering if I will ever see you again after the news of Flight 3911 breaks."

"I've thought of the same thing. It has been fun and we both have been in self-protection mode. You are someone I would like to get to know. Maybe we should see where the next month takes us."

"Are you willing to let your guard down?" she asked.

"Yes, but it's been less than two months for both of us. Are we ready to explore a relationship? We are talking about a relationship, aren't we?"

"I think that would be nice, and yes, I want to get to know you," she said.

"In counseling you learned a lot about my needs. Have I been out of line?"

"No. I've only heard your side, but the things you asked are only common sense and really should not even come up in a committed relationship. Personally and professionally, I'd say Grace has been out of line and inconsiderate. That's what worries me. Someday, she may realize her mistake and when she does, I don't want to be the one hurt."

"I understand. Let's just take it slow and see where it takes us."

"Well, starting right now, we are going to sleep in the same bed, practice self-control and go to sleep."

"That's what I call taking it slow," he said. He leaned toward her and kissed her on the forehead.

"The sun will be up soon, maybe we should try to at least grab a nap before it's time to get up. Now, where's the pillow to put between us?" she asked with a devilish grin.

"Okay, Okay. I'll be a gentleman."

Brandon got up, found a pillow the size of a football and returned to bed.

"Carley, thank you for a wonderful…"

Her kiss interrupted his thanks. This time, he kissed her back. He felt a passion he hadn't felt in months. He kissed her one last time and held her close. Their bodies molded as they held each other. He didn't want to let her go. He felt complete and fell asleep with her in his arms. The knock at the door woke them.

"Mr. Powell?" A voice said.

Brandon got up and answered the door.

"Good morning, Mr. Powell. The president will be ready to see you in an hour."

"Thank you, Walter."

They rose quickly and prepared to meet the man. The morning after they smiled at one another continuously as they put their things together. After breakfast, they would be heading to Andrews to return to Wright-Patterson. Walter returned to take them to the private dining room of the First Family. There was only the president, Brandon, and Carley. The president wanted a few minutes alone before they left. Brandon asked how things were going in the effort to get those responsible for 9/11. The president couldn't talk about it, but the smile he gave Brandon indicated there was progress being made.

"I stay up at night trying to visualize what was in your minds when you took over that airliner. I'm even more terrified of what happened on Flight 93. What were those people thinking? It just haunts me," said the president.

"I still have dreams also. But sir, it all happened so fast. There was no time to be scared. I don't ever remember being really concerned we would crash. It was such a peaceful frame of mind at the time we started the attack. It was as if we knew we would take over the plane."

"Tell me, Brandon," the president asked as he sipped his coffee, "were there any concerns you might not be able to land even if you got in the cockpit?"

"Not really. I've been flying for 25 years. The basics are the same, straight and level flight. It was just a much bigger airplane. I was confident, but nervous, that I could get down with help from the ground. Chief Pilot MacLuskey, the guy who talked me down, did a fantastic job. I made a smooth landing. Most on board said it was a great landing."

"That's what I've been told. You only have a month of being a private person left. Brandon, do you know what's in store for you when the world knows what you did?"

"I know things are going to change, but right now I can't imagine how."

"The TV talk shows, magazines and book and movie deals. You're going to be another real American hero. People everywhere are going to recognize you. I suggest you ask your liaison to arrange to meet with some literary agents and hire yourself a good one. When the cameras zoom in on you after I introduce you, your life will change. Be ready for it."

"Thanks for the warning. I'll do my best."

"Now Carley, please forgive us. We have been ignoring you, but I wanted to prepare him for the days ahead."

"No problem, sir. I've heard things Brandon hasn't mentioned to me. It has been informative, and I am honored to be here."

"How did you like last evening?" the president asked her.

"Most delightful. It was the experience of a lifetime and I am so thrilled Brandon asked me to join him."

"Mr. President, I also enjoyed it and I appreciate including me on the guest list," said Brandon.

"Don't mention it, Brandon. I want you to feel free to get word to me if there is anything I can do for you."

Breakfast was cut short when an aide entered to inform the president of a scheduled meeting. Brandon, Carley, and the president said their goodbyes. The couple returned to the Lincoln Bedroom to gather their bags. When they entered the room and closed the door, Carley put her arms around Brandon and kissed him.

"What was that for?" he asked.

"Oh, I don't know, maybe its infatuation, but I really like you."

"I'm beginning to like you too, Dr. Hollace. But you have me at a disadvantage. You know all my likes and dislikes and most of all my secrets.

"You'll get to know mine. Remember, I am a doctor in these matters. I know we are compatible."

"Then you must remember I am attracted to aggressive women, and you are playing the role well so far."

"This is no role, what you see is what you get," she said smiling again.

Walter knocked on the door.

"We'll continue this later," he promised and opened the door. "Walter, can you take our picture?"

Carley handed him the camera. Brandon grabbed Carley around her waist and held her close. They took one last look around as Walter snapped their photo. At Joint Base Andrews, their jet was waiting and with little delay, their bags were placed on board by an aide. They climbed aboard the jet and in just a few minutes they were off the ground, heading for Wright-Patterson. I could get used to this, Brandon thought.

Their sleepless night began to catch up with them, and as soon as they hit 35,000 feet, they were both asleep. The jolt of the landing woke them up. Brandon got the bags from the captain and walked Carley to her car.

"Brandon, I had an extraordinary weekend. I think it's safe to say that was the best date I've ever had," Carley said.

"I hope so. It's not every day I invite a lady to join me at the White House," Brandon joked. Carley laughed, "Too bad I can't tell anyone about it."

"You can always talk to me," he said.

"If this is what you do on a first date, I can't wait to see what happens on our second date," Carley said.

Chapter 26

At 1201, 17 December the five members of Party Favors were airborne in a CH53 and the big helo was headed for Kabul. They landed at 1322 in the executive terminal, which was now secured by US forces, and immediately enplaned on a C131 waiting with all four propellers turning.

Upon entering the aircraft Cauldwell went forward, entered the cockpit and handed a three-by-five index card to the pilot, an Air Force lieutenant colonel.

"Hey, sir, these are the coordinates for the drop zone. How high are we gonna be comin' in?"

"I was planning on 32,000."

"Thirty-two would be plenty good enough, sir."

"Roger that, 32 it is."

After the aircraft climbed to altitude, leveled off and swung westbound, Cauldwell huddled with his marines.

"Listen up, men. We're gonna bail at 32,000 so I fully expect to hear the plaintive cry of the Ga-Ga Bird."

"The Ga-Ga Bird?" questioned Corporal Gonzales.

Cauldwell looked at Corporal Gonzales with a grin. "Yeah, you know, its call goes this, Ga-Ga-Gaddamn, it's cold up here!"

Everyone laughed.

"Now then, had it been possible, I would have had us do a HAHO, open up early and fly them 'chutes around a bit, but for obvious reasons that isn't possible so it's a HALO which in the dark will serve to greatly increase the pucker factor.

"Back there by the cargo hatch you see five sets of oxygen replenishment gear alongside the stack of 'chutes. When we're twenty seconds out, I want everyone to hyperventilate so that we can easily hold our breaths 'til we're low enough to breathe. All hands will adopt the standard spread eagle freefall position so we hit terminal velocity as soon as possible, that should be 14 seconds for me, 15 for Star, Trenton and LA, and 16 for Apple's scrawny little ass.

213

"You've all done this before so y'all know what it feels like when you hit TV, falling sensation disappears and you're flying. At TV we'll have fallen about two K. We'll be goin' down at about 125 miles per hour or 176 feet per second. That translates into five and one-half seconds for every thousand feet.

"When we hit TV, we'll be about 28 K off the deck. I want all hands to count off 150 seconds before pulling the rip. This should have us open at about 15 or 16 hundred feet.

"When your 'chute fills, get on the risers hard and go down in as tight a left-hand turn as you can manage, any straight-line gliding is gonna create too much separation.

"We're comin' down in farmland and you'll have no deck reference until you're under a hundred feet so keep a good count or the rest of us will be buryin' you right where you hit. Any questions?"

Silence.

"Right. Sit back an' enjoy the flight men. There are box lunches forward on the deck just aft of the starboard side firewall. Help yourselves. Carry on."

A little less than two hours later Cauldwell happened to glance through a port side portal and was surprised to see two FA18 Hornets with marine markings.

"Hey men, we have a couple of escorts off the port wing."

"And two more on this side, Fox," Sergeant Fahmi chimed in.

At that moment, the crew chief appeared. "Hey, sir. Just to let you know, we crossed into Iranian air space and we'll have fighter escorts the rest of the way. We're going to deviate to the northwest to enter Iraqi air space over Kurdish territory then cut southwest for Damascus when we hit the Syrian border. We'll pick up fresh escorts over Iraq."

"Roger, thanks for the info, sergeant. Give us a heads up when we're 30 minutes from the drop zone."

"Roger that, sir. Will do."

Cauldwell stretched out along a section of the canvas bench seats and went to sleep, while one by one the remaining team members followed suit.

When Cauldwell was awakened by the crew chief's voice, his watch showed 2100. Looking out the window he could see the green, starboard running lights of two fighter jets.

"Awright, all hands aft to the cargo hatch. Check gear and strap on those 'chutes."

The five men shuffled rearward and began donning parachute packs with practiced ease.

"Okay, buddy up and check each other. Star, when you're done, check me."

"Aye, aye, Fox."

When all were in readiness they stood in silence, each alone with his thoughts.

"Hey, sir," the crew chief called out, "three minutes to drop zone."

"Roger. Give me 30 seconds out."

"Roger, sir."

"Okay men, grab the oxygen and turn on the tank valves."

All hands complied.

The crew chief pulled his headset mike away from his mouth. "Thirty seconds, sir."

"Roger. Okay, everybody suck on the gas."

As the hydraulic system whined and the cargo ramp opened beneath the aircraft's tail, the five Marines covered mouths and noses with the clear plastic masks and began a series of deep, rapid breaths.

The crew chief began the count down, "Ten..nine..eight..."

When he hit the number five, Cauldwell barked, "Okay, single file on the ramp. Go, go, GO!"

In swift succession the Marines pulled goggles over their eyes and dove headfirst into the blackness with Cauldwell jumping last.

Freezing air numbed his face as he plummeted, face down and with arms and legs spread wide. Within 14 seconds the falling sensation disappeared as he reached terminal velocity, and he began his count.

One an' two an' three an'...

Far below to his left front he could see a dome-shaped, yellowish white halo and knew this was the light cast by the city of Damascus.

One forty-eight an' 149 an' 150.

Cauldwell pulled the ripcord, heard the chute deploy, and was jerked up hard as the nylon wing filled. Immediately he began working the left-side risers so the parachute descended in a tight, left-hand spiral.

Comin' down like a maple-tree seed in October.

Fifty feet below and 20 yards to his right he momentarily faced west, he could barely discern another 'chute also effecting the same turning maneuver. He began to peer down intently, searching for the ground. He never saw it, but what he did see that helped him prepare for the shock of landing was the collapse of the 'chute to his north. Cauldwell leveled his 'chute into linear flight and tried to run to a stop, but the furrows left by a Syrian plow were too many and too deep. He fell on his face after three strides. There was only a slight breeze blowing, but it was enough to drag him ten yards.

Black hearted son of a bitch!

He came to a stop with the lines still pulling. Holding risers in each hand he fought the drag and came to his knees. He leaned back hard, hauling on the lines to create slack, then leaped to his feet, charged forward and dived on top of the 'chute, arms and legs flailing to collapse the wing entirely.

Finally, with the expanse of black material lying inert upon the newly seeded ground, Cauldwell shucked out of the harness, dropped his chest bag and a collapsible entrenching tool. Working swiftly on his knees he dug a shallow hole; stopping when he thought the dimensions to be sufficient.

Leaping to his feet, he stripped off his black gear and threw all, including gloves and goggles into the hole. From the bag he withdrew Arabic clothes and after positioning his shoulder strap, automatic rifle and fighting knife, he donned the costume hurriedly.

Once satisfied, the bag and 'chute also went into the hole. He spent a few seconds stomping on the gear to be buried, making it as compact as possible, then set to work with the e-tool covering everything with a six-inch layer of dirt. He was doing his best to reconstruct the furrows.

Must be winter wheat in here so they won't find this stuff in the spring harvest. But they'll sure as hell find it next time they plow.

He began to move slowly to the northwest.

Within three minutes he heard shoveling and closed upon the sound until he could see Corporal Garcia's bowed back. The corporal was on his knees working with his e-tool.

Cauldwell dropped to one knee and called out in a stage whisper, "Hey, Apple."

The Marine dropped his shovel and whirled about. Cauldwell heard the metallic click of a round being chambered as the young corporal peered into the darkness.

"That you, Trenton?"

"No, it's Fox. I'm comin' to ya."

"Roger, Fox, come ahead."

Cauldwell straightened and approached the still kneeling Garcia, smiling approvingly when he saw the automatic weapon still trained upon him.

"You 'bout done, there Apple?"

"Yes, Fox, just finished."

"Right, well let's be movin' northwest an' see can we collect Trenton."

They moved but a dozen paces when a hushed voice pierced the night. "You guys got Party Favors?"

"Yeah," Cauldwell answered. "We got two of 'em – Fox an' Apple." He stared hard in the direction to find the voice but could see nothing.

"Okay, move slowly to your right front."

Cauldwell and Garcia stepped slowly through the loose dirt for about ten yards before they saw a figure loom between two furrows and with a weapon at the ready. Sergeant Fahmi was arrayed in his Arabic costume and to Cauldwell he looked like the epitome of a Bedouin Sheik.

"Very good, Trenton. Let's put away the weapons and bury these three e-tools."

The shovels were laid in a shallow grave and covered with boot pushed earth.

"Right. Now let's see if we can find the rally point."

The trio, three abreast, began moving steadily west toward the lights of Damascus. After some 1000 meters they entered a fig-tree grove and turned northwest, finding easy footing between the rows. Within 500 meters they halted at the northern edge of the grove. Directly ahead vehicular traffic passed left and right over a main thoroughfare. To their left the road formed a traffic circle around an ornamented garden they recognized as Dawar Al'Matar Square.

"Right men, this is Ibn'Asaker Street and right across the road," he pointed, "is our rally point, the Bab Kissan Church. First, we'll use the streetlights to check each other out an' make sure we look right."

This was quickly done with Sergeant Fahmi making minor adjustments to Garcia's head cloth.

"Now let's wander on over to the square an' grab a bench while we wait for Star and LA to make an appearance." Cauldwell started off.

The three marines walked west, crossed Airport Road and entered the Square. Even here, on the very fringes of the city it was obvious celebration was the order of the day and great multitudes were participating. People were everywhere in groups of two or more, standing, walking or sitting, all were engaged in animated conversations and laughter erupted from many quarters with frequency.

As the strike force members moved along a well maintained, gravel path toward an unoccupied north facing bench, Sergeant Fahmi stayed a pace in front. As they encountered individuals and groups proceeding in the opposite direction, Fahmi gave the greetings in Arabic so Cauldwell and Garcia had only to bow and smile in passing.

They seated themselves and sat very erect, not using the backrest to accommodate the positioning of the weapons beneath their robes. Looking north and just a little to the east across Ibn'Asaker the church was in plain view as was about 400 meters of the wide thoroughfare as it ran Northeast along the edge of the agricultural land whence Sergeant Ayoubi and Corporal Gonzales must come.

The three had been on the bench but seven minutes when they saw two robed figures emerge from the far Northeast edge of the fig grove and begin angling west across Ibn'Asaker in the direction of the church.

Cauldwell grunted. "Awright, there's Star and LA. Let's get close enough to communicate, but remember, we don't know these guys."

Cauldwell, Fahmi and Garcia rose and began moving Northeast pausing several times in the street to allow the passage of vehicles. Behind the church and stretching about a hundred yards to both the north and west was an area of flower gardens and manicured lawns where hordes of people were moving about. After making eye contact with Sergeant Ayoubi, Cauldwell led his contingent into the green space and halted at the edge of a flower bed surrounded by a spiked steel railing.

As they pretended to observe the resplendent botanical offerings, Ayoubi and Gonzales arrived and began to do likewise from five feet away along the railing.

"Listen up Trenton," Cauldwell said in a muffled voice, "talk to Star in Arabic. Tell him we're goin' out the north side of this garden an' heading northwest to Ali Aj'Jammal Street. We'll hang a left an' follow it to the intersection where it becomes Midhat Pacha Souq, then we'll turn right an' head straight north to the mosque. We'll wander about the environs of the mosque an' try to find a couple rooms to rent. Ya got all that?"

"Got it, Fox." Sergeant Fahmi casually moved a couple of feet closer to Ayoubi. He then extended an arm, pointed to the center of the flower bed and began speaking in Arabic as though he were explaining something to Cauldwell. After a time, Ayoubi made a cryptic response as if commenting to Gonzales.

"Okay, Fox, he understands the game plan."

"Right, then let's get goin'."

Separated by several yards, the two groups moved off.

Finding Ali Aj'Jammal was something of a testudinal process requiring the navigation of a myriad of twisting roads and lanes. Progress was also impeded by avenues leading in the desired direction almost devoid of people and these Cauldwell refused to take. It required thirty-two minutes to arrive at the intersection on Midhat Pacha Souq, and another twelve to arrive at the Al'Umawi Mosque.

Having made a positive fix on the mosque, they began to meander among the throngs of celebrants while moving casually west and south.

Along Al Hamidyeh Souq Sergeant Ayoubi, having taken the lead, paused before a bazaar on the north side of the east-west road and tugged thoughtfully at his right ear, the signal for Cauldwell's group to close.

With all hands fingering beads, cloth bolts and robes under the watchful eyes of the leathery-faced proprietor, Ayoubi whispered, "Fox, there's a room rental sign across the street. I'll see if I can get one for me an' LA. If I nod when I come out, it means I was successful. If I rub my nose, it means there's another to be had for you guys."

"Right, Star. Carry on."

Ayoubi and Gonzales crossed the street and disappeared into the four-story building. Fourteen minutes later the two emerged and Ayoubi nodded curtly, then rubbed his nose. Ayoubi and Gonzales faced each other and began a conversation while loitering near the entrance pathway to the rooming house. As Cauldwell and his two marines passed, Ayoubi whispered, "We got 315, 317 is vacant. The two rooms share a head."

Sergeant Fahmi led the way and did all the talking. In short order, room 317 was secured, and a third bed was installed. Payment was made for two weeks in advance, something that obviously pleased the landlord greatly.

When the proprietor departed Cauldwell inquired, "So Trenton, what the hell was all that? Seemed like a long conversation just to be rentin' a damn room."

"Well Fox, he's a very inquisitive guy. I told him we were from Aleppo in the north and here to arrange a company exhibit at the Damascus International Fair in the spring. He seemed satisfied with that."

"Okay. Let's see what kind of a head we've gotta share with Star and LA."

The white-tiled, interconnected bathroom was spacious containing sink, commode, shower, and a claw-foot tub with discolored enamel showing evidence of many years of hard water, iron pipes, or a combination of the two. Cauldwell tried the door leading to the adjoining room and found it locked from the other side.

"Huh! Not very trusting of our two neighbors," he reached up and turned the shower on full, then beckoned the other two to close in. With water sounds masking his words, Cauldwell spoke quickly. "We need to get Star and LA in here ASAP for a bit of a conference. Trenton, you sally forth, give 'em the word, an' get back in here after a reasonable interval."

"Aye, aye, Fox."

Sergeant Fahmi left the head while Cauldwell, after turning off the shower, led the way back into the room and took a seat on the edge of a bed, motioning Garcia to remain silent.

Several minutes passed before they heard footsteps in the hall, followed by the opening and closing of the door to room 315. They continued to wait in silence until their own door opened to admit Fahmi.

Signaling silence, Cauldwell moved once again into the head. As soon as Fahmi and Garcia had joined him, he closed the door, turned on the shower, and rapped lightly on the hatch connecting with 315. The bolt clicked, the door opened, and Sergeant Ayoubi entered, followed closely by Corporal Gonzales. Cauldwell motioned for Ayoubi to shut the door, then began speaking.

"So far, so good boys. Now then, we must get Star and Trenton out there before the kiosks close. We need soap, toothbrushes, toothpaste, deodorant, and two battery powered transistor radios. Each go to different shops and buy only one of each item, except the toothbrushes. Star, you buy two, an' Trenton, you get three.

"We also need to think about robes and head cloths, but you can't be buying different sizes at the same time. If you can, get clothes for yourselves tonight. Tomorrow we'll have the two of you make purchases for another team member, then Trenton can make another trip to get gear for me. You guys got that?"

"Roger that, Fox."

"Roger, Fox."

"Okay, get goin', but since we'll have the rooms manned, leave your weapons here."

"Aye, aye, Fox." Sergeant Ayoubi paused and addressed Fahmi. "Don't pay the price anyone quotes. They love to barter, and the haggle is an expected part of the process. Coughing up the asking price will create suspicion."

"Yeah right, I got it."

Shortly after midnight Fahmi returned bearing a small shopping bag and a bulky, butcher-paper package tied with string. Wordlessly, he deposited his burdens on one of the beds and began removing items from the bag. Two cakes of bar soap taped together and sold as one item, three toothbrushes of red, green, and yellow, a tube of Colgate toothpaste, four D batteries, and two compact transistor radios.

Seeing the radios, Cauldwell immediately grabbed one, inserted two batteries, fired the instrument up and began to adjust the tuner. When he struck a station playing a wailing instrumental, he turned up the volume and set the radio on the deck about a foot from the hallway door.

"Now then, boys," he said in a muffled voice, "we can talk quietly without being overheard from the other side of our damn door. Apple, slam two batteries into the other one, find the same station, an' go show LA where to put it. Keep it just beyond the latch side of the door so Star doesn't smash the damn thing when he comes in."

"Aye, aye, Fox." The corporal hastened to comply.

"So, what's in the parcel, Trenton?"

"A change of clothes for me, Fox, thobe and shumagh, robe, an' head cloth."

"Yeah, I know what the friggin' words mean, Trenton. Anyway, ya did well. We can only hope the same can be said for Star."

Sometime later they heard Ayoubi return. Cauldwell called another meeting in the head. Ayoubi had also foraged successfully and had procured a change of clothes both for himself and Gonzales, telling the shopkeeper the second set was for his younger brother.

"Listen up, men. We are two blocks north of Mu'Awia Street and Sharaf's lair. Tomorrow, in two groups we will begin to insinuate ourselves into the local population. We need to have them become accustomed to seeing us, so they begin to feel like they know us. To that end, all hands will report to the mosque for prayers at least three times each day. Also, each group will take the time to stroll along Mu'Awia and get a hard fix on 461.

"Let Star and Trenton do all the talking, the rest of us will just bow, smile and throw in an Allahu Akbar if absolutely required. Star and Trenton will start trying to identify candidates for friendly personal relationships. We are going to need someone to point out the asshole Sharaf for us."

"In any event, we'll proceed slowly. We have 22 days to get the job done and my guess is that it will take all that time to get properly set up.

"Star and Trenton are obviously going to be our main field agents for getting an ID on Sharaf. They will need to operate individually and alone without the pressure of herding the rest of us around and constantly guarding against someone addressing us directly and discovering we can't speak a damn word of Arabic. When they operate alone, the automatic weapons will be left here and under the continuous supervision of one or more of the remaining three of us. Any questions or comments?"

There were none.

"Awright then, men, carry on. Wash up an' get some sleep."

For the next two weeks the marines of Strike Force Party Favors tried to become known members of the local community. The intelligence gathering was shouldered by Sergeants Ayoubi and Fahmi who quickly discovered Hassan Sharaf was regarded as a demi-god and it was well known that he played a role in several bomb attacks against US installations and personnel. It was also apparent that there was a great protective cooperative among those indigenous to the area. Thus, neither of the Arabic-speaking operatives was able to fix a person and time which they considered safe for asking that Sharaf be pointed out.

They knew he attended prayers at the mosque, but surveillance of his house proved fruitless as seven men always emerged together to attend prayers. Moreover, scrutiny of the group was equally unavailing as by their actions and deportment, none of the seven ever provided a clue as to who among them was preeminent.

After a full month of constant surveillance just before noon on Monday 14 January Sergeant Fahmi returned from his morning patrol and indicated they should hold another head conference as soon as Star got back from his peregrinations.

At 1220 Team Party Favors assembled with a radio playing in each room and the shower gushing water.

"Listen up, men," Cauldwell began, Trenton has something to report. Carry on, there Trenton."

"Aye, aye, Fox. Well, guys, we finally got a break. One of the kiosk owners whom I've been chatting up for a full month now, let it slip the Imam at the mosque is going to have Sharaf himself address the faithful tomorrow at final prayers to update all with Allah's plans for 2002."

"Outstanding!" Cauldwell exclaimed, more loudly than he intended. "This is perfect. We are flat ass running out of time on our end to identify Sharaf before the due date for our mission to end. We can all attend the service and burn that scumbag's face into our memory banks. Start gettin' your heads around the fact we are going to move on this asshole at 2300 on Wednesday.

"I'd go tomorrow after we've identified the prick, but there'll be way too many folks surrounding him after he speaks. Normally everybody around here packs it in at 2200, and we know Taps goes in Sharaf's shit house at 2230 on a normal night."

"If we can get in and out in 15 minutes or less, that will give us plenty of time to make the extraction point under cover of darkness and bring the pickup helo in by strobe light.

"I'll get on the satellite phone today and let Davis know what's up so he can lay on the logistics for us. Trenton, Apple and I will leave 30 minutes before prayers. Star, you, and LA wait ten, then follow. Any questions?"

There were none and the two team sections left for their own rooms.

Twenty minutes later Cauldwell brought out the satellite phone and tried to call Washington.

"Sonofabitch! I can't get a signal in here. I'm gonna have to get up on the roof. Trenton you come with me and once we know the patio up there is clear, you guard the stairs behind me."

"Aye, aye, Fox."

"Apple go through the head an' get the other two in here. I want everybody together in one room with a rag head talker in case someone comes to the door. I have never had any fondness for the way our esteemed landlord continuously oils his way around this place. I don't trust 'im any farther than I can piss over the gunwale in a force-five gale."

When Ayoubi and Gonzales appeared, Cauldwell signaled Fahmi to proceed. The sergeant led the way to the end of the corridor, up a set of stairs to the fourth floor, then up another staircase to the open-air patio on the roof. A quick scan showed the area to be clear and Fahmi retreated to take up station halfway down the stairs.

On the roof, the satellite phone picked up a signal immediately and Cauldwell pushed the Send button.

A three second pause ensued before Cauldwell heard a ring on the other end, a click, and finally "Davis here."

"Hey, Rick, Cauldwell. We're gonna finally launch the boat at 2300 on Wednesday. You ready to copy?"

"Ready. Been worried about you since we haven't heard from you."

"Yeah, been slow sailing here, but we know our timetable for arrival. Okay, the coordinates for the extract point are 3-5-3-9, slash, 3-0-7-2. You copy?"

"Roger, 3-5-3-9, slash, 3-0-7-2."

"That's a solid. Extract time will be 0130, local. You copy?"

"Roger, 0130 local."

"That's a solid. The LZ is a plowed field. We'll fire up a strobe at 0125 You copy?"

"Roger. Strobe at 0125."

"That's a solid. I'll call ya as soon after boat launch as I can. That is all."

Cauldwell depressed the Off button and the phone disappeared beneath his robe.

On Tuesday 15 January 2002, the five marines were kneeling on their prayer mats when the Imam made an announcement, extended a hand and intoned the name Hassan Sharaf.

The black robed figure ascending the podium was about five-nine and built like a fire hydrant. His thick, meticulously trimmed beard was heavily oiled and reflected the light in waves of shimmers as he moved. When Hassan Sharaf began to speak, strong white teeth flashed from the recesses of his luxuriant facial hair.

His harangue lasted forty-seven minutes.

Back in the communal head at their rooming house, Corporal Garcia spoke first. "Jeeze! I swear to God, I thought de damn guy was never gonna shut the hell up!"

Cauldwell chuckled. "Yeah, it was a bit long, still it gave us plenty of time to memorize that sleazy-lookin' face of his. What the hell was he sayin' anyway, Star?"

"Well, Fox, most of it was a diatribe directed against the West in general and US in particular. He referred to the 9/11 attacks and said a much greater evil would soon befall the American pigs."

"Yeah well, we're gonna have something to say about that." Cauldwell snorted in disgust. "Now tomorrow during daylight I want Star and Trenton to make separate excursions along Mu'Awia and recon Sharaf's hovel. Make sure nothing's changed, and we must be sure the maggot returns and stays in there after evening prayers. So, once the scumbag comes home from the mosque, you two make continuous passing patrols and make it so we always have eyes on the house. Once you see lights out at about 2230, haul ass back here and we'll move out. All hands will fire up their radio and insert earpieces.

"Everyone knows their assignments. The two exterior guards, front and rear, are the responsibility of Apple and LA, respectively. Once we know the guards have been eliminated, I'll take the front door with Apple. Simultaneously, Star and Trenton will breach the back door. LA will remain outside and guard the avenues of approach from along Mu'Awia in case anyone tries to respond to noise.

"There shouldn't be any noise since our weapons are silenced and, if we do this right and don't shoot each other, they won't even get off a round. Any questions?"

"Yes, Fox," Corporal Garcia raised a hand, "once we're in, how are we gonna tell who's who in the dark without night vision gear?"

"Good question. I have a chalk block and we're going to put big white crosses on the front and back of our robes. It ain't great but it's better than nothing. When we're done, we'll buddy up an' scrub off the chalk before we hit the street. Also, remember we'll be wearing head cloths and the assholes in bed won't have 'em on, nor robes for that matter. Anything else?"

Silence.

"Okay, carry on an' get some good sleep. Tomorrow's gonna be a long day."

The next morning Cauldwell sounded reveille at 0600. After the five had eaten from the meager rations imported from neighborhood shops, Cauldwell gave an order. "First job of the day is to clean those MP5s."

Immediately all hands set to work dismantling their automatic weapons. The Heckler & Koch MP5K with which all were equipped was a deadly 9mm submachine gun designed for close work. Less than 27 inches long and weighing slightly more than five and one-half pounds, it could spit rounds at the rate of

800 per minute or thirteen per second. There were more than a hundred variations of the weapon, but the K model had no stock and control was effected by means of the pistol grip and a front hand grip. The Party Favors' weapons had all been fitted with screw-on silencers making them thirty inches in overall length. When slung beneath their armpits and under their robes, the tip of the silencer hung down to the outboard side of their kneecaps, a little short of that in Cauldwell's case.

Each team member carried six 15-round magazines and two of the 30-round variety. Firing selections available were single-shot, fully automatic, two-round bursts and three-round bursts.

When the cleaning process concluded, Cauldwell spoke again. "Okay, let's begin the recon. You first, Star. LA, you stay in here with the rest of us."

Sergeant Ayoubi left the room and the rest of the team lounged around listening to the mournful music emanating from the radio.

At 1025 Ayoubi returned with nothing unusual to report and Sergeant Fahmi left to conduct his own patrol.

At 1215 Fahmi, as was his custom, moved silently up the three flights of stairs and quietly opened the corridor door. Twenty-five feet away he saw the landlord with his ear pressed to the door of room 317. The man's back was to him, so the sergeant was able to approach unobserved. From three feet away he inquired in Arabic, "What is happening here?"

The landlord gave a start and whirled around, immediately putting a finger to his lips to demand silence. He then whispered, "These people are not Syrian, they are American! We must inform the police and Sharaf's militia." Suddenly his eyes registered a new awareness. "Wait, you are one of..."

Fahmi smacked his open left palm over the man's mouth and slammed his head against the door, pushing up hard against the Syrian's nose. The would-be informer never saw the knife that flashed briefly before its blade was buried to the hilt on a sharp upward angle through his solar plexus. A look of shock lighted the man's eyes briefly as blood gushed from his mouth and forced its way between Fahmi's fiercely clamped fingers. With his left hand and a firm grip on the knife handle, the sergeant kept the landlord pinned to the wall until the light in the man's eyes went out and breathing ceased. He then rapped three times. "Hey, you guys, it's Trenton. Open the door."

The door was jerked open inward, and the body fell on its back, leaving the bloody knife in Fahmi's hand.

"Jesus H. Christ!" Cauldwell exclaimed. "Haul 'im in an' close the damn door. What the hell happened?"

Fahmi explained.

"Okay. Outstanding job, there Trenton. LA, grab a towel, open the door, make sure the hallway is clear, and check for blood. If ya see any, wipe it up."

"Aye, aye, Fox."

"Awright men, this was a near-run thing, but Trenton saved our asses. Killin' this meathead isn't going to affect us one damn bit. Stow the friggin' body under a bed an' clean up the blood in here. Star, move out on patrol."

Sergeant Ayoubi departed the room at 1232 and returned at 1308.

"Bad news, Fox. Sharaf and four of his assholes got into a Mercedes with quite a lot of luggage and headed east like they were aiming for Airport Road."

"Son of a wicked bitch! Okay, you and Trenton start with the passing patrols on Mu'Awia. If the shithead doesn't return in time for final prayers, we're screwed for today, so y'all can come on back an' I'll call Davis."

Just after sunset Fahmi and Ayoubi returned within five minutes of one another and reported there had been no sign of Sharaf.

"Kiss my sister's black cat's ass!" Cauldwell was visibly angry. "Awright, Trenton, we're goin' up to the patio again."

"Aye, aye, Fox."

In the open air on top of the roof, Cauldwell activated the satellite phone.

"Davis here."

"Rick. Cauldwell. We cannot launch the boat tonight. I say again, no launch tonight."

"I understand no launch. What's the problem?"

"The captain has been called away."

"So, when do you try again? We're almost up against our deadline."

"When the captain returns."

"When will that be?"

"How the hell should I know? I'll call ya when the launch is rescheduled."

"Okay but remember we're less than a week away from deadline."

"Hey! I know all that crap!" Cauldwell interrupted. "We'll do the best we can. That is all." He turned off the phone shaking his head in wonderment at the operational stupidity he had just prevented.

Back in the room Cauldwell's first words were, "The mission is scrubbed. Now we gotta get rid of the body before it stinks us outta here. Any suggestions?"

"Well, Fox," Ayoubi said thoughtfully, 'that restaurant we use a block to our south has a huge dumpster out back that a truck empties every morning before they open. I could go buy one of those giant garbage bags, we could stuff him into that, and a couple of us could lug him down there after midnight an' heave 'im in."

"Sounds like a plan to me. Better get three bags an' we'll triple up. I don't want anything pokin' out when the truck unloads at the dump. Y'all think anyone around here is gonna raise a great outcry about the man bein' missing?"

"Don't know for sure, Fox," Sergeant Fahmi replied, "but I was thinking tomorrow morning I could go down to the first deck and stand outside his room until I see another resident coming, then I'll beat on the hatch an' tell the guy that I'm tryin' to pay the rent again since we have already been here a month, but I can't find the landlord. We can see what the response is and, at the very least, it'll help divert attention away from us."

Cauldwell grunted in approval. "Yer more than just another pretty face, huh, Trenton? Good thinkin'. Do it.

"Now then for the disposal operation, Apple an' LA can carry the bag and I want Star on escort duty. Take your weapon with you."

"Aye, aye, Fox."

By 0120, the three dumpster divers returned to report success and at 0830 Sergeant Fahmi came back up from his station outside the landlord's door.

"Hey Fox, good stuff to report. Three long-time residents happened by together. No one was surprised I couldn't find the landlord. One of 'em said the guy often takes off to visit family up near Hamah and is sometimes gone for several days."

"That's perfect. With any luck, Sharaf will show up an' we can snuff his worthless ass an' get outta here before anyone reports baggie boy as missing. Okay, let's get out there an' keep eyes on the asshole's hootch."

For the next five days the team maintained passing patrols on Mu'Awia Street so 461 was under constant surveillance. There was no sign of their target. Time was running out to complete their mission.

Chapter 27

Brandon and Carley talked every day after the White House Christmas party. Sometimes he would call her throughout the day just to say good morning or make sure she got to work safely or see how her day was going and just to hear her voice or in the evening to say goodnight. Carley liked the extra attention. She made it a point to tell Brandon how much she appreciated his effort. It was bad enough he was in Atlanta. The distance got to them both and made it hard to nurse a relationship. But Carley had a way about her that assured Brandon she might be the one. Brandon was content being the person to travel. It worked out better that way. When the weather was nice, he would hop in the Baron and surprise her for lunch. Or he would schedule a layover to be with her on his way to a book signing or on the way home.

"When can I see you again, I'm missing you," Carley pleaded.

"I have nothing to do this weekend, so what if I fly up there on Saturday?" he suggested.

"I'd love it, can you really come?"

"Sure, I'll see you Saturday around noon."

"You know I have plenty of room, so plan to stay here if you want to," she offered.

"Okay, great, that sounds better than my room in the dignitary quarters," Brandon said.

Saturday morning the weather was perfect for flying. Brandon put his bag in the trunk and slammed it closed. He couldn't wait to see Carley. There wasn't a cloud in the sky, and that's the way he liked it. He went back into the house to check the answering machine one last time and as he was checking a report on CNN caught his attention.

"We are now going to Michael Sigman in Iraq."

"Thank you, Laura. I'm here under the cover of darkness in Fallujah. According to sources, the government has in its possession detailed information on the inner workings of the groups responsible for the September 11 attacks on America. No word how this information was gained. Those are all the details we have at this time, but we will report any new developments. Michael Sigman. Fallujah."

"Thanks Michael. There is also speculation Flight 3911, the plane believed to have crashed in…"

Brandon hit the power button on the remote. He imagined he would be sitting in that same CNN studio setting the record straight. He stood in the middle of his living room, silence around him, enjoying the calm before the storm. The phone rang. Brandon decided to let the answering machine get it. He picked up his keys from the table and set the security alarm.

"Please leave a message after the tone," the answering machine squawked.

"Brandon, this is President Walker."

Brandon made a mad dash for the answering machine.

"I thought you would be home, but I guess you're out," the president said.

Brandon grabbed the phone. "Hello! Hello!"

The alarm continued the count down in the background. He ran to the keypad and punched in his secret code just before the 30-second delay was up.

"Hello," Brandon tried to catch his breath. "I'm sorry about that."

"Screening your calls? I see you're getting ready for the attention coming your way. I'm glad you're there. Did I catch you at an inconvenient time?

"Oh no, Mr. President, I am preparing to fly to Wright-Patterson for a visit." Brandon was glad he was flying the Baron. He wasn't on the same schedule he would be if he were flying commercially.

"Good. I'm following up on the invitation to have you back to the White House. The State of the Union Address is just a little over a week away, and I wanted to make sure you and Carley will be here," the president said.

"Oh, yes. I'm actually on my way to see Carley now," Brandon said.

"Great, be sure to send my regards and tell her I have the Lincoln Bedroom for you," teased the president.

"Thank you, Mr. President, and we thank you for the use of the bedroom again."

"Good. You have a safe trip, and I will see you next week."

Chapter 28

On Monday, January 21 at 1322 Sergeant Ayoubi burst into room 317 to announce Sharaf had finally returned. Right on the deadline date to complete the mission.

With Sergeant Fahmi as his ladder well guard, Cauldwell returned to the rooftop patio with the satellite phone.

"Davis here."

"Rick, this is Cauldwell. The captain has just returned, and boat launch is scheduled for tonight. You copy?"

"Roger, launch tonight."

"Right. All details of time and place remain the same. Any questions?"

"No, but break the link and stand by, I need to talk to the boss. I'll call you back."

"Roger, standing by." Cauldwell terminated the call.

Nine minutes later the phone vibrated in his hand.

"Cauldwell."

"Davis. The boss wants confirmation before his performance. It will be 0130 your time Tuesday 22 January for extract will be 1830 Monday 21 January, so plenty of time for the boss to be informed of launch results. Think you can get to me by then?"

"Shouldn't be a problem," Cauldwell said.

"In the event of a glitch, I'll be in the balcony where the boss can see me, and I'll be plugged into this thing. You understand?"

"I have it. That is all."

On the afternoon of Monday, January 21 at 1:30 Brandon and Carley arrived at the White House. Walter greeted them at the door.

"Mr. Powell. Dr. Holland. How was your flight?" he asked getting the luggage from the trunk.

"It was wonderful." Brandon answered. "How have you been?"

"Fine, sir. If you'll follow me, I'll show you to where you'll be staying. We have prepared the Lincoln Bedroom for you."

"Thank you, Walter."

The walk seemed shorter this time. There were no holiday decorations lining the halls or Christmas music piped through the speakers. There were no trees, and the fragrance of cinnamon wasn't filling the air. There was just the elegance of the house itself, the exquisitely decorated rooms. Brandon took in the view as if it was the first time, he was visiting the White House. It was all so majestic. Walter opened the door to the room, repeated the instructions on how to contact him and left them alone. Carley looked around the room. She felt so comfortable.

"Brandon, where's the cot?" she joked. Brandon grabbed Carley and hugged her. "That little tactic is called avoidance. I know these things; I am a doctor."

There was knock at the door. Carley broke from Brandon's embrace and ran to open it.

"Mr. President!"

"Carley, how are you?" He greeted as they hugged. "Was the flight okay?"

"It was wonderful."

"Where is the man of the hour?"

"I'm right here." Brandon called.

"I'm glad you made it okay. I just wanted to come by and check on you. I have a couple last minute meetings I must attend to prepare for tonight, and this is the only time I have free. So, how are you feeling?"

"I feel great," Brandon said. "Well, I must admit, I am feeling a little nervous."

"I understand. But we are going to hold your hand through this whole process, so there's nothing to be nervous about. Besides, in about three months, you'll be a pro at this. An aide will be in here shortly to go over what will be happening tonight, and we'll be doing a dress rehearsal of sorts later this afternoon.

"I'm really looking forward to announcing to the world what you did on September 11. I have a lot of big announcements I'm going to share with the people of this country. We've been able to make great strides with the information we gained from the terrorists, and I just wanted to thank you, not as your president, but as your friend, for risking your life to save your country."

Brandon felt tears well in his eyes, but he maintained composure.

"On behalf of my fellow passengers, we would like to thank you for taking such good care of us over the months since September."

"It's the least we could do."

"Mr. President, you said your plan was to eliminate the terrorists by the State of the Union address. Have we done it? Have we gotten any closer?"

"Brandon, I can't answer that question right now," the president said as he shot Brandon a sly look. "But know that if it were not for what you and your fellow passengers did on September 11, this country would not be the same."

There was a knock on the door.

"Mr. President?" a voice called from the other side. "It's time."

"Brandon, Carley, you two relax, have lunch. If you need anything, let Walter know. And I will see you tonight."

"Thank you, Mr. President."

Chapter 29

Team Party Favors attended final prayers earlier in the day in two groups and kept Sharaf and his henchmen under constant surveillance until the latter reentered the house on Mu'Awia.

Sergeants Ayoubi and Fahmi continued to stroll back and forth on opposite sides of the street in an aimless fashion until all lights in the domicile were extinguished. They then broke off and ran for the rooming house.

At 2250 the team huddled together in an alley across the street from 461. Cauldwell broke out a block of chalk about the size of a bar of soap. "Okay, all hands buddy up an' get those crosses on the robes, front an' back. Make 'em big an' make 'em bright."

The robes were marked in less than a minute.

"Now then, all hands fire up those radios and secure the earpieces." This required ten seconds.

"Right. All weapons set for two-round bursts. Remember, no rounds fired unless necessary. Even though we have silencers, I'm sure the scumbags in the house are familiar with the sound they make and if one of 'em happens to be lying awake he'll know what's up.

"Now, LA, you get across. Go between 463 and 465 an' circle around to the back of 461.

"Apple give him 30 seconds, then head for the laneway between 461 and 463. There's no dividing fence line, just those gnarly little bushes. They should give ya enough cover to get close."

"Roger that, Fox."

"Okay, LA, go!"

The corporal walked away, angled across the street at a leisurely pace, then darted between two houses and disappeared.

"Apple, go!"

Garcia moved listlessly over the thoroughfare and reached the far sidewalk before vanishing between the shrubs forming the western border of the lot occupied by 461.

In the rear of the house Corporal Gonzales, in a crouch, crept silently along a service lane, carefully avoiding the garbage cans arrayed against backyard fences. As he drew near 461, he smelled cigarette smoke. Cautiously raising his head to peer over the wooden back gate, he saw a man in Arab dress sitting sideways on the steps leading to the rear door. The sentry was facing west with his arms on his knees and an AK-47 propped up on the stairs behind him.

As the gate was 30 feet east of the steps, and a well-trimmed lawn covered the yard, Garcia felt he could move undetected to a position parallel to the steps and then approach the man from behind.

As he began to open the gate, the creak of hinges stopped him cold. He raised his head to look, but the sentry's position remained unchanged. It took the corporal a full minute to move the gate far enough to allow entry. Once inside the yard he slung his MP5 at the ready on its stabilizer strap and drew his fighting knife.

Slowly and steadily, he proceeded north across the grass until he was even with the sentry, then turned ninety degrees to the west and approached the man's bent back.

Garcia reached the edge of the stairs. He was now within two feet of his target. Slowly he unslung his MP5 and laid it on the grass. He then put his left foot on the bottom stair and sprang forward, smacking his open left hand hard across the Arab's mouth and jerking the man's head up and to the rear. The knife swept in an arc from right to left, then viciously reversed direction.

The Syrian's head was half severed from his body. Both the jugular and the carotid artery were cut clean through. Blood spurted forth in a foamy fountain, finally slowing to an ooze when the heart ceased to beat.

Gonzalez took his left hand and pushed the body away, so it tumbled to the ground. Quickly, the Marine dragged the lifeless form hard up against the rear wall of the house, retrieved his MP5 and pushed the talk button on his radio.

"LA reports rear guard gone."

"Roger, copy rear guard gone. Hold your position."

"Roger, holding."

In the meantime, Corporal Garcia crouched in the front yard shrubs and watched his own target pace back and forth in a desultory fashion across the width of the front yard. The man carried an AK47 slung, muzzle-down over his right shoulder and everything in his manner said absolute boredom.

From Garcia's point of view, the problem occurred when the sentry walked west toward him, the man did not come close enough to the bushes before turning to retrace his steps. As the patrol pattern appeared unlikely to change, the corporal determined he would have to exit the bushes and close quickly on the Syrian as the guard moved to the east.

Slowly the marine slid the stabilizer strap of his MP5 down his right arm and set the weapon against a sturdy shrub. He then carefully uncoiled the loops of a stainless-steel, braided wire garrote and, knuckles forward, wrapped all four fingers of each hand around the rear posts of the rectangular, steel four-by-two inch frames to which the ends of the wire were attached.

As soon as the sentry made his next pivot and headed east, Garcia emerged, and cat footed across the grass in pursuit. He held his breath to prevent the target from hearing his respiration and closed to within eighteen inches of the retreating form.

The Syrian was several inches taller than the marine, so Garcia had to leap into the air throwing both hands forward then down to encircle the man's neck with the wire. Still in midair, Garcia twisted his body 180 degrees, so the garrote cable was crossed behind his victim's neck and the two men were back-to-back.

As soon as his boots hit the deck, the corporal pulled the handgrips hard over each shoulder and bent violently forward at the waist, using his own back as a lever against that of the sentry. He heard the AK47 fall to the ground and the man began to thrash and flop like a bloated fish. Blows from the Syrian's boots rained on both Garcia's calf muscles for several seconds, then ceased.

The corporal kept his pose and maintained pressure on the garrote until he felt the body on his back fall limp. He held on for an additional five seconds before releasing the handgrips and stepping swiftly forward to let the body fall on its back.

Quickly Garcia knelt. The carotid artery was devoid of a pulse. He retrieved the garrote and moved rapidly back into the bushes to collect his MP5. He then thumbed his radio switch.

"Apple reports front guard gone."

"Roger, Apple. Copy front guard gone. Hold your position, we're moving now."

"Roger, Apple holding."

In a cat foot run, Cauldwell and the two sergeants moved silently across the street and through the front gate. Conversation was conducted in stage whispers.

"Apple, come to me."

"Aye, aye, Fox."

"Star and Trenton, you guys get to the rear. Send LA forward to cover the front and get positioned at the rear hatch. Apple and I will breach the front door simultaneously with you two going through the rear. We will execute 30 seconds from...Mark, go!"

The two sergeants disappeared around the back of the house while Cauldwell and Garcia moved up to the small porch adjoining the front door.

Fourteen an' 15 an...

"Apple, I'll lead. I have 9-to-twelve; you've got 12-to-three."

Twenty-one an'...29 an'...

"Okay, here we go."

Cauldwell yanked the door open and stepped across the threshold sweeping his weapon through the 90-degree quadrant to his front and left. Garcia followed in a crouch and fixed his gaze straight to the front, as there was ten feet of solid wall to his right before the entrance to a hallway.

Cauldwell's gaze instantly encompassed a twelve-by-fourteen-foot living room with two couches, three armchairs, a large television set, and assorted tables and lamps. In the middle of the wall to his right front was a set of swinging saloon doors he figured must lead to the kitchen. He stepped into the living room at a left oblique and swung his MP5 toward the hallway entrance, signaling Garcia to advance in the passageway.

The corporal moved along the wall, then quickly rounded the corner with his weapon trained into the recess. He gave Cauldwell the clear sign and began advancing into the hall. Cauldwell followed stepping sideways, his eyes covering both the saloon doors and the passageway that led straight from the front door to the back of the house. Once he cleared the corner of the small hallway, he swung around toward Garcia who had halted beside a closed door six feet in on the right-hand side. The sound of snoring roared from the room.

The door was hinged to open inward and Cauldwell signed Garcia should work the doorknob. The young marine flattened his back against the wall just beyond the latch side of the door and, keeping a firm hold on the pistol grip of his MP5, reached sideways with his left hand and began to slowly turn the knob.

Suddenly he froze as both he and Cauldwell heard the "twuu-twuu" of an MP5 in action and a second later another two-round burst. Cauldwell pointed emphatically to the door and Garcia completed the process. Under light pressure from the corporal's fingers, the door swung noiselessly inboard and Cauldwell stepped through the aperture, finger on the trigger.

The bedroom was about ten feet square and had a large window on the north side looking out on Mu'Awia Street. Although the window was curtained, the streetlights cast enough light to illuminate the sleeping space.

There were two beds, one directly beneath the window and another against the west wall, the latter bearing the blanketed form of the snore producer.

The maggot did us a favor masking the sounds of the firing.

Cauldwell looked back at Garcia, pointed to the corporal and then to the sleeper under the window. He trained his submachine gun on the noisemaker and held up three fingers. Garcia returned a thumbs up in acknowledgement and, returning his right hand to his weapon, Cauldwell nodded three times.

At the third nod two rounds from each MP5 smashed into the left chest of each sleeping Syrian. Cauldwell stepped forward quickly and bent down to check for a pulse and scan the face, while Garcia did the same with his victim.

Satisfied that the 9-millimeter slugs had done their work, and that neither was Sharaf, the two marines moved to the door with Garcia leading. As the corporal stepped into the hall, flashes lit the darkness accompanied by the staccato crash of an AK-47. Garcia went down hard and Cauldwell bulled through the door swinging his weapon to the right, just in time to see a door slam shut at the far end. As he moved toward the door, Cauldwell hit his radio Send button. "Apple down, Apple down, front lateral hallway. Render aid. In pursuit of shooter west bedroom."

As he reached the door, Cauldwell heard a window being hurriedly thrown open. He set his feet and, shoulder first, hurled his 235 pounds at the paneled impediment. To the sound of rending wood, the door gave way and Cauldwell saw a figure frantically clambering through the south window.

Cauldwell's MP5 spoke with two bursts and the shadowed form was catapulted over the sill and hit the ground outside with a heavy thump. Cauldwell charged the window and trained his weapon on the huddled form four feet below. It was apparent the wounded man posed no further threat and Cauldwell swung through the aperture and dropped to the ground. He seized the Syrian by the neck of his sleeping shirt and dragged him two yards to the west beyond the corner of the house and to a spot where the light from a streetlamp bathed the grass.

The face glowering up at him with a mixture of pain, rage and hate was that of Hassan Sharaf.

"So, you're the asshole tryin' to attack my country, huh? Tell ya what, ya friggin' murderous pig, you can go talk it over with Allah."

The angry eyes widened momentarily in fear then closed forever as Cauldwell squeezed the trigger twice and four rounds tore into the terrorist's chest blowing his heart to shreds.

As Cauldwell headed for the back door he heard shrill, excited voices from the east. He raced through the door and sped down the passageway to the small hall where he had left Garcia. Sergeants Ayoubi and Fahmi were tending to the wounded Marine.

Ayoubi looked up at Cauldwell's approach. "Hey, Fox, it ain't too bad. One round through the left thigh. We've got pressure bandages in place."

Cauldwell addressed the corporal. "Think ya can walk, there Apple?"

"Yes, Fox. Not sure I can run very well though."

"Awright, get 'im on his feet. We're goin' out the back an' down the service alley. We're gonna have company out front shortly."

Cauldwell raced to the front door and jerked it open. "Hey LA! Get yer ass in here!"

"Aye, aye, Fox." The Californian sprinted across the lawn and through the door.

Cauldwell moved rapidly down the passageway. "Let's go you guys, follow me."

The team boiled out the rear door, crossed the lawn and hustled through the gate into the alley. From Mu'Awia they heard a cacophony of Arabic voices. Streetlights showed a gathering of a dozen men, several bearing shoulder weapons, cautiously approaching the house.

"Let's go!" Cauldwell commanded. "They're gonna start findin' bodies right quick an' they'll be after us full force." He headed east on the service alley and took the first right that presented itself.

They were moving at a recon shuffle as Garcia was limping badly.

"You gonna be okay, there, Apple?"

"Think so, Fox."

They continued south until they hit Midhat Pacha Souq, then turned left along the major thoroughfare. At the intersection where the road became Ali Aj'Jammal they heard shouts to their rear and saw handheld lanterns swinging violently about four blocks behind. With Ayoubi and Fahmi supporting Garcia, they increased their pace and at the intersection where Ali Aj'Jammal became Al Kharab Street the team turned southeast into a maze of twisting laneways. After fourteen minutes and a series of lefts and rights, they came up on the gardens behind the Bab Kissan Church.

As they negotiated the flower beds continuing southeast toward Ibn'Asaker, shouts erupted behind them at the green space perimeter and an AK47 opened with three four-round bursts. Rounds struck an eight-foot statue to their left and the team immediately took cover behind the heavy concrete pedestal.

"Get some rounds on those assholes an' see if we can slow 'em down some," Cauldwell ordered. He then inquired of no one in particular. "How in the hell did they track us through that friggin' labyrinth?"

Sergeant Ayoubi pointed to the grass beside them where Garcia's blood glistened darkly in the moonlight. "That's how, Fox."

Cauldwell grunted as he brought his weapon to bear and unleashed three, two-round bursts. Ayoubi, Fahmi and Gonzales followed suit and the lanterns ceased their advance.

"Right. Now then, I'm gonna hold here an' pin those sonsabitches down for a while. The rest of you haul ass across Ibn'Asaker and into the fig grove. Take up firing positions along the tree line an' make sure none of those assholes put any holes in my butt when I'm on the way to join ya. Okay, go!"

Dragging Garcia whose leg was now virtually useless, the four marines ran for the grove.

Cauldwell eyed the lanterns and when they showed signs of forward movement sighted in on them and gave several squirts with the submachine gun. The weapon was not designed for accuracy at that range, which exceeded a hundred yards, but Cauldwell was gratified to see one lantern extinguished and another tumble through the air.

He alternated his glances between the pursuers and his marines until the time a backward look showed no sign of the rest of Team Party Favors. He climbed from a crouch, moved slightly left from behind the statue and emptied the remainder of his 30-round magazine in the general direction of the single lantern now showing. Turning, he thundered across the grass, over the road and into the grove. About three yards short of the tree line, he saw Fahmi lying prone behind his MP5 and went down in a baseball slide. He plowed through the loamy soil for five yards before coming to a stop behind the prostrate sergeant.

"Any sign of 'em?"

"Not yet, Fox."

"Well, they'll be showin' up directly. Awright men, we'll keep on goin' southeast using the grove for cover an' concealment 'til we hit the farmland, then we'll strike Northeast to the extraction point. Okay, on yer feet, let's go!"

"Ah, sir?"

"Whatchya got, Apple?"

"Sir, I'm slowin' you guys down big time. Let me stay here an' fend 'em off as long as I can. If you all give me a couple magazines, I can hold out until you bring in the chopper."

"No way in hell are we leaving' ya, marine!" Cauldwell walked rapidly to where Garcia was standing on one leg, holding on to a fig tree, and bent down.

"On my back, Apple."

"Shit, sir!"

"That's an order, marine!"

Garcia bent forward over Cauldwell's left shoulder and the major stood up clutching the corporal's legs behind the knees.

"Right. Let's go!"

The team moved swiftly on the packed earth between two rows of trees. In less than ten minutes they hit plowed ground and swung Northeast.

"You got yer GPS goin' there, Star?"

"Roger. Fox."

"Then take the lead an' get us to the EP."

"Aye, aye, Fox."

It was 22 minutes before Sergeant Ayoubi halted. "We're here, Fox."

Cauldwell knelt and laid Garcia on the ground. He looked at his watch, 0120.

"Okay, we got five minutes before we fire up the strobe light. Everybody get down an' remain silent. Those assholes are gonna have a tough time followin' us since Apple's been bleedin' on me instead of the damn deck."

Cauldwell fished out the satellite phone and was about to push the Send button when lanterns suddenly appeared a mile off to the southwest.

"Well, kiss my ass! The little pricks tracked us through the grove. Well, they're gonna have to move awful slow to track us by lantern light. Quick, everyone sit down shoulder to shoulder and face the lanterns."

The two sergeants set Garcia in place, then sat down on either side of him with Gonzalez joining to form the left end of the line.

Cauldwell dropped down behind the barrier of backs and pushed hard on the rubber coated activation button on the strobe light. The instrument gave out a low, high pitched whine and began to flash, sending a blinding white beam skyward. Within twenty seconds they heard the unmistakable whopping of inbound rotor blades.

Another 15 seconds and part of the starry night sky was obliterated by the massive shape of a descending CH53. The rotor wash swept over them and they were enveloped in a great swirl of dust. The chopper settled, ramp down, less than twenty feet to the east. Dragging Garcia, the marines charged through the cloud of airborne dirt and up the ramp into the pitch black interior of the aircraft. The helo lifted, swung its nose to the east and clawed hard for altitude.

Ten minutes later the cabin interior was dimly lit by several red lights. Cauldwell looked around and saw four grinning faces.

"Hey, sir," Sergeant Ayoubi sounded jubilant, "we did it!"

"Yeah men, that we did. Outstanding job by all hands. Break out the first-aid kit an' see what you can do for Corporal Garcia.

"Now then, my two fine sergeants. Why was I hearing MP5s talkin' back there in the hootch when Garcia and I were tryin' to take out our two?"

"Aw hell, sir," Fahmi sounded rueful, "one of them turds woke up an' we had to grease 'em both before they did us injury."

"Okay. Well, guess I better let Davis know what's up."

The satellite phone produced no signal.

"Damn it to hell! What now?" Cauldwell moved forward and leaned through the cockpit door, touching the co-pilot on the shoulder.

"Hey, captain, you got anything I can call Washington with. I can't get a signal on this damn satellite phone."

"Yeah, signal is probably blocked by onboard avionics gear. We haven't got any capability like that, but there's an AWACS bird airborne over northern Iraq, maybe we could patch in through them."

"Well, let me ask ya this, how long before we set down?"

"About two hours."

"That's too long. Okay, ask the pilot if there's any place we can set down along the way. I need to get on the deck an' use the damn phone."

The co-pilot raised his face mike and spoke into it, then listened for several seconds before turning back to Cauldwell.

"The skipper says there's a place he knows about an hour out."

Cauldwell glanced at his watch. "It'll be awful damn close, but if he can get me down in 60 minutes, I can make the deadline."

Chapter 30

Brandon and Carley were overwhelmed by the media frenzy outside the Capitol. Carley counted twenty-three television vans on her side of the limo. Most had call letters she had never seen, but she recognized the CNN van and the reporter standing next to it. Inside the limo, the president sat silently, rehearsing his speech in his head. The first lady held his hand, rubbing her finger back and forth on his wedding band. It was a ritual that they started when he was in law school. It calmed his nerves, and it was working like a charm.

The first lady, never letting go of her husband's hand, turned her attention to making her guests feel at ease. Brandon grew obviously nervous as the car got closer to the Capitol. He closed his eyes and took deep breaths. This breathing technique always calmed him quickly.

"Dave, get the camera," a reporter yelled as the limo turned into the driveway at the Capitol. She grabbed the microphone and ran to her position.

"How do I look?" she asked the photographer.

"Great," Dave said. "You're on in five, four..." He finished the countdown on his fingers and gave the reporter her cue.

"Today is the most anticipated State of the Union address in America's history. The country has not been the same since the events on September 11, and I know many are wondering what the president has to say about restoring peace to this land. It looks like the presidential limousine has just arrived."

The president grabbed Brandon's shoulder. "An aide is waiting to take you to your seats." Brandon and Carley stepped out of the car. The sea of camera lights and flashes blinded them.

"A couple has just stepped out of the presidential limo. This appears to be the same couple that accompanied the president during the holidays. Brandon Powell and Carley Hollace. Mr. Powell is a writer from Atlanta and Carley Hollace is a doctor in Ohio. Tonight we'll find out more about this couple, and the question that has been on the lips of many will finally be answered. Who is this mystery couple?"

***

The helicopter suddenly began a sharp descent. Again, Cauldwell looked at his watch, 0250, 1950 in DC. The president would begin his address in ten minutes.

The aircraft flared and was still five feet off the deck when Cauldwell leaped through the side hatch and raced away from the machine.

As he ran, he turned on the phone and was rewarded with the blue light that indicated a signal. He slammed to a halt and pushed Send.

"Davis here."

"This is Cauldwell. 'The ship has sailed.' I say again, 'The ship has sailed.' You copy?"

"Roger, I copy 'The ship has sailed.'"

"That is all."

Cauldwell put away the phone, retraced his steps, climbed aboard, and stretched out along three seats. As he lay back contentedly, visions of Mary O'Hara flooded his mind. The marines of Party Favors wondered at the huge grin spread over their leader's face.

In the back of the Capitol, Davis, from his place in the balcony, adjusted his tie as he flashed a thumbs up to his president as the latter waited for the introductory applause to die away.

Then, with a smile the president stepped up to the podium and began, "Mister Speaker…"

The applause continued. "Mister Speaker…" The president stepped away from the podium and enjoyed the moment.

Chapter 31

In Albany Georgia, Grace and her friends decided to spend this Tuesday evening at Henry's, a popular local pub. Tuesday was Ladies' Night. As usual, every eye noticed as Grace walked in and sat at her favorite table. The television over the bar was tuned to the State of the Union, as opposed to the usual sports channel. The entire nation anticipated the president's message. Even those in the sports bar and pub anticipated what he might say.

Within minutes of Grace's arrival, Jake Whitmore approached her with an offer to buy her a drink. She gladly accepted with a smile. Jake had an identical twin brother. Both Jake and John played in Brandon's regular golf group. Jake was an awkward goofy guy, but his family was wealthy so Grace could overlook his character traits. Normally he might not have approached her, but word had gotten around she and Brandon had split so he hoped to be the first in line for the rebound. After small talk, she asked him to sit next to her. Just as he got comfortable, all eyes turned to the TV to watch the State of the Union.

"Mr. Speaker, thank you."

"Good evening, America. I stand here tonight to deliver a speech on the state of this union, the state of your union. This country is not the same country it was a year ago. We are a different people. We are a stronger people. The very thing that was sent to cripple us has been used to destroy those who are against this nation. I stand humbled before you, not as your president, but as your next-door neighbor wanting to protect her.

"I have been practicing this speech over the last two weeks, but tonight America, your president is going to speak from his heart, as one American to another. On September 11, 2001, our country was attacked. Since September, we have been diligently working to bring down those behind the attacks. Intelligence has led us to investigating clerks and banking executives in international banks. Through these channels we were able to pinpoint the mastermind behind the attacks. Those involved are being arrested daily, all around the world. And now

243

I am proud to share I just received word a major terrorist leader planning another large scale attack on American soil has been eliminated. This is the first step in wiping out terrorism around the world."

A cheer throughout the audience was followed by a standing ovation.

The 80 people in Henry's cheered.

"I also have the privilege of sharing with you how we were able to obtain this information. We all know what happened on September 11. The attacks on the World Trade Center Towers and the Pentagon, and the courage of the passengers on Flight 93 that went down in Pennsylvania will never be forgotten. So many people paid the ultimate price for freedom.

"But what you don't know is what actually happened on Flight 3911. Around 8:00 a.m. on September 11, five Middle Eastern passengers boarded Northeast Flight 3911, non-stop from NYC to Seattle. By 8:45, the pilot, co-pilot and one flight attendant had been brutally murdered, terrorists had taken over the plane and the hijackers were on a collision course with the White House.

"The passengers aboard this plane thought it to be a worthy cause to try and save other Americans from the fate that lay ahead. They made the decision, as did the brave passengers aboard Flight 93, to take over their plane. They huddled at the back of the airplane to formulate a plan, said a group prayer, and took on the hijackers face to face. Their plan was to subdue the hijackers and land the plane safely. After finishing the Lord's Prayer, Hampton Greene led the charge towards the front of the cabin. A hijacker sliced him from his chest to his navel with a box cutter."

A gasp rose from the audience.

Everyone in Henry's was glued to the television.

"Hampton was able to pin a hijacker to the floor of the aircraft when he fell. Following close behind him were John Dawsett, a former Army Ranger, and Rylander Brookhaven. They were able to make their way to the cockpit. The two engaged in hand-to-hand combat with the other hijackers, killing one and capturing others alive. Once the cockpit was secured, another passenger with flight experience, Brandon Powell, took over the controls. By 9:15 am, Flight 3911 was on its way to Wright-Patterson Air Force Base. Brandon Powell originally from Albany, Georgia, now living in Atlanta, had never flown a commercial airliner before, but with the help of ground control, was able to land the plane safely. Four Americans lost their lives on Flight 3911, and I would like to honor their courage with a moment of silence at this time."

A hush fell over the Capitol.

Several in attendance at Henry's thought they recognized one of the names the president mentioned, Brandon Powell, as their friend in Atlanta. Could it be the same Brandon?

The president continued, "As a result of what these passengers did on that plane, we were able to interrogate the three terrorists captured alive. We learned information that led us directly to the leader Hassan Sharaf in Damascus who was planning a catastrophic event in Washington DC. Just in the last few minutes I received word from a special operations unit and can announce Sharaf was eliminated just one hour ago. Sharaf was the second in command who planned the attacks on 9/11, and he worked with Osama bin Laden who is also now directly in our sights. He is the most important target left to deal with now for the events that took place on 9/11."

Another standing ovation lasted for five minutes.

The president held his hand up trying to hush the applause. He continued, "At this time, I have the honor of introducing you to the passengers of Flight 3911. Please stand."

The passengers all stood. Soon they were lost among the standing ovation in their honor. Grace and others in the bar looked for Brandon as the camera panned across the entire group of passengers but she was unable to find him.

"Please be seated. I would specifically like to introduce you to those who took charge in the attack to take back Flight 3911. John Dawsett, Rylander Brookhaven and Hampton Greene, please stand."

Another standing ovation. For Grace and the others in Henry's, still no sign that the Brandon the president mentioned was also her former Brandon.

"I would also like to introduce you to a man who has become a close friend of mine. One without whom, none of the other passengers would be with us tonight. The man who took control of the 757 airliner and landed it safely, with its precious cargo and wealth of information, Mr. Brandon Powell."

Brandon seated next to the first lady stood up. He felt slaps on his back and shoulders. Those standing around him had tears streaming down their faces. He looked over at the president who was beaming with pride. Carley grabbed his hand, squeezed it, and kissed him on his cheek. His ears were ringing from the cheers and whistles coming from all around him.

Everyone in Henry's stood and cheered for this real American hero. The picture on the television confirmed Grace's question. Yes, it was the same Brandon. There on national TV was the man she let slip out of her life. As he stood in the Capitol being recognized by the President of the United States, he was standing next to a classy, beautiful brunette. She kissed him on national TV! Grace's heart sank as she thought what a fool she had been.

"We staged the crash in Ohio because we didn't want the world to know we had the terrorists in custody. It was important for the passengers to keep this secret so the government could track down those responsible.

"I would like to thank you for assisting us in the cover-up. It played a necessary and integral part in bringing down those responsible for the attacks on 9/11. America, these are real life heroes. I would personally like to ask every one of you to treat them as such. If you see them at the grocery store, thank them, shake their hand, carry their bags. They are prime examples of true Americans, because had it not been for their heroism, the state of this union would not be the same. Thank you, passengers of Flight 3911, thank you America, and good night."

The president tried to make a hasty exit, but everyone wanted to greet him. It took 30 minutes to leave the House Chamber. Once out he went directly to a reception room on the lower floor of the Capitol Building where the passengers gathered. The president spoke to the passengers as a group for the last time before they left DC. He thanked them as a group and wished them well. Then before leaving, he mingled with them and tried to speak to as many of them individually as possible.

When he saw Brandon and Carley, he invited them to ride back to the White House with him in the presidential limousine.

He wanted to get back to the White House for a planned call with Major Cauldwell. Davis planned to have Cauldwell on the satellite phone the minute the president entered the Oval Office. Brandon and Carley left with the president. When they arrived at the White House, the president walked them to the private residence and told them to relax just a few minutes while he attended to other important business.

"I'll be back as soon as I finish a phone call. I want to spend a little time with you before bedtime."

As the president entered his private office, Davis completed the call to Cauldwell and handed the phone to him.

"Cauldwell here."

"Great job. I want to hear all about it," said the president.

"Thank you, Mr. President," Cauldwell replied.

Did you see the State of the Union?" asked the president.

"Sir, no sir. I just returned to base of origin. No reception, but perhaps the president can arrange for a replay, sir."

"Major, get some rest. Davis is working out transportation details to get you back to Washington ASAP. Work out the details for your desired timetable and let him know. I want to invite you to the White House, plan to stay overnight so you can fill me in on the details. We cannot discuss this except in person."

"Sir, yes, sir. I will see you in a few days. Just want to also let you know kudos to Davis, he did an outstanding job."

"Major, your country thanks you for a job well done. Hold for Davis,"

Sir, yes, sir," Cauldwell replied in his usual formal military tone.

The president handed the phone to Davis and left to return to the residence.

"Davis here, do we still have a good signal, Major Cauldwell?" asked Davis.

"Affirmative signal, sir."

"I understand you have had quite a day. Get rest and I will confirm your transport arrangements for return to the White House in 24 hours. The president wants you here as soon as practical once you are fully rested," said Davis.

"Sir, I serve the president. Rest is secondary. Arrangements similar as last time works for me. I need a chopper from location to Kabul, then transport to Washington," requested Cauldwell.

"I am putting assets in position now. As last time, I will have an escort meet your flight at Reagan. Expect full details tomorrow. Also, FYI, the President plans for you to stay in the White House upon your return, so expect an overnight stay here in the Lincoln Bedroom."

"Outstanding, sir. It has been a pleasure working with you. Thanks for your support. I'm looking forward to the unexpected pleasure of the White House overnighter. And Rick, please make sure you take special care of Team Party Favors, those men did one hell of a job for their country. Over until tomorrow, Cauldwell out."

Chapter 32

The air outside Washington was electric. Reporters were on the phone with the networks prepping for live on-air broadcasts.

"After months of speculation, we finally learned the truth about Flight 3911," one reporter announced.

"Brandon Powell, a current resident of Atlanta, originally from Albany, Georgia landed the airplane..." shouted another.

The scene was chaotic. Every news station rushed to be the first to report the truth about Flight 3911. This was the biggest news story since September 11.

Chapter 33

The president returned to the residence to find Brandon and Carley.
"Brandon and Carley," the president interrupted their small talk. "Can I
talk to you two for a minute? Will you go on a short walk with me?"

"Sure," Brandon said.

"Brandon, now that the secret is out, I hope we can still spend time together.
You and Carley could come up to Camp David when things settle down for you.
I'm just letting you know you won't get rid of me. I'm still going to call to check
on you. My family owes their lives to you."

"Mr. President…"

"Brandon, you are my friend. Call me George."

"I can speak for Carley and me when I say, you can call on us anytime for a
visit! We would be happy to spend time with you and the first lady."

Carley smiled. "Sure, Mr. President, I think we can work Camp David into
our calendar most anytime."

"You two make a great looking couple. Good luck to you both in the future!"
the president said. "Let me walk you to your bedroom and maybe even a short
tour as we go."

"Sounds good and it is getting late," Brandon said.

As they left the residence, the president gave Brandon and Carley a private
tour of the residence floor of the White House on their way back to the Lincoln
Bedroom.

As he passed a door he said, "Brandon, that doorway then a quick left takes
you out on the Truman Balcony. It's a magnificent view over the South Lawn
and looking toward the Washington Monument. You have a similar view from
your bedroom window, but the trees obstruct the view."

Like a tour guide, the president continued, "The White House has 132 rooms,
35 bathrooms, and 28 fireplaces, one of which is in your bedroom and Walter
tells me he has a fire already going for you."

251

"Mr. President, how often do you give personal tours?" Carley asked with a smile and a wink.

"Actually, this is my first tour, I hope I get my facts right. Did you know the White House has been called several names other than the White House?" the president asked.

Both Brandon and Carley shook their heads, they did not know this piece of trivia.

"Over the years, it has also been known as "President's Palace," the "President's House," and the "Executive Mansion," but I still like the name White House," the president shared.

He led them into the Treaty Room and pointed out a few historical documents and a sofa presented by England in the early 1800s. The Gettysburg Address normally displayed in the Lincoln Bedroom was on display in preparation of an upcoming event to take place in the Treaty Room.

Before leaving the room, he pointed to another door and said, "That door is another way to get to the Truman Balcony." He led them out and went down the hall to the Queen's Bedroom, which was across the hall from their room, the Lincoln Bedroom.

The president said, "I wanted you to see this room because you might want to use it someday. It is larger and something you might like so you can get a feel for what we have to offer when you visit again."

"So, you really do plan to have us visit again?" asked Brandon.

"Of course, I do."

"We look forward to White House overnighters," said Brandon.

"Brandon, it is the least I can do. You are a national hero. You saved my family, I am forever indebted to you, your country is indebted to you."

"Mr...." Brandon tried to interrupt.

"No, please Brandon, it's true," the president continued. "I understand Walter has a surprise set up for you so perhaps I can now lead you to the Lincoln Bedroom."

The president walked them to the door of their bedroom and gave Brandon a big man hug and kissed Carley on both cheeks.

"Now you two love birds have a good night, and I'll see you before you leave in the morning."

"Good night, Mr. President," said Brandon.

"It's George, remember and get used to it," ordered the president.

"Sorry, sir and thank you, George," Brandon said with a smile.

The president turned and walked away leaving Brandon to let Carley in the room Walter prepared as Brandon had requested.

"Let me get that for you," Brandon said as he opened the door.

Candlelight danced around the room. There were candles everywhere. On the mantle, the dresser, and the nightstands. Walter out did himself. A bottle of champagne sat chilling on a small table in the middle of the room.

"Brandon, this is beautiful, what's this all about?"

"I wanted to make our last night here incredibly special."

"Duh, it's the Lincoln Bedroom. Duh, we are in the White House. I'm glad you wanted to share this experience with me. I don't want this night to end."

Brandon filled two glasses with champagne and returned his attention to Carley.

"I don't know what to say. Brandon, this is all so beautiful."

"You don't have to say anything. Just having you here is enough for me."

"Your life is about to change. Are you ready?"

"Carley, my life has already changed." Brandon kissed her fingers. "Being here, with you. How could I ask for anything more?"

Brandon kissed her.

She abruptly pulled away. "I need to freshen up and powder my nose," she said as she turned and made her way to the bathroom suite, closing the door behind her.

Unsure how to take her abrupt action, Brandon refilled their glasses with champagne and took a place on the antique love seat sofa. As he sat in the candle lit room, he faced the open window looking toward the Washington Monument. Soon he heard the mechanical sound of the bathroom door open, so he turned toward the door. Carley momentarily stood still in the doorway with a Mona Lisa smile. The bright lights in the bathroom provided a brief backlit silhouette of her perfect body through the shear knee length silk nighty just before she turned the light off. She joined him on the sofa. He gave her the champagne. They stared into each other's eyes with the Washington Monument in the distance.

"Is this real? We are in the Lincoln Bedroom. We are in the White House. The President of the United States is a few rooms down the hall. Brandon, he told you to call him George. Can you believe it, you're on a first name basis with the president?"

Brandon gazed into her eyes, "So that's what you find unbelievable?

"Well, yes I do, but I also find it unbelievable I'm here with you," she said.

Carley kissed him. They stared out the window and reminisced over the evening that began six hours earlier. When they realized how late it was, she took him in her arms and led him to the massive Lincoln bed. This time there was no pillow between them.

Neither one wanted to hold back. For the first time he felt her breasts as she unbuttoned his shirt. As she slipped his shirt off, she did not hesitate and explored his body for the first time. She sat up on top of him and very slowly slipped her teddy over her head, revealing her naked body to him and exposing her beautiful breasts.

They melted back into each other arms, with her straddling on top of him. Their hands explored each other's body as she kissed his neck and ears. This was the girl of his dreams. Something about her had him.

They lost their breath as if underwater, drifting through time, weightless and floating in hot scented air. It was as if nothing else existed in the world but the two of them, moving and mingling in a rhythm that rocked the soul.

He kissed her again and in no time, they were making love.

Chapter 34

Rick Davis said "A CH53 will take you to Kabul when you are prepared to leave. A C5 Galaxy is on standby in Kabul to bring you to Joint Base Andrews where you will be met and escorted. Got all that? Over."

"I got it. But curious why it takes the largest cargo jet in the fleet to take me to DC? Over," replied Cauldwell.

Davis laughed, "It's in the area, but most important, it has midair refueling so no stops for fuel, so it cuts four hours off the flight time. You will also like the fact I have ordered the Executive Suite container for the flight. It's like a sea container equipped like a bedroom suite."

"I'll have a special escort meeting you on this end."

"Is that special escort Mary O'Hara?" Cauldwell asked.

"Roger that. Over." Davis had really wanted it to be a surprise.

"Roger, Cauldwell out."

"See you in a couple days. Davis out."

With thoughts of Mary O'Hara, Cauldwell made finalizing his duties and affairs a top priority. As soon as everything was in order, he ordered the CH53 to leave Afghanistan for the final time. He grabbed his bag and left his tent that had been his home for the past two years. He climbed aboard the CH53 to Kabul. As the helicopter landed, he headed toward the huge C5. An Air Force staff sergeant waited his arrival on the tarmac. The sergeant saluted the major and led the way up the rear ramp of the jet.

Cauldwell noted what looked like a sea container secured in the massive cargo bay. Rather than being escorted to the typical seating for a cargo jet, the sergeant opened a door to the container.

"Major, the State Department ordered this for your trip."

Inside the container, it was a luxury apartment, complete with sofa, chairs, bed, TV, and full bathroom. "Sir, this is generally used by dignitaries and must be authorized by the highest levels of the government."

"This will be your home for the next 16 hours or so," said the sergeant.

"Great accommodations! I expect to catch up on sleep."

"Sir, our flying time to Joint Base Andrews will be approximately sixteen hours. We will be refueling over the North Sea. ETA in Washington is 1400 hours tomorrow afternoon. We expect a smooth flight so get some rest and use the phone next to the bed if you need anything. Good night, sir."

Cauldwell replied, "That's great sergeant, thanks."

The sergeant used the intercom and reported to the cockpit. "All secured, ready to roll."

The massive jet lumbered forward. As soon as they were airborne, Cauldwell stretched out at full length and was instantly asleep. Ten hours later he awoke somewhere over the North Atlantic. Using the phone by the bed, he asked for something to eat. The sergeant said he would fix a breakfast plate, service expected at his door in twenty minutes. Meanwhile, the major took a shower and changed into civilian clothes. Dining alone in the massive "condo in the skies," he wondered about his future and decided it was time to retire. Thoughts of Mary O'Hara clouded his mind with anticipation of seeing her in a few hours.

Thirty minutes earlier than the planned ETA, the C5 Galaxy landed at 1330 at Joint Base Andrews. As the big jet rolled to a stop, the sergeant knocked on the door of the suite.

"I'll escort you to your ride, it's just to the rear of the aircraft. As they reached the bottom of the ramp, Cauldwell saw Mary standing next to the door of the limousine. She was hardly able to contain her excitement but did her best to be professional. As he approached her, she gave an unprofessional wink and when she could no longer control herself, Mary ran to him with outstretched arms. He hugged her tight.

"Sir, I am here to escort you to the White House. The president is waiting to see you," she said as they climbed into the back seat of the limo.

"I prefer to see you," he said.

"Not to worry, major, I'll be waiting for you in the Lincoln Bedroom."

"Maybe we should not keep the president waiting," Cauldwell teased. He pulled her close and put his arm around her for the ride. Little was said and they could hardly stop staring at each other. As they pulled up to the south door of the White House, Rick Davis greeted the returning hero and Mary.

"President Walker is waiting, come with me. Mary, I'm giving you the rest of the week off. Follow Walter who will take you upstairs," Rick said.

Walter and Mary went one way and Rick and Cauldwell headed to the Oval Office.

"Mr. President, Major Cauldwell is here," Davis announced.

"Very well, both of you please come in. Major Cauldwell, congratulations on a job well done," the president beamed.

"Thank you, Mr. President, it has been my honor to handle this mission for my country."

"Major, I want to hear all about it, but first we need to take care of some official business. I have instructed Rick to start a process reversing your sham court martial. I have signed all the necessary paperwork. I am reinstating your rank and then promoting you to Major General. Congratulations, Major General Cauldwell."

Cauldwell stood and snapped to attention. "Thank you, Mr. President."

"Major General Cauldwell, please be seated. It is my pleasure. Furthermore, it was clearly a political move and never should have happened. This will hit the news media outlets tomorrow so be prepared!"

"Rick, the major general and I would like to discuss a classified mission, so please excuse us. Be sure to get all the paperwork completed and processed immediately."

"Yes sir," Davis said as he left the Oval Office.

When they were alone, Cauldwell and the president spent an hour talking about the mission. Cauldwell told the President the details that took place over the last three months. The president formed another incredibly special friendship. Cauldwell advised the president of his plans to retire and how he looked forward to trying civilian life.

"Major General, I am happy you accepted our invitation to stay with us here. I hope you enjoy your stay. Walter will assist you with anything you may need so feel free to let him know if you need anything. Meanwhile, I'd be honored to walk you to your room."

"Thank you, Mr. President, but rest is the only thing I need other than catching up with Mary," Cauldwell said.

They left the Oval Office and wandered around, working their way to the second floor. They entered the Lincoln Bedroom to find Mary sitting on the sofa looking over the South Lawn. She turned and was surprised to see her man with the president.

"Hi, Mary, it is nice to see you," the president said as he shook her hand. "I know you are expecting this hero, but I want to be the first to introduce him as Major General Cauldwell."

"Wow, that's quite a promotion," Mary exclaimed.

"Enjoy your stay with us. I must get back to work, good night. Oh, and I will be seeing you again soon Major General Cauldwell, certainly before I let you retire."

"Thank you, Mr. President and good night," said Cauldwell.

As the door closed, Mary jumped into his arms, straddling his hips as he effortlessly held her.

Cauldwell told her he needed to shower and shave in a real bathroom for the first time in three months. He suggested she pour a glass of wine and enjoy the surroundings of the Lincoln Bedroom while he moved to the bathroom.

After a long hot shower, he announced his return. He opened the door and the first thing he saw were her shoes deliberately placed in the middle of the doorway, so he was sure to see them. As he stepped over the shoes and looked toward the sofa, but he didn't see her. His gaze turned toward the Lincoln bed where he noticed her dress crumpled on the floor. Her blouse and bra hung over the foot board of the bed. He approached the bed and pulled the spread back to find Mary wearing nothing but her trademark Irish smile. Beautiful!

They melted into each other's arms, with her on top of him. Their hands were exploring each other's body. She began to kiss him. This was the girl of his dreams. Something about her had him.

Epilogue

Saturday, 8 June 2002. The president planned a special reunion to celebrate the heroes of Flight 3911 and the Delta Force marine team that had eliminated the threat of Hassan Sharaf.

Invitations had been sent in early April for all to mark the date on their calendars to attend the Camp David event billed as a Celebration of Heroes.

Major General Cauldwell and all members of Team Party Favors, along with their spouses or significant others, were incredibly surprised to get the invitation.

Cauldwell, Ayoubi, Fahmi, Garcia, and Gonzales were thrilled to be able to spend time in the presence of the president even if they could not disclose to anyone why they were there attending or being celebrated as heroes.

Acknowledgements

The story of Flight 3911 is fictional. Every effort has been taken to follow the actual timeline of the morning of September 11, 2001, up to the commandeering of Flight 3911. Timelines and events were taken directly from news accounts published that morning.

The seeds were planted for Flight 3911 at a media reception for *Abuse of Process*, the author's first book. Attending that reception were the host Randy Jones, founder of Worth Media, Lorenzo Lamas, Falcon Crest actor, Jan Hopkins, former CNN anchor and Barbara Taylor Bradford, fellow author, who offered congratulations on my first book and encouragement to keep writing. The reception was held on November 1, 2001 when the 9/11 attack was painfully fresh.

During that reception, the heroism shown by the passengers on Flight 93 was discussed and the four of us wondered what the outcome might have been had their attempted takeover been successful.

The storyline for *Flight 3911* was born.

Thanks to my military buddies in the Canadian Forces, Uruguayan Army, and Special Forces of the United States military. For obvious reason, their names must remain anonymous. When I asked for help to put together a story line of the US "using any means necessary to get information," they filled my inbox with ideas and suggestions.

Special thanks to Lt. Col Allen B West. After his retirement in 2003 and when he was in Iraq as a defense contractor, we exchanged email messages and several phone calls. He shared with me the extreme events with an Iraq policeman that resulted in his retirement. These events gave me the inspiration for the character Cauldwell. Col West later became a respected United States congressman.

Thanks to Alice Eachus, my editor. Alice polished my words into an easy to read, interesting and intriguing story of heroism and love for the US.

Much appreciation goes to my reading friends. Steve Severn who spent countless hours proofreading. His encouragement pushed me forward. Ann and Hank Goble and Fred Kelly, who proofed early versions and headed me in the right direction. My mother, Paula Smith, who during the COVID pandemic shutdown, proofed the final versions.

Special thanks to my wife, Drenda Smith, who provided encouragement, plenty of typing, proofing, and fact checking to keep the story as real as possible.